Praise for Harlan Coben

The Woods

'This stand-alone thriller will keep him on the bestseller lists and assures him VIP treatment at this summer's Harrogate Crime Festival'   *Time Out*

'Coben is skilled at weaving this kind of mystery and keeps us guessing till the end'   *Sunday Telegraph*

'Coben's novels are becoming more and more popular with each release, and this one cements his reputation as a top-class mystery writer'   *Independent on Sunday*

'A powerful thriller'   *Sunday Express*

Promise Me

'A story that delivers fully on its promise . . . They say Harlan Coben has a hugely starry fan base, including people from Bruce Springsteen to Bill Clinton. They will be pleased with this latest addition to the list, as will the rest of us. There are light-hearted lessons in life sprinkled throughout . . . But *Promise Me* is not about preaching, it is about catching you by those short hairs on the back of your neck'   *The Times*

'Bolitar is a glorious character, full of the right kind of quips and wise-ass backchat . . . [a] feature of Coben's thrillers is that they always have a dramatic twist at the end, sometimes even two or three, and this does not disappoint on that score'   *Guardian*

'Gripping, violent and original'   *Literary Review*

Harlan Coben is one of the most exciting talents in crime writing. His most recent novels, *No Second Chance*, *Just One Look*, *The Innocent* and *Promise Me*, were all international bestsellers, and are published in thirty-three languages. He was the first ever author to win all three major US crime awards, and established a bestselling series of crime novels starring his powerful creation, Myron Bolitar, before turning to stand-alone books. *The Woods* is his latest novel in Orion paperback. Visit his website at www.harlancoben.com.

By Harlan Coben

The Woods

HARLAN COBEN

An Orion paperback

First published in Great Britain in 2007
by Orion
This paperback edition published in 2008
by Orion Books Ltd,
Orion House, 5 Upper St Martin's Lane,
London WC2H 9EA

An Hachette Livre UK company

10 9 8 7 6 5 4 3 2 1

A CIP catalogue record for this book is available
from the British Library.

ISBN 978-0-7528-8190-4

Printed and bound in Great Britain by
Mackays of Chatham plc, Chatham, Kent

The Orion Publishing Group's policy is to use papers
that are natural, renewable and recyclable products and
made from wood grown in sustainable forests. The logging
and manufacturing processes are expected to conform to
the environmental regulations of the country of origin.

www.orionbooks.co.uk

This one is for

Alek Coben
Thomas Bradbeer
Annie van der Heide

The three joys I'm lucky enough to call
my godchildren

Prologue

I see my father with that shovel.

There are tears streaming down his face. An awful, guttural sob forces its way up from deep in his lungs and out through his lips. He raises the shovel up and strikes the ground. The blade rips into the earth like it's wet flesh.

I am eighteen years old, and this is my most vivid memory of my father – him, in the woods, with that shovel. He doesn't know I'm watching. I hide behind a tree while he digs. He does it with a fury, as though the ground has angered him and he is seeking vengeance.

I have never seen my father cry before – not when his own father died, not when my mother ran off and left us, not even when he first heard about my sister, Camille. But he is crying now. He is crying without shame. The tears cascade down his face in a freefall. The sobs echo through the trees.

This is the first time I've spied on him like this. Most Saturdays he would pretend to be going on fishing trips, but I never really believed that. I think I always knew that this place, this horrible place, was his secret destination.

Because, sometimes, it is mine too.

I stand behind the tree and watch him. I will do this eight more times. I never interrupt him. I never reveal myself. I think he doesn't know that I am there. I am sure of it, in fact. And then one day, as he heads to his car, my father looks at me with dry eyes and says, 'Not today, Paul. Today I go alone.'

I watch him drive off. He goes to those woods for the last time.

On his deathbed nearly two decades later, my father takes my hand. He is heavily medicated. His hands are rough and calloused. He used them his whole life – even in the flusher years in a country that no longer exists. He has one of those tough exteriors where all the skin looks baked and hard, almost like his own tortoise shell. He has been in immense physical pain, but there are no tears.

He just closes his eyes and rides it out.

My father has always made me feel safe, even now, even though I am now an adult with a child of my own. We went to a bar three months ago, when he was still strong enough. A fight broke out. My father stood in front of me, readying to take on anyone who came near me. Still. That is how it is.

I look at him in the bed. I think about those days in the woods. I think about how he dug, how he finally stopped, how I thought he had given up after my mother left.

'Paul?'

My father is suddenly agitated.

I want to beg him not to die, but that wouldn't be

2

right. I had been here before. It doesn't get better – not for anyone.

'It's okay, Dad,' I tell him. 'It's all going to be okay.'

He does not calm down. He tries to sit up. I want to help him, but he shakes me off. He looks deep into my eyes and I see clarity, or maybe that is one of those things that we make ourselves believe at the end. A final false comfort.

One tear escapes his eye. I watch it slowly slide down his cheek.

'Paul,' my father says to me, his voice still thick with a Russian accent. 'We still need to find her.'

'We will, Dad.'

He checks my face again. I nod, assure him. But I don't think that he is looking for assurance. I think, for the first time, he is looking for guilt.

'Did you know?' he asks, his voice barely audible.

I feel my entire body quake, but I don't blink, don't look away. I wonder what he sees, what he believes. But I will never know.

Because then, right then, my father closes his eyes and dies.

Chapter 1

Three Months Later

I was sitting in an elementary school gymnasium, watching my six-year-old daughter, Cara, nervously navigate across a balance beam that hovered maybe four inches off the floor, but in less than an hour, I would be looking at the face of a man who'd been viciously murdered.

That should not shock anyone.

I have learned over the years – in the most horrible ways imaginable – that the wall between life and death, between extraordinary beauty and mind-boggling ugliness, between the most innocent setting and a frightening bloodbath, is flimsy. It takes a second to tear through it. One moment, life appears idyllic. You are in a place as chaste as an elementary school gymnasium. Your little girl is twirling. Her voice is giddy. Her eyes are closed. You see her mother's face there, the way her mother used to close her eyes and smile, and you remember how flimsy that wall really is.

4

'Cope?'

It was my sister-in-law, Greta. I turned to her. Greta looked at me with her normal concern. I smiled through it.

'What are you thinking about?' she whispered.

She knew. I lied anyway.

'Handheld video cameras,' I said.

'What?'

The folding chairs had all been taken by the other parents. I stood in the back, arms crossed, leaning against the cement wall. There were rules posted above the doorway and those annoyingly cute inspirational aphorisms like 'Don't Tell Me the Sky's the Limit When There Are Footprints on the Moon' scattered throughout. The lunch tables were folded in. I leaned against that, feeling the cool of the steel and metal. Elementary school gyms never change as we age. They just seem to grow smaller.

I gestured at the parents. 'There are more video cameras here than kids.'

Greta nodded.

'And the parents, they film everything. I mean, everything. What do they do with all that? Does anybody really watch this again from beginning to end?'

'You don't?'

'I'd rather give birth.'

She smiled at that. 'No,' she said, 'you wouldn't.'

'Okay, yeah, maybe not, but didn't we all grow up in the MTV generation? Quick cuts. Lots of angles. But to just film this straight out like this, to subject an unsuspecting friend or family member to that . . .'

The door opened. The moment the two men stepped into the gym I could tell that they were cops. Even if I didn't have a fair amount of experience – I am the county prosecutor for Essex County, which includes the rather violent city of Newark – I would know. Television does indeed get some stuff right. The way most cops dressed, for example – fathers in the lush suburb of Ridgewood don't dress that way. We don't don suits when we come to see our kids perform quasi-gymnastics. We wear corduroys or jeans with a V-neck over a T-shirt. These two guys wore ill-fitted suits in a brown hue that reminded me of wood chips after a rainstorm.

They were not smiling. Their eyes scanned the room. I know most of the cops in the area, but I didn't know these guys. That troubled me. Something felt wrong. I knew that I hadn't done anything, of course, but there was still a little I'm-innocent-but-I-still-feel-guilty flutter in my stomach.

My sister-in-law, Greta, and her husband, Bob, have three kids of their own. Their youngest daughter, Madison, was six years old and in the same class as my Cara. Greta and Bob have been a tremendous help. After my wife, Jane – Greta's sister – died, they moved to Ridgewood. Greta claims that they had planned on doing that anyway. I doubt it. But I am so grateful that I don't question it much. I can't imagine what it would be like without them.

Usually the other fathers stand in the back with me, but since this was a daytime event, there were very few here. The mothers – except for the one now glaring at me over her video camera because she overheard my anti-video-cam rant – adore me. It is not me, of course, but my story. My wife died five years ago, and I raise my daughter alone. There are other single parents in town, mostly divorced mothers, but I get a ton of slack. If I forget to write a note or pick up my daughter late or leave her lunch on the counter, the other mothers or the

6

staff in the school office chip in and help. They think my male helplessness is cute. When a single mother does any of those things, she is neglectful and on the receiving end of the superior moms' scorn.

The kids continued to tumble or stumble, depending on how you wanted to look at it. I watched Cara. She was big on concentration and did just fine, but I suspected she had inherited her father's lack of coordination. There were high school girls from the gymnastics team helping. The girls were seniors, probably seventeen or eighteen. The one who spotted Cara during her attempted somersault reminded me of my sister. My sister, Camille, died when she was about this teen's age, and the media never lets me forget it. But maybe that was a good thing.

My sister would be in her late thirties now, at least as old as most of these mothers. Weird to think of it that way. I see Camille forever as a teen. It is hard to imagine where she would be now – where she *should* be now, sitting in one of those chairs, the doofy-happy-concerned-I'm-a-mom-first smile on her face, overfilming her own offspring. I wonder what she would look like today, but again all I see is the teenager who died.

It may appear that I'm somewhat obsessed with death, but there is a huge difference between my sister's murder and my wife's premature passing. The first, my sister's, led me to my current job and career projectory. I can fight that injustice in the courtroom. And I do. I try to make the world safer, try to put those who would harm others behind bars, try to bring other families something my family never really had – closure.

With the second death – my wife's – I was helpless and screwed up and no matter what I do now, I will never be able to make amends.

The school principal strapped that faux-concerned smile onto her over-lipsticked mouth and headed in the direction of the two cops. She engaged them in conversation, but neither one of them so much as glanced at her. I watched their eyes. When the taller cop, the lead cop for certain, hit my face, he stopped. Neither of us moved for a moment. He gave his head the slightest tilt, beckoning me outside this safe haven of laughter and tumbling. I made my nod equally slight.

'Where are you going?' Greta asked me.

I don't want to sound unkind, but Greta was the ugly sister. They looked alike, she and my lovely dead bride. You could tell that they were from the same parents. But everything that worked physically with my Jane just doesn't quite make it on Greta. My wife had a prominent nose that somehow made her sexier. Greta has a prominent nose that looks, well, big. My wife's eyes, set far apart, gave her an exotic appeal. On Greta, the wide spacing makes her look somewhat reptilian.

'I'm not sure,' I said.

'Business?'

'Could be.'

She glanced over at the two probable-cops then back at me. 'I was going to take Madison to Friendly's for lunch. Do you want me to bring Cara?'

'Sure, that'd be great.'

'I could also pick her up after school.'

I nodded. 'That might help.'

Greta kissed my cheek gently then – something she rarely does. I headed off. The peals of children's laughter rolled with me. I opened the door and stepped into the corridor. The two policemen followed me. School corridors never change much either. They have an almost haunted-house echo to them, a strange sort of semi-

8

silence and a faint but distinct smell that both soothes and agitates.

'Are you Paul Copeland?' the taller one asked.

'Yes.'

He looked at his shorter partner. The shorter guy was meaty with no neck. His head was shaped like a cinder block. His skin was coarse too, adding to the illusion. From around the corner came a class of maybe fourth graders. They were all red-faced from exertion. Probably had just come from the playground. They made their way past us, trailed by their harried teacher. She gave us a strained smile.

'Maybe we should talk outside,' the taller one said.

I shrugged. I had no idea what this was about. I had the guile of the innocent, but the experience to know that nothing with cops is what it appears to be. This was not about the big, headline-splashing case I was working on. If it had been, they'd have called my office. I'd have gotten word on my cell or BlackBerry.

No, they were here for something else – something personal.

Again I knew that I had done nothing wrong. But I have seen all kinds of suspects in my time and all kinds of reactions. It might surprise you. For example, when the police have a major suspect in custody they often keep them locked in the interrogation room for hours on end. You would think the guilty ones would be climbing walls, but for the most part, it was the opposite. The innocent ones get the most antsy and nervous. They have no idea why they are there or what the police mistakenly think they've done. The guilty often go to sleep.

We stood outside. The sun blazed down. The taller one squinted and raised a hand to shade his eyes. The Cinder Block would not give anyone that satisfaction.

'My name is Detective Tucker York,' the taller one said. He took out his badge and then motioned toward the Cinder Block. 'This is Detective Don Dillon.'

Dillon took out his ID too. They showed them to me. I don't know why they do that. How hard can it be to fake those? 'What can I do for you?' I asked.

'Do you mind telling us where you were last night?' York asked.

Sirens should have gone off at a question like that. I should have right away reminded them of whom I was and that I wouldn't answer any questions without an attorney present. But I am an attorney. A damned good one. And that, of course, just makes you more foolish when you represent yourself, not less so. I was also human. When you are rousted by the police, even with all my experience, you want to please. You can't help that feeling.

'I was home.'

'Anyone who can verify that?'

'My daughter.'

York and Dillon looked back at the school. 'That's the girl who was tumbling in there?'

'Yes.'

'Anyone else?'

'I don't think so. What's this about?'

York was the one who was doing all the talking. He ignored my question. 'Do you know a man named Manolo Santiago?'

'No.'

'Are you sure?'

'Pretty sure.'

'Why only pretty sure?'

'Do you know who I am?'

'Yep,' York said. He coughed into his fist. 'You want us

10

to maybe take a knee or kiss your ring or something?'

'That's not what I meant.'

'Good, then we're on the same page.' I did not like his attitude, but I let it slide. 'So why are you only "pretty sure" you don't know Manolo Santiago?'

'I mean, the name isn't familiar. I don't think I know him. But maybe it's someone I prosecuted or was a witness in one of my cases, or hell, maybe I met him at a fund-raiser ten years ago.'

York nodded, encouraging me to blabber more. I didn't.

'Do you mind coming with us?'

'Where?'

'It won't take long.'

'Won't take long,' I repeated. 'That doesn't sound like a place.'

The two cops exchanged a glance. I tried to look as if I would hold my ground.

'A man named Manolo Santiago was murdered last night.'

'Where?'

'His body was in Manhattan. Washington Heights area.'

'And what does this have to do with me?'

'We think you might be able to help.'

'Help how? I already told you. I don't know him.'

'You said' – York actually referred to his pad, but it was only for effect; he hadn't written anything while I was talking – 'that you were "pretty sure" you didn't know him.'

'I'm sure then. Okay? I'm sure.'

He snapped the pad closed with dramatic flare. 'Mr. Santiago knew you.'

'How do you know that?'

'We'd prefer to show you.'

'And I'd prefer you tell me.'

'Mr. Santiago' – York hesitated as though choosing his next words by hand – 'had certain items on him.'

'Items?'

'Yes.'

'Could you be more specific?'

'Items,' he said, 'that point to you.'

'Point to me as what?'

'Yo, Mr. DA?'

Dillon – the Cinder Block – had finally spoken.

'It's County Prosecutor,' I said.

'Whatever.' He cracked his neck and pointed at my chest. 'You're really starting to itch my ass.'

'Excuse me?'

Dillon stepped into my face. 'Do we look like we're here for a goddamn semantics lesson?'

I thought the question was rhetorical, but he waited. Finally I said, 'No.'

'Then listen up. We got a dead body. The guy is linked to you in a big way. Do you want to come and help clear this up, or do you want to play more word games that make you look suspicious as hell?'

'Who exactly do you think you're talking to, Detective?'

'A guy running for office who wouldn't want us to take this directly to the press.'

'Are you threatening me?'

York stepped in. 'Nobody is threatening anything.'

But Dillon had hit me where I lived. The truth was, my appointment was still only temporary. My friend, the current governor of the Garden State, had made me acting county prosecutor. There was also serious talk of my running for Congress, maybe even the vacant Senate seat. I would be lying if I said I didn't have political ambitions. A scandal, even the fake whiff of one, would not play well.

'I can't see how I can help,' I said.

'Maybe you can't, maybe you can.' Dillon rotated the cinder block. 'But you want to help if you can, don't you?'

'Of course,' I said. 'I mean, I don't want your ass itching any more than it has to.'

He almost smiled at that one. 'Then get in the car.'

'I have an important meeting this afternoon.'

'We'll have you back by then.'

I expected a beat-up Chevy Caprice, but the car was a clean Ford. I sat in the back. My two new friends sat in the front. We did not speak for the ride. There was traffic at the George Washington Bridge, but we just hit our siren and sliced through it. When we were on the Manhattan side, York spoke.

'We think Manolo Santiago might be an alias.'

I said, 'Uh-huh,' because I didn't know what else to say.

'You see, we don't have a positive ID on the victim. We found him last night. His driver's license reads Manolo Santiago. We checked it out. It doesn't appear to be his real name. We ran his prints. No hits. So we don't know who he is.'

'And you think I will?'

They did not bother answering.

York's voice was as casual as a spring day. 'You're a widower, Mr. Copeland, right?'

'Right,' I said.

'Must be tough. Raising a kid on your own.'

I said nothing.

'Your wife had cancer, we understand. You're very

13

involved in some organization to find a cure.'

'Uh-huh.'

'Admirable.'

They should only know.

'This must be weird for you,' York said.

'How's that?'

'Being on the other side. You're usually the one asking the questions, not answering them. That's gotta be a little strange.'

He smiled at me in the rearview mirror.

'Hey, York?' I said.

'What?'

'Do you have a playbill or a program?' I asked.

'A what?'

'A playbill,' I said. 'So I can see your past credits, you know – before you landed the coveted role of Good Cop.'

York chuckled at that. 'I'm just saying, it's weird is all. I mean, have you ever been questioned by the police before?'

It was a setup question. They had to know. When I was eighteen years old, I worked as a counselor at a summer camp. Four campers – Gil Perez and his girlfriend, Margot Green, Doug Billingham and his girlfriend, Camille Copeland (aka my sister) – sneaked into the woods late one night.

They were never seen again.

Only two of the bodies have ever been found. Margot Green, age seventeen, was found with her throat slit within a hundred yards of the campsite. Doug Billingham, also seventeen, was found half a mile away. He had several stab wounds, but cause of death was also a slit throat. The bodies of the other two – Gil Perez and my sister, Camille – have never been found.

The case made headlines. Wayne Steubens, a rich-kid counselor at the camp, was caught two years later – after his third summer of terror – but not until he murdered at least four more teens. He was dubbed the Summer Slasher – an all-too-obvious moniker. Wayne's next two victims were found near a Boy Scout camp in Muncie, Indiana. Another victim was attending one of those all-around camps in Vienna, Virginia. His last victim had been at a sports camp in the Poconos. Most had their throats slit. All had been buried out in the woods, some before death. Yes, as in buried alive. It took a fair amount of time to locate the bodies. The Poconos kid, for example, took six months to be found. Most experts believe that there are others still out there, still underground, deep in the woods.

Like my sister.

Wayne has never confessed, and despite being in a supermaximum-security facility for the past eighteen years, he insists that he had nothing to do with the four murders that started it all.

I don't believe him. The fact that at least two bodies were still out there led to speculation and mystery. It gave Wayne more attention. I think he likes that. But that unknown – that glimmer – still hurts like hell.

I loved my sister. We all did. Most people believe death is the cruelest thing. Not so. After a while, hope is a far more abusive mistress. When you live with it as long as I have, your neck constantly on the chopping block, the axe raised above you for days, then months, then years, you long for it to fall and lop off your head. Most believed that my mother ran off because my sister was murdered. But the truth is the opposite. My mother left us because we could never prove it.

I wished Wayne Steubens would tell us what he did

with her. Not to give her a proper burial or any of that. That would be nice, but beside the point. Death is pure, wrecking-ball destructive. It hits, you're crushed, you start to rebuild. But not knowing – that doubt, that glimmer – made death work more like termites or some sort of relentless germ. It eats away from the inside. You cannot stop the rot. You cannot rebuild because that doubt will just keep gnawing away.

It still does, I think.

That part of my life, much as I want to keep it private, was always picked up by the media. Even the quickest Google search would have brought up my name in connection with the mystery of the Vanished Campers, as they were quickly dubbed. Heck, the story still played on those 'real crime' shows on Discovery or Court TV. I was there that night, in those woods. My name was out there for the finding. I was questioned by the police. Interrogated. Under suspicion even.

So they had to know.

I chose not to answer. York and Dillon didn't push it.

When we arrived at the morgue, they led me down a long corridor. No one spoke. I wasn't sure what to make of this. What York said made sense now. I was on the other side. I had watched plenty of witnesses make walks like this. I had seen every sort of reaction in the morgue. The identifiers usually start off stoic. I'm not sure why. Are they bracing themselves? Or does a smidgeon of hope – that word again – still exist? I'm not sure. Whatever, the hope quickly vanishes. We never make a mistake on the ID. If we think it's your loved one, it is. The morgue is not a place of last-minute miracles. Not ever.

I knew that they were watching me, studying my responses. I became aware of my steps, my posture, my facial expression. I aimed for neutral and then wondered why I bothered.

They brought me to the window. You don't go into the room. You stay behind glass. The room was tiled so that you could just hose it down – no need to get fancy with decor or cleaners. All the gurneys save one were empty. The body was covered with a sheet, but I could see the toe tag. They really used those. I looked at the big toe sticking out from under the sheet – it was wholly unfamiliar. That was what I thought. I do not recognize the man's toe.

The mind does funny things under stress.

A woman wearing a mask rolled the gurney closer to the window. I flashed back to, of all things, the day my daughter was born. I remember the nursery. The window was much the same, with those thin strips of foil forming diamonds. The nurse, a woman about the size of the woman in the morgue, rolled the little cart with my little daughter in it close to the window. Just like this. I guess I would normally have seen something poignant in this – the beginning of life, the end of it – but today I didn't.

She pulled back the top of the sheet. I looked down at the face. All eyes were on me. I knew that. The dead man was about my age, early to midthirties. He had a beard. His head looked shaved. He wore a shower cap. I thought that looked pretty goofy, the shower cap, but I knew why it was there.

'Shot in the head?' I asked.

'Yes.'

'How many times?'

'Twice.'

'Caliber?'

York cleared his throat, as if trying to remind me that

this wasn't my case. 'Do you know him?'

I took another look. 'No,' I said.

'Are you sure?'

I started to nod. But something made me stop.

'What?' York said.

'Why am I here?'

'We want to see if you know—'

'Right, but what made you think I would know him?'

I slid my eyes to the side, saw York and Dillon exchange a glance. Dillon shrugged and York picked up the ball. 'He had your address in his pocket,' York said. 'And he had a bunch of clippings about you.'

'I'm a public figure.'

'Yes, we know.'

He stopped talking. I turned toward him. 'What else?'

'The clippings weren't about you. Not really.'

'What were they about?'

'Your sister,' he said. 'And about what happened in those woods.'

The room dropped ten degrees, but hey, we were in a morgue. I tried to sound nonchalant. 'Maybe he's a real-crime nut. There are lots of them.'

He hesitated. I saw him exchange a glance with his partner.

'What else?' I asked.

'What do you mean?'

'What else did he have on him?'

York turned toward a subordinate I hadn't even noticed was standing there. 'Can we show Mr. Copeland here the personal effects?'

I kept my eye on the dead man's face. There were pockmarks and lines. I tried to smooth them out. I didn't know him. Manolo Santiago was a stranger to me.

Someone pulled out a red plastic evidence bag. They emptied it out onto a table. From the distance I could see a pair of blue jeans and a flannel shirt. There was a wallet and a cell phone.

'You check the cell phone?' I asked.

'Yep. It's a throwaway. The phone log is empty.'

I wrested my gaze away from the dead man's face and walked over to the table. My legs quaked.

There were folded sheets of paper. I carefully opened one up. The article from *Newsweek*. The picture of the four dead teens was there – the Summer Slasher's first victims. They always started with Margot Green because her body was found right away. It took another day to locate Doug Billingham. But the real interest lay in the other two. Blood had been found and torn clothes belonging to both Gil Perez and my sister – but no bodies.

Why not?

Simple. The woods were massive. Wayne Steubens had hidden them well. But some people, those who loved a good conspiracy, didn't buy that. Why had just those two not been found? How could Steubens have moved and buried bodies so quickly? Did he have an accomplice? How had he pulled it off? What were those four doing in those woods in the first place?

Even today, eighteen years after Wayne's arrest, people talk about the 'ghosts' in those woods – or maybe there is a secret cult living in an abandoned cabin or escaped mental patients or men with hook arms or bizarre medical experiments gone wrong. They talk about the boogeyman, finding the remnants of his burned-out campfire, still surrounded by the bones of children he'd eaten. They say how at night they can still hear Gil Perez and my sister, Camille, howl for vengeance.

I spent a lot of nights out there, alone in those woods. I never heard anyone howl.

My eyes moved past Margot Green's picture and Doug Billingham's. The photograph of my sister was next. I had seen this same shot a million times. The media loved it because she looked so wonderfully ordinary. She was the girl-next-door, your favorite babysitter, the sweet teen who lived down the block. That wasn't Camille at all. She was mischievous, with lively eyes and a sideways devil-may-care grin that knocked the boys back a step. This picture was so not her. She was more than this. And maybe that had cost her her life.

I was about to head over to the final picture, the one of Gil Perez, but something made me pull up.

My heart stopped.

I know that sounds dramatic, but that was how it felt. I looked at the pile of coins from Manolo Santiago's pocket and saw it, and it was as if a hand reached into my chest and squeezed my heart so hard it couldn't beat anymore.

I stepped back.

'Mr. Copeland?'

My hand went out as if it were acting on its own. I watched my fingers pluck it up and bring it to my eye level.

It was a ring. A girl's ring.

I looked at the picture of Gil Perez, the boy who'd been murdered with my sister in the woods. I flashed back twenty years. And I remembered the scar.

'Mr. Copeland?'

'Show me his arm,' I said.

'Excuse me?'

'His arm.' I turned back to the window and pointed to the corpse. 'Show me his goddamn arm.'

York signaled to Dillon. Dillon pressed the intercom button. 'He wants to the see the guy's arm.'

'Which one?' the woman in the morgue asked.

They looked at me.

'I don't know,' I said. 'Both, I guess.'

They looked puzzled, but the woman obeyed. The sheet was pulled back.

The chest was hairy now. He was bigger, at least thirty pounds more than he was back in those days, but that wasn't surprising. He had changed. We all had. But that wasn't what I was looking for. I was looking at the arm, for the ragged scar.

It was there.

On his left arm. I did not gasp or any of that. It was as if part of my reality had just been pulled away and I was too numb to do anything about it. I just stood there.

'Mr. Copeland?'

'I know him,' I said.

'Who is he?'

I pointed to the picture in the magazine. 'His name is Gil Perez.'

Chapter 2

There was a time when Professor Lucy Gold, PhD in both English and psychology, loved office hours.

It was a chance to sit one-on-one with students and really get to know them. She loved when the quiet ones who sat in the back with their heads down, taking notes as though it were dictation, the ones who had their hair hanging in front of their faces like a protective curtain – when they arrived at her door and raised their eyes and told her what was in their hearts.

But most of the time, like now, the students who showed up were the brownnosers, the ones who felt that their grade should depend solely on their outward enthusiasm, that the more face time they got, the higher the grade, as though being an extrovert was not rewarded enough in this country.

'Professor Gold,' the girl named Sylvia Potter said. Lucy imagined her a little younger, in middle school. She would have been the annoying girl who arrived the morning of a big test whining that she was going to fail and then ended up being the first one done, smugly handing in her A-plus paper early, and using the rest of the class time to put reinforcements in her notebook.

'Yes, Sylvia?'

'When you were reading that passage from Yeats in class today, I mean, I was so moved. Between the actual words and the way you can use your voice, you know, like a professional actress . . .'

Lucy Gold was tempted to say, 'Do me a favor – just bake me some brownies,' but she kept the smile on instead. No easy task. She glanced at her watch and then felt like crap for doing that. Sylvia was a student trying her best. That was all. We all find our ways to cope, to adapt and survive. Sylvia's way was probably wiser and less self-destructive than most.

'I loved writing that journal piece too,' she said.

'I'm glad.'

'Mine was about . . . well, my first time, if you know what I mean . . .'

Lucy nodded. 'We're keeping them confidential and anonymous, remember?'

'Oh, right.' She glanced down now. Lucy wondered about that. Sylvia never looked down.

'Maybe after I read them all,' Lucy said, 'if you want, we can talk about yours. In private.'

Her head was still down.

'Sylvia?'

The girl's voice was very soft. 'Okay.'

Office hours were over. Lucy wanted to get home. She tried not to sound halfhearted when she asked, 'Do you want to talk about it now?'

'No.'

Sylvia's head was still down.

23

'Okay then,' Lucy said, making a production of look-ing at her watch. 'I have a staff meeting in ten minutes.'

Sylvia stood. 'Thank you for meeting with me.'

'My pleasure, Sylvia.'

Sylvia looked as if she wanted to say something more. But she didn't. Five minutes later, Lucy stood at her win-dow and looked down at the quad. Sylvia walked out the door, wiped her face, set the head high, forced up a smile. She started walk-skipping across campus. Lucy watched her wave at her fellow students, fall in with a group, and blend with the others until Sylvia became an indistinct part of the mass.

Lucy turned away. She caught her reflection in the mirror and did not like what she saw. Had that girl been calling out for help?

Probably, Luce, and you didn't answer. Nice work, superstar.

She sat at her desk and opened the bottom drawer. The vodka was there. Vodka was good. You didn't smell vodka.

Her office door opened. The guy who entered had long black hair tucked behind his ears and several ear-rings. He was unshaven, fashionably so, handsome in an aging-boy-band way. He had the silver stud in his chin, a look that always detracted, low pants barely held up by a studded belt, and a tattoo on the neck that said, 'Breed Often.'

'You,' the guy said, gunning his best smile in her direction, 'look immensely doable.'

'Thanks, Lonnie.'

'Nah, I mean it. Immensely doable.'

Lonnie Berger was her TA, though he was her age. He was permanently caught in that education trap, get-ting a new degree, hanging on campus, the telltale sign of age around the eyes. Lonnie was getting tired of the PC sexual crap on campus, so he was going out of his way to push that boundary and hit on every woman he could.

'You should wear something that shows a little more cleavage, maybe one of those new push-up bras,' Lonnie added. 'Might make the boys pay more attention in class.'

'Yeah, that's what I want.'

'Seriously, chief, when was the last time you got some?'

'It's been eight months, six days, and about' – Lucy checked her watch – 'four hours.'

He laughed. 'You're playing me, right?'

She just stared at him.

'I printed out the journals,' he said.

The confidential, anonymous journals.

She was teaching a class that the university had dubbed Creative Reasoning, a combination of cutting-edge psychological trauma with creative writing and philosophy. Truth be told, Lucy loved it. Current assignment: Each student was supposed to write on a traumatic event in their lives – something that they would not normally share with anyone. No names were to be used. No grades given. If the anonymous student gave permission on the bottom of the page, Lucy might read a few out loud to the class for the purpose of discussion – again keeping the author anonymous.

'Did you start reading them?' she asked.

Lonnie nodded and sat in the seat that Sylvia had occupied a few minutes ago. He threw his feet up on the desk. 'The usual,' he said.

'Bad erotica?'

'I'd say more like soft porn.'

'What's the difference?'

'Damned if I know. Did I tell you about my new chick?'

'No.'

'Delectable.'

'Uh-huh.'

'I'm serious. A waitress. Hottest piece of ass I've ever dated.'

'And I want to hear this because?'

'Jealous?'

'Yeah,' Lucy said. 'That must be it. Give me the journals, will you?'

Lonnie handed her a few. They both started digging in. Five minutes later, Lonnie shook his head.

Lucy said, 'What?'

'How old are most of these kids?' Lonnie asked. 'Maybe twenty, right?'

'Right.'

'And their sexual escapades always last, like, two hours?'

Lucy smiled. 'Active imagination.'

'Did guys last that long when you were young?'

'They don't last that long now,' she said.

Lonnie arched an eyebrow. 'That's because you're so hot. They can't control themselves. It's your fault, really.'

'Hmm.' She tapped the pencil's eraser against her lower lip. 'That's not the first time you've used that line, is it?'

'You think I need a new one? How about: "This has never happened to me before, I swear"?'

Lucy made a buzzing sound. 'Sorry, try again.'

'Damn.'

They went back to reading. Lonnie whistled and shook

his head. 'Maybe we just grew up in the wrong era.'

'Definitely.'

'Luce?' He looked over the paper. 'You really need to get some.'

'Uh-huh.'

'I'm willing to help, you know. No strings attached.'

'What about Ms. Delectable Waitress?'

'We're not exclusive.'

'I see.'

'So what I'm suggesting here is purely a physical thing. A mutual pipe cleaning, if you catch my drift.'

'Shush, I'm reading.'

He caught the hint. Half an hour later, Lonnie sat forward and looked at her.

'What?'

'Read this one,' he said.

'Why?'

'Just read it, okay?'

She shrugged, put down the journal she'd been reading – yet another story of a girl who'd gotten drunk with her new boyfriend and ended up in a threesome. Lucy had read lots of stories of threesomes. None seemed to happen without alcoholic involvement.

But a minute later she forgot all about that. She forgot that she lived alone or that she had no real family left and that she was a college professor or that she was in her office overlooking the quad or that Lonnie was still sitting in front of her. Lucy Gold was gone. And in her place was a younger woman, a girl really, with a different name, a girl on the verge of adulthood but still so very much a girl:

This happened when I was seventeen. I was at summer camp. I worked there as a CIT. That stands for

27

Counselor In Training. It wasn't hard for me to get the job because my dad owned the place . . .

Lucy stopped. She looked at the front sheet. There was no name, of course. The students e-mailed the papers in. Lonnie had printed them out. There was supposed to be no way to know who sent what paper. It was part of the comfort. You didn't even have to risk having your fingerprints on it. You just hit the anonymous Send button:

It was the best summer of my life. At least it was until that final night. Even now I know I will never know a time like it. Weird, right? But I know. I know that I will never, ever, be that happy again. Not ever. My smile is different now. It is sadder, like it is broken and can't be fixed.

I loved a boy that summer. I will call him P for this story. He was a year older than me and a junior counselor. His whole family was at the camp. His sister worked there and his father was the camp doctor. But I barely noticed them because the moment I met P, I felt my stomach clench.

I know what you're thinking. It was just a dumb summer romance. But it wasn't. And now I'm scared I will never love someone like I loved him. That sounds silly. That is what everyone thinks. Maybe they are right. I don't know. I am still so young. But it doesn't feel like that. It feels like I had one chance at happiness and I blew it.

A hole in Lucy's heart started opening, expanding.

One night, we went into the woods. We weren't supposed to. There were strict rules about it. Nobody knew those rules better than me. I had been spending summers here since I was nine. That was when my dad bought the camp. But P was on 'night' duty. And because my dad owned the camp, I had full access. Smart, right? Two kids in love who were supposed to guard the other campers? Give me a break!

He didn't want to go because he thought he should keep watch, but hey, I knew how to entice him. I regret that now, of course. But I did it. So we headed into the woods, just the two of us. Alone. The woods are huge. If you make a wrong turn, you can get lost in there forever. I had heard tales of children going out there and never coming back. Some say they still wander around, living like animals. Some say they died or worse. Well, you know how it is with camp-fire stories.

I used to laugh at stories like that. I never got scared of them. Now I shudder at the thought.

We kept walking. I knew the way. P was holding my hand. The woods were so dark. You can't see more than ten feet in front of you. We heard a rustling noise and realized that someone was in the woods. I froze, but I remember P smiling in the dark and shaking his head in a funny way. You see, the only reason campers met up in the woods was, well, it was a coed camp. There was a boys' side and a girls' side and this finger of the woods stood between them. You figure it out.

P sighed. 'We better check it out,' he said. Or something like that. I don't remember his exact words.

But I didn't want to. I wanted to be alone with him.

My flashlight was out of batteries. I can still remember how fast my heart was beating as we stepped into the trees. There I was, in the dark, holding hands with the guy I loved. He would touch me and I would just melt. You know that feeling? When you can't stand to be away from a guy for even five minutes. When you put everything in context of him. You do something, anything really, and you wonder, 'What would he think about that?' It is a crazy feeling. It is wonderful but it also hurts. You are so vulnerable and raw that it's scary.

'Shh,' he whispers. 'Just stop.'

We do. We stop.

P pulls me behind a tree. He cups my face in both of his hands. He has big hands and I love the way that feels. He tilts my face up and then he kisses me. I feel it everywhere, a fluttering that begins in the center of my heart and then spreads. He takes his hand away from my face. He puts it on my rib cage, right next to my breast. I start to anticipate. I groan out loud.

We kept kissing. It was so passionate. We couldn't get close enough to each other. Every part of me felt on fire. He moved his hand under my shirt. I won't say more about that. I forgot about the rustling in the woods. But now I know. We should have contacted someone. We should have stopped them from going deeper in the woods. But we didn't. We made love instead.

I was so lost in us, in what we were doing, that at first I didn't even hear the screams. I don't think P did either.

But the screams kept coming and you know how people describe near-death experiences? That was what it was like, but kinda in reverse. It was like we were both headed for some wonderful light and the screams were like a rope that was trying to pull us *back, even though we didn't want to go back.*

He stopped kissing me. And here is the terrible thing.

He never kissed me again.

Lucy turned the page, but there were no more. She snapped her head up. 'Where's the rest?'

'That's it. You said to send it in parts, remember? That's all there is.'

She looked at the pages again.

'You okay, Luce?'

'You're good with computers, aren't you, Lonnie?'

He arched the eyebrow again. 'I'm better with da ladies.'

'Do I look like I'm in the mood?'

'Okay, okay, yeah, I'm good with computers. Why?'

'I need to find out who wrote this.'

'But—'

'I need,' she repeated, 'to find out who wrote this.'

He met her eye. He studied her face for a second. She knew what he wanted to say. It betrayed everything that they were about. They had read horrible stories in here, one this year about father-daughter incest even, and they had never tried to track the person down.

Lonnie said, 'Do you want to tell me what this is about?'

'No.'

'But you want me to break all the confidences we've ever set up here?'

'Yes.'

'That bad?'

She just looked at him.

'Ah, what the hell,' Lonnie said. 'I'll see what I can do.'

Chapter 3

'I'm telling you,' I said yet again. 'It's Gil Perez.'

'The guy who died with your sister twenty years ago.'

'Obviously,' I said, 'he didn't die.'

I don't think they believed me.

'Maybe it's his brother,' York tried.

'With my sister's ring?'

Dillon added, 'That ring isn't unusual. Twenty years ago they were all the rage. I think my sister had the same one. Got it for her sweet sixteen, I think. Was your sister's engraved?'

'No.'

'So we don't know for sure.'

We talked for a while, but there was not much to add. I really didn't know anything. They would be in touch, they said. They'd find Gil Perez's family, see if they could make a positive ID. I didn't know what to do. I felt lost and numb and confused.

My BlackBerry and cell phone were going nuts. I was

late now for an appointment with the defense team in the biggest case of my career. Two wealthy collegiate tennis players from the ritzy suburb of Short Hills stood accused of raping a sixteen-year-old African-American girl from Irvington named – and no, her name didn't help – Chamique Johnson. The trial had already started, had hit a delay, and now I hoped to cut a jail-time deal before we had to start up again.

The cops gave me a lift to my office in Newark. I knew that opposing counsel would think my tardiness was a ploy, but there wasn't much to be done about that. When I entered my office, the two lead defense lawyers were already seated.

One, Mort Pubin, stood and started bellowing. 'You son of a bitch! Do you know what time it is? Do you?'

'Mort, did you lose weight?'

'Don't start that crap with me.'

'Wait, no, that's not it. You're taller, right? You grew. Just like a real boy.'

'Up yours, Cope. We've been sitting here for an hour!'

The other lawyer, Flair Hickory, just sat there, legs crossed, not a care in the world. Flair was the one I paid attention to. Mort was loud and obnoxious and showy. Flair was the defense attorney I feared like no other. He was not what anyone expected. In the first place, Flair – he swore it was his real name but I had my doubts – was gay. Okay, that wasn't a big deal. Plenty of attorneys are gay, but Flair was gay gay, like the love child of Liberace and Liza Minnelli, who'd been brought up on nothing but Streisand and show tunes.

Flair did not tone it down for the courtroom – he intentionally ratcheted it up.

He let Mort rant another minute or two. Flair flexed

33

his fingers and studied his manicure. He seemed pleased by it. Then he raised his hand and silenced Mort with a fluttery wave.

'Enough,' Flair said.

He wore a purple suit. Or maybe it was eggplant or periwinkle, some such hue. I'm not good with colors. The shirt was the same color as the suit. So was the solid tie. So was the pocket hanky. So were – good Lord – the shoes. Flair noticed me noticing the clothes.

'You like it?' Flair asked me.

'Barney joins the Village People,' I said.

Flair frowned at me.

'What?'

'Barney, the Village People,' he said, pursing his lips. 'Could you possibly come up with two more dated, overused pop references?'

'I was going to say the purple Teletubby, but I couldn't remember his name.'

'Tinky Winky. And that's still dated.' He crossed his arms and sighed. 'So now that we are all together in this clearly hetero-decorated office, can we just let our clients walk and be done with this?'

I met his eye. 'They did it, Flair.'

He wouldn't deny it. 'Are you really going to put that deranged stripper-cum-prostitute on the stand?'

I was going to defend her, but he already knew the facts. 'I am.'

Flair tried not to smile. 'I will,' he said, 'destroy her.'

I said nothing.

He would. I knew that. And that was the thing about his act. He could slice and dice and still make you like him. I'd seen him do it before. You'd think at least some of the jury would consist of homophobes and that they'd hate or fear him. But that wasn't how it

34

worked with Flair. The female jurists wanted to go shopping with him and tell him about their husbands' inadequacies. The men found him so nonthreatening that they thought there was no way he could pull anything over on them.

It made for a lethal defense.

'What are you looking for?' I asked.

Flair grinned. 'You're nervous, aren't you?'

'I'm just hoping to spare a rape victim from your bullying.'

'Moi?' He put a hand to his chest. 'I'm insulted.'

I just looked at him. As I did, the door opened. Loren Muse, my chief investigator, walked in. Muse was my age, midthirties, and had been a homicide investigator under my predecessor, Ed Steinberg.

Muse sat down without a word or even a wave.

I turned back to Flair. 'What do you want?' I asked again.

'For starters,' Flair said, 'I want Ms. Chamique Johnson to apologize for destroying the reputation of two fine, upstanding boys.'

I looked at him some more.

'But we'll settle for an immediate dropping of all charges.'

'Dream on.'

'Cope, Cope, Cope.' Flair shook his head and tsk-tsked.

'I said no.'

'You're adorable when you're macho, but you know that already, don't you?' Flair looked over at Loren Muse. A stricken expression crossed his face. 'Dear God, what are you wearing?'

Muse sat up. 'What?'

'Your wardrobe. It's like a frightening new Fox

35

reality show: *When Policewomen Dress Themselves.* Dear God. And those shoes . . .'

'They're practical,' Muse said.

'Sweetheart, fashion rule one: The words *shoes* and *practical* should never be in the same sentence.' Without blinking an eye, Flair turned back to me: 'Our clients cop to a misdemeanor and you give them probation.'

'No.'

'Can I just say two words to you?'

'Those two words wouldn't be *shoes* and *practical*, would they?'

'No, something far more dire for you, I'm afraid: Cal and Jim.'

He paused. I glanced at Muse. She shifted in her seat.

'Those two little names,' Flair went on, a lilt in his voice. 'Cal and Jim. Music to my ears. Do you know what I'm saying, Cope?'

I didn't take the bait.

'In your alleged victim's statement . . . you read her statement, didn't you? . . . in her statement she clearly says that her rapists were named Cal and Jim.'

'It means nothing,' I said.

'Well, see, sweetie – and try to pay attention here because I think this could be very important to your case – our clients are named Barry Marantz and Edward Jenrette. Not Cal and Jim. Barry and Edward. Say them out loud with me. Come on, you can do it. Barry and Edward. Now, do those two names sound at all like Cal and Jim?'

Mort Pubin answered that one. He grinned and said, 'No, they don't, Flair.'

I kept still.

'And, you see, that's *your* victim's statement,' Flair

went on. 'It really is so wonderful, don't you think? Hold on, let me find it. I just love reading it. Mort, do you have it? Wait, here it is.' Flair had on half-moon reading glasses. He cleared his throat and changed voices. "The two boys who did this. Their names were Cal and Jim."

He lowered the paper and looked up as if expecting applause.

I said, 'Barry Marantz's semen was found in her.'

'Ah, yes, but young Barry – a handsome boy, by the way, and we both know that matters – admits to a consensual sex act with your eager, young Ms. Johnson earlier in the evening. We all know that Chamique was at their fraternity house – that's not in dispute, is it?'

I didn't like it, but I said, 'No, that's not in dispute.'

'In fact, we both agree that Chamique Johnson had worked there the week before as a stripper.'

'Exotic dancer,' I corrected.

He just looked at me. 'And so she returned. Without the benefit of money being exchanged. We can agree on that too, can't we?' He didn't bother waiting for me. 'And I can get five, six boys to say she was acting very friendly with Barry. Come on, Cope. You've been around this block before. She's a stripper. She's underage. She sneaked into a college fraternity party. She got nailed by the handsome rich kid. He, what, blew her off or didn't call or whatever. She got upset.'

'And plenty of bruises,' I said.

Mort pounded the table with a fist that looked like roadkill. 'She's just looking for a big payday,' Mort said.

Flair said, 'Not now, Mort.'

'Screw that. We all know the deal. She's going after them because they're loaded.' Mort gave me his best flinty-eyed stare. 'You do know the whore has a record, right? Chamique' – he stretched out her name in a mocking way that pissed me off – 'has already got a lawyer too. Going to shake our boys down. This is just a big payday for that cow. That's all. A big friggin' payday.'

'Mort?' I said.

'What?'

'Shh, the grown-ups are talking now.'

Mort sneered. 'You're no better, Cope.'

I waited.

'The only reason you're prosecuting them is because they're wealthy. And you know it. You're playing that rich-versus-poor crap in the media too. Don't pretend you aren't. You know what sucks about that? You know what really burns my butt?'

I had itched an ass this morning and now I had burned a butt. A big day for me.

'Tell me, Mort.'

'It's accepted in our society,' he said.

'What is?'

'Hating rich people.' Mort threw his hands up, outraged. 'You hear it all the time. "I hate him, he's so rich." Look at Enron and those other scandals. It is now an encouraged prejudice – to hate rich people. If I ever said, "Hey, I hate poor people," I'd be strung up. But call the rich names? Well, you have a free pass. Everyone is allowed to hate the rich.'

I looked at him. 'Maybe they should form a support group.'

'Up yours, Cope.'

'No, I mean it. Trump, the Halliburton guys. I mean, the world hasn't been fair to them. A support group. That's what they should have. Maybe hold a telethon or something.'

Flair Hickory rose. Theatrically, of course. I half-expected him to curtsy. 'I think we're done here. See you tomorrow, handsome. And you' – he looked at Loren Muse, opened his mouth, closed it, shuddered.

'Flair?'

He looked at me.

'That Cal and Jim thing,' I said. 'It just proves she's telling the truth.'

Flair smiled. 'How's that, exactly?'

'Your boys were smart. They called themselves Cal and Jim, so she'd say that.'

He raised an eyebrow. 'You think that will fly?'

'Why else would she say that, Flair?'

'Pardon?'

'I mean, if Chamique wanted to set your clients up, why wouldn't she use their correct names? Why would she make up all that dialogue with Cal and Jim? You read the statement. "Turn her this way, Cal." "Bend her over, Jim." "Whoa, Cal, she's loving this." Why would she make that all up?'

Mort took that one. 'Because she's a money-hungry whore who is dumber than dirt?'

But I could see that I'd scored a point with Flair.

'It doesn't make sense,' I said to him.

Flair leaned in toward me. 'Here's the thing, Cope: It doesn't have to. You know that. Perhaps you're right. Perhaps it doesn't make sense. But see, that leads to confusion. And confusion has the major hots for my favorite hunk, Mr. Reasonable Doubt.' He smiled. 'You might have some physical evidence. But, well, you put that girl on the stand, I will not hold back. It will be game, set, match. We both know that.'

They headed to the door.

'Toodles, my friend. See you in court.'

Chapter 4

Muse and I said nothing for a few moments.

Cal and Jim. The names deflated us.

The position of chief investigator was almost always held by some male lifer, a gruff guy slightly burned out by what he'd seen over the years, with a big belly and a heavy sigh and a well-worn trench coat. It would be that man's job to maneuver the guileless county prosecutor, a political appointee like me, through the rings of the Essex County legal system.

Loren Muse was maybe five feet tall and weighed about as much as your average fourth grader. My choosing Muse had caused some nasty ripples among the veterans, but here was my own private prejudice: I prefer hiring single women of a certain age. They worked harder and were more loyal. I know, I know, but I have found this to be true in almost every case. You find a single woman over the age of, say, thirty-three, and she lives for her career and will give you hours and devotion the married ones with kids will never give you.

To be fair, Muse was also an incredibly gifted investigator. I liked talking things out with her. I would say 'muse'-ing them over, but then you'd understandably groan. Right now she was staring down at the floor.

'What's on your mind?' I asked her.

'Are these shoes really that ugly?'

I looked at her and waited.

'Put simply,' she said, 'if we don't find a way to explain Cal and Jim, we're screwed.'

I stared at the ceiling.

'What?' Muse said.

'Those two names.'

'What about them?'

'Why?' I asked for the umpteenth time. 'Why Cal and Jim?'

'Don't know.'

'You questioned Chamique again?'

'I did. Her story is frighteningly consistent. They used those two names. I think you're right. They simply did that as a cover – so her story would sound idiotic.'

'But why those two names?'

'Probably just random.'

I frowned. 'We're missing something, Muse.'

She nodded. 'I know.'

I have always been pretty good about partitioning my life. We all are, but I am especially good at it. I can create separate universes in my own world. I can deal with one aspect of my life and not have it interfere with another in any way. Some people watch a gangster movie and wonder how the mobster can be so violent on the streets and so loving at home. I get that. I have that ability.

I'm not proud of this. It is not necessarily a great attribute. It protects, yes, but I have seen what actions it can justify.

41

So for the past half hour I had been pushing away the obvious questions: If Gil Perez had been alive this whole time, where had he been? What had happened that night in the woods? And of course, the biggest question: If Gil Perez had survived that awful night . . .

Had my sister survived too?

'Cope?'

It was Muse.

'What's going on?'

I wanted to tell her. But now was not the time. I need to sort it through myself first. Figure out what was what. Make sure that body really did belong to Gil Perez. I stood and walked toward her.

'Cal and Jim,' I said. 'We have to figure out what the hell that's all about – and fast.'

My wife's sister, Greta, and her husband, Bob, lived in a McMansion on a new cul-de-sac that looks almost precisely the same as every other new cul-de-sac in North America. The lots are too small for the ginormous brick edifices that stretch across them. The houses have a variety of shapes and shades but somehow still look exactly the same. Everything is a little too brushed, trying to look aged and only looking more faux.

I had met Greta first, before my wife. My mother ran away before I turned twenty, but I remember something she told me a few months before Camille went into those woods. We were the poorest citizens in our rather mixed town. We were immigrants who had come over from the old Soviet Union when I was four. We had started out okay – we had arrived in the USA as heroes – but things turned very bad very quickly.

We were living on the top floor of a three-family dwelling in Newark, though we went to school at Columbia

High in Maplewood. My father, Vladimir Copinsky (he anglicized it to Copeland), who had once been a doctor in Leningrad, couldn't get a license to practice in this country. He ended up working as a house painter. My mother, a frail beauty named Natasha, the once-proud, well-educated daughter of aristocratic college professors, took on a variety of cleaning jobs for the wealthier families in Short Hills and Livingston but could never hold on to one for very long.

On this particular day, my sister, Camille, came home from school and announced in a teasing voice that the town rich girl had a crush on me. My mother was excited by this.

'You should ask her out,' my mother said to me.

I made a face. 'Have you seen her?'

'I have.'

'Then you know,' I said, speaking as a seventeen-year-old would. 'She's a beast.'

'There is an old Russian expression,' my mother countered, raising a finger to clarify her point. 'A rich girl is beautiful when she stands on her money.'

That was the first thought that came through my mind when I met Greta. Her parents – my former in-laws, I guess, still the grandparents of my Cara – are loaded. My wife came from money. It is all in trust for Cara. I'm the executor. Jane and I discussed long and hard the age at which she should get the bulk of the estate. You don't want someone too young inheriting that kind of money, but hey, on the other hand, it is hers.

My Jane was so practical after the doctors had announced her death sentence. I couldn't listen. You learn a lot when someone you love goes down for the count. I learned that my wife had amazing strength and bravery I would have thought unfathomable before her illness. And I found that I had neither.

Cara and Madison, my niece, were playing in the driveway. The days were starting to get longer now. Madison sat on the asphalt and drew with pieces of chalk that resembled cigars. My own daughter rode one of those motorized, slow-moving minicars that are all the rage with today's under-six crowd. The kids who own them never play on them. Only visitors on play-dates do. Playdates. Man, I hated that term.

I stepped out of the car and shouted, 'Hey, kiddos.'

I waited for the two six-year-old girls to stop what they were doing and sprint over to me and wrap me in big hugs. Yeah, right. Madison glanced my way, but she couldn't have looked less interested without some sort of surgical cerebral disconnect. My own daughter pretended not to hear. Cara steered the Barbie Jeep in a circle. The battery was fading fast, the electric vehicle churning at a speed slower than my uncle Morris reaching for the check.

Greta pushed open the screen door. 'Hey.'

'Hey,' I said. 'So how was the rest of the gymnastics show?'

'Don't worry,' Greta said, shading her eyes with her hand in a pseudosalute. 'I have the whole thing on video.'

'Cute.'

'So what was up with those two cops?'

I shrugged. 'Just work.'

She didn't buy it but she didn't press. 'I have Cara's backpack inside.'

She let the door close behind her. There were workers coming around back. Bob and Greta were putting in a swimming pool with matching landscaping. They'd been thinking about it for several years but wanted to wait until Madison and Cara were old enough to be safe.

'Come on,' I said to my daughter, 'we need to go.'

Cara ignored me again, pretending that the whir of the pink Barbie Jeep was overwhelming her aural faculties. I frowned and started toward her. Cara was ridiculously stubborn. I would like to say, 'like her mother,' but my Jane was the most patient and understanding woman you ever met. It was amazing. You see qualities both good and bad in your children. In the case of Cara, all the negative qualities seemed to emanate from her father.

Madison put down the chalk. 'Come on, Cara.'

Cara ignored her too. Madison shrugged at me and gave me that kid-world-weary sigh. 'Hi, Uncle Cope.'

'Hey, sweetie. Have a good playdate?'

'No,' Madison said with her fists on her hips. 'Cara never plays with me. She just plays with my toys.'

I tried to look understanding.

Greta came out with the backpack. 'We already did the homework,' she said.

'Thank you.'

She waved it off. 'Cara, sweetheart? Your father is here.'

Cara ignored her too. I knew that a tantrum was coming. That too, I guess, she gets from her father. In our Disney-inspired worldview, the widowed father–daughter relationship is a magic one. Witness pretty much every kid film – *The Little Mermaid, Beauty and the Beast, A Little Princess, Aladdin* – you get the point. In movies, not having a mother seemed to be a pretty nifty thing, which, when you think about it, is really perverse. In real life, not having a mother was just about the worst thing that could happen to a little girl.

I made my voice firm. 'Cara, we're going now.'

45

Her face was set – I braced for the confrontation – but fortunately the gods interceded. The Barbie battery went totally dead. The pink Jeep stopped. Cara tried to body-language the vehicle another foot or two, but Barbie wouldn't budge. Cara sighed, stepped out of the Jeep, and started for the car.

'Say good-bye to Aunt Greta and your cousin.'

She did so in a voice sullen enough to make a teenager envious.

When we got home, Cara snapped on the TV without asking permission and settled in for an episode of *SpongeBob*. It seems as though *SpongeBob* is on all the time. I wonder if there is an all-*SpongeBob* station. There also only seems to be maybe three different episodes of the show. That did not seem to deter kids, though.

I was going to say something, but I let it go. Right now I just wanted her distracted. I was still trying to put together what was going on with both the Chamique Johnson rape case and now the sudden reemergence and murder of Gil Perez. I confess that my big case, the biggest of my career, was getting the short end of the stick.

I started preparing dinner. We eat out most nights or order in. I do have a nanny-housekeeper, but today was her day off. 'Hot dogs sound good?'

'Whatever.'

The phone rang. I picked it up.

'Mr. Copeland? This is Detective Tucker York.'

'Yes, Detective, what can I do for you?'

'We located Gil Perez's parents.'

I felt my grip tighten on the phone. 'Did they identify the body?'

'Not yet.'

'What did you tell them?'

'Look, no offense, Mr. Copeland, but this isn't the

kind of thing you just say over the phone, you know? "Your dead child might have been alive this whole time – and oh yeah, he's just been murdered"?'

'I understand.'

'So we were pretty vague. We're going to bring them in and see if we can get an ID. But here's the other thing: How sure are you that it's Gil Perez?'

'Pretty sure.'

'You understand that's not really good enough.'

'I do.'

'And anyway, it's late. My partner and I are off duty. So we're going to have one of our men drive the Perezes down tomorrow morning.'

'So this is, what, a courtesy call?'

'Something like that. I understand your interest. And maybe you should be here in the morning, you know, in case any weird questions come up.'

'Where?'

'The morgue again. You need a ride?'

'No, I know my way.'

Chapter 5

A few hours later I tucked my daughter into bed.

Cara never gives me trouble at bedtime. We have a wonderful routine. I read to her. I do not do it because all the parenting magazines tell me to. I do it because she adores it. It never puts her to sleep. I read to her every night and not once has she done as much as doze. I have. Some of the books are awful. I fall asleep right in her bed. She lets me.

I couldn't keep up with her voracious desire for books to be read to her, so I started getting books on audio. I read to her and then she can listen to one side of a tape – usually forty-five minutes – before it is time to close her eyes and go to sleep. Cara understands and likes this rule.

I am reading Roald Dahl to her right now. Her eyes are wide. Last year, when I took her to see the stage production of *The Lion King*, I bought her a terribly overpriced Timon doll. She has it gripped in her right arm. Timon is a pretty avid listener too.

I finished reading and gave Cara a kiss on the cheek. She smelled like baby shampoo. 'Good night, Daddy,' she said.

'Good night, Pumpkin.'

Kids. One moment they're like Medea having a bad mood swing, the next they are God-kissed angels.

I snapped on the tape player and snapped off her light. I headed down to my home office and turned on the computer. I have a hook-up to my work files. I opened up the rape case of Chamique Johnson and started poring over it.

Cal and Jim.

My victim wasn't what we call jury-pool sympathetic. Chamique was sixteen and had a child out of wedlock. She had been arrested twice for solicitation, once for possession of marijuana. She worked parties as an exotic dancer, and yes, that is an euphemism for stripper. People would wonder what she was doing at that party. That sort of thing did not discourage me. It makes me fight harder. Not because I care about political correctness, but because I am into – very into – justice. If Chamique had been a blond student council vice-president from lily-white Livingston and the boys were black, I mean, come on.

Chamique was a person, a human being. She did not deserve what Barry Marantz and Edward Jenrette did to her.

And I was going to nail their asses to the wall.

I went back to the beginning of the case and sifted through it again. The frat house was a ritzy affair with marble columns and Greek letters and fresh paint and carpeting. I checked telephone records. There was a massive amount of them, each kid having his own private line, not to mention cell phones, text messaging, e-mails,

BlackBerrys. One of Muse's investigators had back-tracked every outgoing phone number from that night. There were more than a hundred, but nothing that stuck out. The rest of the bills were ordinary – electric, water, their account at the local liquor store, janitorial services, cable TV, online services, Netflix, pizza delivered via the Internet . . .

Hold up.

I thought about that. I thought about my victim's statement – I didn't have to read it again. It was disgusting and rather specific. The two boys had made Chamique do things, had put her in different positions, had talked the whole time. But something about it all, the way they moved her around, positioned her . . .

My phone rang. It was Loren Muse.

'Good news?' I asked.

'Only if the expression "No news is good news" is really true.'

'It's not,' I said.

'Damn.'

'Anything on your end?' she asked.

Cal and Jim. What the hell was I missing? It was there, just out of reach. You know that feeling, when something you know is right around the corner, like the name of the dog on *Petticoat Junction* or what was the name of the boxer Mr. T played in *Rocky III*? It was like that. Right out of reach.

Cal and Jim.

The answer was here somewhere, just hiding, just around that mental corner. Damned if I wasn't going to keep running until I caught that sumbitch and nailed him to the wall.

'Not yet,' I said. 'But let's keep working on it.'

*

Early the next morning, Detective York sat across from Mr. and Mrs. Perez.

'Thank you for coming in,' he said.

Twenty years ago, Mrs. Perez had worked in the camp's laundry, but I'd only seen her once since the tragedy. There had been a meeting of the victims' families – the wealthy Greens, the wealthier Billinghams, the poor Copelands, the poorer Perezes – in a big fancy law office not far from where we now were. The case had gone class action with the four families against the camp owner. The Perezes had barely spoken that day. They'd sat and listened and let the others rant and take the lead. I remember Mrs. Perez had kept her purse on her lap and clutched it. Now she had it on the table, but both hands were still bolted to its sides.

They were in an interrogation room. At the suggestion of Detective York, I watched from behind one-way glass. He didn't want them to see me yet. That made sense.

'Why are we here?' Mr. Perez asked.

Perez was heavyset, his button-down shirt a size too small so that his gut strained the buttons.

'This isn't easy to say.' Detective York glanced at the mirror and while his gaze was off, I knew that he was seeking me out. 'So I'm just going to come out with it.'

Mr. Perez's eyes narrowed. Mrs. Perez tightened her grip on the purse. I wondered idly if it was the same purse from fifteen years ago. Weird where the mind goes at times like this.

'There was a murder yesterday in the Washington Heights section of Manhattan,' York said. 'We found the body in an alley near 157th Street.'

I kept my eyes on their faces. The Perezes gave away nothing.

'The victim is male and appears to be between the ages of thirty-five and forty years old. He is five-ten and weighs one hundred seventy pounds.' Detective York's voice had fallen into a professional rhythm. 'The man was using an alias, so we are having trouble identifying him.'

York stopped. Classic technique. See if they end up saying something. Mr. Perez did. 'I don't understand what that has to do with us.'

Mrs. Perez's eyes slid toward her husband, but the rest of her did not move.

'I'm getting to that.'

I could almost see York's wheels spinning, wondering what approach to take, start talking about the clippings in the pocket, the ring, what. I could almost imagine him rehearsing the words in his head and realizing how idiotic they sounded. Clippings, rings – they don't really prove anything. Suddenly even I had my doubts. Here we were, at the moment when the Perezes' world was about to be gut-torn open like a slaughtered calf. I was glad that I was behind glass.

'We brought in a witness to identify the body,' York went on. 'This witness seems to feel that the victim could be your son Gil.'

Mrs. Perez closed her eyes. Mr. Perez stiffened. For a few moments no one spoke, no one moved. Perez did not look at his wife. She did not look at him. They just stood there, frozen, the words still hanging in the air.

'Our son was killed twenty years ago,' Mr. Perez said at last.

York nodded, not sure what to say.

'Are you saying that you've finally found his body?'

'No, I don't think so. Your son was eighteen when he vanished, correct?'

'Almost nineteen,' Mr. Perez said.

'This man – the victim – as I mentioned before, he was probably in his late thirties.'

Perez's father sat back. The mother still hadn't moved.

York dove in. 'Your son's body was never found, isn't that correct?'

'Are you trying to tell us . . . ?'

Mr. Perez's voice died off there. No one jumped in and said, 'Yes, that's exactly what we are suggesting – that your son Gil has been alive this whole time, twenty years, and didn't tell you or anyone else, and now, when you finally have the chance to be reunited with your missing child, he's been murdered. Life's a gas, ain't it?'

Mr. Perez said, 'This is crazy.'

'I know what it must sound like—'

'Why do you think it's our son?'

'Like I said before. We have a witness.'

'Who?'

It was the first time that I had heard Mrs. Perez speak. I almost ducked.

York tried to sound reassuring. 'Look, I understand you're upset—'

'Upset?'

The father again.

'Do you know what it's like . . . can you imagine . . . ?'

His voice died off again. His wife put her hand on his forearm. She sat up a little straighter. For a second she turned to the window and I was sure she could see me through it. Then she met York's eye and said, 'I assume you have a body.'

'Yes, ma'am.'

53

'And that's why you brought us here. You want us to look at it and see if it's our son.'

'Yes.'

Mrs. Perez stood. Her husband watched her, looking small and helpless.

'Okay,' she said. 'Why don't we do that?'

Mr. and Mrs. Perez started down the corridor.

I followed at a discreet distance. Dillon was with me. York stayed with the parents. Mrs. Perez held her head high. She still gripped the purse tight against her as though she feared a snatcher. She stayed a step ahead of her husband. So sexist to think it should be the other way around – that the mother should collapse while the father pushed on. Mr. Perez had been the strong one for the 'show' part. Now that the grenade had exploded, Mrs. Perez took the lead while her husband seemed to shrink farther back with every step.

With its worn floor of linoleum and walls of scrape-the-skin concrete, the corridor couldn't have looked more institutional without a bored bureaucrat leaning against it on a coffee break. I could hear the echo of the footsteps. Mrs. Perez wore heavy gold bracelets. I could hear them clank in rhythm with the walking.

When they turned right at the same window I had stood in front of yesterday, Dillon stuck out his hand in front of me, almost in a protective way, as if I were a kid in the front seat and he'd just stopped short. We stayed a good ten yards back, maneuvering so that we stayed out of their line of vision.

It was hard to see their faces. Mr. and Mrs. Perez stood next to each other. They did not touch. I could see Mr. Perez lower his head. He was wearing a blue blazer. Mrs. Perez had on a dark blouse almost the color of dried blood. She wore a lot of gold. I watched a different person – a tall man with a beard this time – wheel the gurney toward the window. The sheet covered the body.

When it was in place, the man with the beard glanced toward York. York nodded. The man carefully lifted the sheet, as if there were something fragile underneath. I was afraid to make a sound, but I still tilted my body a little to the left. I wanted to see some of Mrs. Perez's face, at least a sliver of profile.

I remember reading about torture victims who want to control something, anything, and so they fight hard not to cry out, not to twist up their face, not to show anything, not to give their tormenters any satisfaction whatsoever. Something in Mrs. Perez's face reminded me of that. She had braced herself. She took the blow with a small shudder, nothing more.

She stared a little while. Nobody spoke. I realized that I was holding my breath. I turned my attention toward Mr. Perez. His eyes were on the floor. They were wet. I could see the quake cross his lips.

Without looking away, Mrs. Perez said, 'That's not our son.'

Silence. I had not expected that.

York said, 'Are you sure, Mrs. Perez?'

She did not reply.

'He was a teenager when you last saw him,' York continued. 'I understand he had long hair.'

'He did.'

'This man's head is shaven. And he has a beard. It's been a lot of years, Mrs. Perez. Please take your time.'

Mrs. Perez finally wrested her eyes from the body. She turned her gaze toward York. York stopped speaking.

'That's not Gil,' she said again.

York swallowed, looked toward the father. 'Mr. Perez?'

He managed a nod, cleared his throat. 'There's not even much of a resemblance.' His eyes closed and another quake ran across his face. 'It's just . . .'

'It's the right age,' Mrs. Perez finished for him.

York said, 'I'm not sure I follow.'

'When you lose a son like that, you always wonder. For us, he'll be forever a teenager. But if he had lived, he would be, yes, the same age as this husky man. So you wonder what he'd be like. Would he be married? Have children? What would he look like?'

'And you're certain this man isn't your son?'

She smiled the saddest smile I had ever seen. 'Yes, Detective, I am certain.'

York nodded. 'I'm sorry to bring you out here.'

They began to turn away when I said, 'Show them the arm.'

Everyone turned in my direction. Mrs. Perez's laser gaze zeroed in on me. There was something there, a strange sense of cunning, a challenge maybe. Mr. Perez spoke first.

'Who are you?' he asked.

I had my eyes on Mrs. Perez. Her sad smile returned. 'You're the Copeland boy, aren't you?'

'Yes, ma'am.'

'Camille Copeland's brother.'

'Yes.'

'Are you the one who made the identification?'

I wanted to explain about the clippings and the ring, but it felt as though I was running out of time. 'The arm,' I said. 'Gil had that awful scar on his arm.'

She nodded. 'One of our neighbors kept llamas. He had a barbed-wire fence. Gil was always a good climber. He tried to get into the pen when he was eight years old.

He slipped and the wire dug deep into his shoulder.' She turned to her husband. 'How many stitches did he need, Jorge?'

Jorge Perez had the sad smile now too. 'Twenty-two.'

That was not the story Gil had told us. He had weaved a tale about a knife fight that sounded like something out of a bad production of *West Side Story*. I hadn't believed him then, even as a kid, so this inconsistency hardly surprised me.

'I remembered it from camp,' I said. I gestured with my chin back toward the glass. 'Look at his arm.'

Mr. Perez shook his head. 'But we already said—'

His wife put a hand up, quieting him. No question about it. She was the leader here. She nodded in my direction before turning back to the glass.

'Show me,' she said.

Her husband looked confused, but he joined her at the window. This time she took his hand and held it. The bearded man had already wheeled the gurney away. York knocked on the glass. The bearded man startled upright. York beckoned him to bring the gurney back toward the window. He did.

I moved closer to Mrs. Perez. I could smell her perfume. It was vaguely familiar, but I didn't remember from where. I stood maybe a foot behind them, looking between their heads.

York hit the white intercom button. 'Please show them his arms.'

The bearded man pulled back the sheet, again using that gentle, respectful technique. The scar was there, an angry slash. A smile returned to Mrs. Perez's face, but what type – sad, happy, confused, fake, practiced, spontaneous? – I couldn't say.

'The left,' she said.

'What?'

She turned to me. 'This scar is on the left arm,' she said. 'Gil's was on the right. And Gil's wasn't that long or deep.'

Mrs. Perez turned to me and put a hand on my arm. 'It's not him, Mr. Copeland. I understand why you'd so much want it to be Gil. But it's not. He isn't coming back to us. And neither is your sister.'

Chapter 6

When I got back to my house, Loren Muse was pacing like a lion near a wounded gazelle. Cara was in the backseat. She had dance class in an hour. I wasn't taking her. Our nanny, Estelle, was back today. She drove. I overpay Estelle and don't care. You find someone good who also drives? You pay them whatever they want.

I pulled into my driveway. The house was a three-bedroom split-level that had all the personality of that morgue corridor. It was supposed to be our 'starter' house. Jane had wanted to upgrade to a McMansion, maybe in Franklin Lakes. I didn't care much where we lived. I'm not into houses or cars and would pretty much let Jane have her way on that kind of stuff.

I missed my wife.

Loren Muse had a something-eating grin locked onto her face. No poker player was Muse, that was for certain. 'I got all the bills. Computer records too. The works.' Then she turned to my daughter. 'Hi, Cara.'

'Loren!' Cara shouted. She jumped out of the car. Cara liked Muse. Muse was good with kids. Muse had never been married, never had any of her own. A few weeks ago I met her most recent boyfriend. The guy wasn't in her league, but that again seemed to be the norm for single women of a certain age.

Muse and I spread everything out on the den floor – witness statements, police reports, phone records, all the fraternity's bills. We started with the frat bills, and man, there were a ton. Every cell phone. Every beer order. Every online purchase.

'So,' Muse said, 'what are we looking for?'

'Damned if I know.'

'I thought you had something.'

'Just a feeling.'

'Oh, gag me. Please don't tell me you're playing a hunch.'

'I would never,' I said.

We kept looking.

'So,' she said, 'basically we're going through these papers looking for a sign saying, 'Big Clue This Way'?'

'We are looking,' I said, 'for a catalyst.'

'Good word. In what way?'

'I don't know, Muse. But the answer is here. I can almost see it.'

'Ooookay,' she said, managing with great effort not to roll her eyes.

So we searched. They ordered pizza pretty much every night, eight pies, from Pizza-To-Go, directly billed to their credit card. They had Netflix so that they could rent regular DVD movies, three at a time delivered to your door, and something called HotFlixxx, so they could do the same with dirty ones. They ordered fraternity frat-logo golf shirts. The frat logo was also on golf balls, tons of them.

We tried to put them in some kind of order. I don't have a clue why.

I lifted the HotFlixxx bill and showed it to Muse. 'Cheap,' I said.

'The Internet makes porn readily accessible and thus affordable to the masses.'

'Good to know,' I said.

'But this might be an opening,' Muse said.

'What is?'

'Young boys, hot women. Or in this case, woman.'

'Explain,' I said.

'I want to hire someone outside the office.'

'Who?'

'A private eye named Cingle Shaker. Have you heard of her?'

I nodded. I had.

'Forget heard,' she said. 'Have you seen her?'

'No.'

'But you've heard?'

'Yeah,' I said. 'I've heard.'

'Well, it's no exaggeration. Cingle Shaker has a body that not only stops traffic, it pulls up the road and bulldozes highway dividers. And she's very good. If anyone can get lawyered-up frat boys to spill, it's Cingle.'

'Okay,' I said.

Hours later – I can't even tell you how many – Muse started to rise. 'There's nothing here, Cope.'

'Seems that way, doesn't it?'

'You have Chamique's direct first thing in the morning?'

'Yes.'

She stood over me. 'Your time would be better spent working on that.'

I did a mock 'yes, sir' salute in her direction. Chamique and I had worked on her testimony already, but not as hard as one might imagine. I didn't want her to sound practiced. I had another strategy in mind.

'I'll get you what I can,' Muse said.

She stomped out the door in her best lick-da-world mode.

Estelle made us all dinner – spaghetti and meatballs. Estelle is not a great cook, but it went down. I took Cara out for Van Dyke's ice cream afterward, a special treat. She was chattier now. In the rearview mirror, I could see her strapped into the car seat. When I was a kid, we were allowed to sit in the front seat. Now you had to be of drinking age before that was permissible.

I tried to listen to what she was saying but Cara was just yakking pure nonsense the way kids do. It seems Brittany had been mean to Morgan so Kyle threw an eraser and how come Kylie, not Kylie G, Kylie N – there were two Kylies in her class – how come Kylie N didn't want to go on the swings at recess unless Kiera was on one too? I kept glancing at her animated face, scrunched up as though imitating an adult. I got hit with that overwhelming feeling. It sneaked up on me. Parents get it from time to time. You are looking at your child and it is an ordinary moment, not like they are onstage or hitting a winning shot, just sitting there and you look at them and you know that they are your whole life and that moves you and scares you and makes you want to stop time.

I had lost a sister. I had lost a wife. And most recently, I had lost my father. In all three cases I had gotten off the canvas. But as I looked at Cara, at the way she talked with her hands and widened her eyes, I knew that there was indeed one blow from which I could never rise.

I thought about my father. In the woods. With that shovel. His heart broken. Searching for his little girl. I thought about my mother. She had run away. I didn't know where she was. Sometimes I still think about searching her out. But not that often anymore. For years I had hated her. Maybe I still do. Or maybe now that I have a child I understand a little better about the pain she must have been going through.

When we walked back into the house, the phone rang. Estelle took Cara from me. I picked it up and said hello.

'We got a problem, Cope.'

It was my brother-in-law, Bob, Greta's husband. He was chairman of the charitable fund JaneCare. Greta, Bob and I had founded it after my wife's death. I had gotten lots of wonderful press for it. My living memorial to my lovely, beautiful, gentle wife.

My, what a wonderful husband I must have been.

'What's the matter?' I asked.

'Your rape case is costing us big-time. Edward Jenrette's father has gotten several of his friends to back out of their commitments.'

I closed my eyes. 'Classy.'

'Worse, he's making noises that we've embezzled funds. EJ Jenrette is a well-connected son of a bitch. I'm already getting calls.'

'So we open our books,' I said. 'They won't find anything.'

'Don't be naive, Cope. We compete with other charities for the giving dollar. If there is even a whiff of a scandal, we're finished.'

'Not much we can do about it, Bob.'

'I know. It's just that . . . we're doing a lot of good here, Cope.'

'I know.'

'But funding is always tough.'

'So what are you suggesting?'

'Nothing.' Bob hesitated and I could tell he had more to say. So I waited. 'But come on, Cope, you guys plea-bargain all the time, right?'

'We do.'

'You let a lesser injustice slide so you can nail someone for a bigger one.'

'When we have to.'

'These two boys. I hear they're good kids.'

'You hear wrong.'

'Look, I'm not saying that they don't deserve to be punished, but sometimes you have to trade. The greater good. JaneCare is making big strides. It might be the greater good. That's all I'm saying.'

'Good night, Bob.'

'No offense, Cope. I'm just trying to help.'

'I know. Good night, Bob.'

I hung up. My hands were shaking. Jenrette, that son of a bitch, hadn't gone after me. He had gone after my wife's memory. I started upstairs. Rage consumed me. I would channel it. I sat at my desk. There were only two pictures on it. One was the current school photo of my daughter, Cara. It had a prized spot, dead center.

The second photograph was a grainy picture of my Noni and Popi from the old country, Russia – or, as it was called when they died in that gulag, the Soviet Union. They died when I was very young, when we still lived in Leningrad, but I have vague recollections of them, especially my Popi's big shock of white hair.

Why, I often wondered, do I keep this picture out?

Their daughter, my mother, had abandoned me, right? Dumb when you thought about it. But somehow, despite the obvious pain intertwined, I find the picture oddly relevant. I would look at it, at my Noni and Popi, and I would wonder about ripples and family curses and where it all might have started.

I used to keep out pictures of Jane and Camille. I liked having them in view. They brought me comfort. But just because I found comfort in the dead, that didn't mean my daughter did. It was a hard balance with a six-year-old. You want to talk about her mother. You want her to know about Jane, her wonderful spirit, how much she would have loved her little girl. You want to offer some kind of comfort, too, that her mother was up in heaven looking down on her. But I didn't believe in that. I want to. I want to believe that there is a glorious afterlife and that above us, my wife, my sister and my father are all smiling down. But I can't make myself believe it. And when I peddle it to my daughter, I feel as though I'm lying to her. I do it anyway. For now it feels like Santa Claus or the Easter Bunny, something temporary and soothing, but in the end, she, like all children, will learn it is yet another parental lie with minimum justification. Or maybe I'm wrong and they are up there looking down on us. Maybe that is what Cara will conclude someday.

At midnight I finally allowed my mind to go where it wanted to – my sister, Camille, Gil Perez, that awful, magical summer. I flashed back to camp. I thought about Camille. I thought about that night. And for the first time in several years, I let myself think about Lucy.

A sad smile crossed my face. Lucy Silverstein had been my first real girlfriend. We'd had it so good, a fairy-tale summer romance, until that night. We never had the chance to break up – we were, instead, ripped apart by bloody murders. We were torn away while still enmeshed in each other, at a point where our love – as silly and immature as it was supposed to have been – was still rising and growing.

Lucy was the past. I had given myself an ultimatum and shut her out. But the heart doesn't really know from ultimatums. Over the years, I have tried to see what Lucy is up to, harmlessly Googling her name and stuff, though I doubt I would ever have the courage to contact her. I never found anything. My bet is, after all that happened, she'd wisely changed her name. Lucy was probably married now – like I had been. She was probably happy. I hoped so.

I pushed that all away. Right now I needed to think about Gil Perez. I closed my eyes and went back. I thought about him at camp, how we horsed around, how I used to fun-punch him in the arm, the way he'd say, 'Wimp! I didn't even feel that . . .'

I could see him now, with the skinny torso, his shorts too baggy before that was a fashionable look, the smile that needed major orthodontia, the . . .

My eyes opened. Something felt wrong.

I headed into the basement. I found the cardboard box right away. Jane had been good about marking everything. I saw her extraneat handwriting on the side of the box. It made me pause. Handwriting is so damn personal. My fingertips drifted over it. I touched her lettering and pictured her with the big Magic Marker in her hand, the top in her mouth as she wrote boldly: PHOTOGRAPHS – COPELANDS.

I had made many mistakes in my life. But Jane . . . it was my one great break. Her good transformed me, made me better and stronger in every way. Yes, I loved her and there was passion, but more than that, she had the ability to make me my best. I was neurotic and insecure, the financial-aid kid at a school with very few of them, and there she was, this nearly perfect creature who saw something in me. How? How could I be so awful and worthless if a creature this magnificent loved me?

Jane was my rock. And then she got sick. My rock crumbled. And so did I.

I found the photographs from that long-ago summer. There were none of Lucy. I had wisely thrown them all away years ago. Lucy and I had our songs too – Cat Stevens, James Taylor – stuff that was syrupy enough to be gag worthy. I have trouble listening to them. Still. To this day. I make sure that they are nowhere near my iPod. If they come on the radio, I switch stations at a dizzying speed.

I sifted through a stack of pictures from that summer. Most of them were of my sister. I pushed through them until I found one that was taken three days before she died. Doug Billingham was in the picture – her boyfriend. A rich kid. Mom had approved, of course. The camp was an odd social mix of privileged and poor. Inside that camp, the upper and lower classes mingled on about as level a playing field as you could find. That was how the hippie who ran the camp, Lucy's fun-loving hippie dad, Ira, wanted it.

Margot Green, another rich kid, was smack in the middle. She always was. She had been the camp hottie and knew it. She was blond and busty and worked it constantly. She always dated older guys, until Gil anyway, and to the mere mortals around her, Margot's life was like something on TV, a melodrama we all watched with fascination. I looked at her now and pictured her throat slit. I closed my eyes for a second.

Gil Perez was in the photograph too. And that was why I was here.

I pointed my desk light and took a closer look.

Upstairs, I'd remembered something. I am right-handed, but when I fun-punched Gil on the arm, I used my left hand. I did this to avoid touching that awful scar. True, it was healed up, but I was afraid to go near it. Like it might tear open anew and start spewing blood. So I used my left hand and hit his right arm. I squinted and moved closer.

I could see the bottom of the scar peaking out beneath the T-shirt.

The room began to spin.

Mrs. Perez had said that her son's scar was on his right arm. But then I would have punched him with my right hand, ergo, hitting his left shoulder. But I hadn't done that. I had punched him with my left hand – on his right shoulder.

Now I had the proof.

Gil Perez's scar was on his left arm.

Mrs. Perez had lied.

And now I had to wonder why.

Chapter 7

arrived in my office early the next morning. In half an hour, I would have Chamique Johnson, the victim, on the stand. I was going over my notes. When the clock struck nine, I had enough. So I called Detective York.

'Mrs. Perez lied,' I said.

He listened to my explanation.

'Lied,' York repeated when I finished. 'Don't you think that's a little strong?'

'What would you call it?'

'Maybe she just made a mistake?'

'A mistake about which one of her son's arms was scarred?'

'Sure, why not. She knew it wasn't him already. Natural.'

I wasn't buying it. 'Have you got anything new on the case?'

'We think Santiago was living in New Jersey.'

'You have an address?'

'Nope. But we have a girlfriend. Or at least we think she's a girlfriend. A friend anyway.'

'How did you find her?'

'That empty cell phone. She called it looking for him.'

'So who is he really? Manolo Santiago, I mean?'

'Don't know.'

'The girlfriend won't tell you?'

'The girlfriend only knew him as Santiago. Oh, something else important.'

'What?'

'His body was moved. I mean, we were sure of that in the first place. But now we have it confirmed. And our ME says, based on the bleeding out and some other nonsense I don't quite understand or care to, Santiago was probably dead an hour before he got dumped. There are some carpet fibers, stuff like that. Preliminary shows that they're from a car.'

'So Santiago was murdered, stuck in a trunk, and then dumped in Washington Heights?'

'That's our working theory.'

'Do you have a make on the car?'

'Not yet. But our guy says it's something old. That's all he knows. But they're working on it.'

'How old?'

'I don't know. Not new. Come on, Copeland, give me a break here.'

'I have a pretty big personal interest in this case.'

'Speaking of which.'

'What?'

'Why don't you jump in and help?'

'Meaning?'

'Meaning I have a psychotic caseload. We now have a possible New Jersey connection – Santiago probably lived there. Or at least his girlfriend does. And that's where she saw him exclusively – in New Jersey.'

'My county?'

'No, I think it's Hudson. Or maybe Bergen. Hell, I don't know. But it's close enough. But let me add something else into the mix.'

'I'm listening.'

'Your sister lived in New Jersey, right?'

'Yes.'

'That's not my jurisdiction. You can probably claim it as your own, even if it's out of your county. Open up the old case – it's not like anybody else wants it.'

I thought about that. I was being played, in part. He was hoping I'd do some of his legwork and hand off the glory – all of which was fine for me.

'This girlfriend,' I said. 'Do you have a name?'

'Raya Singh.'

'How about an address?'

'You're going to talk to her?'

'You mind?'

'As long as you don't screw up my case, you can do whatever you want. But can I give you a piece of friendly advice?'

'Sure.'

'That lunatic, the Summer Slasher. I forget his real name.'

'Wayne Steubens,' I said.

'You knew him, didn't you?'

'Have you read the case file?' I asked.

'Yep. They looked at you hard for it, didn't they?'

I still remember that Sheriff Lowell, that look of skepticism. Understandable, of course.

'What's your point?'

71

'Just this: Steubens is still looking to overturn his conviction.'

'He was never tried for those first four murders,' I said. 'They didn't need them – they had better evidence in the other cases.'

'I know. But still. He was linked. If it really is Gil Perez and Steubens was to hear, well, it would help him. You know what I'm saying?'

He was saying to keep it quiet until I knew something for sure. I got that. The last thing I wanted to do was help Wayne Steubens.

We hung up. Loren Muse stuck her head in my office.

'You got anything new for me?' I asked.

'Nope. Sorry.' She checked her watch. 'You ready for your big direct?'

'I am.'

'Then come on. It's show time.'

'The People call Chamique Johnson.'

Chamique was dressed on the conservative side but not ridiculously so. You could still see the street. You could still see the curves. I even had her wear high heels. There are times you try to obstruct the jury's view. And there are times, like this, when you know that your only chance is for them to see the entire picture, warts and all.

Chamique kept her head high. Her eyes shifted right and left, not in a dishonest-Nixon way but in a where-is-the-next-blow-coming-from way. Her makeup was a little heavy. But that was okay too. It made her look like a girl trying to look like a grown-up.

There were those in my office who disagreed with this strategy. But I believed that if you are going to go down, go down with the truth. So that was what I was prepared to do now.

Chamique stated her name and swore on the Bible and sat down. I smiled at her and met her eye. Chamique offered me a little nod, giving me the okay to go ahead.

'You work as a stripper, isn't that right?'

Opening up with a question like that – without any preliminaries – surprised the gallery. There were a few gasps. Chamique blinked. She had some idea of what I was going to do here, but I had intentionally not been specific.

'Part time,' she said.

I didn't like that answer. It seemed too wary.

'But you do take off your clothes for money, right?'

'Yeah.'

That was more like it. No hesitation.

'Do you strip in clubs or at private parties?'

'Both.'

'What club do you strip out of?'

'Pink Tail. It's in Newark.'

'How old are you?' I asked.

'Sixteen.'

'Don't you have to be eighteen to strip?'

'Yeah.'

'So how do you get around that?'

Chamique shrugged. 'I got a fake ID, says I'm twenty-one.'

'So you break the law?'

'Guess so.'

'Do you break the law or not?' I asked. There was a hint of steel in my voice. Chamique understood. I wanted her to be honest. I wanted her to – pardon the pun, her being a stripper and all – expose herself totally. The steel was a reminder.

'Yeah. I break the law.'

I looked over at the defense table. Mort Pubin stared at me as if I were out of my mind. Flair Hickory had his palms pressed together, his index finger resting on his lips. Their two clients, Barry Marantz and Edward Jenrette, wore blue blazers and pale faces. They did not look smug or confident or evil. They looked contrite and scared and very young. The cynic would say that this was intentional – that their lawyers had told them how to sit and what expressions to wear on their faces. But I knew better. I just didn't let it matter to me.

I smiled at my witness. 'You're not the only one, Chamique. We found a bunch of fake IDs at your rapists' frat house – so that they could all go out and do a little underage partying. At least you broke the law to make a living.'

Mort was on his feet. 'Objection!'

'Sustained.'

But it was in. As the old saw goes, 'You can't unring a bell.'

'Miss Johnson,' I continued, 'you're not a virgin, are you?'

'No.'

'In fact, you have a son out of wedlock.'

'I do.'

'How old is he?'

'Fifteen months.'

'Tell me, Miss Johnson. Does the fact that you're not a virgin and have a son out of marriage make you less of a human being?'

'Objection!'

'Sustained.' The judge, a bushy-eyed man named Arnold Pierce, frowned at me.

'I'm just pointing out the obvious, Your Honor. If

Miss Johnson were an upper-class blonde from Short Hills or Livingston—'

'Save it for the summation, Mr. Copeland.'

I would. And I had used it in the opening. I turned back to my victim.

'Do you enjoy stripping, Chamique?'

'Objection!' Mort Pubin was up again. 'Irrelevant. Who cares if she likes stripping or not?'

Judge Pierce looked at me. 'Well?'

'Tell you what,' I said, looking at Pubin. 'I won't ask about her stripping if you don't.'

Pubin went still. Flair Hickory still had not spoken. He did not like to object. By and large, juries don't like objections. They think you're hiding something from them. Flair wanted to stay liked. So he had Mort do the hatchet work. It was the attorney version of good cop, bad cop.

I turned back to Chamique. 'You weren't stripping the night you were raped, were you?'

'Objection!'

'Alleged rape,' I corrected.

'No,' Chamique said. 'I was invited.'

'You were invited to a party at the frat house where Mr. Marantz and Mr. Jenrette live?'

'That's right.'

'Did either Mr. Marantz or Mr. Jenrette invite you?'

'No.'

'Who did?'

'Another boy who lived there.'

'What's his name?'

'Jerry Flynn.'

'I see. How did you meet Mr. Flynn?'

'I worked the frat the week before.'

'When you say you worked the frat—'

'I stripped for them,' Chamique finished for me. I liked that. We were getting a rhythm.

'And Mr. Flynn was there?'

'They all were.'

'When you say "they all" – '

She pointed at the two defendants. 'They were there too. A bunch of other guys.'

'How many would you say?'

'Twenty, twenty-five maybe.'

'Okay, but it was Mr. Flynn who invited you to the party a week later?'

'Yes.'

'And you accepted the invitation?'

Her eyes were wet now, but she held her head high. 'Yes.'

'Why did you choose to go?'

Chamique thought about that. 'It would be like a billionaire inviting you on his yacht.'

'You were impressed with them?'

'Yeah. 'Course.'

'And their money?'

'That too,' she said.

I loved her for that answer.

'And,' she went on, 'Jerry was sweet to me when I was stripping.'

'Mr. Flynn treated you nicely?'

'Yeah.'

I nodded. I was entering trickier territory now, but I went for it. 'By the way, Chamique, going back on the night you were hired to strip . . .' I felt my breath go a little shallow. 'Did you perform other services on any of the men in attendance?'

I met her eye. She swallowed, but she held it together. Her voice was soft. The edges were gone now. 'Yeah.'

'Were these favors of a sexual nature?'

'Yeah.'

She lowered her head.

'Don't be ashamed,' I said. 'You needed the money.' I gestured toward the defense table. 'What's their excuse?'

'Objection!'

'Sustained.'

But Mort Pubin wasn't done. 'Your Honor, that statement was an outrage!'

'It is an outrage,' I agreed. 'You should castigate your clients immediately.'

Mort Pubin turned red. His voice was a whine. 'Your Honor!'

'Mr. Copeland.'

I held my palm up to the judge, signaling he was right and I would cease. I am a firm believer in getting out all the bad news during direct, albeit in my own way. You take the wind out of their cross.

'Were you interested in Mr. Flynn as a potential boyfriend?'

Mort Pubin again: 'Objection! Relevance?'

'Mr. Copeland?'

'Of course it's relevant. They are going to say that Miss Johnson is making up these charges to shake down their clients financially. I'm trying to establish her frame of mind on that night.'

'I'll allow it,' Judge Pierce said.

I repeated the question.

Chamique squirmed a little and it made her look her age. 'Jerry was out of my league.'

'But?'

'But, I mean, yeah, I don't know. I never met anyone like him. He held a door for me. He was so nice. I'm not used to that.'

'And he's rich. I mean, compared with you.'

'Yeah.'

'Did that mean something to you?'

'Sure.'

I loved the honesty.

Chamique's eyes darted toward the jury box. The defiant expression was back. 'I got dreams too.'

I let that echo a few moments before following up. 'And what was your dream that night, Chamique?'

Mort was about to object again but Flair Hickory put his hand on Mort's forearm.

Chamique shrugged. 'It's stupid.'

'Tell me anyway.'

'I thought maybe . . . it was stupid . . . I thought maybe he'd like me, you know?'

'I do,' I said. 'How did you get to the party?'

'Took a bus from Irvington and then I walked.'

'And when you arrived at the frat house, Mr. Flynn was there?'

'Yes.'

'Was he still sweet?'

'At first, yeah.' Now a tear escaped. 'He was real sweet. It was—'

She stopped.

'It was what, Chamique?'

'In the beginning' – another tear ran down her cheek – 'it was the best night of my life.'

I let the words hang and echo. A third tear escaped.

'Are you okay?' I asked

Chamique wiped the tear. 'I'm fine.'

'You sure?'

Her voice was hard again. 'Ask your question, Mr. Copeland,' she said.

She was wonderful. The jury all had their heads up,

78

listening to – and believing, I thought – every word.

'Was there a time when Mr. Flynn's behavior toward you changed?'

'Yeah.'

'When?'

'I saw him whispering with that one over there.' She pointed toward Edward Jenrette.

'Mr. Jenrette?'

'Yeah. Him.'

Jenrette tried not to shrink from Chamique's gaze. He was half successful.

'You saw Mr. Jenrette whisper something to Mr. Flynn?'

'Yeah.'

'And then what happened?'

'Jerry asked me if I wanted to take a walk.'

'By Jerry, you mean Jerry Flynn?'

'Yeah.'

'Okay, tell us what happened.'

'We walked outside. They had a keg. He asked me if I wanted a beer. I said no. He was acting all jumpy and stuff.'

Mort Pubin was up. 'Objection.'

I spread my arm and looked exasperated. 'Your Honor.'

'I'll allow it,' the judge said.

'Go on,' I said.

'Jerry got a beer from the keg and he kept looking at it.'

'Looking at his beer?'

'Yeah, a little, I guess. He wouldn't look at me no more. Something was different. I asked him if he was okay. He said, sure, everything was great. And then' – her voice didn't catch, but it came awfully close –

79

'he said I had a hot bod and that he liked watching me take off my clothes.'

'Did that surprise you?'

'Yeah. I mean, he never talked like that before. His voice was all rough now.' She swallowed. 'Like the others.'

'Go on.'

'He said, "You wanna go upstairs and see my room?"'

'What did you say?'

'I said okay.'

'Did you want to go to his room?'

Chamique closed her eyes. Another tear leaked out. She shook her head.

'You need to answer out loud.'

'No,' she said.

'Why did you go?'

'I wanted him to like me.'

'And you thought he would like you if you went upstairs with him?'

Chamique's voice was soft. 'I knew he wouldn't if I said no.'

I turned away and moved back to my table. I pretended to look at notes. I just wanted to give the jury time to digest. Chamique had her back straight. She kept her chin high. She tried to show nothing, but you could feel the hurt emanating from her.

'What happened when you got upstairs?'

'I walked past a door.' She turned her eyes back to Jenrette. 'And then he grabbed me.'

Again I made her point out Edward Jenrette and identify him by name.

'Was anyone else in the room?'

'Yeah. Him.'

She pointed to Barry Marantz. I noticed the two families behind the defendants. The parents had those death-mask faces, where the skin looks as if it were being pulled from behind, the cheekbones appear too prominent, the eyes sunken and shattered. They were the sentinels, lined up to shelter their offspring. They were devastated. I felt bad for them. But too bad. Edward Jenrette and Barry Marantz had people to protect them.

Chamique Johnson had no one.

Yet part of me understood what really happened here. You start drinking, you get out of control, you forget about the consequences. Maybe they would never do this again. Maybe they had indeed learned their lesson. But again too bad.

There were some people who were bad to the bone, who would always be cruel and nasty and hurt others. There were others, maybe most that came through my office, who just messed up. It is not my job to differentiate. I leave that to the judge during sentencing.

'Okay,' I said, 'what happened next?'

'He closed the door.'

'Which one?'

She pointed to Marantz.

'Chamique, to make this easier, could you call him Mr. Marantz and the other one Mr. Jenrette?'

She nodded.

'So Mr. Marantz closed the door. And then what happened?'

'Mr. Jenrette told me to get on my knees.'

'Where was Mr. Flynn at this point?'

'I don't know.'

'You don't know?' I feigned surprise. 'Hadn't he walked up the stairs with you?'

'Yeah.'

'Hadn't he been standing next to you when Mr. Jenrette grabbed you?'

'Yeah.'

'And then?'

'I don't know. He didn't come in the room. He just let the door close.'

'Did you see him again?'

'Not till later.'

I took a deep breath and dove in. I asked Chamique what happened next. I walked her through the assault. The testimony was graphic. She spoke matter-of-factly – a total disconnect. There was much to get in, what they had said, how they had laughed, what they had done to her. I needed specifics. I don't think the jury wanted to hear it. I understood that. But I needed her to try to be as specific as possible, to remember every position, who had been where, who had done what.

It was numbing.

When we finished the testimony on the assault, I gave it a few seconds and then approached our trickiest problem. 'In your testimony, you claimed your attackers used the names Cal and Jim.'

'Objection, Your Honor.'

It was Flair Hickory, speaking up for the first time. His voice was quiet, the kind of quiet that draws all ears.

'She did not claim they *used* the names Cal and Jim,' Flair said. 'She claimed, in both her testimony and prior statements, that they *were* Cal and Jim.'

'I'll rephrase,' I said with a tone of exasperation, as if to say to the jury, can you believe how picky he's being? I turned back to Chamique. 'Which one *was* Cal and which one *was* Jim?'

Chamique identified Barry Marantz as Cal and Edward Jenrette as Jim.

'Did they introduce themselves to you?' I asked.

'No.'

'So how did you know their names?'

'They used them with each other.'

'Per your testimony. For example, Mr. Marantz said, 'Bend her over, Jim.' Like that?'

'Yeah.'

'You are aware,' I said, 'that neither of the defendants is named Cal or Jim.'

'I know,' she said.

'Can you explain that?'

'No. I'm just telling you what they said.'

No hesitation, no trying to make excuses – it was a good answer. I left it alone.

'What happened after they raped you?'

'They made me clean up.'

'How?'

'They stuck me in a shower. They used soap on me. The shower had one of those hoses. They made me scrub off.'

'Then what?'

'They took my clothes – they said they were going to burn them. Then they gave me a T-shirt and shorts.'

'What happened next?'

'Jerry walked me to the bus stop.'

'Did Mr. Flynn say anything to you during the walk?'

'No.'

'Not one word?'

'Not one word.'

'Did you say anything to him?'

'No.'

Again I looked surprised. 'You didn't tell him you were raped?'

She smiled for the first time. 'You don't think he knew that?'

I let that go too. I wanted to shift gears again.

'Have you hired a lawyer, Chamique?'

'Kinda.'

'What do you mean, kinda?'

'I didn't really hire him. He found me.'

'What's his name?'

'Horace Foley. He don't dress nice like Mr. Hickory over there.'

Flair smiled at that one.

'Are you suing the defendants?'

'Yeah.'

'Why are you suing them?'

'To make them pay,' she said.

'Isn't that what we're doing here?' I asked. 'Finding a way to punish them?'

'Yeah. But the lawsuit is about money.'

I made a face as though I didn't understand. 'But the defense is going to claim that you made up these charges to extort money. They're going to say that your lawsuit proves, in fact, that you're interested in money.'

'I am interested in money,' Chamique said. 'Did I ever say I wasn't?'

I waited.

'Aren't you interested in money, Mr. Copeland?'

'I am,' I said.

'So?'

'So,' I said, 'the defense is going to claim it's a motive to lie.'

'Can't do nothing about that,' she said. 'See, if I say I don't care about money, that would be a lie.' She looked at the jury. 'If I sat here and told you, money means nothing to me, would you believe me? 'Course not. Same as if you told me you didn't care about money. I cared about money before they raped me. I care about it now. I'm not lying. They raped me. I want them to go to jail for that. And if I can get some money from them too, why not? I could use it.'

I stepped back. Candor – real candor – smells like nothing else.

'Nothing further,' I said.

Chapter 8

The trial broke for lunch.

Lunch is usually a time to discuss strategy with my subordinates. But I didn't want that right now. I wanted to be alone. I wanted to rework the direct in my head, see what I missed, figure out what Flair was going to do.

I ordered a cheeseburger and a beer from a waitress who looked as though she wanted to be in one of those want-to-get-away? commercials. She called me hon. I love when a waitress calls me hon.

A trial is two narratives competing for your attention. You need to make your protagonist a real person. Real was much more important than pure. Attorneys forget that. They think they need to make their clients sweet and perfect. They don't. So I try to never dumb it down for the jury. People are pretty good judges of character. They are more likely to believe you if you show your foibles. At least on my side – the prosecution's. When you're doing defense, you want to muddy up the waters.

As Flair Hickory had made abundantly clear, you want to bring forth that beautiful mistress known as Reasonable Doubt. I was the opposite. I needed it clear.

The waitress reappeared and said, 'Here, hon,' as she dropped the burger in front of me. I eyed it. It looked so greasy I almost ordered a side of angiogram. But in truth, this mess was just what I'd wanted. I put both hands on it and felt my fingers sink into the bun.

'Mr. Copeland?'

I didn't recognize the young man standing over me.

'You mind?' I said. 'I'm trying to eat here.'

'This is for you.'

He dropped a note on the table and left. It was a sheet from a legal yellow pad folded into a small rectangle. I opened it up.

Please meet me in the back booth on your right.
EJ Jenrette

It was Edward's father. I looked down at my beloved burger. It looked back at me. I hate eating cold food or anything reheated. So I ate it. I was starving. I tried not to wolf it down. The beer tasted damn good.

When I was done I rose and headed toward the back booth on my right. EJ Jenrette was there. A glass of what looked like Scotch sat on the table in front of him. He had both hands surrounding the glass, as if he were trying to protect it. His eyes were transfixed on the liquor.

He did not look up as I slid into the booth. If he was upset by my tardiness – heck, if he noticed it – EJ Jenrette was hiding it well.

'You wanted to see me?' I said.

EJ nodded. He was a big man, ex-athlete type, with

designer shirts that still looked as though the collar was strangling the neck. I waited.

'You have a child,' he said.

I waited some more.

'What would you do to protect her?'

'For one,' I said, 'I'd never let her go to a party at your son's frat house.'

He looked up. 'That's not funny.'

'Are we done here?'

He took a long pull on his drink.

'I will give that girl a hundred thousand dollars,' Jenrette said. 'I will give your wife's charity another one hundred thousand.'

'Great. Do you want to write the checks now?'

'You'll drop the charges?'

'No.'

He met my eye. 'He's my son. Do you really want him to spend the next ten years in prison?'

'Yes. But the judge will decide the sentence.'

'He's just a kid. At worst, he got carried away.'

'You have a daughter, don't you, Mr. Jenrette?'

Jenrette stared at his drink.

'If a couple of black kids from Irvington grabbed her, dragged her into a room and did those things to her, would you want it swept under the rug?'

'My daughter isn't a stripper.'

'No, sir, she isn't. She has all the privileges in life. She has all the advantages. Why would she strip?'

'Do me a favor,' he said. 'Don't hand me that socio-economic crap. Are you saying that because she was disadvantaged she had no choice but to choose whoredom? Please. It's an insult to any disadvantaged person who ever worked their way out of the ghetto.'

I raised my eyebrows. 'Ghetto?'

He said nothing.

'You live in Short Hills, don't you, Mr. Jenrette?'

'So?'

'Tell me,' I said, 'how many of your neighbors choose stripping or, to use your term, whoredom?'

'I don't know.'

'What Chamique Johnson does or doesn't do is totally irrelevant to her being raped. We don't get to choose like that. Your son doesn't get to decide who deserves to be raped or not. But either way, Chamique Johnson stripped because she had limited options. Your daughter doesn't.' I shook my head. 'You really don't get it.'

'Get what?'

'The fact that she's forced to strip and sell herself doesn't make Edward less culpable. If anything, it makes him more so.'

'My son didn't rape her.'

'That's why we have trials,' I said. 'Are we done now?'

He finally lifted his head. 'I can make it hard on you.'

'Seems like you're already trying that.'

'The fund stoppage?' He shrugged. 'That was nothing. A muscle flex.'

He met my eye and held it. This had gone far enough.

'Good-bye, Mr. Jenrette.'

He reached out and grabbed my forearm. 'They're going to get off.'

'We'll see.'

'You scored points today, but that whore still needs to be crossed. You can't explain away the fact that she got their names wrong. That will be your downfall. You know that. So listen to what I'm suggesting.'

I waited.

'My son and the Marantz boy will plead to whatever charge you come up with so long as there is no jail time. They'll do community service. They can be on strict probation for as long as you want. That's fair. But in addition, I will help support this troubled woman and I will make sure that JaneCare gets the proper funding. It's a win-win-win.'

'No,' I said.

'Do you really think these boys will do something like this again?'

'Truth?' I said. 'Probably not.'

'I thought prison was about rehabilitation.'

'Yeah, but I'm not big on rehabilitation,' I said. 'I'm big on justice.'

'And you think my son going to prison is justice?'

'Yes,' I said. 'But again, that's why we have juries and judges.'

'Have you ever made a mistake, Mr. Copeland?'

I said nothing.

'Because I'm going to dig. I'm going to dig until I find every mistake you ever made. And I'll use them. You got skeletons, Mr. Copeland. We both know that. If you keep up this witch hunt, I'm going to drag them out for all the world to see.' He seemed to be gaining confidence now. I didn't like that. 'At worst, my son made a big mistake. We're trying to find a way to make amends for what he did without destroying his life. Can you understand that?'

'I have nothing more to say to you,' I said.

He kept hold of my arm.

'Last warning, Mr. Copeland. I will do whatever I can to protect my child.'

I looked at EJ Jenrette and then I did something that surprised him. I smiled.

'What?' he said.

'It's nice,' I said.

'What is?'

'That your son has so many people who will fight for him,' I said. 'In the courtroom too. Edward has so many people on his side.'

'He is loved.'

'Nice,' I said again, pulling away my arm. 'But when I look at all those people sitting behind your son, you know what I can't help but notice?'

'What?'

'Chamique Johnson,' I said, 'has no one sitting behind her.'

'I would like to share this journal entry with the class,' Lucy Gold said.

Lucy liked having her students form a big circle with their desks. She stood in the center of it. Sure, it was hokey, her stalking around the 'ring of learning' like the bad-guy wrestler, but she found it worked. When you put the students in a circle, no matter how large, they all had front-row seats. There was no place to hide.

Lonnie was in the room. Lucy had considered letting him read the entry so she could better study the faces, but the narrator was female. It wouldn't sound right. Besides, whoever wrote this *knew* that Lucy would be watching for a reaction. Had to know. Had to be screwing with her mind. So Lucy decided that she would read it while Lonnie searched for reactions. And of course, Lucy would look up a lot, pausing during the reading, hoping something would give.

Sylvia Potter, the brownnoser, was directly in front of her. Her hands were folded and her eyes were wide. Lucy met her eye and gave her a small smile. Sylvia brightened up. Next to her was Alvin Renfro, a big-time slacker. Renfro sat the way most students did, as though they had no bones and might slide off their chairs and become a puddle on the floor.

'This happened when I was seventeen,' Lucy read. 'I was at summer camp. I worked there as a CIT. That stands for Counselor In Training . . .'

As she continued to read about the incident in the woods, the narrator and her boyfriend, 'P,' the kiss against the tree, the screams in the woods, she moved around the tight circle. She had read the piece at least a dozen times already, but now, reading out loud to others, she felt her throat start to constrict. Her legs turned rubbery. She shot a quick glance at Lonnie. He had heard something in her tone too, was looking at her. She gave him a look that said, 'You're supposed to be watching them, not me,' and he quickly turned away.

When she finished, Lucy asked for comments. This request pretty much always followed the same route. The students knew that the author was right there, in this very room, but because the only way to build yourself up is to tear others down, they ripped into the work with a fury. They raised their hands and always started with some sort of disclaimer, like, 'Is it just me?' or 'I could be wrong about this, but,' and then it began:

'The writing is flat. . . .'

'I don't feel her passion for this P, do you? . . .'

'Hand under the shirt? Please . . .'

'Really, I thought it was just dreck.'

'The narrator says, "We were kissing, it was so passionate." Don't *tell* me it was passionate. *Show* me . . .'

Lucy moderated. This was the most important part of the class. It was hard to teach students. She often thought back to her own education, the hours of mind-numbing

92

lectures, and could not remember one thing from any of them. The lessons she had truly learned, the ones she internalized and recalled and put to use, were the quick comments a teacher would make during discussion time. Teaching was about quality, not quantity. You talk too much, you become Muzak – annoying background music. If you say very little, you can actually score.

Teachers also like attention. That can be a danger too. One of her early professors had given her sound and simple advice on this: It's not all about you. She kept that front and center at all times. On the other hand, students didn't want you floating above the fray. So when she did tell the occasional anecdote, she tried to make it one where she messed up – there were plenty of those anyway – and how, despite that, she ended up okay.

Another problem was that students did not say what they truly believed as much as what they hoped would impress. Of course this was true at the faculty meetings too – the priority was sounding good, not telling the truth.

But right now Lucy was being a bit more pointed than usual. She wanted reactions. She wanted the author to reveal him- or herself. So she pushed.

'This was supposed to be memoir,' she said. 'But does anybody really believe this happened?'

That quieted the room. There were unspoken rules here. Lucy had pretty much called out the author, called her a liar. She backtracked. 'What I mean to say is, it reads like fiction. That is usually a good thing, but does it make it difficult in this case? Do you start to question the veracity?'

The discussion was lively. Hands shot up. Students debated one another. This was the high of the job. Truth was, she had very little in her life. But she loved these kids. Every semester she fell in love all over again. They were her family, from either September through December or January through May. Then they left her. Some came back. Very few. And she was always glad to see them. But they were never her family again. Only the current students achieved that status. It was weird.

During some point, Lonnie headed out. Lucy wondered where he was going, but she was lost in the class. On some days, it ended too quickly. This was one of them. When time ran out and the students started packing their backpacks, she was no closer to knowing who had sent her that anonymous journal.

'Don't forget,' Lucy said. 'Two more pages of the journals. I'd like them in by tomorrow.' Then she added, 'Uh, you can send more than two pages, if you want. Whatever you have for me.'

Ten minutes later, she arrived at her office. Lonnie was already there.

'You see anything in their faces?' she asked.

'No,' he said.

Lucy started packing her stuff, jamming papers into her laptop bag.

'Where are you going?' Lonnie asked.

'I have an appointment.'

Her tone kept him from asking any more. Lucy kept this particular 'appointment' once a week, but she didn't trust anyone with that information. Not even Lonnie.

'Oh,' Lonnie said. His eyes were on the floor. She stopped.

'What is it, Lonnie?'

'Are you sure you want to know who sent the journal? I mean, I don't know, this whole thing is such a betrayal.'

'I need to know.'

'Why?'

'I can't tell you.'

He nodded. 'Okay, then.'

'Okay, what?'

'When will you be back?'

'An hour, maybe two.'

Lonnie checked his watch. 'By then,' he said, 'I should know who sent it.'

Chapter 9

The trial was postponed for the afternoon.

There were those who would argue that this made a difference in the case – that the jury would be left overnight with my direct and that it would settle in, blah, blah, blah. That sort of strategizing was nonsense. It was the life cycle of a case. If there was a positive in this development, it would be offset by the fact that Flair Hickory would now have more time to prepare his cross. Trials work like that. You get hysterical about it, but stuff like this tends to even out.

I called Loren Muse on my cell. 'You have anything yet?'

'Still working on it.'

I hung up and saw there was a message from Detective York. I wasn't sure what to do anymore about Mrs. Perez lying about the scar on Gil's arm. If I confronted her with it, she would probably say she just got mixed up. No harm, no foul.

But why would she have said it in the first place?

Was she, in fact, telling what she believed to be the truth – that this body did not belong to her son? Were both Mr. and Mrs. Perez merely making a grievous (but understandable) mistake here – that it was so hard to fathom that their Gil had been alive this whole time that they could not accept what their own eyes were showing them?

Or were they lying?

And if they were lying, well, why?

Before I confronted them, I needed to have more facts on hand. I would have to provide definitive proof that the corpse in the morgue with the alias Manolo Santiago was really Gil Perez, the young man who had disappeared into the woods with my sister and Margot Green and Doug Billingham nearly twenty years ago.

York's message said: 'Sorry it took me so long to get this. You asked about Raya Singh, the victim's girlfriend. We only had a cell on her, believe it or not. Anyway, we called up. She works at an Indian restaurant on Route 3 near the Lincoln Tunnel.' He gave me the name and address. 'She's supposed to be there all day. Hey, if you learn anything about Santiago's real name, let me know. Far as we can tell, he's had the alias for a while. We got some hits on him out in the Los Angeles area from six years ago. Nothing heavy. Talk to you later.'

I wondered what to make of that. Not much. I headed to my car, and as soon as I started to slide in, I knew something was very wrong.

There was a manila envelope sitting on the driver's seat.

I knew it wasn't mine. I knew I hadn't left it here. And I knew that I had locked my car doors.

Someone had broken into my car.

I stopped and picked up the envelope. No address,

97

no postage. The front was totally blank. It felt thin. I sat down in the front seat and closed the door behind me. The envelope was sealed. I slit it open with my index finger. I reached in and plucked out the contents.

Ice poured in my veins when I saw what it was:

A photograph of my father.

I frowned. What the . . . ?

On the bottom, neatly typed on the white border, was his name and the year: 'Vladimir Copeland.' That was all.

I didn't get it.

I just sat there for a moment. I stared at the photograph of my beloved father. I thought about how he had been a young doctor in Leningrad, how so much had been taken away from him, how his life ended up being an endless series of tragedies and disappointments. I remember him arguing with my mother, both of them wounded with no one to strike at but each other. I remembered my mother crying by herself. I remembered sitting some of those nights with Camille. She and I never fought – weird for a brother and sister – but maybe we had seen enough. Sometimes she would take my hand or say that we should take a walk. But most of the time we would go into her room and Camille would put on one of her favorite dopey pop songs and tell me about it, about why she liked it, as if it had hidden meanings, and then she'd tell me about some boy she liked at school. I would sit there and listen and feel the strangest contentment.

I didn't get it. Why was this photograph . . . ?

There was something else in the envelope.

I turned it upside down. Nothing. I dug with my hand to the bottom. It felt like an index card. I pulled it into view. Yep, an index card. White with red lines. That side

– the lined side – was left blank. But on the other side – the side that was plain white – someone had typed three words all in caps:

THE FIRST SKELETON

'You know who sent the journal?' Lucy asked.

'Not yet,' Lonnie said. 'But I will.'

'How?'

Lonnie kept his head down. Gone was the confident swagger. Lucy felt bad about that. He didn't like what she was making him do. She didn't like it either. But there was no choice here. She had worked hard to conceal her past. She had changed her name. She had not let Paul find her. She had gotten rid of her naturally blond hair – man, how many women her age had naturally blond hair? – and replaced it with this brown mess.

'Okay,' she said. 'You'll be here when I get back?'

He nodded. Lucy headed down the stairs to her car.

On TV it seems so easy to get a new identity. Maybe it was, but Lucy hadn't found that to be the case. It was a slow process. She started by changing her last name from Silverstein to Gold. Silver to Gold. Clever, no? She didn't think so, but somehow it worked for her, still gave her a link to the father she had so loved.

She had moved around the country. The camp was long gone. So were all her father's assets. And so, in the end, was most of her father.

What remained of Ira Silverstein, her father, was housed in a halfway house ten miles from the campus of Reston University. She drove, enjoying the time alone. She listened to Tom Waits sing that he hoped he didn't fall in love, but of course, he does. She pulled into the lot. The house, a converted mansion on a large tract of land, was nicer than most. Lucy's entire salary pretty much went here.

She parked near her father's old car, a rusted-out yellow VW Beetle. The Beetle was always in the exact same spot. She doubted that it had moved from there in the past year. Her father had freedom here. He could leave anytime. He could check himself in and check out. But the sad fact was, he almost never left his room. The leftist bumper stickers that had adorned the vehicle had all faded away. Lucy had a copy of the VW key and every once in a while she started it up, just to keep the battery in operating order. Doing that, just sitting in the car, brought flashbacks. She saw Ira driving it, the full beard, the windows open, the smile, the wave and honk to everyone he passed.

She never had the heart to take it out for a spin.

Lucy signed in at the front desk. This house was fairly specialized, catering to older residents with lifelong drug and mental issues. There seemed to be a tremendous range in here, everything from those who appeared totally 'normal' to people who could double as extras in *One Flew Over the Cuckoo's Nest*.

Ira was a little of both.

She stopped in his doorway. Ira's back was to her. He wore the familiar hemp poncho. His gray hair was an every-direction shock. 'Let's Live for Today' by The Grass Roots, a classic from 1967, boomed from what her father still called a 'hi-fi.' Lucy paused as Warren Entner did the big '1, 2, 3, 4' countdown before the group blasted in for another 'sha-la-la-la-la, let's live for today.' She closed her eyes and mouthed along with the words.

Great, great stuff.

There were beads in the room and tie-dye and a

'Where Have All the Flowers Gone' poster. Lucy smiled, but there was little joy in it. Nostalgia was one thing – a deteriorating mind another.

Early dementia had crept in – from age or drug use, no one could say – and staked a claim. Ira had always been spacey and living in the past, so it was hard to say how gradual the slide had been. That was what the doctors said. But Lucy knew that the initial break, the initial push down the slide, had occurred that summer. Ira took a lot of the blame for what happened in those woods. It was his camp. He should have done more to protect his campers.

The media went after him but not as hard as the families. Ira was too sweet a man to handle it. It broke him.

Ira barely left his room now. His mind bounced around decades, but this one – the sixties – was the only one he felt comfortable in. Half the time he actually thought it was still 1968. Other times he knew the truth – you could see it in his expression – but he just didn't want to face it. So as part of the new 'validation therapy,' his doctors let his room, for all intents and purposes, be 1968.

The doctor had explained that this sort of dementia did not improve with age, so you want the patient to be as happy and stress free as possible, even if that means living something of a lie. In short, Ira wanted it to be 1968. That was where he was happiest. So why fight it?

'Hey, Ira.'

Ira – he had never wanted her to call him 'Dad' – did the slow 'meds' turn toward her voice. He raised his hand, as though underwater, and waved. 'Hey, Luce.'

She blinked away the tears. He always recognized her, always knew who she was. If the fact that he was living in 1968 and his daughter hadn't even been born then seemed like a contradiction, well, it was. But that never shattered Ira's illusion.

He smiled at her. Ira had always been too big-hearted, too generous, too childlike and naive, for a world this cruel. She would refer to him as an 'ex-hippie' but that implied that at some point Ira gave up being a hippie. Long after everyone else had turned in their tie-dyes and flower power and peace beads, after the others had gotten haircuts and shaved off their beards, Ira stayed true to the cause.

During Lucy's wonderful childhood, Ira had never raised his voice to her. He had almost no filter, no boundaries, wanting his daughter to see and experience everything, even what was probably inappropriate. Weirdly enough, that lack of censorship had made his only child, Lucy Silverstein, somewhat prudish by the day's standards.

'I'm so happy you're here . . . ,' Ira said, half stumbling toward her.

She took a step in and embraced him. Her father smelled of age and body odor. The hemp needed to be cleaned.

'How are you feeling, Ira?'

'Great. Never better.'

He opened a bottle and took a vitamin. Ira did that a lot. Despite his noncapitalist ways, her father had made a small fortune in vitamins during the early seventies. He cashed out and bought that property on the Pennsylvania/New Jersey border. For a while he ran it as a commune. But that didn't last. So he turned it into a summer camp.

'So how are you?' she asked.

'Never better, Luce.'

And then he started crying. Lucy sat with him and held his hand. He cried, then he laughed, then he cried again. He kept telling her over and over how much he loved her.

'You're the world, Luce,' he said. 'I see you . . . I see everything that should be. You know what I mean?'

'I love you too, Ira.'

'See? That's what I mean. I'm the richest man in the world.'

Then he cried again.

She couldn't stay long. She needed to get back to her office and see what Lonnie had learned. Ira's head was on her shoulder. The dandruff and odor were getting to her. When a nurse came in, Lucy used the interruption to extricate herself from him. She hated herself for it.

'I'll be back next week, okay?'

Ira nodded. He was smiling when she left.

In the corridor the nurse – Lucy forgot her name – was waiting for her. 'How has he been?' Lucy asked.

This was normally a rhetorical question. These patients were all bad, but their families didn't want to hear that. So the nurse would normally say, 'Oh, he's doing just fine,' but this time, she said, 'Your father has been more agitated lately.'

'How so?'

'Ira is normally the sweetest, most gentle man in the universe. But his mood swings—'

'He's always had mood swings.'

'Not like these.'

'Has he been nasty?'

'No. It's not that . . .'

'Then what?'

She shrugged. 'He's been talking about the past a lot.'

'He always talks about the sixties.'

'No, not that far in the past.'

'What then?'

'He talks about a summer camp.'

Lucy felt a slow thud in her chest. 'What does he say?'

'He says he owned a summer camp. And then he loses it. He starts ranting about blood and the woods and the dark, stuff like that. Then he clams up. It's creepy. And before last week, I never even heard him say a word about a camp, let alone that he owned one. Unless, of course, well, Ira's mind does wander. Maybe he's just imagining he did?'

It was said as a question, but Lucy didn't answer it. From down the hall another nurse called, 'Rebecca?'

The nurse, whom she now realized was named Rebecca, said, 'I have to run.'

When Lucy was alone in the corridor, she looked back in the room. Her father's back was to her. He was staring at the wall. She wondered what was going on in his head. What he wasn't telling her.

What he really knew about that night.

She tore herself away and headed toward the exit. She reached the receptionist who asked her to sign out. Each patient had his own page. The receptionist flipped to Ira's and spun the book for Lucy to sign. She had the pen in her hand and was about to do the same absentminded scribble she had done on the way in when she stopped.

There was another name there.

Last week. Ira had another visitor. His first and only visitor besides, well, her. Ever. She frowned and read the name. It was wholly unfamiliar.

Who the hell was Manolo Santiago?

Chapter 10

THE FIRST SKELETON

My father's photograph was still in my hand.

I needed now to make a detour on the way to my visit with Raya Singh. I looked at the index card. The First Skeleton. Implication: There would be more than one.

But let's start with this one – my father.

There was only one person who could help me when it came to my dad and his potential skeletons. I took out my cell phone and held down the number six. I rarely called this number, but it was still on my speed dial. My guess is, it would always be.

He answered on the first ring in his low rumble of a voice. 'Paul.'

Even the one word was thick with accent.

'Hi, Uncle Sosh.'

Sosh wasn't really my uncle. He was a close family friend from the old country. I hadn't seen him in three months, not since my father's funeral, but as soon as I heard his voice, I instantly saw the big bear of a man. My father said that Uncle Sosh had been the most powerful and feared man in Pulkovo, the town on the outskirts of Leningrad where they'd both been raised.

'It's been too long,' he said.

'I know. I'm sorry about that.'

'Acch,' he said, as though disgusted by my apology. 'But I thought that you would call today.'

That surprised me. 'Why?'

'Because, my young nephew, we need to talk.'

'About what?'

'About why I never talk about anything over the phone.'

Sosh's business was, if not illegal, on the shadier side of the street.

'I'm at my place in the city.' Sosh had an expansive penthouse on 36th Street in Manhattan. 'When can you be here?'

'Half an hour if there's no traffic,' I said.

'Splendid. I will see you then.'

'Uncle Sosh?'

He waited. I looked at the photograph of my father on the passenger seat.

'Can you give me an idea what it's about?'

'It's about your past, Pavel,' he said through that thick accent, using my Russian name. 'It's about what should stay in your past.'

'What the hell does that mean?'

'We'll talk,' he said again. And then he hung up.

There was no traffic, so the ride to Uncle Sosh's was closer to twenty-five minutes. The doorman wore one of those ridiculous uniforms with rope tassels. The look, interestingly enough with Sosh living here, reminded me of something Brezhnev would have worn for the May

Day parade. The doorman knew my face and had been told that I was arriving. If the doorman isn't told in advance, he doesn't ring up. You just don't get in.

Sosh's old friend Alexei stood at the elevator door. Alexei Kokorov had worked security for Sosh, had for as long as I could remember. He was probably in his late sixties, a few years younger than Sosh, and as ugly a man as you'd ever see. His nose was bulbous and red, his face filled with spider veins from, I assumed, too much drink. His jacket and pants didn't fit right, but his build was not the kind made for haute couture.

Alexei didn't seem happy to see me, but he didn't look like lots of laughs in general. He held the elevator door open for me. I stepped in without saying a word. He gave me a curt nod and let the door close. I was alone.

The elevator opened into the penthouse.

Uncle Sosh stood a few feet from the door. The room was huge. The furniture was cubist. The picture window showed off an incredible view, but the walls had this thick wallpaper, tapestry-like, in a color that probably had some fancy name like 'Merlot' but looked to me like blood.

Sosh's face lit up when he saw me. He spread his hands wide. One of my most vivid childhood memories was the size of those hands. They were still huge. He had grayed over the years, but even now, when I calculated that he was probably in his early seventies, you still felt the size and power and something approaching awe.

I stopped outside the elevator.

'What,' he said to me, 'you too old for a hug now?'

We both stepped toward each other. The embrace was, per his Russian background, a true bear hug. Strength emanated from him. His forearms were still thick coils. He pulled me close, and I felt as though he could simply tighten his grip and snap my spine.

After a few seconds, Sosh grabbed my arms near the biceps and held me at arm's length so he could take a good look.

'Your father,' he said, his voice thick with more than accent this time. 'You look just like your father.'

Sosh had arrived from the Soviet Union not long after we did. He worked for InTourist, the Soviet tour company, in their Manhattan office. His job was to help facilitate American tourists who wished to visit Moscow and what was then called Leningrad.

That was a long time ago. Since the fall of the Soviet government, he dabbled in that murky enterprise people labeled 'import-export.' I never knew what that meant exactly, but it had paid for this penthouse.

Sosh looked at me another moment or two. He wore a white shirt buttoned low enough to see the V-neck undershirt. A huge tuft of gray chest hair jutted out. I waited. This would not take long. Uncle Sosh was not one for casual talk.

As if reading my mind, Sosh looked me hard in the eye and said, 'I have been getting calls.'

'From?'

'Old friends.'

I waited.

'From the old country,' he said.

'I'm not sure I follow.'

'People have been asking questions.'

'Sosh?'

'Yes?'

'On the phone you were worried about being overheard. Are you worried about that here?'

'No. Here it is completely safe. I have the room swept weekly.'

'Great, then how about stopping with the cryptic and telling me what you're talking about?'

He smiled. He liked that. 'There are people. Americans. They are in Moscow and throwing money around and asking questions.'

I nodded to myself. 'Questions about what?'

'About your father.'

'What kind of questions?'

'You remember the old rumors?'

'You're kidding me.'

But he wasn't. And in a weird way, it made sense. The First Skeleton. I should have guessed.

I remembered the rumors, of course. They had nearly destroyed my family.

My sister and I were born in what was then called the Soviet Union during what was then called the Cold War. My father had been a medical doctor but lost his license on charges of incompetence trumped up because he was Jewish. That was how it was in those days.

At the same time, a reform synagogue here in the United States – Skokie, Illinois, to be more specific – was working hard on behalf of Soviet Jewry. During the mid-seventies, Soviet Jewry was something of a cause célèbre in American temples – getting Jews out of the Soviet Union.

We got lucky. They got us out.

For a long time we were heralded in our new land as heroes. My father spoke passionately at Friday night services about the plight of the Soviet Jew. Kids wore buttons in support. Money was donated. But about a year into our stay, my father and the head rabbi had a falling out, and suddenly there were whispers that my father had gotten out of the Soviet Union because he was actually KGB, that he wasn't even Jewish, that it was all a ruse. The charges were pathetic and contradictory and false and now, well, more than twenty-five years old.

I shook my head. 'So they're trying to prove that my father was KGB?'

'Yes.'

Friggin' Jenrette. I got it, I guessed. I was something of a public figure now. The charges, even if ultimately proven false, would be damaging. I should know. Twenty-five years ago, my family had lost pretty much everything due to those accusations. We left Skokie, moved east to Newark. Our family was never the same.

I looked up. 'On the phone you said you'd thought I'd call.'

'If you hadn't, I would have called you today.'

'To warn me?'

'Yes.'

'So,' I said, 'they must have something.'

The big man did not reply. I watched his face. And it was as if my entire world, everything I grew up believing, slowly shifted.

'Was he KGB, Sosh?' I asked.

'It was a long time ago,' Sosh said.

'Does that mean yes?'

Sosh smiled slowly. 'You don't understand how it was.'

'And again I say: Does that mean yes?'

'No, Pavel. But your father . . . maybe he was supposed to be.'

'What's that supposed to mean?'

'Do you know how I came to this country?'

'You worked for a travel company.'

'It was the Soviet Union, Pavel. There were no companies. InTourist was run by the government. Everything was run by the government. Do you understand?'

'I guess.'

'So when the Soviet government had a chance to send someone to live in New York City, do you think they sent the man who was most competent in booking vacations? Or do you think they sent someone who might help them in other ways?'

I thought about the size of his hands. I thought about his strength. 'So you were KGB?'

'I was a colonel in the military. We didn't call it KGB. But yes, I guess you would call me' – he made quote marks with his fingers – ' "a spy." I would meet with American officials. I would try to bribe them. People always think we learn important things – things that can change the balance of power. That's such nonsense. We learned nothing relevant. Not ever. And the American spies? They never learned anything about us either. We passed nonsense from side to side. It was a silly game.'

'And my father?'

'The Soviet government let him out. Your Jewish friends think that they applied enough pressure. But please. Did a bunch of Jews in a synagogue really think they could pressure a government that answered to no one? It's almost funny when you think about it.'

'So you're saying . . . ?'

'I'm just telling you how it was. Did your father promise he would help the regime? Of course. But it was just to get out. It's complicated, Pavel. You can't imagine what it was like for him. Your father was a good doctor and a better man. The government made up charges that he committed medical malpractice. They took away his license. Then your grandmother and grandfather . . . my God, Natasha's wonderful parents . . . you're too young to remember—'

'I remember,' I said.

'Do you?'

I wondered if I really did. I have that image of my grandfather, my Popi, and the shock of white hair and maybe his boisterous laugh, and my grandmother, my Noni, gently scolding him. But I was three when they were taken away. Did I really remember them, or has that old photo I still keep out come to life? Was it a real memory or something I'd created from my mother's stories?

'Your grandparents were intellectuals – university professors. Your grandfather headed the history department. Your grandmother was a brilliant mathematician. You know this, yes?'

I nodded. 'My mother said she learned more from the debates at the dinner table than at school.'

Sosh smiled. 'Probably true. The most brilliant academics sought out your grandparents. But, of course, that drew the attention of the government. They were labeled radicals. They were considered dangerous. Do you remember when they were arrested?'

'I remember,' I said, 'the aftermath.'

He closed his eyes for a long second. 'What it did to your mother?'

'Yes.'

'Natasha was never the same. You understand that?'

'I do.'

'So here he was, your father. He had lost so much – his career, his reputation, his license and now your mother's parents. And suddenly, down like he was, the government gave your father a way out. A chance for a fresh start.'

'A life in the USA.'

'Yes.'

'And all he had to do was spy?'

Sosh waved a dismissive hand in my direction. 'Don't

112

you get it? It was a big game. What could a man like your father learn? Even if he tried – which he didn't. What could he tell them?'

'And my mother?'

'Natasha was just a woman to them. The government cared nothing for the woman. She was a problem for a while. Like I said, her parents, your grandparents, were radicals in their eyes. You say you remembered when they were taken?'

'I think I do.'

'Your grandparents formed a group, trying to get the human rights abuses out to the public. They were making headway until a traitor turned them in. The agents came at night.'

He stopped.

'What?' I said.

'This isn't easy to talk about. What happened to them.'

I shrugged. 'You can't hurt them now.'

He did not reply.

'What happened, Sosh?'

'They were sent to a gulag – a work camp. The conditions were terrible. Your grandparents were not young. You know how it ended?'

'They died,' I said.

Sosh turned away from me then. He moved over to the window. He had a great view of the Hudson. There were two mega-cruise ships in port. You could turn to the left and even see the Statue of Liberty. Manhattan is so small, eight miles from end to end, and like with Sosh, you just always feel its power.

'Sosh?'

When he spoke again, his voice was soft. 'Do you know how they died?'

'Like you said before. The conditions were terrible. My grandfather had a heart condition.'

He still hadn't turned toward me. 'The government wouldn't treat him. Wouldn't even give him his medicine. He was dead within three months.'

I waited.

'So what aren't you telling me, Sosh?'

'Do you know what happened to your grandmother?'

'I know what my mother told me.'

'Tell me,' he said.

'Noni got sick too. With her husband gone, her heart sorta gave out. You hear about it all the time in longterm couples. One dies, then the other gives up.'

He said nothing.

'Sosh?'

'In a sense,' he said, 'I guess that was true.'

'In a sense?'

Sosh kept his eyes on whatever was out the window. 'Your grandmother committed suicide.'

My body stiffened. I started shaking my head.

'She hung herself with a sheet.'

I just sat there. I thought of that picture of my Noni. I thought of that knowing smile. I thought of the stories my mother told me about her, about her sharp mind and sharper tongue. Suicide.

'Did my mother know?' I asked.

'Yes.'

'She never told me.'

'Maybe I shouldn't have either.'

'Why did you?'

'I need you to see how it was. Your mother was a beautiful woman. So lovely and delicate. Your father adored her. But when her parents were taken and then, well, put to death really, she was never the same. You sensed it, yes? A melancholy there? Even before your sister.'

I said nothing, but I had indeed sensed it.

'I guess I wanted you to know how it was,' he said. 'For your mother. So maybe you'd understand more.'

'Sosh?'

He waited. He still had not turned from the window.

'Do you know where my mother is?'

The big man didn't answer for a long time.

'Sosh?'

'I used to know,' he said. 'When she first ran away.'

I swallowed. 'Where did she go?'

'Natasha went home.'

'I don't understand.'

'She ran back to Russia.'

'Why?'

'You can't blame her, Pavel.'

'I don't. I want to know why.'

'You can run away from your home like they did. You try to change. You hate your government but never your people. Your homeland is your homeland. Always.'

He turned to me. Our eyes locked.

'And that's why she ran?'

He just stood there.

'That was her reasoning?' I said, almost shouting. I felt something in my blood tick. 'Because her homeland was always her homeland?'

'You're not listening.'

'No, Sosh, I'm listening. Your homeland is your homeland. That's a load of crap. How about your family is your family? How about your husband is your husband – or more to the point, how about your son is your son?'

He did not reply.

'What about us, Sosh? What about me and Dad?'

'I don't have an answer for you, Pavel.'

'Do you know where she is now?'

'No.'

'Is that the truth?'

'It is.'

'But you could find her, couldn't you?'

He didn't nod but he didn't shake his head either.

'You have a child,' Sosh said to me. 'You have a good career.'

'So?'

'So this is all so long ago. The past is for the dead, Pavel. You don't want to bring the dead back. You want to bury them and move on.'

'My mother isn't dead,' I said. 'Is she?'

'I don't know.'

'So why are you talking about the dead? And Sosh? While we're talking about the dead, here's one more thing to chew over' – I couldn't stop myself, so I just said it – 'I'm not even sure my sister is dead anymore.'

I expected to see shock on his face. I didn't. He barely seemed surprised.

'To you,' he said.

'To me, what?'

'To you,' he said, 'they should both be dead.'

Chapter 11

shook off Uncle Sosh's words and headed back through the Lincoln Tunnel. I needed to focus on two things and two things only: Focus One, convict those two damned sons of bitches who had raped Chamique Johnson. And Focus Two, find out where the hell Gil Perez had been for the past twenty years.

I checked the address Detective York had given me for the witness/girlfriend. Raya Singh worked at an Indian restaurant called Curry Up and Wait. I hate pun titles. Or do I love them? Let's go with love.

I was on my way.

I still had the picture of my father in the front seat. I didn't much worry about those KGB allegations. I had almost expected it after my conversation with Sosh. But now I read the index card again:

THE FIRST SKELETON

The First. That again implied that more would be

coming. Clearly Monsieur Jenrette, probably with financial help from Marantz, was sparing no expense. If they found out about those old accusations against my father – more than twenty-five years old now – they were clearly desperate and hungry.

What would they find?

I was not a bad guy. But I wasn't perfect either. No one was. They would find something. They would blow it out of proportion. It could seriously damage JaneCare, my reputation, my political ambition – but then again Chamique had skeletons too. I had convinced her to take them all out and show them to the world.

Could I ask less of myself?

When I arrived at the Indian restaurant, I threw the car into Park and turned off the ignition. I was not in my jurisdiction, but I didn't think that would matter much. I took a look out the car window, thought again about that skeleton and called Loren Muse. When she answered I identified myself and said, 'I may have a small problem.'

'What's that?' Muse asked.

'Jenrette's father is coming after me.'

'How?'

'He's digging into my past.'

'Will he find anything?'

'You dig into anybody's past,' I said, 'you find something.'

'Not mine,' she said.

'Really? How about those dead bodies in Reno?'

'Cleared of all charges.'

'Great, terrific.'

'I'm just playing with you, Cope. Making a funny.'

'You're hilarious, Muse. Your comic timing. It's pro-like.'

'Okay, cut to the chase then. What do you need from me?'

'You're friends with some of the local private eyes, right?'

'Right.'

'Call around. See if you can find out who's on me.'

'Okay, I'm on it.'

'Muse?'

'What?'

'This isn't a priority. If the manpower isn't there, don't worry about it.'

'It's there, Cope. Like I said, I'm on it.'

'How do you think we did today?'

'It was a good day for the good guys,' she said.

'Yeah.'

'But probably not good enough.'

'Cal and Jim?'

'I'm in the mood to gun down every man with those names.'

'Get on it,' I said and hung up.

In terms of interior decorating, Indian restaurants seem to break down into two categories – very dark and very bright. This one was bright and colorful in the pseudostyle of a Hindu temple, albeit a really cheesy one. There were faux-mosaic and lit-up statues of Ganesh and other deities with which I am wholly unfamiliar. The waitresses were costumed in belly-revealing aqua; the outfits reminded me of what the evil sister wore on *I Dream of Jeannie*.

We all hold on to our stereotypes, but the whole scene looked as if a Bollywood musical number were about to break out. I try to have an appreciation for various foreign cultures, but no matter how hard I try, I detest the music they play in Indian restaurants. Right now it sounded like a sitar was torturing a cat.

The hostess frowned when I entered. 'How many?' she asked.

'I'm not here to eat,' I said.

She just waited.

'Is Raya Singh here?'

'Who?'

I repeated the name.

'I don't . . . oh, wait, she's the new girl.' She folded her arms across her chest and said nothing.

'Is she here?' I said.

'Who wants to know?'

I did the eyebrow arch. I wasn't good with it. I was going for rakish but it always came out more like constipation. 'The President of the United States.'

'Huh?'

I handed her a business card. She read it and then surprised me by shouting out, 'Raya! Raya Singh!'

Raya Singh stepped forward and I stepped back. She was younger than I'd expected, early twenties, and absolutely stunning. The first thing you noticed – couldn't help but notice in that aqua getup – was that Raya Singh had more curves than seemed anatomically possible. She stood still but it looked as though she were moving. Her hair was tousled and black and begged to be touched. Her skin was more gold than brown and she had almond eyes that a man could slip into and never find his way back out.

'Raya Singh?' I said.

'Yes.'

'My name is Paul Copeland. I'm the prosecutor for Essex County in New Jersey. Could we talk a moment?'

'Is this about the murder?'

'Yes.'

'Then of course.'

Her voice was polished with a hint of a New England-boarding-school accent that shouted refinement over geographical locale. I was trying not to stare. She saw that and smiled a little. I don't want to sound like some kind of pervert because it wasn't like that. Female beauty gets to me. I don't think I'm alone in that. It gets to me like a work of art gets to me. It gets to me like a Rembrandt or Michelangelo. It gets to me like night views of Paris or when the sun rises on the Grand Canyon or sets in the turquoise of an Arizona sky. My thoughts were not illicit. They were, I self-rationalized, rather artistic.

She led me outside onto the street, where it was quieter. She wrapped her arms around herself as though she were cold. The move, like pretty much every move she made, was nearly a double entendre. Probably couldn't help it. Everything about her made you think about moonlit skies and four-poster beds – and that, I guess, shoots down my 'rather artistic' reasoning. I was tempted to offer her my coat or something, but it wasn't cold at all. Oh, and I wasn't wearing a coat.

'Do you know a man named Manolo Santiago?' I asked.

'He was murdered,' she said.

Her voice had a strange lilt to it, as if she were reading for a part.

'But you knew him?'

'I did, yes.'

'You were lovers?'

'Not yet.'

'Not yet?'

'Our relationship,' she said, 'was platonic.'

My eyes moved to the pavement and then across the street. Better. I didn't really care so much about the murder or who had committed it. I cared about finding out about Manolo Santiago.

'Do you know where Mr. Santiago lived?'

'No, I'm sorry, I don't.'

'How did you two meet?'

'He approached me on the street.'

'Just like that? He just walked up to you on the street?'

'Yes,' she said.

'And then?'

'He asked me if I would like to grab a cup of coffee.'

'And you did?'

'Yes.'

I risked another look at her. Beautiful. That aqua against the dark skin . . . total killer. 'Do you always do that?' I asked.

'Do what?'

'Meet a stranger and accept his invitation to grab coffee with him?'

That seemed to amuse her. 'Do I need to justify my behavior to you, Mr. Copeland?'

'No.'

She said nothing.

I said, 'We need to learn more about Mr. Santiago.'

'May I ask why?'

'Manolo Santiago was an alias. I'm trying to find out his real name, for one thing.'

'I wouldn't know it.'

'At the risk of overstepping my bounds,' I said, 'I'm having trouble understanding.'

'Understanding what?'

'Men must hit on you all the time,' I said.

The smile was crooked and knowing. 'That's very flattering, Mr. Copeland, thank you.'

I tried to stay on message. 'So why did you go with him?'

'Does it matter?'

'It might tell me something about him.'

'I can't imagine what. Suppose, for example, I told you that I found him handsome. Would that help?'

'Did you?'

'Did I what – find him handsome?' Another smile. A tousled lock dropped across her right eye. 'You almost sound jealous.'

'Ms. Singh?'

'Yes?'

'I'm investigating a murder. So maybe we can stop now with the head games.'

'Do you think we can?' She tucked the hair back. I held my ground. 'Well, okay then,' she said. 'Fair enough.'

'Can you help me figure out who he really was?'

She thought about it. 'Maybe through his cell-phone records?'

'We checked the one he had on him. Your call was the only one on it.'

'He had another number,' she said. 'Before that.'

'Do you remember it?'

She nodded and gave it to me. I took out a small pen and wrote it on the back of one of my cards.

'Anything else?'

'Not really.'

I took out another card and wrote down my mobile phone number. 'If you think of anything else, will you call me?'

'Of course.'

I handed it to her. She just looked at me and smiled.

'What?'

'You're not wearing a wedding band, Mr. Copeland.'

'I'm not married.'

'Divorced or widowed?'

'How do you know I'm not a lifelong bachelor?'

Raya Singh did not bother replying.

'Widowed,' I said.

'I'm sorry.'

'Thank you.'

'How long has it been?'

I was going to tell her none of her goddamn business, but I wanted to keep her in my good graces. And damned if she wasn't beautiful. 'Nearly six years.'

'I see,' she said.

She looked at me with those eyes.

'Thank you for your cooperation,' I said.

'Why don't you ask me out?' she asked.

'Excuse me?'

'I know you think I'm pretty. I'm single, you're single. Why don't you ask me out?'

'I don't mix my work life with my personal,' I said.

'I came here from Calcutta. Have you been?'

The change in subjects threw me for a second. The accent also didn't seem to match that locale, but that didn't mean much nowadays. I told her I had never been, but I obviously knew of it.

'What you've heard,' she said. 'It's even worse.'

Again I said nothing, wondering where she was going with this.

'I have a life plan,' she said. 'The first part was getting here. To the United States.'

'And the second part?'

'People here will do anything to get ahead. Some play the lottery. Some have dreams of being, I don't know, professional athletes. Some turn to crime or strip or sell themselves. I know my assets. I am beautiful. I am also a nice person and I have learned how to be' – she stopped and considered her words – 'good for a man. I will make a man incredibly happy. I will listen to him. I will be by his side. I will lift his spirits. I will make his nights special. I will give myself to him whenever he wants and in whatever way he wants. And I will do it gladly.'

Oookay, I thought.

We were in the middle of a busy street but I swear there was so much silence I could hear a cricket chirp. My mouth felt very dry.

'Manolo Santiago,' I said in a voice that sounded far away. 'Did you think he might be that man?'

'I thought he might be,' she said. 'But he wasn't. You seem nice. Like you would treat a woman well.' Raya Singh might have moved toward me, I can't be sure. But she suddenly seemed closer. 'I can see that you are troubled. That you don't sleep well at night. So how do you know, Mr. Copeland?'

'How do I know what?'

'That I'm not the one. That I'm not the one who will make you deliriously happy. That you wouldn't sleep soundly next to me.'

Whoa.

'I don't,' I said.

She just looked at me. I felt the look in my toes. Oh, I was being played. I knew that. And yet this direct line, her lay-it-out-with-no-BS approach . . . I found it oddly endearing.

Or maybe it was the blinded-by-beauty thing again.

'I have to go,' I said. 'You have my number.'

'Mr. Copeland?'

I waited.

'Why are you really here?'

'Excuse me?'

'What is your interest in Manolo's murder?'

'I thought I explained that. I'm the county prosecutor—'

'That's not why you're here.'

I waited. She just stared at me. Finally I asked, 'What makes you say that?'

Her reply landed like a left hook. 'Did you kill him?'

'What?'

'I said—'

'I heard you. Of course not. Why would you ask that?'

But Raya Singh shook it off. 'Good-bye, Mr. Copeland.' She gave me one more smile that made me feel like a fish dropped on a dock. 'I hope you find what you're looking for.'

Chapter 12

L ucy wanted to Google the name 'Manolo Santiago' – he was probably a reporter doing a story on that son of a bitch, Wayne Steubens, the Summer Slasher – but Lonnie was waiting for her in the office. He didn't look up when she entered. She stopped over him, aiming for mild intimidation.

'You know who sent the journals,' she said.

'I can't be sure.'

'But?'

Lonnie took a deep breath, readying himself, she hoped, to take the plunge. 'Do you know much about tracing e-mail messages?'

'No,' Lucy said, moving back to her desk.

'When you receive an e-mail, you know how there's all this gobbledygook about paths and ESMTP and Message IDs?'

'Pretend I do.'

'Basically it shows how the e-mail got to you. Where it went, where it came from, what route via what Internet mail service to get from point A to point B. Like a bunch of postmarks.'

'Okay.'

'Of course, there are ways of sending it out anonymously. But usually, even if you do that, there are some footprints.'

'Great, Lonnie, super.' He was stalling. 'So can I assume you found some of these footprints in the e-mail with that journal attached?'

'Yes,' Lonnie said. He looked up now and managed a smile. 'I'm not going to ask you why you want the name anymore.'

'Good.'

'Because I know you, Lucy. Like most hot chicks, you're a major pain in the ass. But you're also frighteningly ethical. If you need to betray the trust of your class – betray your students and me and everything you believe – there must be a good reason. A life-or-death reason, I'm betting.'

Lucy said nothing.

'It is life or death, right?'

'Just tell me, Lonnie.'

'The e-mail came from a bank of computers at the Frost Library.'

'The library,' she repeated. 'There must be, what, fifty computers in there?'

'About that.'

'So we'll never figure out who sent it.'

Lonnie made a yes-and-no gesture with a head tilt. 'We know what time it was sent. Six forty-two p.m. the day before yesterday.'

'And that helps us how?'

'The students who use the computer. They need to sign in. They don't have to sign in to a particular computer – the staff did away with that two years ago – but in order to get a computer, you reserve it for the hour. So I went to the library and got the time sheets. I compared a list of students in your class with students who had signed up for a computer during the hour between six and seven p.m. the day before yesterday.'

He stopped.

'And?'

'There was only one hit with a student in this class.'

'Who?'

Lonnie walked over to the window. He looked down at the quad. 'I'll give you a hint,' he said.

'Lonnie, I'm not really in the mood – '

'Her nose,' he said, 'is brown.'

Lucy froze. 'Sylvia Potter?'

His back was still to her.

'Lonnie, are you telling me that Sylvia Potter wrote that journal entry?'

'Yes,' he said. 'That's exactly what I'm telling you.'

On the way back to the office, I called Loren Muse.

'I need another favor,' I said.

'Shoot.'

'I need you to find out all you can about a phone number. Who owned the phone. Who the guy called. Everything.'

'What's the number?'

I gave her the number Raya Singh had told me.

'Give me ten minutes.'

'That's it?'

'Hey, I didn't become chief investigator because I have a hot ass.'

'Says who?'

She laughed. 'I like when you're a little fresh, Cope.'

129

'Don't get used to it.'

I hung up. My line had been inappropriate – or was it a justifiable comeback to her 'hot ass' joke? It is simplistic to criticize political correctness. The extremes make it an easy target for ridicule. But I've also seen what it's like in an office workplace when that stuff is allowed to go on. It can be intimidating and dark.

It's like those seemingly overcautious kid-safety rules nowadays. Your child has to wear a bike helmet no matter what. You have to use a special mulch in playgrounds and you can't have any jungle gym where a kid could climb too high and oh yeah, your child shouldn't walk three blocks without an escort and wait, where is your mouth guard and eye protection? And it is so easy to poke fun at that stuff and then some wiseass sends out a random e-mail saying, 'Hey, we all did that and survived.' But the truth is, a lot of kids didn't survive.

Kids did have a ton of freedom back then. They did not know what evil lurked in the darkness. Some of them went to sleepaway camp in the days when security was lax and you let kids be kids. Some of those kids sneaked into the woods at night and were never seen again.

Lucy Gold called Sylvia Potter's room. There was no answer. Not surprising. She checked the school phone directory, but they didn't list mobile numbers. Lucy remembered seeing Sylvia using a BlackBerry, so she e-mailed a brief message asking Sylvia to call her as soon as possible.

It took less than ten minutes to get a response.

'You wanted me to call, Professor Gold?'

'I did, Sylvia, thank you. Do you think you could stop by my office?'

'When?'

'Now, if that's possible.'

Several seconds of silence.

'Sylvia?'

'My English lit class is about to start,' she said. 'I'm presenting my final project today. Can I come by when I'm done?'

'That would be fine,' Lucy said.

'I should be there in about two hours.'

'Great, I'll be here.'

More silence.

'Can you tell me what this is about, Professor Gold?'

'It can keep, Sylvia, don't worry about it. I'll see you after your class.'

'Hey.'

It was Loren Muse. I was back in the courthouse the next morning. Flair Hickory's cross would start in a few minutes.

'Hey,' I said.

'You look like hell.'

'Wow, you are a trained detective.'

'You worried about this cross?'

'Of course.'

'Chamique will be fine. You did a helluva job.'

I nodded, tried to get my head back into the game. Muse walked next to me.

'Oh,' she said, 'that phone number you gave me? Bad news.'

I waited.

'It's a throwaway.'

Meaning someone bought it with cash with a preset number of minutes on it and didn't leave a name. 'I don't need to know who bought it,' I said. 'I just need to know what calls the phone made or received.'

'Tough to do,' she said. 'And impossible through the normal sources. Whoever it was, he bought it online from some fly-by-night posing as another fly-by-night. It'll take me a while to track it all down and apply enough pressure to get records.'

I shook my head. We entered the courtroom.

'Another thing,' she said. 'You heard of MVD?'

'Most Valuable Detection,' I said.

'Right, biggest private-eye firm in the state. Cingle Shaker, the woman I have on the frat boys, used to work there. Rumor has it they got a no-expense-spared, seek-'n'-destroy investigation going on with you.'

I reached the front of the courtroom. 'Super.' I handed her an old picture of Gil Perez.

She looked at it. 'What?'

'Do we still have Farrell Lynch doing the computer work?'

'We do.'

'Ask him to do an age progression on this. Age him twenty years. Tell him to give him a shaved head too.'

Loren Muse was about to follow up, but something in my face stopped her. She shrugged and peeled off. I sat down. Judge Pierce came in. We all rose. And then Chamique Johnson took the stand.

Flair Hickory stood and carefully buttoned his jacket. I frowned. The last time I'd seen a powder-blue suit in that shade was in a prom picture from 1978. He smiled at Chamique.

'Good morning, Miss Johnson.'

Chamique looked terrified. 'Morning,' she managed.

Flair introduced himself as if they'd just stumbled across each other at a cocktail party. He segued into Chamique's criminal record. He was gentle but firm. She had been arrested for prostitution, correct? She had been arrested for drugs, correct? She had been accused of rolling a john and taking eighty-four dollars, correct?

I didn't object.

This was all part of my warts-and-all strategy. I had raised much of this during my own examination, but Flair's cross was effective. He didn't ask her yet to explain any of her testimony. He simply warmed up by sticking to facts and police records.

After twenty minutes, Flair began his cross in earnest. 'You have smoked marijuana, have you not?'

Chamique said, 'Yeah.'

'Did you smoke any the night of your alleged attack?'

'No.'

'No?' Flair put his hand on his chest as though this answer shocked him to the core. 'Hmm. Did you imbibe any alcohol?'

'Im-what?'

'Did you drink anything alcoholic? A beer or wine maybe?'

'No.'

'Nothing?'

'Nothing.'

'Hmm. How about a regular drink? Maybe a soda?'

I was going to object, but again my strategy was to let her handle this as much as she could.

'I had some punch,' Chamique said.

'Punch, I see. And it was nonalcoholic?'

'That's what they said.'

'Who?'

'The guys.'

'Which guys?'

She hesitated. 'Jerry.'

'Jerry Flynn?'

133

'Yeah.'

'And who else?'

'Huh?'

'You said guys. With an s at the end. As in more than one? Jerry Flynn would constitute one guy. So who else told you that the punch you consumed – by the way, how many glasses did you have?'

'I don't know.'

'More than one.'

'I guess.'

'Please don't guess, Miss Johnson. Would you say more than one?'

'Probably, yeah.'

'More than two?'

'I don't know.'

'But it's possible?'

'Yeah, maybe.'

'So maybe more than two. More than three?'

'I don't think so.'

'But you can't be sure.'

Chamique shrugged.

'You'll need to speak up.'

'I don't think I had three. Probably two. Maybe not even that much.'

'And the only person who told you that the punch was nonalcoholic was Jerry Flynn. Is that correct?'

'I think.'

'Before you said "guys" as in more than one. But now you're saying just one person. Are you changing your testimony?'

I stood. 'Objection.'

Flair waved me off. 'He's right, small matter, let's move on.' He cleared his throat and put a hand on his right hip. 'Did you take any drugs that night?'

'No.'

'Not even a puff from, say, a marijuana cigarette?'

Chamique shook her head and then remembering that she needed to speak, she leaned into the microphone and said, 'No, I did not.'

'Hmm, okay. So when did you last do any sort of drugs?'

I stood again. 'Objection. The word *drugs* could be anything – aspirin, Tylenol . . .'

Flair looked amused. 'You don't think everyone here knows what I'm talking about?'

'I would prefer clarification.'

'Ms. Johnson, I am talking about illegal drugs here. Like marijuana. Or cocaine. Or LSD or heroin. Something like that. Do you understand?'

'Yeah, I think so.'

'So when did you last take any illegal drug?'

'I don't remember.'

'You said that you didn't take any the night of the party.'

'That's right.'

'How about the night before the party?'

'No.'

'The night before that?'

Chamique squirmed just a little bit and when she said, 'No,' I wasn't sure that I believed her.

'Let me see if I can help nail down the timetable. Your son is fifteen months old, is that correct?'

'Yeah.'

'Have you done any illegal drugs since he's been born?'

Her voice was very quiet. 'Yeah.'

'Can you tell us what kind?'

I stood yet again. 'I object. We get the point.

Ms. Johnson has done drugs in the past. No one denies that. That doesn't make what Mr. Hickory's clients did any less horrible. What's the difference when?'

The judge looked at Flair. 'Mr. Hickory?'

'We believe that Ms. Johnson is a habitual drug user. We believe that she was high that night and the jury should understand that when assessing the integrity of her testimony.'

'Ms. Johnson has already stated that she had not taken any drugs that night or *imbibed*' – I put the sarcastic emphasis this time – 'any alcohol.'

'And I,' Flair said, 'have the right to cast doubt on her recollections. The punch was indeed spiked. I will produce Mr. Flynn, who will testify that the defendant knew that when she drank it. I also want to establish that this is a woman who did not hesitate to do drugs, even when she was mothering a young child—'

'Your Honor!' I shouted.

'Okay, enough.' The judge cracked the gavel. 'Can we move along, Mr. Hickory?'

'We can, Your Honor.'

I sat back down. My objection had been stupid. It looked as if I was trying to get in the way and worse, I had given Flair the chance to offer more narrative. My strategy had been to stay silent. I had lost my discipline, and it had cost us.

'Ms. Johnson, you are accusing these boys of raping you, is that correct?'

I was on my feet. 'Objection. She's not a lawyer or familiar with legal definitions. She told you what they did to her. It is the court's job to find the correct terminology.'

Flair looked amused again. 'I'm not asking her for a legal definition. I'm curious about her own vernacular.'

'Why? Are you going to give her a vocabulary test?'

'Your Honor,' Flair said, 'may I please question this witness?'

'Why don't you explain what you're after, Mr. Hickory?'

'Fine, I'll rephrase. Miss Johnson, when you are talking to your friends, do you tell them that you were raped?'

She hesitated. 'Yeah.'

'Uh-huh. And tell me, Ms. Johnson, do you know anyone else who has claimed to be raped?'

Me again. 'Objection. Relevance?'

'I'll allow it.'

Flair was standing near Chamique. 'You can answer,' he said, like he was helping her out.

'Yeah.'

'Who?'

'Coupla the girls I work with.'

'How many?'

She looked up as if trying to remember. 'I can think of two.'

'Would these be strippers or prostitutes?'

'Both.'

'One of each or—'

'No, they both do both.'

'I see. Did these crimes occur while they were working or while they were on their leisure time?'

I was up again. 'Your Honor, I mean, enough. What's the relevance?'

'My distinguished colleague is right,' Flair said, gesturing with a full arm swing in my direction. 'When he's right, he's right. I withdraw the question.'

He smiled at me. I sat down slowly, hating every moment of it.

'Ms. Johnson, do you know any rapists?'

Me again. 'You mean, besides your clients?'

Flair just gave me a look and then turned to the jury as if to say, *My, wasn't that the lowest cheap shot ever?* And truth: It was.

For her part, Chamique said, 'I don't understand what you mean.'

'No matter, my dear,' Flair said, as if her answer would bore him. 'I'll get back to that later.'

I hate when Flair says that.

'During this purported attack, did my clients, Mr. Jenrette and Mr. Marantz, did they wear masks?'

'No.'

'Did they wear disguises of any sort?'

'No.'

'Did they try to hide their faces?'

'No.'

Flair Hickory shook his head as if this was the most puzzling thing he had ever heard.

'And according to your testimony, you were grabbed against your will and dragged into the room. Is that correct?'

'Yes.'

'The room where Mr. Jenrette and Mr. Marantz resided?'

'Yes.'

'They didn't attack you outside, in the dark, or some place that couldn't be traced back to them. Isn't that correct?'

'Yes.'

'Odd, don't you think?'

I was about to object again, but I let it go.

'So it is your testimony that two men raped you, that they didn't wear masks or do anything to disguise themselves, that they in fact showed you their faces, that they did this in their room with at least one witness watching you being forced to enter. Is that correct?'

I begged Chamique not to sound wishy-washy. She didn't. 'That sounds right, yeah.'

'And yet, for some reason' – again Flair looked like the most perplexed man imaginable – 'they used aliases?'

No reply. Good.

Flair Hickory continued to shake his head as though someone had demanded he make two plus two equal five. 'Your attackers used the names Cal and Jim instead of their own. That's your testimony, is it not, Miss Johnson?'

'It is.'

'Does that make any sense to you?'

'Objection,' I said. 'Nothing about this brutal crime makes sense to her.'

'Oh, I understand that,' Flair Hickory said. 'I was just hoping, being that she was there, that Ms. Johnson might have a theory on why they would let their faces be seen and attack her in their own room – and yet use aliases.' He smiled sweetly. 'Do you have one, Miss Johnson?'

'One what?'

'A theory on why two boys named Edward and Barry would call themselves Jim and Cal?'

'No.'

Flair Hickory walked back to his desk. 'Before I asked you if you knew any rapists. Do you remember that?'

'Yeah.'

'Good. Do you?'

'I don't think so.'

Flair nodded and picked up a sheet of paper. 'How about a man currently being incarcerated in Rahway on charges of sexual battery named – and please pay attention, Ms. Johnson – Jim Broodway?'

Chamique's eyes grew wide. 'You mean James?'

'I mean, Jim – or James, if you want the formal name – Broodway who used to reside at 1189 Central Avenue in the city of Newark, New Jersey. Do you know him?'

'Yeah.' Her voice was soft. 'I used to know him.'

'Did you know that he is now in prison?'

She shrugged. 'I know a lot of guys who are now in prison.'

'I'm certain you do' – for the first time, there was bite in Flair's voice – 'but that wasn't my question. I asked you if you knew that Jim Broodway was in prison.'

'He's not Jim. He's James – '

'I will ask one more time, Miss Johnson, and then I will ask the court to demand an answer – '

I was up. 'Objection. He's badgering the witness.'

'Overruled. Answer the question.'

'I heard something about it,' Chamique said, and her tone was meek.

Flair did the dramatic sigh. 'Yes or no, Miss Johnson, did you know that Jim Broodway is currently serving time in a state penitentiary?'

'Yes.'

'There. Was that so hard?'

Me again. 'Your Honor . . .'

'No need for the dramatics, Mr. Hickory. Get on with it.'

Flair Hickory walked back to his chair. 'Have you ever had sex with Jim Broodway?'

'His name is James!' Chamique said again.

'Let's call him 'Mr. Broodway' for the sake of this discussion, shall we? Have you ever had sex with Mr. Broodway?'

I couldn't just let this go. 'Objection. Her sex life is

irrelevant to this case. The law is clear here.'

Judge Pierce looked at Flair. 'Mr. Hickory?'

'I am not trying to besmirch Miss Johnson's reputation or imply that she is a woman of loose morals,' Flair said. 'Opposing counsel already explained very clearly that Miss Johnson has worked as a prostitute and has engaged in a variety of sexual activities with a wide variety of men.'

When will I learn to keep my mouth shut?

'The point I am trying to raise is a different one and will not at all embarrass the defendant. She has admitted having sex with men. The fact that Mr. Broodway might be one of them is hardly stapling a scarlet letter to her chest.'

'It's prejudicial,' I countered.

Flair looked at me as if I'd just dropped out of the backside of a horse. 'I just explained to you why it is very much not. But the truth is, Chamique Johnson has accused two youths of a very serious crime. She has testified that a man named Jim raped her. What I am asking, plain and simple, is this: Did she ever have sex with Mr. Jim Broodway – or James, if she prefers – who is currently serving time in a state penitentiary for sexual battery?'

I saw now where this was going. And it wasn't good.

'I'll allow it,' the judge said.

I sat back down.

'Miss Johnson, have you ever had sexual relations with Mr. Broodway?'

A tear rolled down her cheek. 'Yeah.'

'More than once?'

'Yeah.'

It looked like Flair was going to try to be more specific, but he knew better than to pile on. He changed directions a little. 'Were you ever drunk or high while having sex with Mr. Broodway?'

'Might have been.'

'Yes or no?'

His voice was soft but firm. There was a hint of outrage now too.

'Yes.'

She was crying harder now.

I stood. 'Quick recess, Your Honor.'

Flair dropped the hammer before the judge could reply. 'Was there ever another man involved in your sexual encounters with Jim Broodway?'

The courtroom exploded.

'Your Honor!' I shouted.

'Order!' The judge used the gavel. 'Order!'

The room quieted quickly. Judge Pierce looked down at me. 'I know how hard this is to listen to, but I'm going to allow this question.' He turned to Chamique. 'Please answer.'

The court stenographer read the question again. Chamique sat there and let the tears spill down her face. When the stenographer finished, Chamique said, 'No.'

'Mr. Broodway will testify that—'

'He let some friend of his watch!' Chamique cried out. 'That's all. I never let him touch me! You hear me? Not ever!'

The room was silent. I tried to keep my head up, tried not to close my eyes.

'So,' Flair Hickory said, 'you had sex with a man named Jim—'

'James! His name is James!'

' – and another man was in the room and yet you don't know how you came up with the names Jim and Cal?'

'I don't know no Cal. And his name is James.'

Flair Hickory moved closer to her. His face showed concern now, as if he were reaching out to her. 'Are you sure you didn't imagine this, Miss Johnson?'

His voice sounded like one of those TV help doctors.

She wiped her face. 'Yeah, Mr. Hickory. I'm sure. Damned sure.'

But Flair did not back down.

'I don't necessarily say you're lying,' he went on, and I bit back my objection, 'but isn't there a chance that maybe you had too much punch – not your fault, of course, you thought it was nonalcoholic – and then you engaged in a consensual act and just flashed back to some other time period? Wouldn't that explain your insisting that the two men who raped you were named Jim and Cal?'

I was up on my feet to say that was two questions, but Flair again knew what he was doing.

'Withdrawn,' Flair Hickory said, as if this whole thing was just the saddest thing for all parties involved. 'I have no further questions.'

Chapter 13

While Lucy waited for Sylvia Potter, she tried to Google the name from Ira's visitor's log: Manolo Santiago. There were lots of hits, but nothing that helped. He wasn't a reporter – or no hits showed that to be the case anyhow. So who was he? And why would he visit her father?

She could ask Ira, of course. If he remembered.

Two hours passed. Then three and four. She called Sylvia's room. No answer. She tried e-mailing the BlackBerry again. No response.

This wasn't good.

How the hell would Sylvia Potter know about her past?

Lucy checked the student directory. Sylvia Potter lived in Stone House down in the social quad. She decided to walk over and see what she could find.

There was an obvious magic to a college campus. There is no entity more protected, more shielded, and while it was easy to complain about that, it was also how it should be. Some things grow better in a vacuum. It was a place to feel safe when you're young – but when you're older, like she and Lonnie, it started becoming a place to hide.

Stone House used to be Psi U's fraternity house. Ten years ago, the college did away with fraternities, calling them 'anti-intellectual.' Lucy didn't disagree that fraternities had plenty of negative qualities and connotations, but the idea of outlawing them seemed heavy-handed and a tad too fascist for her taste. There was a case going on at a nearby college involving a fraternity and a rape. But if it isn't a fraternity, then it would be a lacrosse team or a group of hard hats in a strip club or rowdy rockers at a nightclub. She wasn't sure of the answer, but she knew that it wasn't to rid yourself of every institution you didn't like.

Punish the crime, she thought, not the freedom.

The outside of the house was still a gorgeous Georgian brick. The inside had been stripped of all personality. Gone were the tapestries and wood paneling and rich mahogany of its storied past, replaced with off-whites and beiges and all things neutral. Seemed a shame.

Students meandered about. Her entrance drew a few stares but not too many. Stereos – or more likely, those iPod speaker systems – blared. Doors were open. She saw posters of Che on the wall. Maybe she was more like her father than she realized. University campuses were also caught in the sixties. Styles and music might change, but that sentiment was always there.

She took the center stairwell, also scrubbed of its originality. Sylvia Potter lived in a single on the second floor. Lucy found her door. There was one of those erasable boards, the kind where you write notes with a marker, but there wasn't a blemish on it. The board had been put on straight and perfectly centered. On the top, the name 'Sylvia' was written in a script that almost looked like professional calligraphy. There was a pink flower next to her name. It seemed so out of place, this whole door, separate and apart and from another era.

Lucy knocked on the door. There was no reply. She tried the knob. It was locked. She thought about leaving a note on the door – that was what those erasable boards were there for – but she didn't want to mar it up. Plus it seemed a little desperate. She had called already. She had e-mailed. Stopping by like this was going a step too far.

She started back down the stairs when the front door of Stone House opened. Sylvia Potter entered. She saw Lucy and stiffened. Lucy took the rest of the steps and stopped in front of Sylvia. She said nothing, trying to meet the girl's eyes. Sylvia looked everywhere but directly at Lucy.

'Oh hi, Professor Gold.'

Lucy kept silent.

'Class ran late, I'm so sorry. And then I had this other project due tomorrow. And I figured it was late and you'd be gone and it could just wait till tomorrow.'

She was babbling. Lucy let her.

'Do you want me to stop by tomorrow?' Sylvia asked.

'Do you have time now?'

Sylvia looked at her watch without really looking at it. 'I'm really so crazy with this project. Can it wait until tomorrow?'

'Who is the project for?'

'What?'

'What professor assigned you the project, Sylvia? If I take up too much of your time, I can write them a note.'

Silence.

'We can go to your room,' Lucy said. 'Talk there.'

Sylvia finally met her eye. 'Professor Gold?'

Lucy waited.

'I don't think I want to talk to you.'

'It's about your journal.'

'My . . . ?' She shook her head. 'But I sent it in anonymously. How would you know which is mine?'

'Sylvia—'

'You said! You promised! They were anonymous. You said that.'

'I know what I said.'

'How did you . . . ?' She straightened up. 'I don't want to talk to you.'

Lucy made her voice firm. 'You have to.'

But Sylvia wasn't backing down. 'No, I don't. You can't make me. And . . . my God, how could you do that? Tell us it's anonymous and confidential and then . . .'

'This is really important.'

'No, it's not. I don't have to talk to you. And if you say anything about it, I will tell the dean what you did. You'll get fired.'

Other students were staring now. Lucy was losing control of the situation. 'Please, Sylvia, I need to know—'

'Nothing!'

'Sylvia—'

'I don't have to tell you a thing! Leave me alone!'

Sylvia Potter turned, opened the door, and ran away.

Chapter 14

After Flair Hickory finished with Chamique, I met with Loren Muse in my office.

'Wow,' Loren said. 'That sucked.'

'Get on that name thing,' I said.

'What name thing?'

'Find out if anyone called Broodway "Jim," or if, as Chamique insists, he went by James.'

Muse frowned.

'What?'

'You think that's going to help?'

'It can't hurt.'

'You still believe her?'

'Come on, Muse. This is a smoke screen.'

'It's a good one.'

'Your friend Cingle learn anything?'

'Not yet.'

The judge called the court day over, thank God. Flair had handed me my head. I know that it is supposed to be about justice and that it's not a competition or anything like that, but let's get real.

Cal and Jim were back and stronger than ever.

My cell phone rang. I looked at the caller ID. I didn't recognize the number. I put the phone to my ear and said, 'Hello?'

'It is Raya.'

Raya Singh. The comely Indian waitress. I felt my throat go dry.

'How are you?'

'Fine.'

'Did you think of something?'

Muse looked at me. I tried to look at her as if to say, this is private. For an investigator, Muse could be slow on the pickup. Or maybe that was intentional.

'I probably should have said something earlier,' Raya Singh said.

I waited.

'But you showing up like that. It surprised me. I'm still not sure what the right thing to do is.'

'Ms. Singh?'

'Please call me Raya.'

'Raya,' I said, 'I have no idea what you're talking about.'

'It was why I asked why you were really there. Do you remember?'

'Yes.'

'Do you know why I asked that – about what you really wanted?'

I thought about it and went with honest: 'Because of the unprofessional way I was ogling you?'

'No,' she said.

'Okay, I'm game. Why did you ask? And come to think of it, why did you ask if I killed him?'

Muse arched an eyebrow. I didn't much care.

Raya Singh didn't reply.

'Miss Singh?' Then: 'Raya?'

'Because,' she said, 'he mentioned your name.'

I thought that maybe I'd heard wrong, so I asked something stupid. 'Who mentioned my name?'

Her voice had a hint of impatience. 'Who are we talking about?'

'Manolo Santiago mentioned my name?'

'Yes, of course.'

'And you didn't think you should tell me this before?'

'I didn't know if I could trust you.'

'And what changed your mind?'

'I looked you up on the Internet. You really are the county prosecutor.'

'What did Santiago say about me?'

'He said you lied about something.'

'About what?'

'I don't know.'

I pushed ahead. 'Who did he say it to?'

'A man. I don't know his name. He also had clippings about you in his apartment.'

'His apartment? I thought you said you didn't know where he lived.'

'That's when I didn't trust you.'

'And you do now?'

She did not reply to that one directly. 'Pick me up at the restaurant in one hour,' Raya Singh said, 'and I'll show you where Manolo lived.'

Chapter 15

When Lucy came back to her office, Lonnie was there, holding up sheets of paper.

'What's that?' she asked.

'More of that journal.'

She tried hard not to snap the pages from his hand.

'Did you find Sylvia?' he asked.

'Yes.'

'And?'

'And she went crazy on me and won't talk.'

Lonnie sat in the chair and threw his feet up on her desk. 'You want me to try?'

'I don't think that's a good idea.'

Lonnie gave her the winning smile. 'I can be pretty persuasive.'

'You're willing to put out just to help me?'

'If I must.'

'I would worry so about your reputation.' She sat back, gripping the pages. 'Did you read this already?'

'Yep.'

She just nodded and started in for herself:

P broke our embrace and darted toward the scream.

I called after him, but he didn't stop. Two seconds later, it was like the night had swallowed him whole. I tried to follow. But it was dark. I should have known these woods better than P. This was his first year here.

The screaming voice had been a girl's. That much I could tell. I trekked through the woods. I didn't call out anymore. For some reason I was scared to. I wanted to find P, but I didn't want anyone to know where I was. I know that doesn't make much sense, but that was how I felt.

I was scared.

There was moonlight. Moonlight in the woods changes the color of everything. It is like one of those poster lights my dad used to have. They called them black lights, even though they were more like purple. They changed the color of everything around them. So did the moon.

So when I finally found P and I saw the strange color on his shirt, I didn't recognize what it was at first. I couldn't tell the shade of crimson. It looked more like liquid blue. He looked at me. His eyes were wide.

'We have to go,' he said. 'And we can't tell anyone we were ever out here . . .'

That was it. Lucy read it two more times. Then she put the story down. Lonnie was watching her.

'So,' he said, dragging out the word, 'I assume that you are the narrator of this little tale?'

'What?'

'I've been trying to figure this out, Lucy, and I've only

come up with one possible explanation. You're the girl in the story. Someone is writing about you.'

'That's ridiculous,' she said.

'Come on, Luce. We have tales of incest in that pile, for crying out loud. We aren't even searching those kids out. Yet you're all uptight about this scream-in-the-woods story?'

'Let it go, Lonnie.'

He shook his head. 'Sorry, sweetie, not my nature. Even if you weren't superfine and I didn't want to get in your pants.'

She didn't bother with a retort.

'I'd like to help if I can.'

'You can't.'

'I know more than you think.'

Lucy looked up at him.

'What are you talking about?'

'You, uh, you won't get mad at me?'

She waited.

'I did a little research on you.'

Her stomach dropped, but she kept it off her face.

'Lucy Gold isn't your real name. You changed it.'

'How do you know that?'

'Come on, Luce. You know how easy it is with a computer?'

She said nothing.

'Something about this journal kept bugging me,' he went on. 'This stuff about a camp. I was young, but I remember hearing about the Summer Slasher. So I did a little more research.' He tried to give her the cocky smile. 'You should go back to blond.'

'It was a tough time in my life.'

'I can imagine.'

'That's why I changed my name.'

'Oh, I get that. Your family took a big hit. You wanted to get out from under that.'

'Yes.'

'And now, for some weird reason, it's coming back.'

She nodded.

'Why?' Lonnie asked.

'I don't know.'

'I'd like to help.'

'Like I said, I'm not sure how.'

'Can I ask you something?'

She shrugged.

'I did a little digging. You know that the Discovery Channel did a special on the murders a few years ago.'

'I know,' she said.

'They don't talk about you being there. In the woods that night, I mean.'

She said nothing.

'So what gives?'

'I can't talk about it.'

'Who is P? It's Paul Copeland, right? You know he's a DA or something now.'

She shook her head.

'You're not making this easy,' he said.

She kept her mouth closed.

'Okay,' he said, standing. 'I'll help anyway.'

'How?'

'Sylvia Potter.'

'What about her?'

'I'll get her to talk.'

'How?'

Lonnie headed for the door. 'I got my ways.'

On the way back to the Indian restaurant, I took a detour and visited Jane's grave.

I was not sure why. I did not do it that often – maybe three times a year. I don't really feel my wife's presence here. Her parents picked out the burial site with Jane. 'It means a lot to them,' she'd explained on her death-bed. And it did. It distracted her parents, especially her mother, and made them feel as though they were doing something useful.

I didn't much care. I was in denial about Jane ever dying – even when it got bad, *really* bad, I still thought she'd somehow pull through. And to me death is death – final, the end, nothing coming after, the finish line, no more. Fancy caskets and well-tended graveyards, even ones as well tended as Jane's, don't change that.

I parked in the lot and walked the path. Her grave had fresh flowers on it. We of the Hebrew faith do not do that. We put stones on the marker. I liked that, though I am not sure why. Flowers, something so alive and bright, seemed obscene against the gray of her tomb. My wife, my beautiful Jane, was rotting six feet below those freshly cut lilies. That seemed like an outrage to me.

I sat on a concrete bench. I didn't talk to her. It was so bad in the end. Jane suffered. I watched. For a while anyway. We got hospice – Jane wanted to die at home – but then there was her weight loss and the smell and the decay and the groans. The sound that I remembered most, the one that still invaded my sleep, was the awful coughing noise, more a choke really, when Jane couldn't get the phlegm up and it would hurt so much and she would be so uncomfortable and it went on for months and months and I tried to be strong but I wasn't as strong as Jane and she knew that.

There was a time early in our relationship when she knew that I was having doubts. I had lost a sister. My mother had run off on me. And now, for the first time in a long time, I was letting a woman into my life. I remember late one night when I couldn't sleep and I was staring at the ceiling and Jane was sleeping next to me. I remember that I heard her deep breath, then so sweet and perfect and so different from what it would be in the end. Her breathing shortened as she slowly came awake. She put her arms around me and moved close.

'I'm not her,' she said softly, as if she could read my thoughts. 'I will never abandon you.'

But in the end, she did.

I had dated since her death. I have even had some fairly intense emotional commitments. One day I hope to find someone and remarry. But right now, as I thought about that night in our bed, I realized that it would probably not happen.

I'm not her, my wife had said.

And of course, she meant my mother.

I looked at the tombstone. I read my wife's name. Loving Mother, Daughter and Wife. There were some kind of angel wings on the sides. I pictured my in-laws picking those out, just the right size angel wings, just the right design, all that. They had bought the plot next to Jane's without telling me. If I didn't remarry, I guess, it would be mine. If I did, well, I don't know what my in-laws would do with it.

I wanted to ask my Jane for help. I wanted to ask her to search around up wherever she was and see if she could find my sister and let me know if Camille was alive or dead. I smiled like a dope. Then I stopped.

I'm sure cell phones in graveyards are no-nos. But I didn't think Jane would mind. I took the phone out of my pocket and pressed down on that six button again.

Sosh answered on the first ring.

'I have a favor to ask,' I said.

'I told you before. Not on the phone.'

'Find my mother, Sosh.'

Silence.

'You can do it. I'm asking. In the memory of my father and sister. Find my mother for me.'

'And if I can't?'

'You can.'

'Your mother has been gone a long time.'

'I know.'

'Have you considered the fact that maybe she doesn't want to be found?'

'I have,' I said.

'And?'

'And tough,' I said. 'We don't always get what we want. So find her for me, Sosh. Please.'

I hung up the phone. I looked at my wife's stone again.

'We miss you,' I said out loud to my dead wife. 'Cara and I. We miss you very, very much.'

Then I stood up and walked back to my car.

Chapter 16

Raya Singh was waiting for me in the restaurant parking lot. She had turned in the aqua waitress uniform for jeans and a dark blue blouse. Her hair was pulled back in a ponytail. The effect was no less dazzling. I shook my head. I had just visited my wife's grave. Now I was inappropriately admiring the beauty of a young woman.

It was an interesting world.

She slipped into the passenger seat. She smelled great.

'Where to?' I asked.

'Do you know where Route 17 is?'

'Yes.'

'Take it north.'

I pulled out of the lot. 'Do you want to start telling me the truth?' I asked.

'I have never lied to you,' she said. 'I decided not to tell you certain things.'

'Are you still claiming you just met Santiago on the street?'

'I am.'

I didn't believe her.

'Have you ever heard him mention the name Perez?'

She did not reply.

I pressed. 'Gil Perez?'

'The exit for 17 is on the right.'

'I know where the exit is, Raya.'

I glanced at her in perfect profile. She stared out the window, looking achingly beautiful.

'Tell me about hearing him say my name,' I said.

'I told you already.'

'Tell me again.'

She took a deep, silent breath. Her eyes closed for a moment.

'Manolo said you lied.'

'Lied about what?'

'Lied about something involving' – she hesitated – 'involving woods or a forest or something like that.'

I felt my heart lurch across my chest. 'He said that? About woods or a forest?'

'Yes.'

'What were his exact words?'

'I don't remember.'

'Try.'

'"Paul Copeland lied about what happened in those woods."' Then she tilted her head. 'Oh, wait.'

I did.

Then she said something that almost made me turn off the road. She said, 'Lucy.'

'What?'

'That was the other name. He said, "Paul Copeland lied about what happened in those woods. So did Lucy."'

Now it was my turn to be struck silent.

'Paul,' Raya said, 'who is this Lucy?'

We took the rest of the ride in silence.

I was lost in thoughts of Lucy. I tried to remember the feel of her flaxen hair, the wondrous smell of it. But I couldn't. That was the thing. The memories seemed so clouded. I couldn't remember what was real and what my imagination had conjured up. I just remembered the wonder. I remembered the lust. We were both new, both clumsy, both inexperienced, but it was like something in a Bob Seger song or maybe Meat Loaf's 'Bat Out of Hell.' God, that lust. How had it started? And when did that lust seemingly segue into something approaching love?

Summer romances come to an end. That was part of the deal. They are built like certain plants or insects, not able to survive more than one season. I thought Luce and I would be different. We were, I guess, but not in the way that I thought. I truly believed that we would never let each other go.

The young are so dumb.

The AmeriSuites efficiency unit was in Ramsey, New Jersey. Raya had a key. She opened the door to a room on the third floor. I would describe the decor to you except that the only word to describe it would be *nondescript*. The furnishing had all the personality of, well, an efficiency unit on a road called Route 17 in northern New Jersey.

When we stepped into the room, Raya let out a little gasp.

'What?' I said.

Her eyes took in the whole room. 'There were tons of papers on that table,' she said. 'Files, magazines, pens, pencils.'

'It's empty now.'

Raya opened a drawer. 'His clothes are gone.'

We did a pretty thorough search. Everything was gone – there were no papers, no files, no magazine articles, no toothbrush, no personal items, nothing. Raya sat on the couch. 'Someone came back and cleared this place out.'

'When were you here last?'

'Three days ago.'

I started for the door. 'Come on.'

'Where are you going?'

'I'm going to talk to someone at the front desk.'

But there was a kid working there. He gave us pretty much nothing. The occupant had signed in as Manolo Santiago. He had paid in cash, leaving a cash deposit. The room was paid for until the end of the month. And no, the kid didn't remember what Mr. Santiago looked like or anything about him. That was one of the problems with these kinds of units. You don't have to go in through the lobby. It was easy to be anonymous.

Raya and I headed back to Santiago's room.

'You said there were papers?'

'Yes.'

'What did they say?'

'I didn't pry.'

'Raya,' I said.

'What?'

'I have to be honest here. I'm not fully buying the ignorant act.'

She just looked at me with those damn eyes.

'What?'

'You want me to trust you.'

'Yes.'

'Why should I?'

I thought about that.

'You lied to me when we met,' she said.

161

'About what?'

'You said you were just investigating his murder. Like a regular detective or something. But that wasn't true, was it?'

I said nothing.

'Manolo,' she went on. 'He didn't trust you. I read those articles. I know something happened to all of you in those woods twenty years ago. He thought you lied about it.'

I still said nothing.

'And now you expect me to tell you everything. Would you? If you were in my position, would you tell everything you knew?'

I took a second, gathered my thoughts. She had a point. 'So you saw those articles?'

'Yes.'

'Then you know that I was at that camp that summer.'

'I do.'

'And you know that my sister disappeared that night too.'

She nodded.

I turned to her. 'That's why I'm here.'

'You're here to avenge your sister?'

'No,' I said. 'I'm here to find her.'

'But I thought she was dead. Wayne Steubens murdered her.'

'That was what I used to think.'

Raya turned away for a moment. Then she looked right through me. 'So what did you lie about?'

'Nothing.'

The eyes again. 'You can trust me,' she said.

'I do.'

She waited. I waited too.

162

'Who is Lucy?'

'She's a girl who was at the camp.'

'What else? What's her connection to this?'

'Her father owned the camp,' I said. Then I added, 'She was also my girlfriend at the time.'

'And how did you both lie?'

'We didn't lie.'

'So what was Manolo talking about?'

'Damned if I know. That's what I'm trying to find out.'

'I don't understand. What makes you so sure your sister is alive?'

'I'm not sure,' I said. 'But I think there's a decent enough chance.'

'Why?'

'Because of Manolo.'

'What about him?'

I studied her face and wondered if I was getting played here. 'You clammed up before when I mentioned the name Gil Perez,' I said.

'His name was in those articles. He was killed that night too.'

'No,' I said.

'I don't understand.'

'Do you know why Manolo was looking into what happened that night?'

'He never said.'

'Weren't you curious?'

She shrugged. 'He said it was business.'

'Raya,' I said. 'Manolo Santiago wasn't his real name.'

I hesitated, seeing if she would jump in, volunteer something. She didn't.

'His real name,' I went on, 'was Gil Perez.'

She took a second to process this. 'The boy from the woods?'

'Yes.'

'Are you sure?'

Good question. But I said, 'Yes,' without any hesitation.

She thought about it. 'And what you're telling me now – if it's true – was that he was alive this whole time.'

I nodded.

'And if he was alive . . .' Raya Singh stopped. So I finished it for her.

'Maybe my sister is too.'

'Or maybe,' she said, 'Manolo – Gil, whatever you call him – killed them all.'

Strange. I hadn't thought of that. It actually made some sense. Gil kills them all, leaves evidence he was a victim too. But was Gil clever enough to pull something like that off? And how do you explain Wayne Steubens?

Unless Wayne was telling the truth . . .

'If that's the case,' I said, 'then I'll find that out.'

Raya frowned. 'Manolo said you and Lucy were lying. If he killed them, why would he say something like that? Why would he have all this paperwork and be looking into what happened? If he did it, he would know the answers, wouldn't he?'

She crossed the room and stood directly in front of me. So damn young and beautiful. I actually wanted to kiss her.

'What aren't you telling me?' she asked.

My cell phone rang. I glanced at the caller ID. It was Loren Muse. I hit the On button and said, 'What's up?'

'We got a problem,' Muse said.

I closed my eyes and waited.

'It's Chamique. She wants to recant.'

My office is in the center of Newark. I keep hearing that there is a revitalization going on in this city. I don't see it. The city has been decaying for as long as I can remember. But I have gotten to know this city well. The history is still there, beneath the surface. The people are wonderful. We as a society are big on stereotyping cities the way we do ethnic groups or minorities. It is easy to hate them from a distance. I remember Jane's conservative parents and their disdain for all things gay. Her college roommate, Helen, unbeknownst to them, was gay. When they met her, both her mother and father simply loved Helen. When they learned Helen was a lesbian, they still loved her. Then they loved her partner.

That was how it often was. It was easy to hate gays or blacks or Jews or Arabs. It was more difficult to hate individuals.

Newark was like that. You could hate it as a mass, but so many neighborhoods and shopkeepers and citizens had a charm and strength that you couldn't help but be drawn in and care about and want to make it better.

Chamique sat in my office. She was so damned young, but you could see the hard written on her face. Life had not been easy for this girl. It would probably not get any easier. Her attorney, Horace Foley, wore too much cologne and had eyes spaced too widely apart. I am an attorney, so I don't like the prejudices that are made against my profession, but I was fairly confident that if an ambulance drove by, this guy would jump through my third-floor window to slow it down.

'We would like to see you drop the charges on Mr.

165

Jenrette and Mr. Marantz,' Foley said.

'Can't do that,' I said. I looked at Chamique. She did not have her head down, but she wasn't exactly clamoring for eye contact. 'Did you lie on the stand yesterday?' I asked her.

'My client would never lie,' Foley said.

I ignored him, met Chamique's eyes. She said, 'You're never going to convict them anyway.'

'You don't know that.'

'You serious?'

'I am.'

Chamique smiled at me, as if I were the most naive creature that God had ever created. 'You don't understand, do you?'

'Oh, I understand. They're offering money if you recant. The sum has now reached a level where your attorney here, Mr. Who-Needs-A-Shower-When-There's-Cologne, thinks it makes sense to do it.'

'What did you call me?'

I looked at Muse. 'Open a window, will you?'

'Got it, Cope.'

'Hey! What did you call me?'

'The window is open. Feel free to jump out.' I looked back at Chamique. 'If you recant now, that means your testimony today and yesterday was a lie. It means you committed perjury. It means you had this office spend millions of tax dollars on your lie – your perjury. That's a crime. You'll go to jail.'

Foley said, 'Talk to me, Mr. Copeland, not my client.'

'Talk to you? I can't even breathe around you.'

'I won't stand for this – '

'Shh,' I said. Then I cupped my ear with my hand. 'Listen to the crinkling sound.'

166

'To what?'

'I think your cologne is peeling my wallpaper. If you listen closely, you can hear it. Shh, listen.'

Even Chamique smiled a little.

'Don't recant,' I said to her.

'I have to.'

'Then I'll charge you.'

Her attorney was ready to do battle again, but Chamique put her hand on his arm. 'You won't do that, Mr. Copeland.'

'I will.'

But she knew better. I was bluffing. She was a poor, scared rape victim who had a chance of cashing in – making more money than she would probably see again in her lifetime. Who the hell was I to lecture her on values and justice?

She and her attorney stood. Horace Foley said, 'We sign the agreement in the morning.'

I didn't say anything. Part of me felt relief, and that shamed me. JaneCare would survive now. My father's memory – okay, my political career – wouldn't take an unnecessary hit. Best off, I was off the hook. It wasn't my doing. It was Chamique's.

Chamique offered me her hand. I took it. 'Thank you,' she said.

'Don't do this,' I said, but there was nothing left in my try. She could see that. She smiled. Then they left my office. First Chamique, then her attorney. His cologne stayed behind as a memento.

Muse shrugged and said, 'What can you do?'

I was wondering that myself.

I got home and had dinner with Cara. She had a 'homework' assignment that consisted of finding things that were red in magazines and cutting them out. This would seem like a very easy task, but of course, nothing we found together would work for her. She didn't like the red wagon or the model's red dress or even the red fire engine. The problem, I soon realized, was that I was showing enthusiasm for what she'd find. I would say, 'That dress *is* red, sweetie! You're right! I think that would be perfect!'

After about twenty minutes of this, I saw the error of my ways. When she stumbled across a picture of a bottle of a ketchup, I made my voice flat and shrugged my shoulders and said, 'I don't really like ketchup.'

She grabbed the scissors with the safety handles and went to work.

Kids.

Cara started singing a song as she cut. The song was from a cartoon TV show called *Dora the Explorer* and basically consisted of singing the word *backpack* over and over again until the head of a nearby parent exploded into a million pieces. I had made the mistake about two months ago of buying her a Dora the Explorer Talking Backpack ('backpack, backpack,' repeat) with matching talking Map (song: 'I'm the map, I'm the map, I'm the map,' repeat). When her cousin, Madison, came over, they would often play Dora the Explorer. One of them would play the role of Dora. The other would be a monkey with the rather interesting moniker 'Boots.' You don't often meet monkeys named for footwear.

I was thinking about that, about Boots, about the way Cara and her cousin would argue over who would be Dora and who would be Boots, when it struck me like the proverbial thunderbolt.

I froze. I actually stopped and just sat there. Even Cara saw it.

'Daddy?'

'One second, kitten.'

I ran upstairs, my footsteps shaking the house. Where the hell were those bills from the frat house? I started tearing apart the room. It took me a few minutes to find them – I had been ready to throw them all away after my meeting this morning.

Bang, there they were.

I rifled through them. I found the online charges, the monthly ones, and then I grabbed the phone and called Muse's number. She answered on the first ring.

'What's up?'

'When you were in college,' I asked, 'how often did you pull all-nighters?'

'Twice a week minimum.'

'How did you keep yourself awake?'

'M&Ms. Lots of them. The oranges are amphetamines, I swear.'

'Buy as many as you need. You can even expense them.'

'I like the tone of your voice, Cope.'

'I have an idea, but I don't know if we have the time.'

'Don't worry about the time. What's the idea concerning?'

'It concerns,' I said, 'our old buddies Cal and Jim.'

Chapter 17

I got Cologne Lawyer Foley's home number and woke him up.

'Don't sign those papers until the afternoon,' I said.

'Why?'

'Because if you do, I will make sure my office comes down on you and your clients as hard as they can. I will let it be known that we don't cut deals with Horace Foley, that we always make sure the client serves the maximum time.'

'You can't do that.'

I said nothing.

'I have an obligation to my client.'

'Tell her I asked for the extra time. Tell her it's in her best interest.'

'And what do I say to the other side?'

'I don't know, Foley, find something wrong with the paperwork maybe, whatever. Just stall until the afternoon.'

'And how is that in my client's best interest?'

'If I get lucky and hurt them, you can renegotiate. More moola in your pockets.'

He paused. Then: 'Hey, Cope?'

'What?'

'She's a strange kid. Chamique, I mean.'

'How so?'

'Most of them would have taken the money right away. I've had to push her because, frankly, taking the money early is her best move. We both know that. But she wouldn't hear of it until they sandbagged her with that Jim/James thing yesterday. See, before that, despite what she said in court, she was more interested in them going to jail than the financial payoff. She really wanted justice.'

'And that surprises you?'

'You're new on this job. Me, I've been doing this for twenty-seven years. You grow cynical. So yeah, she surprised the hell out of me.'

'Is there a point to your telling me all this?'

'Yeah, there is. Me, you know what I'm all about. Getting my one-third of the settlement. But Chamique is different. This is life-changing money for her. So whatever you're up to, Mr. Prosecutor, don't screw it up for her.'

Lucy drank alone.

It was night. Lucy lived on campus in faculty housing. The place was beyond depressing. Most professors worked hard and long and saved money in the hopes that they could move the hell out of faculty housing. Lucy had lived here for a year now. Before her, an English-lit professor named Amanda Simon had spent three decades of spinsterhood in this very unit. Lung cancer cut her down at the age of fifty-eight. Her remnants remained in the smoky smell left behind. Despite ripping up the wall-to-wall carpeting and repainting the entire place, the cigarette stench remained. It was a little like living in an ashtray.

Lucy was a vodka girl. She looked out the window. In the distance, she heard music. This was a college campus. There was always music playing. She checked her watch. Midnight.

She flipped on her own tinny-speaker iPod stereo and set it on a playlist she called 'Mellow.' Each song was not only slow but a total heart ripper. So she would drink her vodka and sit in her depressing apartment and smell the smoke from a dead woman and listen to aching songs of loss and want and devastation. Pitiful, but sometimes it was enough to feel. It didn't matter if it hurt or not. Just to feel.

Right now, Joseph Arthur was singing 'Honey and the Moon.' He sang to his true love that if she weren't real, he would make her up. Wow, what a thing. Lucy tried to imagine a man, a worthy man, saying that to her. It made her shake her head in wonder.

She closed her eyes and tried to put the pieces together. Nothing fit. The past was rising up again. Lucy had spent her entire adult life running away from those damn woods at her father's camp. She had fled across the country, all the way to California, and she had fled all the way back again. She had changed her name and hair color. But the past always followed. Sometimes it would let her gain a comfortable lead – lulled her into thinking that she had put enough distance between that night and the present day – but the dead always closed the gap.

In the end that awful night always found her.

But this time . . . how? Those journal entries . . . how could they exist? Sylvia Potter had barely been born when the Summer Slasher struck Camp PLUS (Peace Love Understanding Summer). What could she know about it? Of course, like Lonnie, she might have gone online, done some research, figured out that Lucy had a past. Or maybe someone, someone older and wiser, had told her something.

But still. How would she know? For that matter, how would anyone know? Only one person knew that Lucy had lied about what happened that night.

And, of course, Paul wouldn't say anything.

She stared through the clear liquid in her glass. Paul. Paul Copeland. She could still see him with those gangly arms and legs, that lean torso, that long hair, that knock-a-girl-back smile. Interestingly enough, they had met through their fathers. Paul's old man, an ob-gyn in his old country, had escaped repression in the Soviet Union only to find plenty of it here in the good ol' USA. Ira, Lucy's bleeding-heart father, could never resist a tale of woe like that. So Ira hired Vladimir Copeland to be camp doctor. Gave his family a chance to escape Newark in the summer.

Lucy could still see it – their car, a broken-down Oldsmobile Ciera, kicking up the dirt road, coming to a stop, the four doors opening seemingly at the same time, the family of four stepping out as one. At that moment, when Lucy first saw Paul and their eyes met, it was boom, crack, thunderbolt. And she could see that he felt the same. There are those rare moments in life – when you feel that jolt and it feels great and it hurts like hell, but you're feeling, really feeling, and suddenly colors seem brighter and sounds have more clarity and foods taste better and you never, not even for a minute, stop thinking about him and you know, just know, that he is feeling exactly the same way about you.

'Like that,' Lucy said out loud and took another swig of her vodka and tonic. Like with these pathetic songs she played over and over. A feeling. A rush of emotion. A high or a low, didn't matter. But it wasn't the same anymore. What had Elton John sung, via those Bernie Taupin lyrics, about vodka and tonic? Something about taking a couple of vodka and tonics to set you on your feet again.

That hadn't worked for Lucy. But hey, why give up now?

The little voice in her head said, *Stop drinking*.

The much bigger voice told the little voice to shut up or get its ass kicked.

Lucy made a fist and put it in the air. 'Go, Big Voice!'

She laughed, and that sound, the sound of her own laugh alone in this still room, frightened her. Rob Thomas came on her 'Mellow' list, asking if he could just hold her while she falls apart, if he could just hold her while they both fall down. She nodded. Yes, he could. Rob reminded her that she was cold and scared and broken, and damn her, she wanted to listen to this song with Paul.

Paul.

He would want to know about these journals.

It had been twenty years since she'd seen him, but six years ago, Lucy had looked him up on the Internet. She had not wanted to. She knew that Paul was a door best left closed. But she had gotten drunk – big surprise – and while some people 'drunk dialed,' Lucy had 'drunk Googled.'

What she'd found was both sobering and unsurprising. Paul was married. He worked as an attorney. He had a young daughter. Lucy had even managed to find a picture of his gorgeous wife from a well-to-do family at some charity function. Jane – that was his wife's name – was tall and lean and wore pearls. She looked good in pearls. She had that whole meant-for-pearls thing going on.

Another swig.

Things might have changed in six years, but back then Paul was living in Ridgewood, New Jersey, a scant twenty miles from where Lucy now was. She looked across the room at her computer.

Paul should be told, shouldn't he?

And it would be no problem to do another quick Google search. Just get a phone number for him – home or, better, office. She could contact him. Warn him, really. Totally on the up-and-up. No agenda, no hidden meanings, nothing like that.

She put down the vodka and tonic. Rain fell outside the window. Her computer was already on. Her screen saver was, yep, the Windows default one. No family vacation picture. No slideshow of the kids or even that spinster staple: photograph of a pet. Just that Windows logo bopping around, like the monitor was sticking its tongue out at her.

Beyond pathetic.

She brought up her home page and was about to type when she heard the knock on the door. She stopped, waited.

Another knock. Lucy checked the small clock in the bottom right-hand corner of her computer.

Twelve-seventeen a.m.

Awfully late for a visitor.

'Who is it?'

No reply.

'Who—'

'It's Sylvia Potter.'

There were tears in that voice. Lucy stood and stumbled to the kitchen. She dumped the rest of her drink into the sink and put the bottle back in its cabinet. Vodka didn't smell, at least not much, so she was okay on that count. She took a quick look in the mirror. The image in it looked like hell, but there wasn't much she could do about that now.

'Coming.'

She opened the door and Sylvia tumbled in as if she'd been leaning against it. The girl was soaked. The air-conditioning was set on high. Lucy almost made some comment about her catching her death, but it sounded like something a mother would say. She closed the door.

Sylvia said, 'I'm sorry it's so late.'

'Don't worry about it. I was up.'

She stopped in the center of the room. 'I'm sorry about before.'

'That's okay.'

'No, it's just . . .' Sylvia looked around. She wrapped her arms around her body.

'Do you want a towel or something?'

'No.'

'Can I get you something to drink?'

'I'm okay.'

Lucy gestured for Sylvia to have a seat. Sylvia collapsed on the Ikea couch. Lucy hated Ikea and their graphics-only instruction manuals, seemingly designed by NASA engineers. Lucy sat next to her and waited.

'How did you find out I wrote that journal?' Sylvia asked.

'It's not important.'

'I sent it anonymously.'

'I know.'

'And you said they would be confidential.'

'I know. I'm sorry about that.'

Sylvia wiped her nose and looked off. Her hair was still dripping.

'I even lied to you,' Sylvia said.

'How's that?'

'About what I wrote. When I visited your office the other day. Do you remember?'

'Yes.'

'Do you remember what I said my paper was about?'

Lucy thought for a second. 'Your first time.'

Sylvia smiled but there was nothing behind it. 'I guess, in a sick way, that was true.'

Lucy thought about that too. Then she said, 'I'm not sure I follow, Sylvia.'

Sylvia did not say anything for a long time. Lucy remembered that Lonnie said he would help get her to talk. But he was supposed to wait until the morning.

'Did Lonnie visit you tonight?'

'Lonnie Berger? From class?'

'Yes.'

'No. Why would Lonnie visit me?'

'It's not important. So you just came here on your own?'

Sylvia swallowed and looked unsure of herself. 'Was I wrong to?'

'No, not at all. I'm glad you're here.'

'I'm really scared,' Sylvia said.

Lucy nodded, tried to appear reassuring, encouraging. Forcing this issue would only backfire. So she waited. She waited for a full two minutes before breaking.

'There's no reason to be scared,' Lucy said.

'What do you think I should do?'

'Tell me everything, okay?'

'I have. I mean, the majority of it.'

Lucy wondered how to play this. 'Who is P?'

Sylvia frowned. 'What?'

'In your journal. You talk about a boy named P. Who is P?'

'What are you talking about?'

Lucy stopped. Tried again.

'Tell me exactly why you're here, Sylvia.'

But now Sylvia was being cagey. 'Why did you come to my room today?'

'Because I wanted to talk about your journal.'

'Then why are you asking me about a guy named P? I didn't call anyone P. I said straight out that it was . . .' The words stuck in her throat. She closed her eyes and whispered, '. . . my father.'

The dam broke. The tears came down like the rain, in sheets.

Lucy closed her eyes. The incest story. The one that had struck her and Lonnie with such horror. Damn. Lonnie had gotten it wrong. Sylvia hadn't written the journal about that night in the woods.

'Your father molested you when you were twelve,' Lucy said.

Sylvia's face was in her hands. Her sobs sounded as if they were being ripped out of her chest. Her entire body quaked as she nodded her head. Lucy looked at this poor girl, so anxious to please, and pictured the father. She reached out her hand and put it on Sylvia's. Then she moved closer and put her arms around the girl. Sylvia leaned into her chest and cried. Lucy shushed her and rocked her and held her.

Chapter 18

hadn't slept. Neither had Muse. I managed a quick electric shave. I smelled so bad I debated asking Horace Foley if I could borrow his cologne.

'Get me that paperwork,' I told Muse.

'As soon as I can.'

When the judge called us to order, I called a – gasp – surprise witness.

'The People call Gerald Flynn.'

Flynn had been the 'nice' boy who'd invited Chamique Johnson to the party. He looked the part, too, what with his too-smooth skin, nicely parted blond locks, wide blue eyes that seemed to gaze at everything with naïveté. Because there was a chance I would end my side of the case at any time, the defense had made sure Flynn was waiting. He was, after all, supposed to be their key witness.

Flynn had steadfastly backed his fraternity brothers. But it was one thing to lie to the police and even in depositions. It was another to do it during 'the show.' I looked back at Muse. She sat in the last row and tried to keep a straight face. The results were mixed. Muse would not be my first choice as a poker buddy.

I asked him to say his name for the record.

'Gerald Flynn.'

'But you go by Jerry, isn't that correct?'

'Yes.'

'Fine, let's start from the beginning, shall we? When did you first meet the defendant, Ms. Chamique Johnson?'

Chamique had come today. She was sitting near the center in the second to last row with Horace Foley. Interesting spot to sit. Like she didn't want to commit. I had heard some screaming in the corridors earlier in the morning. The Jenrette and Marantz families were not pleased with the last-minute snafu in their Chamique retraction. They had tried to nail it down, but it hadn't worked out. So we were starting late. Still they were ready. Their court faces, concerned, serious, engaged, were back in place.

It was a temporary delay, they figured. Just a few more hours.

'When she came to the fraternity house on October twelfth,' he replied.

'You remember the date?'

'Yes.'

I made a face like, *My, my, isn't that interesting*, even though it wasn't. Sure, he would know the date. This was a part of his life now too.

'Why was Ms. Johnson at your fraternity house?'

'She was hired as an exotic dancer.'

'Did you hire her?'

'No. Well, I mean, the whole fraternity did. But I wasn't the one who made the booking or anything.'

'I see. So she came to your fraternity house and performed an exotic dance?'

'Yes.'

'And you watched this dance?'

'I did.'

'What did you think of it?'

Mort Pubin was up. 'Objection!'

The judge was already scowling in my direction. 'Mr. Copeland?'

'According to Ms. Johnson, Mr. Flynn here invited her to the party where the rape took place. I am trying to understand why he would do that.'

'So ask him that,' Pubin said.

'Your Honor, may I please do this in my own way?'

Judge Pierce said, 'Try to rephrase.'

I turned back to Flynn. 'Did you think Ms. Johnson was a good exotic dancer?' I asked.

'I guess.'

'Yes or no?'

'Not great. But yeah, I thought she was pretty good.'

'Did you think she was attractive?'

'Yeah, I mean, I guess so.'

'Yes or no?'

'Objection!' Pubin again. 'He doesn't have to answer a question like that yes or no. Maybe he thought she was mildly attractive. It isn't always yes or no.'

'I agree, Mort,' I said, surprising him. 'Let me rephrase, Mr. Flynn – how would you describe her attractiveness?'

'Like on a one-to-ten scale?'

'That would be splendid, Mr. Flynn. On a one-to-ten scale.'

He thought about it. 'Seven, maybe an eight.'

'Fine, thank you. And at some point in the evening, did you talk to Ms. Johnson?'

'Yes.'

'What did you talk about?'

'I don't know.'

'Try to remember.'

'I asked her where she lived. She said Irvington. I asked her if she went to school or if she had a boyfriend. That kinda thing. She told me about having a kid. She asked me what I was studying. I said I wanted to go to medical school.'

'Anything else?'

'It was like that.'

'I see. How long would you say you talked with her?'

'I don't know.'

'Let me see if I can help you then. Was it more than five minutes?'

'Yes.'

'More than an hour?'

'No, I don't think so.'

'More than a half an hour?'

'I'm not sure.'

'More than ten minutes?'

'I think so.'

Judge Pierce interrupted, telling me that we got the point and that I should move it along.

'How did Ms. Johnson depart that particular event, if you know?'

'A car came and picked her up.'

'Oh, was she the only exotic dancer there that evening?'

'No.'

'How many others were there?'

'There were three altogether.'

'Thank you. Did the other two leave with Ms. Johnson?'

'Yes.'

'Did you talk with either of them?'

'Not really. Maybe a hello.'

'Would it be fair to say that Chamique Johnson was the only one of the three exotic dancers you had a conversation with?'

Pubin looked as though he wanted to object but then he decided to let it go.

'Yes,' Flynn said. 'That would be fair.'

Enough prelims. 'Chamique Johnson testified that she made extra money by performing a sexual act on several of the young men at the party. Do you know if that's true?'

'I don't know.'

'Really? So you didn't engage her services?'

'I did not.'

'And you never heard a word mentioned by any of your fraternity brothers about Ms. Johnson performing acts of a sexual nature on them?'

Flynn was trapped. He was either going to lie or admit an illegal activity was going on. He did the dumbest thing of all – he took the middle road. 'I may have heard some whispers.'

Nice and wishy-washy, making him look like a total liar.

I put on my best incredulous tone. 'May have heard some whispers?'

'Yes.'

'So you're not sure if you heard some whispers,' I said, as if this was the most ridiculous thing I had ever heard in my life, 'but you may have. You simply cannot remember if you heard whispers or not. Is that your testimony?'

Flair stood this time. 'Your Honor?'

The judge looked at him.

'Is this a rape case or is Mr. Copeland now working vice?' He spread his hands. 'Is his rape case so weak now, so far-fetched, that he is now fishing to indict these boys on soliciting a prostitute?'

I said, 'That's not what I'm after.'

Flair smiled at me. 'Then please ask this witness questions that concern this alleged assault. Don't ask him to recite every misbehavior he's ever seen a friend commit.'

The judge said, 'Let's move on, Mr. Copeland.'

Friggin' Flair.

'Did you ask Ms. Johnson for her phone number?'

'Yes.'

'Why?'

'I thought I might call her.'

'You liked her?'

'I was attracted to her, yes.'

'Because she was a seven, maybe an eight?' I waved before Pubin could move. 'Withdrawn. Did there come a time when you called Ms. Johnson?'

'Yes.'

'Can you tell us when, and as best as you can, please tell us what was said in that conversation?'

'Ten days later I called and asked her if she wanted to come to a party at the fraternity.'

'Did you want her to dance exotically again?'

'No,' Flynn said. I saw him swallow and his eyes were a little wet now. 'I asked her as a guest.'

I let that sit. I looked at Jerry Flynn. I let the jury look at him. There was something in his face. Had he liked Chamique Johnson? I let the moment linger. Because I was confused. I had thought that Jerry Flynn was part of it – that he had called Chamique and set her up. I tried to work it through in my head.

The judge said, 'Mr. Copeland.'

'Did Ms. Johnson accept your invitation?'

'Yes.'

'When you say you invited her as your' – I made quote marks with my fingers – ' "guest," do you really mean "date"?'

'Yes.'

I followed him through meeting her and getting her punch.

'Did you tell her it was spiked with alcohol?' I asked.

'Yes.'

It was a lie. And it looked like a lie, but I wanted to emphasize the ridiculousness of that claim.

'Tell me how that conversation went,' I said.

'I don't understand the question.'

'Did you ask Ms. Johnson if she wanted something to drink?'

'Yes.'

'And did she say yes?'

'Yes.'

'And then what did you say?'

'I asked her if she wanted some punch.'

'And what did she say?'

'She said yes.'

'And then what?'

He shifted in his chair. 'I said it was spiked.'

I arched the eyebrow. 'Just like that?'

'Objection!' Pubin rose. 'Just like what? He said it was spiked. Asked and answered.'

He was right. Leave them with the obvious lie. I waved to the judge that I would let it go. I started walking him through the night. Flynn stuck to the story he'd already told, about how Chamique got drunk, how she started flirting with Edward Jenrette.

'How did you react when that happened?'

He shrugged. 'Edward is a senior, I'm a freshman. It happens.'

'So you think Chamique was impressed because Mr. Jenrette was older?'

Again Pubin decided to not object.

'I don't know,' Flynn said. 'Maybe.'

'Oh, by the way, have you ever been in Mr. Marantz's and Mr. Jenrette's room?'

'Sure.'

'How many times?'

'I don't know. A lot.'

'Really? But you're just a freshman.'

'They're still my friends.'

I made my skeptical face. 'Have you been in there more than once?'

'Yes.'

'More than ten times?'

'Yes.'

I made my face even more skeptical. 'Okay then, tell me: What sort of stereo or music system do they have in the room?'

Flynn answered it immediately. 'They have a Bose speakers iPod system.'

I knew that already. We had searched the room. We had pictures.

'How about the television in their room? How big is it?'

He smiled as if he'd seen my trap. 'They don't have one.'

'No television at all?'

'None.'

'Okay then, back to the night in question . . .'

Flynn continued to weave his tale. He started partying with his friends. He saw Chamique start up the stairs holding hands with Jenrette. He didn't know what happened after that, of course. Then later that night, he met up with Chamique again and walked her to the bus stop.

'Did she seem upset?' I asked.

Flynn said no, just the opposite. Chamique was 'smiling' and 'happy' and light as air. His Pollyanna description was overkill.

'So when Chamique Johnson talked about going out to the keg with you and then walking upstairs and being grabbed in the corridor,' I said, 'that was all a lie?'

Flynn was smart enough not to bite. 'I'm telling you what I saw.'

'Do you know anyone named Cal or Jim?'

He thought about it. 'I know a couple of guys named Jim. I don't think I know any Cals.'

'Are you aware that Ms. Johnson claimed the men who raped her were named' – I didn't want Flair objecting with his semantics game but I did roll my eyes a little when I said the word named – 'Cal and Jim?'

He was wondering how to handle that one. He went with the truth. 'I heard that.'

'Was there anyone named Cal or Jim at the party?'

'Not that I'm aware of.'

'I see. And would you know any reason why Mr. Jenrette and Mr. Marantz would call themselves that?'

'No.'

'Ever heard those two names together? I mean, before the alleged rape?'

'Not that I can recall.'

'So you can't shine a light on why Ms. Johnson would

testify that her attackers were named Cal and Jim?'

Pubin shouted his objection. 'How could he possibly know why this deranged, intoxicated woman would lie?'

I kept my eyes on the witness. 'Nothing comes to mind, Mr. Flynn?'

'Nothing,' he said firmly.

I looked back at Loren Muse. Her head was down, fiddling with her BlackBerry. She glanced up, met my eye, nodded once.

'Your Honor,' I said, 'I have more questions for this witness but this might make a good place to break for lunch.'

Judge Pierce agreed.

I tried not to sprint over to Loren Muse.

'We got it,' she said with a grin. 'The fax is in your office.'

Chapter 19

Lucy was lucky that she had no morning class. Between the amount she drank and the late night with Sylvia Potter, she had stayed in bed until noon. When she rose she placed a call to one of the school counselors, Katherine Lucas, a therapist Lucy had always thought was really good. She explained the situation with Sylvia. Lucas would have a better idea what to do.

She thought about the journal entry that had started this all. The woods. The screams. The blood. Sylvia Potter hadn't sent it. So who had?

No clue.

Last night, she had decided to call Paul. He needed to know about this, she'd concluded. But had that been the booze talking? Now that it was sobering daylight, did that still seem to be a good idea?

An hour later, she found Paul's work number on the computer. He was the Essex County prosecutor – and, alas, a widower. Jane had died of cancer. Paul had set up a charity in her name. Lucy wondered how she felt about all that, but there was no way she could sort through that right now.

With a shaking hand she dialed the number. When she reached the switchboard operator, she asked to speak to Paul Copeland. It hurt when she said that. She realized that she hadn't said his name out loud in twenty years.

Paul Copeland.

A woman answered and said, 'County prosecutor.'

'I would like to speak to Paul Copeland, please.'

'May I ask who's calling?'

'I'm an old friend,' she said.

Nothing.

'My name is Lucy. Tell him it's Lucy. From twenty years ago.'

'Do you have a last name, Lucy?'

'Just tell him that, okay?'

'Prosecutor Copeland isn't in the office at the moment. Would you like to leave a number so he can return your call?'

Lucy gave her the numbers for her home, her office, her mobile.

'May I tell him what this is in reference to?'

'Just tell him that it's Lucy. And that it's important.'

Muse and I were in my office. The door was closed. We had ordered in deli sandwiches for lunch. I was having chicken salad on whole wheat. Muse was downing a meatball sub that was the approximate size of a surfboard.

I had the fax in my hands. 'Where is your private eye? Cingle whatever?'

'Shaker. Cingle Shaker. She'll be here.'

I sat and looked over my notes.

'Do you want to talk it out?' she asked.

'No.'

She had a big grin on her face.

'What?' I said.

'I hate to say this, Cope, you being my boss and all, but you're a doggone genius.'

'Yeah,' I said. 'I guess I am.'

I went back to my notes.

Muse said, 'You want me to leave you alone?'

'No. I may think of something I need you to do.'

She lifted the sandwich. I was surprised that she could do it without the use of an industrial crane. 'Your predecessor,' Muse said, teeth-diving into the sandwich. 'With big cases, sometimes he would sit there and stare and say he was getting into a zone. Like he was Michael Jordan. You do that?'

'No.'

'So' – more chewing, some swallowing – 'would it distract you if I raised another issue?'

'You mean something that doesn't involve this case?'

'That's what I mean.'

I looked up. 'Actually, I could use the distraction. What's on your mind?'

She looked off to the right, took a moment or two. Then she said, 'I have friends in Manhattan homicide.'

I had an idea where this was going. I took a delicate bite of my chicken-salad sandwich. 'Dry,' I said.

'What?'

'The chicken salad. It's dry.' I put it down and wiped my finger with the napkin. 'Let me guess. One of your homicide friends told you about the murder of Manolo Santiago?'

'Yeah.'

'Did they tell you what my theory was?'

'About him being one of the boys who the Summer Slasher murdered at that camp, even though his parents say it's not him?'

'That would be the one.'

'Yeah, they told me.'

'And?'

'And they think you're crackers.'

I smiled. 'What about you?'

'I would have thought you were crackers. Except now' – she pointed to the fax – 'I see what you're capable of. So I guess what I'm saying is, I want in.'

'In on what?'

'You know what. You're going to investigate, right? You're going to see if you can figure out what really happened in those woods?'

'I am,' I said.

She spread her hands. 'I want in.'

'I can't have you taking up county business with my personal affairs.'

'First off,' Muse said, 'while everyone is sure that Wayne Steubens killed them all, the homicide file is technically still open. In fact, a quadruple homicide, when you think about it, remains unsolved.'

'That did not take place in our county.'

'We don't know that. We only know where the bodies were found. And one victim, your sister, lived in this very city.'

'That's stretching it.'

'Second, I am hired to work forty hours a week. I do closer to eighty. You know that. It is why you promoted me. So what I do outside of those forty hours is up to me. Or I'll up it to one hundred, I don't care. And before you ask, no, this isn't just a favor for my boss. Let's face it, I'm an investigator. Solving it would be a heck of a feather in my cap. So what do you say?'

I shrugged. 'What the hell.'

'I'm in?'

'You're in.'

She looked very pleased. 'So what's step one?'

I thought about it. There was something I had to do. I had avoided it. I couldn't avoid it any longer.

'Wayne Steubens,' I said.

'The Summer Slasher.'

'I need to see him.'

'You knew him, right?'

I nodded. 'We were both counselors at that camp.'

'I think I read that he doesn't allow visitors.'

'We need to change his mind,' I said.

'He's in a maximum security facility in Virginia,' Muse said. 'I can make some calls.'

Muse already knew where Steubens was being held. Incredible.

'Do that,' I said.

There was a knock on my door and my secretary, Jocelyn Durels, stuck her head in the door. 'Messages,' she said. 'You want me to stick them on your desk?'

I waved my fingers for her to hand them to me. 'Anything important?'

'Not really. A fair amount from media. You'd think they'd know you're in court, but they still call.'

I took the messages and started sorting through them. I looked up at Muse. She was glancing around. There was almost nothing personal in this office. When I first moved in, I put a picture of Cara on my credenza. Two days later we arrested a child molester who had done unspeakable things to a girl around Cara's age. We talked about it in this office and I kept looking over at my daughter and finally I had to turn the picture around so it faced the wall. That night, I brought the picture back home.

This was no place for Cara. This was not even a place for her picture.

I was pawing through the messages when something caught my eye.

My secretary uses the old-fashioned pink note sheets, the ones where she can keep a yellow copy in her book, and writes the messages by hand. Her handwriting is impeccable.

The caller, according to my pink message, was:

Lucy ??

I stared at the name for a moment. Lucy. It couldn't be.

There was a work number, a home number and a mobile. All three had area codes that indicated Lucy Double-Question-Mark lived, worked and, uh, mobilized in New Jersey.

I grabbed the phone and hit the intercom. 'Jocelyn?'

'Yes?'

'I'm seeing a message here from someone named Lucy,' I said.

'Yes. She called about an hour ago.'

'You didn't write a last name.'

'She wouldn't give one. That's why I put the question marks.'

'I don't understand. You asked her for a last name and she wouldn't give one?'

'That's right.'

'What else did she say?'

'On the bottom of the page.'

'What?'

'Did you read my notes on the bottom of the page?'

'No.'

She just waited, not saying the obvious. I scanned down the sheet and read:

Says she's an old friend from twenty years ago.

I read the words again. And again.

'Ground control to Major Cope.'

It was Muse. She hadn't said the words – she sang them, using the old David Bowie tune. I startled up. 'You sing,' I said, 'like you pick out shoes.'

'Very funny.' She gestured at my message and arched one eyebrow. 'So who is this Lucy, big guy? An old lover?'

I said nothing.

'Oh, damn.' Her arched eyebrow dropped. 'I was just messing around. I didn't mean to . . .'

'Don't worry about it, Muse.'

'Don't you worry about it either, Cope. At least not until later.'

Her gaze turned to the clock behind me. I looked too. She was right. Lunch was over. This would have to wait. I didn't know what Lucy wanted. Or maybe I did. The past was coming back. All of it. The dead, it seemed, were digging their way out of the ground now.

But that was all for later. I grabbed the fax and stood.

Muse rose too. 'Showtime,' she said.

I nodded. More than showtime. I was going to destroy those sons of bitches. And I was going to try like hell not to enjoy it too much.

On the stand after lunch, Jerry Flynn looked fairly composed. I had done little damage in the morning. There was no reason to think the afternoon would be any different.

'Mr. Flynn,' I began, 'do you like pornography?'

I didn't even wait for the obvious. I turned to Mort Pubin and made a sarcastic hand gesture, as though I had just introduced him and was ushering him onstage.

'Objection!'

Pubin didn't even need to elaborate. The judge gave me a disapproving look. I shrugged and said, 'Exhibit eighteen.' I picked up the sheet of paper. 'This is a bill sent to the fraternity house for online expenses. Do you recognize it?'

He looked at it. 'I don't pay the bills. The treasurer does.'

'Yes, Mr. Rich Devin, who testified that this is indeed the fraternity bill.'

The judge looked over to Flair and Mort. 'Any objection?'

'We will stipulate that it is a bill from the fraternity house,' Flair said.

'Do you see this entry here?' I pointed to a line near the top.

'Yes.'

'Can you read what it says?'

'Netflix.'

'That's with one x at the end.' I spelled 'Netflix' out loud. 'What's Netflix, if you know?'

'It's a DVD rental service. You do it through the mail. You get to keep three DVDs at all times. When you mail one back, you get another sent to you.'

'Good, thank you.' I nodded and moved my fingers down a few rows. 'Could you read this line to me?'

He hesitated.

'Mr. Flynn?' I said.

He cleared his throat. 'HotFlixxx,' he said.

'With three x's at the end, correct?' Again I spelled it out loud.

'Yes.'

He looked as though he was about to be sick.

'Can you tell me what HotFlixxx is?'

'It's like Netflix,' he said.

'It's a DVD movie rental service?'

'Yes.'

'How is it different from Netflix, if you know?'

He turned red. 'They rent, uh, different kinds of movies.'

'What kind?'

'Um, well, adult movies.'

'I see. So before I asked if you liked pornography – perhaps a better question would have been, do you ever watch pornographic movies?'

He squirmed. 'Sometimes,' he said.

'Nothing wrong with that, son.' Without looking behind me, knowing he was up, I pointed at opposing counsel's chair. 'And I bet Mr. Pubin is standing to tell us he enjoys them too, especially the plots.'

'Objection!' Pubin said.

'Withdrawn,' I said. I turned back to Flynn. 'Is there any pornographic movie in particular that you like?'

The color drained from his face. It was as if the question had turned a spigot. His head swiveled toward the defense table. I moved just enough to block his view. Flynn coughed into his fist and said, 'Can I plead the Fifth?'

'For what?' I asked.

Flair Hickory stood. 'The witness has asked for counsel.'

'Your Honor,' I said, 'when I went to law school, we

197

learned that the Fifth Amendment was to be used to prevent self-incrimination and – correct me if I'm wrong here – but, well, is there a law on the books against having a favorite pornographic movie?'

Flair said, 'Can we have a ten-minute recess?'

'No way, Your Honor.'

'The witness,' Flair went on, 'has asked for counsel.'

'No, he didn't. He asked to plead the Fifth. And tell you what, Mr. Flynn – I will give you immunity.'

'Immunity for what?' Flair asked.

'For whatever he wants. I don't want this witness off the stand.'

Judge Pierce looked back at Flair Hickory. He took his time. If Flair got ahold of him, I would be in trouble. They would come up with something. I glanced behind me at Jenrette and Marantz. They hadn't moved, hadn't warned counsel.

'No recess,' the judge said.

Flair Hickory wilted back into his seat.

I went back to Jerry Flynn. 'Do you have a favorite pornographic movie?'

'No,' he said.

'Have you ever heard of a pornographic movie called' – I pretended now to be checking a piece of paper but I knew the name by heart – 'a movie called *Romancing His Bone?*'

He must have seen it coming, but the question still zapped him like a cattle prod. 'Uh, can you repeat that title?'

I repeated it. 'Have you seen or heard of it?'

'I don't think so.'

'Don't think so,' I repeated. 'So you may have?'

'I'm not sure. I'm not good with movie titles.'

'Well, let's see if I can refresh your recollection.'

I had the fax Muse had just given me. I passed a copy to opposing counsel and made it an exhibit. Then I started back in: 'According to HotFlixxx, a copy of that DVD had been in the possession of the fraternity house for the past six months. And again according to HotFlixxx's records, the movie was mailed back to them the day *after* Ms. Johnson reported the assault to the police.'

Silence.

Pubin looked as though he'd swallowed his tongue. Flair was too good to show anything. He read the fax as though it were an amusing ditty from *The Family Circus*.

I moved closer to Flynn. 'Does that refresh your memory?'

'I don't know.'

'You don't know? Then let's try something else.'

I looked toward the back of the room. Loren Muse was standing by the door. She was grinning. I nodded. She opened the door and a woman who looked like a gorgeous Amazon in a B movie stepped forward.

Muse's private eye, Cingle Shaker, strutted into the room as if it were her favorite watering hole. The room itself seemed to gasp at the sight.

I said, 'Do you recognize the woman who just walked into the room?'

He did not reply. The judge said, 'Mr. Flynn?'

'Yes.' Flynn cleared his throat to gain time. 'I recognize her.'

'How do you know her?'

'I met her at a bar last night.'

'I see. And did you two talk about the movie *Romancing His Bone*?'

Cingle had pretended to be an ex–porno actress. She

199

had gotten several frat boys to open up in a hurry. Like Muse had said – it must have been *really* difficult, a woman with a figure so shapely it could draw a citation, getting frat boys to talk.

Flynn said, 'We might have said something about it.'

' "It" being the movie?'

'Yes.'

'Hmm,' I said, again as if this were a curious development. 'So now, with Ms. Shaker out there as a catalyst, do you remember the film *Romancing His Bone*?'

He tried not to drop his head, but the shoulders went. 'Yeah,' Flynn said, 'I guess I remember it.'

'Glad I could help,' I said.

Pubin rose to object, but the judge waved him to sit.

'In fact,' I went on, 'you told Ms. Shaker that *Romancing His Bone* was the entire fraternity's favorite porno flick, didn't you?'

He hesitated.

'It's okay, Jerry. Three of your brothers told Ms. Shaker the same thing.'

Mort Pubin: 'Objection!'

I looked back at Cingle Shaker. So did everyone else. Cingle smiled and waved as though she were a celebrity in the audience and had just been introduced. I wheeled out the TV with a DVD player attached. The offending DVD was already in it. Muse had keyed it up to the relevant scene.

'Your Honor, last night one of my investigators visited King David's Smut Palace in New York City.' I looked at the jury and said, 'See, it's open twenty-four hours, though why someone might need to go there at, say, three in the morning is beyond me – '

'Mr. Copeland.'

The judge correctly stopped me with a disapproving

gaze, but the jury had smiled. That was good. I wanted the mood loose. And then, when the contrast came, when they saw what was on that DVD, I wanted to wallop them.

'Anyway, my investigator purchased all of the X-rated movies ordered on HotFlixxx by the frat house in the past six months, including *Romancing His Bone*. I would now like to show a scene I believe is relevant.'

Everything stopped. All eyes turned toward the judge's bench. Arnold Pierce took his time. He stroked his chin. I held my breath. There wasn't a sound. Everyone leaned forward. Pierce stroked his chin some more. I wanted to wring the answer out of him.

Then he simply nodded and said, 'Go ahead. I'll allow it.'

'Wait!' Mort Pubin objected, did everything he could, wanted voir dire and all that. Flair Hickory joined in. But it was a waste of energy. Eventually the courtroom curtains were closed so that there would be no glare. And then, without explaining what they were about to see, I hit the Play button.

The setting was a run-of-the-mill bedroom. Looked like a king-size bed. Three participants. The scene opened with very little foreplay. A rough ménage à trois started up. There were two men. There was one girl.

The two men were white. The girl was black.

The white men tossed her about like a plaything. They sneered and laughed and talked to each other throughout:

'*Turn her over, Cal. . . . Yeah, Jim, like that . . . Flip her, Cal . . .*'

I watched the jury's reaction rather than the screen. Children playact. My daughter and niece acted out Dora the Explorer. Jenrette and Marantz, as sick as it was, had acted out a scene from a pornographic movie. The courtroom was tomb still. I watched the faces in the gallery collapse, even those behind Jenrette and Marantz, as the black girl in the movie screamed, as the two white men used their names and laughed cruelly.

'Bend her over, Jim. . . . Whoa, Cal, the bitch is loving it. . . . Do her, Jim, yeah, harder . . .'

Like that. Cal and Jim. On and on. Their voices were cruel, awful, hell spawned. I looked toward the back of the room and found Chamique Johnson. Her spine was straight. Her head was high.

'Woo hoo, Jim . . . Yeah, my turn . . .'

Chamique met my eye and nodded. I nodded back. There were tears on her cheeks.

I couldn't be sure, but I think there were tears on mine too.

Chapter 20

Flair Hickory and Mort Pubin got a half-hour recess. When the judge rose to leave, the courtroom exploded. I no-commented my way back to my office. Muse followed me. She was this tiny thing but she played like she was my Secret Service agent.

When we closed the office door, she put up her palm. 'High five!'

I just looked at her. She put down her hand.

'It's over, Cope.'

'Not quite yet,' I said.

'But in a half hour?'

I nodded. 'It will be over. But in the meantime, there's still work to do.'

I moved back around to the conference table. The message from Lucy was sitting there. I had managed to do my brain-partition thing during my Flynn questioning. I had kept Lucy out. But now, as much as I wanted to spend a few minutes basking in the glory of the moment, the message was calling out to me again.

Muse saw me looking down at the note.

'A friend from twenty years ago,' Muse said. 'That's when the Camp PLUS incident occurred.'

I looked at her.

'It's connected, isn't it?'

'I don't know,' I said. 'But probably.'

'What's her last name?'

'Silverstein. Lucy Silverstein.'

'Right,' Muse said, sitting back and crossing her arms. 'That's what I figured.'

'How did you figure that?'

'Come on, Cope. You know me.'

'That you're too nosy for your own good?'

'Part of what makes me so attractive.'

'Nosiness and maybe your footwear. So when did you read up on me?'

'Soon as I heard you were taking over as county prosecutor.'

I wasn't surprised.

'Oh, and I brushed up on the case before I told you I wanted in.'

I looked at the message again.

'She was your girlfriend,' Muse said.

'Summer romance,' I said. 'We were kids.'

'When was the last time you heard from her?'

'It's been a long time.'

We just sat there for a moment. I could hear the commotion outside the door. I ignored it. So did Muse. Neither one of us spoke. We just sat there with that message on the table.

Finally Muse stood. 'I got some work to do.'

'Go,' I said.

'You'll be able to make it back to court without me?'

'I'll muddle through,' I said.

When Muse reached the door, she turned back to me. 'Are you going to call her?'

'Later.'

'You want me to run her name? See what I come up with?'

I thought about it. 'Not yet.'

'Why not?'

'Because she used to mean something to me, Muse. I don't feel like having you poke around in her life.'

Muse put her hands up. 'Okay, okay, sheesh, don't bite my head off. I wasn't talking about dragging her in here with cuffs. I was talking about running a routine background check.'

'Don't, okay? At least, not yet.'

'I'll get to work on your prison visit to Wayne Steubens then.'

'Thank you.'

'This Cal and Jim thing. You're not going to let it slip away, are you?'

'Not a chance.'

My one worry was that the defense would claim that Chamique Johnson had watched the movie too and made up her story based on it or had deluded herself into thinking the movie was real. I was helped by several factors, however. One, it was easy to establish that the movie had not been playing on the fraternity's big-screen TV in the public room. Enough witnesses would back that up. Second, I had established via Jerry Flynn and photographs taken by the police that Marantz and Jenrette did not have a television set in their room, so she couldn't have seen it there.

Still, it was the only direction I could see them going in. A DVD could be played on a computer. Flimsy, true, but I really didn't want to leave much of an out. Jerry Flynn was what I refer to as a 'bullfight' witness. In a bullfight, the bull comes out and a bunch of guys – not the matador – wave capes around. The bull charges until exhausted. Then picadors on horseback come out with long lances and jam them into a gland behind the bull's neck muscle, drawing blood and swelling the neck so that the bull can't turn his head much. Then some other guys run up and throw banderillas – gaily decorated daggers – into the bull's flanks, near his shoulders. More blood. The bull is half-dead already.

After all that, the matador – from the Spanish *matar* or 'to kill' – comes in and finishes the job with a sword.

That was my job now. I had made my witness run into exhaustion and jammed a lance into his neck and stuck some colorful darts into him. So now it was time to bring out the sword.

Flair Hickory did everything in his considerable power to prevent this. He called for a recess, claiming that we had never produced this film before and that it was unfair and that it should have been given to them during discovery, blah, blah, blah. I fought back. The film had been in the possession of his clients, after all. We only found a copy ourselves last night. The witness had confirmed that it had been watched in the fraternity house. If Mr. Hickory wants to claim his clients never saw it, he could put them on the stand.

Flair took his time arguing. He stalled, asked and got some sidebars with the judge, tried with some success to give Jerry Flynn a chance to catch his breath.

But it didn't work.

I could see that the moment Flynn sat in that chair. He had been too seriously wounded by those darts and that lance. The movie had been the final blow. He had shut his eyes while it played, shut them so tightly that I think he was trying to close his ears.

I could tell you that Flynn probably wasn't a bad kid. The truth was, as he now testified, he had liked Chamique. He had asked her out legitimately on a date. But when the upperclassmen got wind of it, they teased and bullied him into going along with their sick 'movie reenactment' plan. And Flynn the Freshman folded.

'I hated myself for doing it,' he said. 'But you have to understand.'

No, I don't, I wanted to say. But I didn't. Instead I just looked at him until he lowered his eyes. Then I looked at the jury with a slight challenge in my eyes. Seconds passed.

Finally I turned to Flair Hickory and said, 'Your witness.'

It took me a while to get alone.

After my ridiculous act of indignation at Muse, I decided to do some amateur sleuthing. I Googled Lucy's phone numbers. Two gave me nothing, but the third, her work number, showed me that it was the direct line to a professor at Reston University named Lucy Gold.

Gold. *Silver*-stein. Cute.

I had already known it was 'my' Lucy, but this pretty much confirmed it. The question was, what do I do about it? The answer was fairly simple. Call her back. See what she wants.

I was not big on coincidence. I hadn't heard a word from this woman in twenty years. Now suddenly she calls and won't leave a last name. It had to be connected to Gil Perez's death. It had to be connected to the Camp PLUS incident.

That was obvious.

Partitioning your life. It should have been easy to leave her behind. A summer fling, even an intense one, is just that – a fling. I might have loved her, probably did, but I was just a kid. Kid love doesn't survive blood and dead bodies. There are doors. I closed that one. Lucy was gone. It took me a long time to accept that. But I did and I kept that damn door shut.

Now I would have to open it.

Muse had wanted to run a background check. I should have said yes. I let emotion dictate my decision. I should have waited. Seeing her name was a blow. I should have taken my time, dealt with the blow, seen things more clearly. But I didn't.

Maybe I shouldn't call yet.

No, I told myself. Enough with the stalling.

I picked up the phone and dialed her home. On the fourth ring, the phone was picked up. A woman's voice said, 'I'm not home, but at the beep please leave a message.'

The beep came too fast. I wasn't ready for it. So I hung up.

Very mature.

My head swam. Twenty years. It had been twenty years. Lucy would be thirty-seven now. I wondered if she was still as beautiful. When I think back on it, she had the kind of looks that would do well with maturity. Some women are like that.

Get your head in the game, Cope.

I was trying. But hearing her voice, sounding exactly the same . . . it was the aural equivalent of hooking up with your old college roommate: After ten seconds, the years melt away and it's like you're back in the dorm room and nothing has changed. That was how this was. She sounded the same. I was eighteen again.

I took a few deep breaths. There was a knock on the door.

'Come in.'

Muse stuck her head in the room. 'Did you call her yet?'

'I tried her home number. No answer.'

'You probably won't get her now,' Muse said. 'She's in class.'

'And you know this because?'

'Because I'm chief investigator. I don't have to listen to everything you say.'

She sat and threw her practical-shoed feet up on the table. She studied my face and didn't speak. I kept quiet too. Finally she said, 'Do you want me to leave?'

'Tell me what you got first.'

She tried hard not to smile. 'She changed her name seventeen years ago. It's Lucy Gold now.'

I nodded. 'That would have been right after the settlement.'

'What settlement? Oh, wait, you guys sued the camp, right?'

'The victims' families.'

'And Lucy's father owned the camp.'

'Right.'

'Nasty?'

'I don't know. I wasn't that involved.'

'But you guys won?'

'Sure. It was a summer camp with practically no security.' I squirmed when I said that. 'The families got Silverstein's biggest asset.'

'The camp itself.'

'Yep. We sold the land to a developer.'

'All of it?'

'There was a provision involving the woods. It's fairly

209

unusable land, so it's held in some kind of public trust. You can't build on it.'

'Is the camp still there?'

I shook my head. 'The developer tore down the old cabins and built some gated community.'

'How much did you guys get?'

'After lawyer fees, each family ended up with more than eight hundred grand.'

Her eyes widened. 'Wow.'

'Yeah. Losing a child is a great moneymaker.'

'I didn't mean—'

I waved her off. 'I know. I'm just being an ass.'

She didn't argue. 'It must have changed things,' Muse said.

I didn't answer right away. The money had been held in a joint account. My mother took off with a hundred grand. She left the rest for us. Generous of her, I guess. Dad and I moved out of Newark, moved to a decent place in Montclair. I had already gotten a scholarship to Rutgers, but now I set my sights on Columbia Law in New York. I met Jane there.

'Yeah,' I said. 'It changed things.'

'Do you want to know more about your old flame?'

I nodded.

'She went to UCLA. Majored in psychology. She got a graduate degree from USC in the same, another in English from Stanford. I don't have her entire work history yet, but she's currently down the road at Reston U. Started last year. She, uh, she got two DUIs when she lived in California. One in 2001. Another in 2003. Pleaded out both times. Other than that, her record is clean.'

I sat there. DUI. That didn't sound like Lucy. Her father, Ira, the head counselor, had been a major stoner

– so much so that she'd had no interest in anything that would provide a high. Now she had two DUIs. It was hard to fathom. But of course, the girl I knew was not even of legal drinking age. She had been happy and a little naive and well-adjusted, and her family had money and her father was a seemingly harmless free spirit.

All that had died that night in the woods too.

'Another thing,' Muse said. She shifted in the seat, aiming for nonchalance. 'Lucy Silverstein, aka Gold, isn't married. I haven't done all the checking yet, but from what I see, she's never been married either.'

I didn't know what to make of that. It certainly had no bearing on what was going on now. But it still pierced me. She was such a lively thing, so bright and energetic and so damn easy to love. How could she have remained single all these years? And then there were those DUIs.

'What time does her class end?' I asked.

'Twenty minutes.'

'Okay. I'll call her then. Anything else?'

'Wayne Steubens doesn't allow visitors, except for his immediate family and lawyer. But I'm working on it. I got some other coals in the fire, but that's about it for now.'

'Don't spend too much time on it.'

'I'm not.'

I looked at the clock. Twenty minutes.

'I should probably go,' Muse said.

'Yeah.'

She stood. 'Oh, one more thing.'

'What?'

'Do you want to see a picture of her?'

I looked up.

'Reston University has faculty pages. There are pictures of all the professors.' She held up a small piece of paper. 'I got the URL right here.'

She didn't wait for my reply. She dropped the address on the table and left me alone.

I had twenty minutes. Why not?

I brought up my default page. I use one with Yahoo where you can choose a lot of your content. I had news, my sports teams, my two favorite comic strips – *Doonesbury* and *FoxTrot* – stuff like that. I typed in the Reston University Web site page Muse had given me.

And there she was.

It wasn't Lucy's most flattering photograph. Her smile was tight, her expression grim. She had posed for the picture, but you could see that she really didn't want to. The blond hair was gone. That happens with age, I know, but I had a feeling that it was intentional. The color didn't look right on her. She was older – duh – but as I had predicted, it worked on her. Her face was thinner. The high cheekbones were more pronounced.

And damn if she didn't still look beautiful.

Looking at her face, something long dormant came alive and started twisting in my gut. I didn't need that now. There were enough complications in my life. I didn't need those old feelings resurfacing. I read her short bio, learned nothing. Nowadays students rank classes and professors. You could often find that information online. I did. Lucy was clearly beloved by her students. Her rankings were incredible. I read a few of the student comments. They made the class sound life altering. I smiled and felt a strange sense of pride.

Twenty minutes passed.

I gave it another five, pictured her saying good-bye to students, talking to a few who loitered behind, packing her lessons and sundries in some beat-up faux leather bag.

I picked up my office phone. I buzzed out to Jocelyn. 'Yes?'

'No calls,' I said. 'No interruptions.'

'Okay.'

I pressed for an outside line. I dialed Lucy's cell phone. On the third ring I heard her voice say, 'Hello?'

My heart leapt into my throat but I managed to say, 'It's me, Luce.'

And then, a few seconds later, I heard her start to cry.

Chapter 21

'Luce?' I said into the phone. 'You okay?'

'I'm fine. It's just . . .'

'Yeah, I know.'

'I can't believe I did that.'

'You always were an easy cry,' I said, regretting it the moment it came out. But she snorted a laugh.

'Not anymore,' she said.

Silence.

Then I said, 'Where are you?'

'I work at Reston University. I'm walking across the commons.'

'Oh,' I said, because I didn't know what else to say.

'I'm sorry about leaving such a cryptic message. I don't go by Silverstein anymore.'

I didn't want her to know I already knew this. But I didn't want to lie either. So again I gave a noncommittal 'Oh.'

More silence. She broke it this time.

'Man, this is awkward.'

I smiled. 'I know.'

'I feel like a big dope,' she said. 'Like I'm sixteen again and worried about a new zit.'

'Same here,' I said.

'We never really change, do we? I mean, inside, we're always a scared kid, wondering what we're going to be when we grow up.'

I was still smiling, but I thought about her never being married and the DUIs. We don't change, I guess, but our path certainly does.

'It's good to hear your voice, Luce.'

'Yours too.'

Silence.

'I was calling because . . .' Lucy stopped. Then: 'I don't even know how to say this, so let me ask a question. Has anything strange happened to you lately?'

'Strange how?'

'Strange as in about-that-night strange.'

I should have expected her to say something like that – knew it was coming – but the smile still fled as if I'd been punched. 'Yes.'

Silence.

'What the hell is going on, Paul?'

'I don't know.'

'I think we need to figure it out.'

'I agree.'

'Do you want to meet?'

'Yes.'

'It's going to be weird,' she said.

'I know.'

'I mean, I don't want it to be. And that's not why I called. To see you. But I think we should meet up and discuss this, don't you?'

'I do,' I said.

'I'm babbling. I babble when I get nervous.'

'I remember,' I said. And then, again, I regretted saying that, so I quickly added, 'Where should we meet?'

'Do you know where Reston University is?'

'Yes.'

'I have another class and then student appointments until seven-thirty,' Lucy said. 'Do you want to meet me at my office? It's in the Armstrong Building. Say, eight o'clock?'

'I'll be there.'

When I arrived home I was surprised to find the press camped out in front of my house. You often hear about that – about the press doing stuff like that – but this was my first experience with it. The local cops were on hand, clearly excited to be doing something that seemed quasi-big time. They stood on either side of the driveway so that I could pull in. The press didn't try to stop them. In fact, when I pulled in, the press barely seemed to notice.

Greta gave me the conquering-hero welcome. She was full of kisses and quick hugs and congratulations. I love Greta. There are some people you know are pure good, who are always on your side. There aren't many of them. But there are some. Greta would jump in the way of a bullet for me. And she made me want to protect her.

In that way she reminded me of my sister.

'Where's Cara?' I asked.

'Bob took Cara and Madison to Baumgart's for dinner.'

Estelle was in the kitchen, doing laundry. 'I need to go out tonight,' I said to her.

'No problem.'

Greta said, 'Cara can sleep over at our house.'

'I think I'd rather she slept at home tonight, thanks.'

She followed me into the den. The front door opened and Bob came in with the two girls. Again I envisioned my daughter sprinting into my arms while screaming, 'Daddy! You're home!' That didn't happen. But she did smile and she did come over to me. I swept her up in my arms and kissed her hard. She held the smile but wiped her cheek. Hey, I'll take it.

Bob slapped my back. 'Congrats on the trial,' he said.

'It's not over yet.'

'That's not what the media is saying. Either way it should get that Jenrette off our back.'

'Or more desperate.'

His face paled a little. If you were to cast Bob in a movie, he'd be the bad-guy rich Republican. His complexion was ruddy, his jowls thick, his fingers short and stubby. Here was another example of where appearances could be deceiving. Bob's background was totally blue collar. He studied and worked hard. Nothing had ever been given to him or made easy.

Cara came back into the room carrying a DVD. She held it up as though it were an offering. I closed my eyes, and remembering what day of the week it was, I cursed to myself. Then I said to my little girl, 'It's movie night.'

She still held up the DVD. Her eyes were wide. She was smiling. On the cover was something animated or computer-generated with talking cars or maybe farm animals or zoo animals, something from Pixar or Disney, something I had seen a hundred times already.

'That's right. Will you make popcorn?'

I took a knee so I was at her eye level. I put a hand on either shoulder. 'Honey,' I said, 'Daddy has to go out tonight.'

No reaction.

'I'm sorry, sweetie.'

I waited for the tears. 'Can Estelle watch it with me?'

'Sure, honey.'

'And she can make popcorn?'

'Of course.'

'Cool.'

I'd been hoping for a little crestfallen. No go.

Cara skipped away. I looked at Bob. He looked at me as if to say, *Kids – what can you do?*

'Inside,' I said, gesturing toward my daughter. 'On the inside, she's really crushed.'

Bob laughed as my cell phone buzzed. The read-out simply said, new jersey, but I recognized the number and felt a little jolt. I picked it up and said, 'Hello?'

'Nice job today, All-Star.'

'Mr. Governor,' I said.

'That's not correct.'

'Excuse me?'

'Mr. Governor. You would properly address the President of the United States as Mr. President, but governors are addressed as either Governor or by their last name, for example, Governor Stallion or Governor Chick Magnet.'

'Or,' I said, 'how about Governor Anal Compulsive.'

'There's that.'

I smiled. During my freshman year at Rutgers, I first met (now Governor) Dave Markie at a party. He intimidated me. I was the immigrant's son. His father was a United States senator. But that was the beauty of college. It is made for strange bedfellows. We ended up becoming close friends.

Dave's critics could not help but notice this friendship when he appointed me to my current post as Essex County prosecutor. The guv shrugged and pushed me through. I had gotten very good press already, and at the risk of caring about what I shouldn't care about, today should have helped my possible bid for a congressional seat.

'So, big day, no? You da man. Woo hoo. Go, Cope, go, Cope, it's your birthday.'

'Trying to appeal to your hip-hop constituency?'

'Trying to understand my teenage daughter. Anyway, congrats.'

'Thanks.'

'I'm still no-commenting this case to death.'

'I've never heard you say no-comment in your life.'

'Sure you have, just in creative ways: I believe in our judicial system, all citizens are innocent until proven guilty, the wheels of justice will turn, I am not judge and jury, we should wait for all the facts to come in.'

'Cliché as no comment.'

'Cliché as no comment and every comment,' he corrected. 'So how is everything, Cope?'

'Fine.'

'You dating?'

'Some.'

'Dude, you're single. You're good-looking. You got some money in the bank. Do you see where I'm going with this?'

'You're subtle, Dave, but I think I can follow.'

Dave Markie had always been a lady slayer. He was okay-looking, but the man had a gift for pick-up that could be conservatively called dazzling. He had that sort of charisma where he made every woman feel as though she was the most beautiful and fascinating person in the world. It was all an act. He just wanted to nail them.

Nothing but. Still, I had never seen anybody better at picking up women.

Dave was married now, of course, had two polished children, but I had little doubt that there was some side action. Some men can't help it. It is instinctive and primitive. The idea of Dave Markie not hitting on a woman was simply anathema.

'Good news,' he said. 'I'm coming up to Newark.'

'What for?'

'Newark is the largest city in my state, that's why, and I value all my constituents.'

'Uh-huh.'

'And I want to see you. It's been too long.'

'I'm kinda busy with this case.'

'You can't make time for your governor?'

'What's up, Dave?'

'It involves what we talked about before.'

My possible congressional run. 'Good news?' I said.

'No.'

Silence.

'I think there's a problem,' he said.

'What kind of problem?'

His voice switched back to jovial. 'Could be nothing, Cope. We'll talk. Let's make it your office. Say, lunchtime?'

'Okay.'

'Get those sandwiches. From that place on Brandford.'

'Hobby's.'

'Exactly. The fully dressed turkey breast on homemade rye. Get yourself one too. See you then.'

Lucy Gold's office building was the otherwise-lovely quad's resident eyesore, a seventies 'mod' structure that was supposed to look futuristic but somehow looked dated three years after completion. The rest of the quad edifices were handsome brick that begged for more ivy. I parked in the lot in the southwest corner. I tilted the rearview mirror and then, to paraphrase Springsteen, I checked my look in that mirror and wanted to change my clothes, my hair, my face.

I parked and walked across the commons. I passed a dozen students. The girls were much prettier than I remembered, but that was probably my aging. I nodded at them as I walked by. They didn't nod back. When I went to college there was a guy in my class who was thirty-eight years old. He'd gone to the military and skipped getting his BA. I remembered how he stuck out on campus because he looked so goddamn old. That was my age now. Hard to fathom. I was the same age as that seemingly old geezer.

I continued to think such inane thoughts because they helped me ignore where I was going. I wore an untucked white dress shirt, blue jeans, blue blazer, Ferragamo loafers without socks. Mr. Casual Chic.

When I approached the building, I could actually feel my body shaking. I scolded myself. I was a grown man. I had been married. I was a father and a widower. I had last seen this woman more than half my life ago.

When do we grow out of this?

I checked the directory, even though Lucy had told me that her office was on the third floor, door B. There it was. Professor Lucille Gold. Three-B. I managed to press the right button in the elevator. I turned left when I got out on the third floor, even though the sign with the 'A–E' had an arrow pointing right.

I found her door. There was a sign-up sheet with her office hours. Most of the time slots were taken. There was also a class schedule and something about when assignments were due. I almost breathed into my hand and smelled it, but I was already working a peppermint Altoid.

I knocked, two sharp raps with the knuckles. Confident, I thought. Manly.

God, I'm pathetic.

'Come in.'

Her voice made my stomach drop. I opened the door and stepped into the room. She stood near the window. The sun was still out, and a shadow cut across her. She was still damn beautiful. I took the hit and stayed where I was. For a moment we just stood there, fifteen feet apart, neither moving.

'How's the lighting?' she said.

'Excuse me?'

'I was trying to figure out where to be. You know, when you knocked. Do I answer the door? Nah, too much of an early close-up. Do I stay at my desk with a pencil in my hand? Should I look up at you over my half-moon reading glasses? Anyway, I had a friend of mine help me test out all the angles. He thought I looked best with this one – across the room, the shade half drawn.'

I smiled. 'You look terrific.'

'So do you. How many outfits did you try on?'

'Only this one,' I said. 'But I've been told in the past it's my A-game look. You?'

'I tried on three blouses.'

'I like this one,' I said. 'You always looked good in green.'

'I had blond hair back then.'

'Yeah, but you still have the green eyes,' I said. 'Can I come in?'

She nodded. 'Close the door.'

'Should we, I don't know, hug or something?'

'Not yet.'

Lucy sat at her desk chair. I sat in the chair in front of the desk.

'This is so messed up,' she said.

'I know.'

'I have a million things I want to ask you.'

'Me too.'

'I saw online about your wife,' she said. 'I'm sorry.'

I nodded. 'How's your father?'

'Not well.'

'I'm sorry to hear that.'

'All that free love and drugs – eventually they take a toll. Ira also . . . he never got over what happened, you know?'

I guessed that I did.

'How about your parents?' Lucy asked.

'My father died a few months ago.'

'I'm sorry to hear that. I remember him so well from that summer.'

'It was the last time he was happy,' I said.

'Because of your sister?'

'Because of a lot of things. Your father gave him the chance to be a doctor again. He loved that – practicing medicine. He never got to do it again.'

'I'm sorry.'

'My father really didn't want to be part of the lawsuit – he adored Ira – but he needed to blame someone and my mom pushed him. All the other families were on board.'

'You don't need to explain.'

I stopped. She was right.

'And your mother?' she asked.

'Their marriage didn't survive.'

223

The answer did not seem to surprise her.

'Do you mind if I put on my professional hat?' she asked.

'Not at all.'

'Losing a child is a ridiculous strain on a marriage,' Lucy said. 'Most people think that only the strongest marriages survive that sort of blow. That's not true. I've studied it. I've seen marriages one might describe as 'crappy' endure and even improve. I've seen ones that seemed destined to last forever crack apart like cheap plaster. Do you two have a good relationship?'

'My mother and I?'

'Yes.'

'I haven't seen her in eighteen years.'

We sat there.

'You've lost a lot of people, Paul.'

'You're not going to psychoanalyze me, are you?'

'No, nothing like that.' She sat back and looked up and away. It was a look that sent me right back. We would sit out in the camp's old baseball field, where the grass was overgrown, and I would hold her and she would look up and away like that.

'When I was in college,' Lucy began, 'I had this friend. She was a twin. Fraternal, not identical. I guess that doesn't make much of a difference, but with the identical, there seems to be a stronger bond. Anyway, when we were sophomores her sister died in a car crash. My friend had the strangest reaction. She was devastated, of course, but part of her was almost relieved. She thought, well, that's it. God got me. That was my turn. I'm okay for now. I gave at the office. You lose a twin sister like that, you're sorta safe the rest of your life. One heart-breaking tragedy per person. You know what I mean?'

'I do.'

'But life isn't like that. Some get a lifetime pass. Others, like you, get more than your share. Much more. And the worst part is, it doesn't make you immune to even more.'

'Life ain't fair,' I said.

'Amen.' Then she smiled at me. 'This is so weird, isn't it?'

'Yes.'

'I know we were together for, what, six weeks?'

'Something like that.'

'And it was just a summer fling, when you think about it. You've probably had dozens of girls since then.'

'Dozens?' I repeated.

'What, more like hundreds?'

'At the very least,' I said.

Silence. I felt something well up in my chest.

'But you were special, Lucy. You were . . .'

I stopped.

'Yeah, I know,' she said. 'So were you. That's why this is awkward. I want to know everything about you. But I'm not sure now is the time.'

It was as if a surgeon was at work, a time-warping plastic surgeon maybe. He had snipped off the last twenty years, pulled my eighteen-year-old self up to meet my thirty-eight-year-old one, done it almost seamlessly.

'So what made you call me?' I asked.

'The strange thing?'

'Yeah.'

'You said you had one too.'

I nodded.

'Would you mind going first?' she asked. 'You know, like when we messed around?'

'Ouch.'

'Sorry.' She stopped, crossed her arms over her chest

225

as if cold. 'I'm babbling like a ditz. Can't help it.'

'You haven't changed, Luce.'

'Yeah, Cope. I've changed. You wouldn't believe how much I've changed.'

Our eyes met, really met, for the first time since I entered the room. I'm not big on reading people's eyes. I have seen too many good liars to believe much of what I see. But she was telling me something there, a tale, and the tale had a lot of pain in it.

I didn't want any lies between the two of us.

'Do you know what I do now?' I asked.

'You're the county prosecutor. I saw that online too.'

'Right. That gives me access to information. One of my investigators did a quick background check on you.'

'I see. So you know about my drinking and driving.'

I said nothing.

'I drank too much, Cope. Still do. But I don't drive anymore.'

'Not my business.'

'No, it's not. But I'm glad you told me.' She leaned back, folded her hands, placed them in her lap. 'So tell me what happened, Cope.'

'A few days ago, a couple of Manhattan homicide detectives showed me an unidentified male victim,' I said. 'I think the man – a man they said was in his mid to late thirties – was Gil Perez.'

Her jaw dropped. 'Our Gil?'

'Yes.'

'How the hell is that possible?'

'I don't know.'

'He's been alive all this time?'

'Apparently.'

She stopped and shook her head. 'Wait, did you tell his parents?'

226

'The police brought them in to ID him.'

'What did they say?'

'They said it wasn't Gil. That Gil died twenty years ago.'

She collapsed back in the chair. 'Wow.' I watched her tap her lower lip as she mulled it over. Another gesture straight back from our camp days. 'So what has Gil been doing all this time?'

'Wait, you're not going to ask me if I'm sure it's him?'

'Of course you're sure. You wouldn't have said it if you weren't. So his parents are either lying or, more likely, in denial.'

'Yes.'

'Which one?'

'I'm not sure. But I'm leaning toward lying.'

'We should confront them.'

'We?'

'Yes. What else have you learned about Gil?'

'Not much.' I shifted in my seat. 'How about you? What happened?'

'My students write anonymous journals. I got one that pretty much described what happened to us that night.'

I thought I was hearing wrong. 'A student journal?'

'Yep. They had a lot of it right. How we went into the woods. How we were messing around. How we heard the scream.'

I was still having trouble understanding. 'A journal written by one of your students?'

'Yeah.'

'And you have no idea who wrote it?'

'Nope.'

I thought about it. 'Who knows your real identity?'

'I don't know. I didn't change identities, just my name. It wouldn't be that hard to find.'

'And when did you get this journal?'

'Monday.'

'Pretty much the day after Gil was murdered.'

We sat and let that settle.

I asked, 'Do you have the journal here?'

'I made you a copy.'

She handed the pages across the desk. I read them. It brought it back. It hurt, reading it. I wondered about the heart stuff, about never getting over the mysterious 'P.' But when I put it down, the first thing I said to her was, 'This isn't what happened.'

'I know.'

'But it's close.'

She nodded.

'I met this young woman who knew Gil. She said she overheard him talking about us. He said that we lied.'

Lucy kept still for a moment. She spun the chair so that now I saw her profile. 'We did.'

'Not about anything that mattered,' I said.

'We were making love,' she said, 'while they were being murdered.'

I said nothing. I partitioned again. That was how I got through my day. Because if I didn't partition, I would remember that I was the counselor on guard duty that night. That I shouldn't have sneaked off with my girlfriend. That I should have watched them better. That if I had been a responsible kid, if I had done what I was supposed to, I wouldn't have said I had done head counts when I hadn't. I wouldn't have lied about it the next morning. We would have known that they were gone since the night before, not just that morning. So maybe, while I put check marks next to cabin inspections that I had never done, my sister was having her throat slashed.

Lucy said, 'We were just kids, Cope.'

Still nothing.

'They sneaked out. They would have sneaked out if we were there or not.'

Probably not, I thought. I would have been there. I would have spotted them. Or I would have noticed empty beds when I did my rounds. I did none of that. I went off and had a good time with my girlfriend. And the next morning, when they weren't there, I figured that they were just having fun. Gil had been dating Margot, though I thought they'd broken up. My sister was seeing Doug Billingham, though they weren't too serious. They had run off, were having fun.

So I lied. I said I'd checked the cabins and that they'd been safely tucked away. Because I didn't realize the danger. I said I was alone that night – I stuck to that lie for too long – because I wanted to protect Lucy. Isn't that strange? I didn't know all the damage. So yeah, I lied. Once Margot Green was found, I admitted most of the truth – that I'd been negligent on guard duty. But I left off Lucy's role. And once I stuck with that lie, I was afraid to go back and tell the whole truth. They were suspicious of me already – I still remember Sheriff Lowell's skeptical face – and if I admitted it later, the police would wonder why I lied in the first place. It was irrelevant anyway.

What difference did it make if I was alone or with somebody? Either way, I didn't watch out for them.

During the lawsuit, Ira Silverstein's office tried to lay some of the blame on me. But I was only a kid. There were twelve cabins on the boys' side of the camp alone. Even if I had been in position, it would have been easy enough to sneak out. The security was inadequate. That was true. Legally, it wasn't my fault.

Legally.

'My father used to go back to those woods,' I said.

She turned toward me.

'He would go digging.'

'For what?'

'For my sister. He told us he was going fishing. But I knew. He did it for two years.'

'What made him stop?'

'My mother left us. I think he figured that his obsession had cost him too much already. He hired private eyes instead. Called some old friends. But I don't think he dug anymore.'

I looked at her desk. It was a mess. Papers were scattered, some half-tumbling off like a frozen waterfall. There were open textbooks sprawled out like wounded soldiers.

'That's the problem when you don't have a body,' I said. 'I assume you've studied the stages of grief?'

'I have.' She nodded, seeing it. 'The first step is denial.'

'Exactly. In a sense, we never got past that.'

'No body, ergo, denial. You needed proof to move on.'

'My father did. I mean, I was sure Wayne had killed her. But then I would see my father going out like that.'

'It made you doubt.'

'Let's just say it kept the possibility alive in my mind.'

'And what about your mother?'

'She grew more and more distant. My parents never had the greatest marriage. There were cracks already. When my sister died – or whatever the hell happened

– she totally withdrew from him.'

We both went quiet. The last remnants of sunlight were fading away. The sky was turning into a purple swirl. I looked out the window to my left. She looked out too. We sat there, the closest we had been to each other in twenty years.

I said before that the years had been surgically removed. They seemed to return now. The sadness was back. I could see it on her. The long-lasting destruction to my family from that night was obvious. I had hoped that Lucy had been able to get past it. But she hadn't. There hadn't been closure for her either. I don't know what else had happened to her over the last twenty years. To blame that one incident for the sadness I saw in her eyes would be too pat. But I could see it now. I could see myself pulling away from her that very night.

The student journal had talked about how she had never gotten over me. I don't flatter myself to that degree. But she had never gotten over that night. What it did to her father. What it did to her childhood.

'Paul?'

She was still looking out the window.

'Yes?'

'What do we do now?'

'We find out what really happened in those woods.'

Chapter 22

I remember on a trip to Italy seeing tapestries that seem to change perspective depending on where you stand. If you move to the right, the table appears to be facing the right. If you move to the left, the table follows you.

Governor Dave Markie was the human embodiment of that. When he walked into the room he had the ability to make every person feel as though he were facing and looking at them. In his youth I had seen him score with so many women, again not because of his looks, but because he seemed so interested in them. There was a hypnotic intensity in his gaze. I remember a lesbian friend at Rutgers who said, 'When Dave Markie looks at you like that, heck, I'd switch teams for the night.'

He brought that into my office. Jocelyn Durels, my secretary, tittered. Loren Muse's face flushed. Even the U.S. Attorney, Joan Thurston, had a smile on her face that showed me what she must have looked like when she had her first kiss in the seventh grade.

Most would say that it was the power of the office. But I'd known him before the office. The office was a power enhancer, not creator.

We greeted each other with a hug. I noticed that guys did that now – hugged as a greeting. I liked it, the true human contact. I don't have a lot of real friends, so the ones I do have are hugely important to me. They were specially picked, and I love every one of them.

'You don't want all these people here,' Dave whispered to me.

We pulled back from the embrace. He had a smile on his face, but I got the message. I cleared everyone out of my office. Joan Thurston stayed behind. I knew her pretty well. The U.S. Attorney's office was right down the street. We tried to cooperate, help each other out. We had similar jurisdiction – Essex County had plenty of crime in it – but she was only interested in the big stuff. Right now that mostly meant terrorism and political corruption. When her office stumbled across other crimes, they let us handle it.

As soon as the door closed, leaving the three of us alone, the smile slipped off Dave's face. We sat at my conference table. I was on one side. They took the other.

'Bad?' I said.

'Very.'

I put my hands out and gestured with my fingers for them to bring it on. Dave looked at Joan Thurston. She cleared her throat.

'As we speak, my detectives are entering the offices of the charitable institution known as JaneCare. They have a warrant. We'll be taking records and files. I had hoped to keep it quiet, but the media already has a hold of it.'

I felt my pulse do a two-step. 'This is crap.'

Neither one of them spoke.

'It's Jenrette. He's pressuring me to go easy on his son.'

'We know,' Dave said.

'So?'

He looked over at Thurston.

'So that doesn't make the charges untrue.'

'What the hell are you talking about?'

'Jenrette's investigators went places where we never would. They found improprieties. They brought them to the attention of one of my best people. My guy did more digging. We tried to keep it quiet. We know what charges can do to a charity.'

I didn't like where this was going. 'You found something?'

'Your brother-in-law has been skimming.'

'Bob? No way.'

'He's diverted at least a hundred grand.'

'To what?'

She handed me two sheets of paper. I scanned down them.

'Your brother-in-law is putting in a pool, right?'

I said nothing.

'Fifty grand was given to Marston Pools in various payments and listed here as a building expansion. Did JaneCare have a building expansion?'

I said nothing.

'Another almost thirty grand was given to Barry's Landscaping. The expense is listed as beautifying the surrounding areas.'

Our office was half a converted two-house dwelling in downtown Newark. There were no plans to expand or beautify. We didn't need more space. We were concentrating on raising money for treatments and cures. That had been our focus. I saw too much abuse in the charity system, what with fund-raising expenses far outpacing the amount that went into the good works. Bob and I had talked about that. We had the same vision.

I felt sick.

Dave said, 'We can't play favorites. You know that.'

'I do,' I said.

'And even if we wanted to keep it quiet for friendship's sake, we couldn't. The media has been tipped off. Joan here is about to hold a press conference.'

'Are you going to arrest him?'

'Yes.'

'When?'

She looked at Dave. 'He's in custody now. We picked him up an hour ago.'

I thought about Greta. I thought about Madison. A pool. Bob had stolen from my wife's charity to build a goddamn pool.

'You spared him the perp walk?'

'No. They're going to run him through the gauntlet in about ten minutes. I'm here as a friend, but we both agreed we would go after cases like this. I can't play favorites.'

I nodded. We had agreed. I didn't know what to think.

Dave rose. Joan Thurston followed. 'Get him somebody good, Cope. It's going to be ugly, I think.'

I flicked on the TV and watched Bob's perp walk. No, it wasn't carried live on CNN or Fox, but News 12 New Jersey, our local twenty-four-hour news station, carried it. There would be pictures in all the big Jersey papers like the *Star-Ledger* and the *Bergen Record*. Some of the local major network affiliates might run something, though I doubted it.

The perp walk lasted seconds. Bob was cuffed. He didn't duck his head. He looked, as so many do, dazed and childlike. I felt nauseous. I called Greta at home and on her cell. No answer. I left messages on both.

Muse sat with me throughout. When they moved on to another story, she said, 'That sucked.'

'It did.'

'You should ask Flair to rep him.'

'Conflict of interest.'

'Why? Because of this case?'

'Yes.'

'I don't see how. They're unconnected.'

'His client's father, EJ Jenrette, started the investigation.'

'Oh, right.' She sat back. 'Damn.'

I said nothing.

'You in the mood to talk about Gil Perez and your sister?'

'I am.'

'As you know, twenty years ago they found their ripped clothes and blood in the woods.'

I nodded.

'All the blood was O positive. So were both of the missing. Four out of ten people are, so it's not that surprising. They didn't have DNA tests back then, so there was no way to know for certain. I checked. Even if we rush it, the DNA tests will take a minimum of three weeks. Probably longer.'

I was only half listening. I kept flashing to Bob, to his face during that perp walk. I thought about Greta, sweet, kind Greta, and how this was going to destroy her. I thought about my wife, my Jane, how this name-sake charity was about to be leveled. I had set it up as a memorial to the wife I'd failed in life. Now, again, I had failed her.

'Plus with DNA tests, we need something to compare it to. We could use your blood for your sister, but we'd need a member of the Perez family to cooperate too.'

'What else?'

'You don't really need the DNA on Perez.'

'Why's that?'

'Farrell Lynch finished the age progression.'

She handed me two photographs. The first was the morgue shot of Manolo Santiago. The second was the age-progression shot derived from the photograph I'd given her of Gil Perez.

A total match.

'Wow,' I said.

'I got you the address for Perez's parents.' She handed me a slip of paper. I looked at it. They lived in Park Ridge. Less than an hour from here.

'Are you going to confront them?' Muse asked me.

'Yes.'

'You want me to go?'

I shook my head. Lucy had already insisted on joining me. That would be enough.

'I also have a thought,' she said.

'What's that?'

'The technology in finding buried bodies is much better now than it was twenty years ago. Do you remember Andrew Barrett?'

'Lab guy at John Jay? Talkative and strange.'

'And a genius. Right, that's him. Anyway, he's probably the country's top expert with this new ground-penetrating radar machine. He pretty much invented it and claims he can cover a lot of ground quickly.'

'The area is too large.'

'But we can try some of it, right? Look, Barrett is dying to try this new baby out. He says he needs the fieldwork.'

'You already talked to him?'

'Sure, why not?'

I shrugged. 'You're the investigator.'

I glanced back at the TV. They were already replaying Bob's perp walk. He looked even more pathetic this time. My hands tightened into fists.

'Cope?'

I looked at her.

'We gotta go to court,' she said.

I nodded, rose without speaking. She opened the door. A few minutes later, I spotted EJ Jenrette in the lobby. He was purposely standing in my path. He was also grinning at me.

Muse stopped and tried to steer me. 'Let's move to the left. We can go in through—'

'No.'

I kept walking straight. Rage consumed me. Muse rushed to catch up with my steps. EJ Jenrette stayed still, watching my approach.

Muse put a hand on my shoulder. 'Cope . . .'

I didn't break stride. 'I'm fine.'

EJ kept grinning. I met his eye. He stayed in my path. I walked up and stopped so that our faces were inches apart. The idiot was still grinning at me.

'I warned you,' EJ said.

I matched his grin and leaned in very close.

'The word has been passed around,' I said.

'What?'

'Any inmate who gets Little Edward to service him receives preferential treatment. Your boy is going to be the bitch of his block.'

238

I walked away without waiting for a reaction. Muse stumbled after me.

'That was classy,' she said.

I kept moving. It was a false threat, of course – the sins of the father should never fall to the son – but if that image stuck when EJ laid his head on his goose-down pillow, so be it.

Muse jumped in front of me. 'You gotta calm down, Cope.'

'I forget, Muse – are you my investigator or my shrink?'

She put her hands up in a surrender gesture and let me pass. I sat at my seat and waited for the judge.

What the hell had Bob been thinking?

Some days, court is about sound and fury signifying nothing. This was one of them. Flair and Mort knew that they were in deep trouble. They wanted to exclude the pornographic DVD because we hadn't produced it earlier. They tried for a mistrial. They made motions and handed in findings and research and papers. Their interns and paralegals must have been up all night.

Judge Pierce listened, the bushy eyebrows low. He had his hand on his chin and looked very, well, judicial. He did not comment. He used terms like 'under advisement.' I wasn't worried. They had nothing. But a thought began to worm its way in and gnaw. They had gone after me. They had gone after me hard.

Might they not do the same with the judge?

I watched his face. It gave away nothing. I looked at his eyes, looked for some sort of telltale sign that he wasn't sleeping. There was nothing there, but that didn't mean anything.

We finished up by three p.m. I went back to my office and checked my messages. Nothing from Greta. I called her again. Still no answer. I tried Bob's cell too. More nothing. I left a message.

I looked at those two photographs – the aged Gil Perez, the dead Manolo Santiago. Then I called Lucy. She picked up on the first ring.

'Hey,' Lucy answered. And unlike last night, there was a lilt in her voice. I was thrown back again.

'Hey.'

There was a weird, almost happy pause.

'I got the address for Mr. and Mrs. Perez,' I said. 'I want to take another run at them.'

'When?'

'Now. They don't live far from you. I can pick you up on the way.'

'I'll be ready.'

Chapter 23

Lucy looked fabulous.

She wore a green snug pullover that clung exactly as it should. Her hair was tied back in a ponytail. She tucked a strand behind her ear. She wore glasses tonight, and I liked the way they looked.

As soon as she got into the car, Lucy checked out the CDs. 'Counting Crows,' she said. '*August and Everything After.*'

'You like it?'

'Best debut of the past two decades.'

I nodded.

She slid it into the slot. 'Round Here' came on. We drove and listened. When Adam Duritz sang about a woman saying you should take a shot, that her walls were crumbling, I risked a glance. Lucy's eyes were wet.

'You okay?'

'What other CDs you got?'

'What do you want?'

'Something hot and sexy.'

'Meat Loaf.' I lifted the CD case into view. 'A little *Bat Out of Hell*?'

'Oh my,' she said. 'You remember?'

'I rarely travel without it.'

'God, you always were a hopeless romantic,' she said.

'How about a little "Paradise By The Dashboard Light"?'

'Yes, but skip to the part where she makes him promise to love her forever before she gives it up.'

'Gives it up,' I repeated. 'Love that phrase.'

She turned so her body faced me. 'What line did you use on me?'

'Probably my patented seducer.'

'Which is?'

I put a whine in my voice. 'Please? Come on, *pretty* please?'

She laughed.

'Hey, it worked on you.'

'But I'm easy.'

'Right, forgot that.'

She playfully slapped my arm. I smiled. She turned away. We listened to Meat Loaf in silence for a little while.

'Cope?'

'What?'

'You were my first.'

I almost slammed on the brakes.

'I know I pretended otherwise. My father and I and that whole crazy free-love lifestyle. But I never. You were my first. You were the first man I ever loved.'

The silence was heavy.

'Of course, after you, I boinked everybody.'

242

I shook my head, looked to my right. She was smiling again.

I made the right turn per the perky voice of my navigation system.

The Perezes lived in a condo development in Park Ridge.

'Are they expecting us?' Lucy asked.

'No.'

'How do you know they're home?' she asked.

'I called right before I picked you up. My number comes up private on caller ID. When I heard Mrs. Perez answer, I disguised my voice and asked for Harold. She said I had the wrong number. I said I was sorry and hung up.'

'Wow, you're good at this.'

'I try to remain humble.'

We headed out of the car. The property was neatly landscaped. The air was syrupy with some kind of blossom. I couldn't place it. Lilacs maybe. The smell was too strong, cloying, like someone had spilled cheap shampoo.

Before I knocked, the door opened. It was Mrs. Perez. She did not say hi or offer up much of a greeting. She looked at me with hooded eyes and waited.

'We need to talk,' I said.

Her eyes moved toward Lucy. 'Who are you?'

'Lucy Silverstein,' she said.

Mrs. Perez closed her eyes. 'Ira's daughter.'

'Yes.'

Her shoulders seemed to sag.

'May we come in?' I said.

'If I say no?'

I met her eye. 'I'm not letting this go.'

'What go? That man was not my son.'

'Please,' I said. 'Five minutes.'

Mrs. Perez sighed and stepped back. We entered. The shampoo smell was even stronger in here. Too strong. She closed the door and led us to a couch.

'Is Mr. Perez home?'

'No.'

There were noises coming from one of the bedrooms. In the corner were some cardboard boxes. The inscription on the side indicated that they were medical supplies. I looked around the room. Everything, other than those boxes, was so in place, so coordinated, you would swear they bought the model unit.

The unit had a fireplace. I stood and walked over to the mantel. There were family photographs. I looked at them. There were no pictures of the Perez parents. There were no pictures of Gil. The mantel was full of images of people I assumed to be Gil's two brothers and one sister.

One brother was in a wheelchair.

'That's Tomás,' she said, pointing to a picture of the smiling boy in the wheelchair graduating from Kean University. 'He has CP. Do you know what that is?'

'Cerebral palsy.'

'Yes.'

'How old is he?'

'Tomás is thirty-three now.'

'And who's that?'

'Eduardo,' she said. Her expression said not to press it. Eduardo looked like a hard case. I remembered Gil telling me that his brother was a gang member or something, but I didn't believe it.

I pointed to the girl. 'I remember Gil talking about her,' I said. 'She was, what, two years older? I remember he said that she was trying to get into college or something.'

'Glenda is a lawyer,' Mrs. Perez said, and her chest puffed out. 'She went to Columbia Law School.'

'Really? So did I,' I said.

Mrs. Perez smiled. She moved back to the couch. 'Tomás lives in the unit next door. We knocked down a common wall.'

'He can live on his own?'

'I take care of him. We also have nursing.'

'Is he home now?'

'Yes.'

I nodded, sat back down. I didn't know why I cared about that. I wondered though. Did he know about his brother, about what had happened to him, about where he'd been the past twenty years?

Lucy had not left her seat. She remained quiet, letting me take the lead. She was soaking in everything, studying the house, probably putting on her psychology suit.

Mrs. Perez looked at me. 'Why are you here?'

'The body we found belonged to Gil.'

'I already explained to you – '

I held up the manila envelope.

'What's that?'

I reached in and slipped out the top photograph. It was the old one, from camp. I put it on the coffee table. She stared down at the image of her son. I watched her face to see the reaction. Nothing seemed to move or change, or maybe it was just happening so subtly that I couldn't see the transformation. One moment she looked okay. Then, seamlessly, everything collapsed. The mask cracked, laying the devastation bare.

She closed her eyes. 'Why are you showing me this?'

'The scar.'

Her eyes stayed closed.

'You said Gil's scar was on the right arm. But look at this photograph. It was on the left.'

She didn't speak.

'Mrs. Perez?'

'That man was not my son. My son was murdered by Wayne Steubens twenty years ago.'

'No.'

I reached into the envelope. Lucy leaned in. She hadn't seen this picture yet. I took out the photograph. 'This is Manolo Santiago, the man from the morgue.'

Lucy startled up. 'What was his name?'

'Manolo Santiago.'

Lucy looked stunned.

'What?' I said.

She shook me off. I continued.

'And this' – I plucked out the final photograph – 'is a computer rendering using age-progression software. In other words, my lab guy took the old photograph of Gil and aged him twenty years. Then he matched the shaved head and facial hair of Manolo Santiago.'

I put the pictures next to one another.

'Take a look, Mrs. Perez.'

She did. She looked for a long time. 'He looks like him maybe. That's all. Or maybe you just think all Latinos look alike.'

'Mrs. Perez?'

It was Lucy, speaking directly to Gil's mother for the first time since we entered. 'Why don't you keep any pictures of Gil up there?'

Lucy pointed to the fireplace mantel. Mrs. Perez did not follow the finger. She stared at Lucy. 'Do you have any children, Ms. Silverstein?'

'No.'

'Then you wouldn't understand.'

246

'With all due respect, Mrs. Perez, that's a load of crap.'

Mrs. Perez looked like she'd just been slapped.

'You have pictures up there from when the children were young, when Gil was still alive. But not one photograph of your son? I've counseled parents who are grieving. All of them kept a picture out. All of them. Then you lied about which arm was scarred. You didn't forget. A mother doesn't make that mistake. You can see the pictures here. They don't lie. And lastly, Paul hasn't hit you with the coup de grace.'

I had no idea what the coup de grace was. So I stayed silent.

'The DNA test, Mrs. Perez. We got the results on the way over here. They're just preliminary, but it's a match. It's your son.'

Man, I thought, she's good.

'DNA?' Mrs. Perez shouted. 'I didn't give anyone permission to run a DNA test.'

'The police don't need your permission,' Lucy said. 'After all, according to you, Manolo Santiago is not your son.'

'But . . . but how did they get my DNA?'

I took that one. 'We're not at liberty to say.'

'You . . . you can do that?'

'We can, yes.'

Mrs. Perez sat back. For a long time she didn't speak. We waited her out.

'You're lying.'

'What?'

'The DNA test is wrong,' she said, 'or you are lying. That man is not my son. My son was murdered twenty years ago. So was your sister. They died at your father's summer camp because no one watched them. You are both chasing ghosts, that's all.'

I looked over at Lucy, hoping she would have a clue here.

Mrs. Perez rose.

'I want you to leave now.'

'Please,' I said. 'My sister disappeared that night too.'

'I can't help you.'

I was going to say more, but Lucy shook me off. I decided that it might be better to regroup, see what she thought and had to say before I pressed.

When we were outside the door, Mrs. Perez said, 'Don't come back. Let me grieve in peace.'

'I thought your son died twenty years ago.'

'You never get over it,' Mrs. Perez said.

'No,' Lucy went on. 'But at some point, you don't want to be left to grieve in peace anymore.'

Lucy didn't follow up after that. I headed back to her. The door closed. After we slipped into my car, I said, 'Well?'

'Mrs. Perez is definitely lying.'

'Nice bluff,' I said.

'The DNA test?'

'Yeah.'

Lucy let that go. 'In there. You mentioned the name Manolo Santiago.'

'That was Gil's alias.'

She was processing. I waited another moment or two and then said, 'What?'

'I visited my father yesterday. At his, uh, home. I checked the logbook. He's had only one visitor other than me in the past month. A man named Manolo Santiago.'

'Whoa,' I said.

'Yes.'

I tried to let it settle. It wouldn't. 'So why would Gil Perez visit your father?'

'Good question.'

I thought about what Raya Singh had said, about Lucy and me lying. 'Can you ask Ira?'

'I'll try. He's not well. His mind has a habit of wandering.'

'Worth a try.'

She nodded. I made a right turn, decided to change subjects.

'What makes you so sure Mrs. Perez is lying?' I asked.

'She's grieving, for one thing. That smell? It's candles. She was wearing black. You could see the red in the eyes, the slump of the shoulders. All that. Second, the pictures.'

'What about them?'

'I wasn't lying in there. It is very unusual to have pictures dating back to childhood and leaving out a dead child. On its own, it wouldn't mean much, but did you notice the funny spacing? There weren't enough pictures for that mantel. My guess is, she took away the pictures with Gil in them. Just in case something like this happened.'

'You mean if someone came by?'

'I don't know exactly. But I think Mrs. Perez was getting rid of evidence. She figured that she was the only one with pictures to use for identification. She couldn't have thought that you'd still have one from that summer.'

I thought about it.

'Her reactions were all wrong, Cope. Like she was playing a role. She's lying.'

'So the question is, what was she lying about?'

'When in doubt, go with the most obvious.'

'Which is?'

Lucy shrugged. 'Gil helped Wayne kill them. That would explain everything. People always assumed that Steubens had an accomplice – how else did he bury those bodies so fast? But maybe it was only one body.'

'My sister's.'

'Right. Then Wayne and Gil staged it to look like Gil died too. Maybe Gil has always been helping Wayne. Who knows?'

I said nothing.

'If that's the case,' I said, 'then my sister is dead.'

'I know.'

I said nothing.

'Cope?'

'What?'

'It's not your fault.'

I said nothing.

'If anything,' she said, 'it's mine.'

I stopped the car. 'How do you figure that?'

'You wanted to stay there that night. You wanted to work guard duty. I'm the one who lured you into the woods.'

'Lured?'

She said nothing.

'You're kidding, right?'

'No,' she said.

'I had a mind of my own, Lucy. You didn't make me do anything.'

She stayed quiet. Then she said, 'You still blame yourself.'

I felt my grip tighten on the wheel. 'No, I don't.'

'Yeah, Cope, you do. Come on. Despite this recent revelation, you knew that your sister had to be dead.

You were hoping for a second chance. You were hoping to still find redemption.'

'That psychology degree of yours,' I said. 'It's really paying off, huh?'

'I don't mean to – '

'How about you, Luce?' My voice had more bite than I intended. 'Do you blame yourself? Is that why you drink so damn much?'

Silence.

'I shouldn't have said that,' I said.

Her voice was soft. 'You don't know anything about my life.'

'I know. I'm sorry. It's none of my business.'

'Those DUIs were a long time ago.'

I said nothing. She turned away from me and looked out the window. We drove in silence.

'You may be right,' I said.

Her eyes stayed on the window.

'Here is something I've never told anyone,' I said. I felt my face flush and the tears push against my eyes. 'After the night in the woods, my father never looked at me the same.'

She turned toward me.

'I could have been projecting. I mean, you're right. I did blame myself to some degree. What if we hadn't gone off? What if I had just stayed where I was supposed to? And maybe the look on his face was just the pure devastation of a parent losing a child. But I always thought there was something more in it. Something almost accusatory.'

She put a hand on my arm. 'Oh, Cope.'

I kept driving. 'So maybe you're on to something. Maybe I do need to make amends for the past. But what about you?'

'What about me?'

'Why are you delving into this? What do you hope to gain after all these years?'

'Are you kidding?'

'No. What are you after exactly?'

'The life I knew ended that night. Don't you get that?'

I said nothing.

'The families – including yours – dragged my father into court. You took away everything we had. Ira wasn't built for that kind of hit. He couldn't take the stress.'

I waited for her to say more. She didn't.

'I understand that,' I said. 'But what are you after now? I mean, like you said, I'm trying to rescue my sister. Short of that, I'm trying to find out what really happened to her. What are you after?'

She didn't reply. I drove some more. The skies were starting to darken.

'You don't know how vulnerable I feel being here,' she said.

I wasn't sure how to answer that. So I said, 'I would never hurt you.'

Silence.

'Part of it is,' she said, 'it feels like I lived two lives. The one before that night, where things were going pretty well, and the one after, where things aren't. And yeah, I know how pathetic that sounds. But sometimes it feels like I was pushed down a hill that night and I've been stumbling down ever since. That sometimes I sort of get my bearings but the hill is so steep that I can never really get balanced again and then I start tumbling again. So perhaps – I don't know – but perhaps if I figure out what really happened that night, if I can make some good out of all that bad, I'll stop tumbling.'

She had been so magnificent when I knew her. I wanted to remind her of that. I wanted to tell her that she was being overly melodramatic, that she was still beautiful and successful and that she still had so much going for her. But I knew that it would sound too patronizing.

So instead I said, 'It's so damn good to see you again, Lucy.'

She squeezed her eyes shut as though I had struck her. I thought about what she said, about not wanting to be too vulnerable. I thought about that journal, all that talk about not finding another love like that, not ever. I wanted to reach out and take her hand, but I knew for both of us right now, it was too raw, that even a move like that would be too much and not enough.

Chapter 24

I dropped off Lucy back at her office.

'In the morning,' she said, 'I'll visit Ira and see what he can tell me about Manolo Santiago.'

'Okay.'

Lucy reached for the door handle. 'I have a bunch of papers to correct.'

'I'll walk you in.'

'Don't.'

Lucy slipped out of the car. I watched her walk toward the door. My stomach tightened. I tried to sort through what I was feeling right now, but it just felt like a rush of emotion. Hard to distinguish what was what.

My cell phone rang. I looked at the caller ID and saw it was Muse.

'How did it go with Perez's mother?' Muse asked.

'I think she's lying.'

'I got something you might find interesting.'

'I'm listening.'

'Mr. Perez hangs at a local bar called Smith Brothers.

He likes hanging out with the boys, plays some darts, that kind of thing. Moderate drinker from what I hear. But the last two nights, he got really lit up. Started crying and picking fights.'

'Grieving,' I said.

At the morgue, Mrs. Perez had been the strong one. He had leaned on her. I remember that I could see the cracks there.

'And either way, liquor loosens the tongue,' Muse said.

'True enough.'

'Perez is there now, by the way. At the bar. Might be a good place to take a run at him.'

'On my way.'

'There is one more thing.'

'I'm listening.'

'Wayne Steubens will see you.'

I think I stopped breathing. 'When?'

'Tomorrow. He's serving his time at Red Onion State Prison in Virginia. I also hooked you up to meet with Geoff Bedford at the FBI office afterward. He was the special agent in charge of Steubens's case.'

'Can't. We have court.'

'Can. One of your associates can handle it for a day. I have you booked on the morning flight.'

I don't know what I expected the bar to be. Something tougher, I guessed. The place could have been a chain restaurant like T.G.I. Friday's or Bennigan's, something like that. The bar was bigger than in most of those places, the dining area obviously smaller. They had wood paneling and free-popcorn machines and loud music from the eighties. Right now Tears for Fears was singing 'Head Over Heels.'

In my day, they would have called this a yuppie bar. There were young men in loosened ties and women trying hard to look business-y. The men drank beer out of bottles, trying hard to look like they were having a good time with their buddies while checking out the ladies. The ladies drank wine or faux Martinis and eyed the guys more surreptitiously. I shook my head. The Discovery Channel should film a mating special in here.

This didn't look like a hangout for a guy like Jorge Perez, but I found him toward the back. He sat at the bar with four or five comrades in arms, men who knew how to drink, men who hulked over their alcohol as though it were a baby chick in need of protection. They watched the twenty-first-century yuppies milling about them with hooded eyes.

I came up behind Mr. Perez and put a hand on his shoulder. He turned toward me slowly. So did his comrades. His eyes were red and runny. I decided to try a direct route.

'My condolences,' I said.

He seemed puzzled. The other guys with him, all Latino men in their late fifties, looked at me as though I'd been ogling their daughters. They wore work clothes. Mr. Perez had on a Polo shirt and khaki pants. I wondered if that meant anything, but I couldn't imagine what.

'What do you want?' he asked me.

'To talk.'

'How did you find me?'

I ignored the question. 'I saw your face at the morgue. Why are you lying about Gil?'

His eyes narrowed. 'Who you calling a liar?'

The other men stared at me a little harder.

'Maybe we could talk in private.'

He shook his head. 'No.'

'You know that my sister disappeared that night, right?'

He turned away from me and grabbed his beer. His back was to me when he said, 'Yeah, I know.'

'That was your son in the morgue.'

He still kept his back to me.

'Mr. Perez?'

'Get out of here.'

'I'm not going anywhere.'

The other men, tough men, men who had spent their lives working outdoors and with their hands, glared at me. One slid off his bar stool.

'Sit down,' I said to him.

He didn't move. I met his eyes and held it. Another man stood and folded his arms at me.

'Do you know who I am?' I said.

I reached into my pocket and pulled out my prosecutor badge. Yes, I have one. The truth is, I am the top law-enforcement officer for Essex County. I didn't like being threatened. Bullies piss me off. You know the old yarn about standing up to a bully? It was only true if you could back it up. I could.

'You all better be legal,' I said. 'Your family better be legal, your friends better be legal. People you accidentally bump into on the streets – they all better be legal.'

The narrow eyes opened a little wider.

'Let me see some ID,' I said. 'All of you.'

The one who had stood first put up his hands. 'Hey, we don't want no trouble.'

'Then get lost.'

They threw down some bills and left. They didn't run, didn't hurry, but they didn't want to stick around either. I would normally feel bad about making idle threats, quasi-abusing my power like that, but they had more or less asked for it.

Perez turned to me, clearly unhappy.

'Hey,' I said, 'what's the point of carrying a badge if I don't use it?'

'Haven't you done enough?' he asked me.

The bar stool next to him was open. I took it. I signaled for the bartender and ordered a draft of 'whatever he's having,' pointing to Jorge Perez's mug.

'That was your son in the morgue,' I said. 'I could show you the proof, but we both know it.'

He drained his beer and signaled for another. It arrived with mine. I picked up my mug as though to offer a toast. He just looked at me and kept his beer on the bar. I took a deep sip. The first sip of beer on a hot day is like that first finger-dip when you open a new jar of peanut butter. I enjoyed what could only be called God's nectar.

'There are two ways to play it,' I went on. 'You keep pretending it's not him. I've already ordered a DNA test. You know about those, don't you, Mr. Perez?'

He looked out over the crowd. 'Who doesn't anymore?'

'Right, I know. *CSI*, all those cop shows on TV. So you know it won't be a problem for us to prove that Manolo Santiago was Gil.'

Perez took another sip. His hand shook. His face had fault lines now. I pressed on.

'So the question is, once we prove it's your son, what happens? My guess is, you and your wife will try to peddle some 'gasp! – we had no idea' crap. But that won't hold. You start off looking like liars. Then my people start investigating for real. We check all the phone records, all the bank records, we knock on doors, we ask your friends and neighbors about you, we ask about your children—'

'Leave my children out of it.'

'No way,' I said.

'That's not right.'

'What's not right is you lying about your son.'

He shook his head. 'You don't understand.'

'Like hell I don't. My sister was in those woods that night too.'

Tears filled his eyes.

'I'll go after you, your wife, your children. I will dig and dig and trust me, I will find something.'

He stared at his beer. The tears escaped and trickled down his face. He didn't wipe them away. 'Damn,' he said.

'What happened, Mr. Perez?'

'Nothing.'

He lowered his head. I moved so that my face was close to his.

'Did your son kill my sister?'

He looked up. His eyes searched my face as if desperately seeking some kind of solace that would never be there. I held my ground.

'I'm not talking to you anymore,' Perez said.

'Did he? Is that what you're trying to cover up?'

'We're not covering up anything.'

'I'm not making idle threats here, Mr. Perez. I'll go after you. I'll go after your children.'

His hand moved so fast I didn't have time to react. He grabbed my lapels with both hands and pulled me close. He had a good twenty years on me, but I could feel his strength. I got my bearings quickly enough and, remembering one of the few martial arts moves I learned when I was a kid, slashed down on his forearms.

He released me. I don't know if my blow did it or it was just a decision on his part. But he let go. He stood. I stood too. The bartender was watching us now.

'You need help, Mr. Perez?' he asked.

I had the badge out again. 'You reporting all your tips to the IRS?'

He backed off. Everyone lies. Everyone has stuff they keep buried. Everyone breaks laws and keeps secrets.

Perez and I stared at each other. Then Perez said to me, 'I'm going to make this simple for you.'

I waited.

'If you go after my children, I'll go after yours.'

I felt my blood tick. 'What the hell does that mean?'

'It means,' he said, 'I don't care what sort of badge you carry. You don't threaten to go after a man's children.'

He walked out the door. I thought about his words. I didn't like them. Then I picked up my cell phone and called Muse.

'Dig up everything you can on the Perezes,' I said.

Chapter 25

Greta finally returned my call.

I was on my way home, still in the car, and I struggled to find that damn 'hands-free' so that the Essex County prosecutor would not be caught breaking the law.

'Where are you?' Greta asked.

I could hear the tears in her voice.

'I'm on my way home.'

'Do you mind if I meet you there?'

'Of course not. I called before—'

'I was down at the courthouse.'

'Did Bob make bail?'

'Yes. He's upstairs getting Madison to bed.'

'Did he tell you—'

'What time will you be home?'

'Fifteen, twenty minutes tops.'

'I'll see you in an hour, okay?'

Greta hung up before I could answer.

Cara was still awake when I got home. I was glad for

that. I put her to bed and we played her new favorite game, called 'Ghost.' Ghost is basically hide-and-seek and tag combined. One person hides. When that person is found, he tries to tag the finder before the finder gets back to home base. What made our version of the game extra-silly was that we played it in her bed. This severely limited your hiding spots and chances to reach home base. Cara would duck under the covers and I would pretend I couldn't find her. Then she would close her eyes and I would put my head under the pillow. She was as good at pretending as I was. Sometimes I would hide by putting my face right in front of her eyes, so she would see me the second she opened them. We both laughed, well, like children. It was dumb and silly and Cara would outgrow it very soon and I didn't ever want her to.

By the time Greta arrived, using the key I had given her years ago, I was so lost in the bliss of my daughter that I'd almost forgotten everything – young men who rape, young girls who vanish in the woods, serial killers who slit throats, brothers-in-law who betray your trust, grieving fathers who threaten little girls. But the jangle in the door brought it all back to me.

'I have to go,' I told Cara.

'One more turn,' she pleaded.

'Your aunt Greta is here. I need to talk to her, okay?'

'One more? Please?'

Children will always beg for one more. And if you give in, they will do it again and again. Once you give in, they will never stop. They will always ask for one more. So I said, 'Okay, one more.'

Cara smiled and hid and I found her and she tagged me and then I said I had to go and she begged for one more, but I'm nothing if not consistent so I kissed her cheek and left her begging, nearly in tears.

Greta stood at the bottom of the steps. She wasn't pale. Her eyes were dry. Her mouth was a straight line that accentuated her already too-prominent jowls.

'Isn't Bob coming?' I asked.

'He's watching Madison. And his lawyer is coming over.'

'Who does he have?'

'Hester Crimstein.'

I knew her. She was very good.

I came down the stairs. I usually kissed her cheek. I didn't today. I wasn't sure what to do exactly. I also didn't know what to say. Greta moved toward the den. I followed. We sat on the couch. I took her hands in mine. I looked at that face, that plain face, and, as always, saw angels. I adored Greta. I really did. My heart broke for her.

'What's going on?' I asked.

'You need to help Bob,' she said. Then: 'Help us.'

'I will do whatever I can. You know that.'

Her hands felt ice cold. She lowered her head and then looked straight at me.

'You have to say you loaned us the money,' Greta said in pure monotone. 'That you knew about it. That we agreed to pay you back with interest.'

I just sat there.

'Paul?'

'You want me to lie?'

'You just said you would do whatever you could.'

'Are you saying' – I had to stop – 'Are you saying Bob took the money? That he stole from the charity?'

Her voice was firm. 'He borrowed the money, Paul.'

'You're kidding, right?'

Greta took her hands away from mine. 'You don't understand.'

263

'Then explain it to me.'

'He'll go to jail,' she said. 'My husband. Madison's father. Bob will go to jail. Do you get that? It will ruin all our lives.'

'Bob should have thought of that before he stole from a charity.'

'He didn't steal. He borrowed. It's been tough for him at work. Did you know he lost his two biggest accounts?'

'No. Why didn't he tell me?'

'What was he going to say?'

'So he thought the answer was to steal?'

'He didn't . . .' She stopped mid-denial, shook her head. 'It's not that simple. We had signed the papers and committed to the pool. We made a mistake. We overextended.'

'What about your family money?'

'After Jane died, my parents thought it best to keep everything in trust. I can't touch it.'

I shook my head. 'So he stole?'

'Will you stop saying that? Look.' She handed me photocopied sheets. 'Bob was keeping tabs on every cent he took. He was using six percent interest. He would pay it all back once he got on his feet. It was just a way of tiding us over.'

I scanned through the papers, tried to see something that would help them, show me that he hadn't truly done what they said. But there was nothing. There were handwritten notes that could have been put there at any time. My heart sank.

'Did you know about this?' I asked her.

'That's not relevant.'

'Like hell it isn't. Did you know?'

'No,' she said. 'He didn't tell me where the money

264

came from. But listen, do you know how many hours Bob put into JaneCare? He was director. A man in that position should have had a full-time salary. Six figures at least.'

'Please tell me you're not going to justify it that way.'

'I will justify it any way I can. I love my husband. You know him. Bob's a good man. He borrowed the money and would have returned it before anybody noticed. This type of thing is done all the time. You know that. But because of who you are and this damn rape case, the police stumbled across it. And because of who you are, they will make an example of him. They'll destroy the man I love. And if they destroy him, they destroy me and my family. Do you get that, Paul?'

I did get it. I had seen it done before. She was right. They would put the entire family through the wringer. I tried to push past my anger. I tried to see it Greta's way, tried to accept her excuses.

'I don't know what you want me to do,' I said.

'This is my life we're talking about.'

I flinched when she said that.

'Save us. Please.'

'By lying?'

'It was a loan. He just didn't have time to tell you.'

I closed my eyes and shook my head. 'He stole from a charity. He stole from your sister's charity.'

'Not my sister's,' she said. 'Yours.'

I let that one go. 'I wish I could help, Greta.'

'You're turning your back on us?'

'I'm not turning my back. But I can't lie for you.'

She just stared at me. The angel was gone. 'I would do it for you. You know that.'

I said nothing.

'You've failed everyone in your life,' Greta said. 'You didn't look out for your sister at that camp. And in the end, when my sister was suffering the most . . .' She stopped.

The room temperature dialed down ten degrees. That sleeping snake in my belly woke up and started to slither.

I met her eye. 'Say it. Go ahead, say it.'

'JaneCare wasn't about Jane. It was about you. It was about your guilt. My sister was dying. She was in pain. I was there, at her deathbed. And you weren't.'

The unending suffering. Days turned to weeks, weeks to months. I was there. I watched it all. Most of it anyway. I watched the woman I adored, my tower of strength, wither away. I watched the light dim from her eyes. I smelled death on her, on the woman who smelled of lilacs when I had made love to her outside on a rainy afternoon. And toward the end, I couldn't take it. I couldn't watch the final light go out. I cracked. The worst moment of my life. I cracked and ran and my Jane died without me. Greta was right. I had failed to stay on watch. Again. I will never get over it – and the guilt did indeed drive me to start up JaneCare.

Greta knew what I'd done, of course. As she just pointed out, she alone was there in the end. But we'd never talked about it. Not once had she thrown my greatest shame in my face. I always wanted to know if Jane asked for me in the end. If she knew that I wasn't there. But I never have. I thought about asking now, but what difference would it make? What answer would satisfy me? What answer did I deserve to hear?

Greta stood. 'You won't help us?'

'I'll help. I won't lie.'

'If it could save Jane, would you lie?'

I said nothing.

'If lying would have saved Jane's life – if lying would bring back your sister – would you do it?'

'That's a hell of a hypothetical.'

'No, it's not. Because this is my life we're talking about. You won't lie to save it. And that's pretty typical of you, Cope. You're willing to do anything for the dead. It's the living you're not so good with.'

Chapter 26

Muse had faxed me a three-page summary on Wayne Steubens.

Count on Muse. She didn't send me the entire file. She had read it herself and given me the main points. Most of it I knew. I remember that when Wayne was arrested, many wondered why he decided to kill campers. Did he have a bad experience at a summer camp? One psychiatrist explained that while Steubens hadn't talked, he believed that he had been sexually molested at a summer camp during his childhood. Another psychiatrist, however, surmised that it was just the ease of the kill: Steubens had slaughtered his first four victims at Camp PLUS and gotten away with it. He associated that rush, that thrill, with summer camps and thus continued the pattern.

Wayne hadn't worked at the other camps. That would have been too obvious, of course. But circumstances had been his undoing. A top FBI profiler named Geoff Bedford had nailed him that way. Wayne had been under moderate suspicion for those first four murders. By the time the boy was slaughtered in Indiana, Bedford started to look at anyone who could have been in all those spots at the same time. The most obvious place to start was with the counselors at the camp.

Including, I knew, me.

Originally Bedford found nothing in Indiana, the site of the second murder, but there had been an ATM withdrawal in Wayne Steubens's name two towns away from the murder of the boy in Virginia. That was the big break. So Bedford did more serious digging. Wayne Steubens hadn't made any ATM withdrawals in Indiana, but there was one in Everett, Pennsylvania, and another in Columbus, Ohio, in a pattern that suggested that he had driven his car from his home in New York out that way. He had no alibi and eventually they found a small motel owner near Muncie who positively identified him. Bedford dug some more and got a warrant.

They found souvenirs buried in Steubens's yard.

There were no souvenirs from that first group of murders. But those, the theory went, were probably his first killings and he either had no time for souvenirs or didn't think to collect them.

Wayne refused to talk. He claimed innocence. He said that he'd been set up.

They convicted him of the Virginia and Indiana murders. That was where the most evidence was. They didn't have enough for the camp. And there were problems with that case. He had only used a knife. How had he managed to kill four of them? How had he gotten them into the woods? How had he disposed of two of the bodies? They could all be explained – he only had time to get rid of two bodies, he chased them deep in the woods – but the case wasn't neat. With the murders in

Indiana and Virginia, it was open and shut.

Lucy called at near midnight.

'How did it go with Jorge Perez?' she asked.

'You're right. They're lying. But he wouldn't talk either.'

'So what's the next step?'

'I meet with Wayne Steubens.'

'For real?'

'Yep.'

'When?'

'Tomorrow morning.'

Silence.

'Lucy?'

'Yeah.'

'When he was first arrested, what did you think?'

'What do you mean?'

'Wayne was, what, twenty years old that summer?'

'Yes.'

'I was a counselor in the red cabin,' I said. 'He was two down at the yellow. I saw him every day. We worked that basketball court for a week straight, just the two of us. And, yeah, I thought he was off. But a killer?'

'It's not like there's a tattoo or something. You work with criminals. You know that.'

'I guess. You knew him too, right?'

'I did.'

'What did you think?'

'I thought he was a dickhead.'

I smiled in spite of myself. 'Did you think he was capable of this?'

'Of what, slitting throats and burying people alive? No, Cope. I didn't think that.'

'He didn't kill Gil Perez.'

'But he killed those other people. You know that.'

270

'I guess.'

'And come on, you know he had to be the one who killed Margot and Doug. I mean, what other theory is there – he happened to be a counselor at a camp where murders took place and then took up killing himself?'

'It's not impossible,' I said.

'Huh?'

'Maybe those murders set Wayne off somehow. Maybe he had that potential and that summer, being a counselor at a camp where throats were slit, maybe that was the catalyst.'

'You really buy that?'

'Guess not, but who knows?'

'One other thing I remember about him,' she said.

'What?'

'Wayne was a pathological liar. I mean, now that I have that big-time psychology degree I know the technical term for it. But even then. Do you remember that at all? He would lie about anything. Just to lie. It was his natural reaction. He'd lie about what he had for breakfast.'

I thought about it. 'Yeah, I do remember. Part of it was normal camp boasting. He was this rich kid and he'd try to fit in with us wrong-siders. He was a drug dealer, he said. He was in a gang. He had this girlfriend from home who posed in *Playboy*. Everything he said was crap.'

'Remember that,' she said, 'when you talk to him.'

'I will.'

Silence. The sleeping snake was gone. Now I felt other dormant feelings stir. There was still something there, with Lucy. I don't know if it was real or nostalgia or a result of all this stress, but I felt it and I didn't want to ignore it and I knew I'd have to.

'You still there?' she said.

'I am.'

'This is still weird, isn't it? Us, I mean.'

'Yes, it is.'

'Just so you know,' Lucy said, 'you're not alone. I'm there too, okay?'

'Okay.'

'Does that help?'

'Yes. Does it help you?'

'It does. It would suck if I was the only one feeling this way.'

I smiled.

'Good night, Cope.'

'Good night, Luce.'

Serial killing – or at least, having a severely compromised conscience – must be pretty stress free, because Wayne Steubens had barely aged in twenty years. He had been a good-looking guy back when I knew him. He still was. He had a buzz cut now as opposed to those wavy, out-sailing-with-Mummy locks, but it looked good on him. I knew that he only got out of his cell an hour a day, but he must have spent it in the sun because he had none of that typical prison pallor.

Wayne Steubens gave me a winning, near-perfect smile. 'Are you here to invite me to a camp reunion?'

'We're having it in the Rainbow Room in Manhattan. Gosh, I hope you can attend.'

He howled with laughter as if I had just cracked the gem of gems. It wasn't, of course, but this interrogation was going to be a dance. He had been questioned by the best federal officers in the land. He had been probed by psychiatrists who knew every trick in The Psychopath's Handbook. Normal venues wouldn't work here. We had a past. We had even been somewhat friendly. I needed to use that.

His laughter segued into a chuckle and then the smile slipped away. 'They still call you Cope?'

'Yes.'

'So how are you, Cope?'

'Groovy,' I said.

'Groovy,' Wayne repeated. 'You sound like Uncle Ira.'

At camp we used to call the elders Uncle and Aunt.

'Ira was one crazy dude, wasn't he, Cope?'

'He was out there.'

'That he was.' Wayne looked off. I tried to focus in on his powder blue eyes, but they kept darting around. He seemed a bit manic. I wondered if he was medicated – probably – and then I wondered why I hadn't checked on that.

'So,' Wayne said, 'are you going to tell me why you're really here?' And then, before I could answer, he held up his palm. 'Wait, no, don't tell me. Not yet.'

I had expected something different. I don't know what exactly. I expected him to be more outwardly crazy or obvious. By crazy, I meant like the raving lunatics you conjure up when you think of serial killers – the piercing gaze, the scenery chewing, the intensity, the lip smacking, the hands clenching and unclenching, the rage right under the surface. But I didn't feel any of that with Wayne. By obvious, I meant the type of sociopaths we stumble across every day, the smooth guys you know are lying and capable of horrible things. I wasn't getting that vibe either.

What I got from Wayne was something far more frightening. Sitting here and talking to him – the man who in all likelihood had murdered my sister and at least seven others – felt normal. Okay, even.

'It's been twenty years, Wayne. I need to know what happened in those woods.'

'Why?'

'Because my sister was there.'

'No, Cope, that's not what I meant.' He leaned in a little. 'Why now? As you pointed out, it's been twenty years. So why, old friend, do you need to know now?'

'I'm not sure,' I said.

His eyes settled and met mine. I tried to stay steady. Role reversal: The psychotic was trying to read me for a lie.

'The timing,' he said, 'is very interesting.'

'Why's that?'

'Because you're not my only recent surprise visitor.'

I nodded slowly, trying not to seem too anxious. 'Who else came?'

'Why should I tell you?'

'Why not?'

Wayne Steubens sat back. 'You're still a good-looking guy, Cope.'

'So are you,' I said. 'But I think us dating is out of the question.'

'I should be angry with you, really.'

'Oh?'

'You spoiled that summer for me.'

Partitioning. I talked about that before. I know that my face showed nothing, but it was like razors were slicing through my gut. I was making small talk with a mass murderer. I looked at his hands. I imagined the blood. I imagined the blade up against the exposed throat. Those hands. Those seemingly innocuous hands that now sat folded on the steel tabletop. What had they done?

I kept my breath steady.

'How did I do that?' I asked.

'She would have been mine.'

'Who would have been yours?'

'Lucy. She was bound to hook up with somebody that summer. If you weren't there, I had more than an inside track, if you know what I mean.'

I wasn't sure what to say to that, but I waded in. 'I thought you were interested in Margot Green.'

He smiled. 'She had some bod, huh?'

'Indeed.'

'Such a major tease. You remember that time when we were on the basketball court?'

I did remember. Instantly. Funny how that worked. Margot was the camp va-va-voom, and man, did she know it. She always wore these excruciating halter tops whose sole purpose was to be more obscene than actual nudity. On that day, some girl had gotten hurt on the volleyball court. I don't remember the girl's name. I think she ended up with a broken leg, but who remembers anymore? What we all remember – the image I was sharing with this sicko – was a panicked Margot Green sprinting past the basketball court in that damn halter top, everything jiggling, screaming for help, and all of us, maybe thirty, forty boys on the basketball court, just stopping and staring slack jawed.

Men are pigs, yes. But so are adolescents. It is an odd world. Nature demands that males between the ages of, say, fourteen and seventeen become walking hormonal erections. You can't help it. Yet, according to society, you are too young to do anything about it other than suffer. And that suffering increased tenfold around a Margot Green.

God has some sense of humor, don't you think?

'I remember,' I said.

'Such a tease,' Wayne said. 'You do know that she dumped Gil?'

'Margot?'

'Yep. Right before the murder.' He arched an eyebrow. 'Makes you wonder, doesn't it?'

I didn't move, let him talk, hoped he'd say more. He did.

'I had her, you know. Margot. But she wasn't as good as Lucy.' He put his hand to his mouth as though he had said too much. Quite a performance. I stayed very still.

'You do know that we had a fling before you arrived that summer, right? Lucy and me.'

'Uh-huh.'

'You look a little green, Cope. You aren't jealous, are you?'

'It was twenty years ago.'

'It was, yes. And to be honest, I only got to second base. Bet you got farther, Cope. Bet you popped that cherry, didn't you?'

He was trying to get a rise out of me. I wouldn't play that game.

'A gentleman never kisses and tells,' I said.

'Right, sure. And don't get me wrong. You two were something. A blind man could see it. You and Lucy were the real deal. It was very special, wasn't it?'

He smiled at me and blinked rapidly.

'It was,' I said, 'a long time ago.'

'You don't really believe that, do you? We get older, sure, but in most ways, we still feel exactly the same as we did back then. Don't you think?'

'Not really, Wayne.'

'Well, life does march on, I guess. They give us Internet access, you know. No porno sites or anything like that, and they check all our communications. But I did a Web search on you. I know you're a widower with a six-year-old girl. I couldn't find her name online though. What is it?'

Couldn't help it this time – the effect was visceral. Hearing this psycho mention my daughter was worse than having her photograph in my office. I bit back and got to the point.

'What happened in those woods, Wayne?'

'People died.'

'Don't play games with me.'

'Only one of us is playing games, Cope. If you want the truth, let's start with you. Why are you here now? Today. Because the timing is not coincidental. We both know that.'

I looked behind me. I knew that we were being watched. I had requested no eavesdropping. I signaled for someone to come in. A guard opened the door.

'Sir?' he said to me.

'Has Mr. Steubens had any visitors over the past, say, two weeks?'

'Yes, sir. One.'

'Who?'

'I can get that name for you, if you'd like.'

'Please do.'

The guard left. I looked back at Wayne. Wayne did not appear upset. 'Touché,' he said. 'But there's no need. I will tell you. A man named Curt Smith.'

'I don't know that name.'

'Ah, but he knows you. You see, he works for a company called MVD.'

'A private detective?'

'Yes.'

'And he came because he wanted' – I saw it now, those damn sons of bitches – 'he wanted dirt on me.'

277

Wayne Steubens touched his nose and then pointed at me.

'What did he offer you?' I asked.

'His boss used to be a big fed. He said that he could get me better treatment.'

'Did you tell him anything?'

'No. For two reasons. One, his offer was total nonsense. An ex-fed can't do anything for me.'

'And two?'

Wayne Steubens leaned forward. He made sure I was looking him square in the eye. 'I want you to listen to me, Cope. I want you to listen to me very carefully.'

I held his gaze.

'I have done a lot of bad things in my life. I won't go into details. There is no need. I have made mistakes. I have spent the past eighteen years in this hellhole paying for them. I don't belong here. I really don't. I won't talk about Indiana or Virginia or any of that. The people who died there – I didn't know them. They were strangers.'

He stopped, closed his eyes, rubbed his face. He had a wide face. The complexion was shiny, waxy even. He opened his eyes again, made sure that I was still looking at him. I was. I couldn't have moved if I wanted to.

'But – and here's your number-two reason, Cope – I have no idea what happened in those woods twenty years ago. Because I wasn't there. I don't know what happened to my friends – not *strangers*, Cope, friends – Margot Green or Doug Billingham or Gil Perez or your sister.'

Silence.

'Did you kill those boys in Indiana and Virginia?' I asked.

'Would you believe me if I said no?'

'There was a lot of evidence.'

278

'Yes, there was.'

'But you're still proclaiming your innocence.'

'I am.'

'Are you innocent, Wayne?'

'Let's focus on one thing at a time, shall we? I am talking to you about that summer. I am talking to you about that camp. I didn't kill anyone there. I don't know what happened in those woods.'

I said nothing.

'You are a prosecutor now, right?'

I nodded.

'People are digging into your past. I understand that. I wouldn't really pay too much attention. Except now you're here too. Which means something happened. Something new. Something involving that night.'

'What's your point, Wayne?'

'You always thought I killed them,' he said. 'But now, for the first time, you're not so sure, are you?'

I said nothing.

'Something has changed. I can see it in your face. For the first time you seriously wonder if I had something to do with that night. And if you have learned something new, you have an obligation to tell me about it.'

'I have no obligations, Wayne. You weren't tried for those murders. You were tried and convicted for murders in Indiana and Virginia.'

He spread his arms. 'Then where's the harm in telling me what you learned?'

I thought about that. He had a point. If I told him that Gil Perez was still alive, it would do nothing to overturn his convictions – because he wasn't convicted of killing Gil. But it would cast a long shadow. A serial killer case is a bit like the proverbial and literal house of corpses: If you learn that a victim wasn't murdered – at least, not

279

then and not by your serial killer – then that house of corpses could easily implode.

I chose discretion for now. Until we had a positive ID on Gil Perez, there was no reason to say anything anyway. I looked at him. Was he a lunatic? I thought so. But how the hell could I be sure? Either way I had learned all I could today. So I stood.

'Good-bye, Wayne.'

'Good-bye, Cope.'

I started for the door.

'Cope?'

I turned.

'You know I didn't kill them, don't you?'

I did not reply.

'And if I didn't kill them,' he went on, 'you have to wonder about everything that happened that night – not only to Margot, Doug, Gil and Camille. But what happened to me. And to you.'

Chapter 27

'Ira, look at me a second.'

Lucy had waited until her father seemed his most lucid. She sat across from him in his room. Ira had broken out his old vinyls today. There were covers with a long-haired James Taylor on *Sweet Baby James* and another of the Beatles crossing Abbey Road (with a barefoot and therefore 'dead' Paul). Marvin Gaye wore a scarf for *What's Going On* and Jim Morrison moped sexuality on the cover of the original Doors album.

'Ira?'

He was smiling at an old picture from their camp days. The yellow VW Beetle had been decorated by the oldest-girl bunk. They put flowers and peace signs all over it. Ira was standing in the middle with his arms crossed. The girls surrounded the car. Everyone wore shorts and T-shirts and sun-kissed smiles. Lucy remembered that day. It had been a good one, one of those you stick in a box and put in a bottom drawer and take out and look at when you're feeling particularly blue.

'Ira?'

He turned toward her. 'I'm listening.'

Barry McGuire's classic 1965 antiwar anthem, 'Eve of Destruction,' was playing. Troubling as this song was, it had always comforted Lucy. The song paints a devastatingly bleak picture of the world. He sings about the world exploding, about bodies in the Jordan River, about the fear of a nuclear button being pushed, about hate in Red China and Selma, Alabama (a forced rhyme, but it worked), about all the hypocrisy and hate in the world – and in the chorus he almost mockingly asks how the listener can be naive enough to think that we aren't on the eve of destruction.

So why did it comfort her?

Because it was true. The world was this terrible, awful place. The planet was on the brink back then. But it had survived – some might even say thrived. The world seems pretty horrible today too. You can't believe that we will get through it. McGuire's world had been just as scary. Maybe scarier. Go back twenty years earlier – World War II, Nazism. That must have made the sixties look like Disneyland. We got through that too.

We always seem to be on the eve of destruction. And we always seem to get through it.

Maybe we all survive the destruction we have wrought.

She shook her head. How naïve. How Pollyannaish. She should know better.

Ira's beard was trimmed today. His hair was still unruly. The gray was taking on an almost blue tinge. His hands shook and Lucy wondered if maybe Parkinson's was on the horizon. His last years, she knew, would not be good. But then again, there really hadn't been many good ones in the past twenty.

'What is it, honey?'

His concern was so apparent. It had been one of Ira's great and honest charms – he so genuinely cared about people. He was a terrific listener. He saw pain and wanted to find a way to ease it. Everyone felt that empathy with Ira – every camper, every parent, every friend. But when you were his only child, the person he loved above all else, it was like the warmest blanket on the coldest day.

God, he'd been such a magnificent father. She missed that man so much.

'In the logbook, it says that a man named Manolo Santiago visited you.' She tilted her head. 'Do you remember that, Ira?'

His smile slid away.

'Ira?'

'Yeah,' he said. 'I remember.'

'What did he want?'

'To talk.'

'To talk about what?'

He wrapped his lips over his teeth, as if forcing them to stay closed.

'Ira?'

He shook his head.

'Please tell me,' she said.

Ira's mouth opened but nothing came out. When he finally spoke his voice was a hush. 'You know what he wanted to talk about.'

Lucy looked over her shoulder. They were alone in the room. 'Eve of Destruction' was over. The Mamas and the Papas came on to tell them that all the leaves were brown.

'The camp?' she said.

He nodded.

'What did he want to know?'

He started to cry.

'Ira?'

'I didn't want to go back there,' he said.

'I know you didn't.'

'He kept asking me.'

'About what, Ira? What did he ask you about?'

He put his face in his hands. 'Please . . .'

'Please what?'

'I can't go back there anymore. Do you understand? I can't go back there.'

'It can't hurt you anymore.'

He kept his face in his hands. His shoulders shook. 'Those poor kids.'

'Ira?' He looked so damn terrified. She said, 'Daddy?'

'I let everyone down.'

'No, you didn't.'

His sobs were uncontrollable now. Lucy got on her knees in front of him. She felt the tears push against her eyes too. 'Please, Dad, look at me.'

He wouldn't. The nurse, Rebecca, stuck her head in the doorway.

'I'll go get something,' the nurse said.

Lucy held a hand up. 'No.'

Ira let out another cry.

'I think he needs something to calm him down.'

'Not yet,' Lucy said. 'We're just . . . please leave us alone.'

'I have a responsibility.'

'He's fine. This is a private conversation. It's getting emotional, that's all.'

'I'll get the doctor.'

Lucy was about to tell her not to, but she was gone.

'Ira, please listen to me.'

'No . . .'

'What did you say to him?'

'I could only protect so many. Do you understand?'

She didn't. She put her hands on his cheeks and tried to lift his head. His scream almost knocked her backward. She let go. He backed up, knocking the chair to the ground. He huddled in the corner. 'No . . . !'

'It's okay, Dad. It's—'

'No!'

Nurse Rebecca came back with two other women. One Lucy recognized as the doctor. The other, another nurse, Lucy figured, had a hypodermic needle.

Rebecca said, 'It's okay, Ira.'

They started to approach him. Lucy stepped in the way. 'Get out,' she said.

The doctor – her name tag read Julie Contrucci – cleared her throat. 'He's very agitated.'

'So am I,' Lucy said.

'Excuse me?'

'You said he's agitated. Big deal. Being agitated is a part of life. I feel agitated sometimes. You feel agitated sometimes, right? Why can't he?'

'Because he's not well.'

'He's fine. I need him lucid for a few more minutes.'

Ira let out another sob.

'You call this lucid?'

'I need time with him.'

Dr. Contrucci folded her arms across her chest. 'It's not up to you.'

'I'm his daughter.'

'Your father is here voluntarily. He can come and go as he pleases. No court has ever declared him incompetent. It's up to him.'

Contrucci looked to Ira. 'Do you want a sedative, Mr. Silverstein?'

Ira's eyes darted back and forth like the cornered animal he suddenly was.

'Mr. Silverstein?'

He stared at his daughter. He started crying again. 'I didn't say anything, Lucy. What could I tell him?'

He started sobbing again. The doctor looked at Lucy. Lucy looked at her father. 'It's okay, Ira.'

'I love you, Luce.'

'I love you too.'

The nurses went over. Ira stuck out his arm. Ira smiled dreamily when the needle went in. It reminded Lucy of her childhood. He had smoked grass in front of her without worry. She could remember him inhaling deeply, his smile like that, and now she wondered why he'd needed it. She remembered how it had picked up after the camp. During her childhood years the drugs were just a part of him – a part of the 'movement.' But now she wondered. Like with her drinking. Was there some kind of addiction gene working? Or was Ira, like Lucy, using outside agents – drugs, booze – to escape, to numb, to not face the truth?

Chapter 28

'Please tell me you're joking.'

FBI Special Agent Geoff Bedford and I were sitting at a regulation-size diner, the kind with the aluminum on the outside and signed photographs of local anchors on the inside. Bedford was trim and sported a handlebar mustache with waxed tips. I'm sure that I had seen one of those in real life before, but I couldn't recall where. I kept expecting three other guys to join him for a little barbershop quartet work.

'I'm not,' I said.

The waitress came by. She didn't call us hon. I hate that. Bedford had been reading the menu for food, but he just ordered coffee. I got the meaning and ordered the same. We handed her the menus. Bedford waited until she was gone.

'Steubens did it, no question. He killed all those people. There was never any doubt in the past. There is no doubt now. And I'm not just talking about reasonable doubt here. There is absolutely no doubt at all.'

'The first killings. The four in the woods.'

'What about them?'

'There was no evidence linking him to those,' I said.

'No physical evidence, no.'

'Four victims,' I said. 'Two were young women. Margot Green and my sister?'

'That's right.'

'But none of Steubens's other victims were female.'

'Correct.'

'All were males between the ages of sixteen and eighteen. Don't you find that odd?'

He looked at me as if I had suddenly grown a second head. 'Look, Mr. Copeland, I agreed to see you because, one, you're a county prosecutor, and two, your own sister died at the hands of this monster. But this line of questioning . . .'

'I just visited Wayne Steubens,' I said.

'I am aware of that. And let me tell you, he is one damn good psychopath and pathological liar.'

I thought about how Lucy had said the same thing. I also thought about how Wayne had said that he and Lucy had a little fling before I got to camp.

'I know that,' I said.

'I'm not sure you do. Let me explain something to you. Wayne Steubens has been a part of my life for nearly twenty years. Think about that. I've seen how convincing a liar he can be.'

I wasn't sure what tack to take here, so I just started tramping around. 'New evidence has come to light,' I said.

Bedford frowned. The tips of the mustache down-turned with his lips. 'What are you talking about?'

'You know who Gil Perez is?'

'Of course I do. I know everything and everyone involved in this case.'

'You never found his body.'

'That's right. We didn't find your sister's either.'

'How do you explain that?'

'You went to that camp. You know that area.'

'I do.'

'Do you know how many square miles of woods there are out there?'

'I do.'

He lifted his right hand and looked at it. 'Hello, Mr. Needle?' Then he did the same with his left. 'Meet my friend Mr. Haystack.'

'Wayne Steubens is a relatively small man.'

'So?'

'So Doug was over six feet tall. Gil was a tough kid. How do you think Wayne surprised or overpowered all four of them?'

'He had a knife, that's how. Margot Green was tied up. He simply sliced her throat. We aren't sure of the order of the others. They may have been tied up too – in different places in the woods. We just don't know. He ran down Doug Billingham. Billingham's body was in a shallow grave half a mile from Margot's. He had several stab wounds, some defensive wounds on the hands too. We found blood and clothes belonging to your sister and Gil Perez. You know all this.'

'I do.'

Bedford tilted his chair way back so that his feet went up on the toes. 'So tell me, Mr. Copeland. What is the new evidence that has suddenly come to light?'

'Gil Perez.'

'What about him?'

'He didn't die that night. He died this week.'

The chair dropped forward. 'Pardon me?'

I told him about Manolo Santiago being Gil Perez. I would say that he looked skeptical, but that makes it sound more in my favor than the reality. In reality, Agent Bedford stared at me as if I were trying to convince him that the Easter Bunny was real.

'So let me get this straight,' he said when I finished. The waitress came back with our coffees. Bedford added nothing to it. He lifted the cup carefully and managed to keep the rim off his mustache. 'Perez's parents deny it's him. Manhattan homicide doesn't believe it's him. And you're telling me – '

'It's him.'

Bedford chuckled. 'I think you've taken up enough of my time, Mr. Copeland.'

He put down his coffee and started to slide out of the booth.

'I know it's him. It's just a question of time before I prove it.'

Bedford stopped. 'Tell you what,' he said. 'Let's play your game. Let's say it is indeed Gil Perez. That he survived that night.'

'Okay.'

'That doesn't let Wayne Steubens off the hook. Not at all. There are many' – he looked at me hard now – 'who believed that maybe Steubens had an accomplice for the first murders. You yourself asked how he could have taken out so many. Well, if there were two of them and only three victims, it makes it all a lot easier, don't you think?'

'So now you think maybe Perez was an accomplice?'

'No. Hell, I don't even believe he survived that night. I'm just playing hypotheticals. If that body in the Manhattan morgue did end up being Gil Perez.'

I added a packet of Splenda and some milk to my

coffee. 'Are you familiar with Sir Arthur Conan Doyle?' I asked.

'The guy who wrote Sherlock Holmes.'

'Exactly. One of Sherlock's axioms goes something like this: 'It is a big mistake to theorize before one has data – because one begins to twist facts to suit theories, instead of theories to suit facts."

'You're starting to try my patience, Mr. Copeland.'

'I gave you a new fact. Rather than trying to rethink what happened, you just immediately found a way to twist that fact to suit your theory.'

He just stared at me. I didn't blame him. I was coming on hard, but I needed to push.

'Do you know anything about Wayne Steubens's past?' he asked.

'Some.'

'He fits the profile to a tee.'

'Profiles aren't evidence,' I said.

'But they help. For instance, do you know that neighborhood animals went missing when Steubens was a teen?'

'Really? Well, that's all the proof I need.'

'May I give you an example to illustrate?'

'Please.'

'We have an eyewitness to this. A boy named Charlie Kadison. He didn't say anything back then because he was too scared. When Wayne Steubens was sixteen, he buried a small white dog – what's the breed, something French . . .'

'Bichon Frise?'

'That's it. He buried the dog up to its neck. So only its head was sticking out. The thing couldn't move.'

'Pretty sick.'

'No, it gets worse.'

He took another dainty sip. I waited. He put the coffee back down and dabbed his mouth with a napkin.

'So after he buries the body, your old camp buddy goes to this Kadison kid's house. You see his family had one of those riding lawn mowers. He asks to borrow it . . .'

He stopped, looked at me, and nodded.

'Eeuw,' I said.

'I have other cases like that. Maybe a dozen.'

'And yet Wayne Steubens managed to land a job working at that camp – '

'Big surprise. I mean, that Ira Silverstein seemed like such a stickler for background checks.'

'And no one thought of Wayne when those murders first occurred?'

'We didn't know any of this. First off, the locals were on the Camp PLUS case, not us. It wasn't federal. Not at first. On top of that, people were too scared to come forward during Steubens's formative years. Like Charlie Kadison. You have to also remember that Steubens came from a rich family. His father died when he was young, but his mother shielded him, paid people off, whatever. She was overprotective, by the way. Very conservative. Very strict.'

'Another check mark in your little serial killer profile kit?'

'It isn't just about his profile, Mr. Copeland. You know the facts. He lived in New York yet somehow managed to be in all three areas – Virginia, Indiana, Pennsylvania – when the murders occurred. What are the odds of that? And the kicker, of course: After we got a search warrant, we found items – classic trophies – belonging to all the victims on his property.'

'Not all the victims,' I said.

'Enough of them.'

'But none from those first four campers.'

'That's correct.'

'Why not?'

'My guess? He probably was in a rush. Steubens was still disposing of the bodies. He ran out of time.'

'Again,' I said, 'it sounds a bit like fact twisting.'

He sat back and studied me. 'So what is your theory, Mr. Copeland? Because I am dying to hear it.'

I said nothing.

He spread his arms. 'That a serial killer who slit campers' throats in Indiana and Virginia happened to be a counselor at a summer camp where at least two other victims had their throats slit?'

He had a point. I had been thinking about that from the get-go, and I couldn't get around it.

'You know the facts, twisted or not. You're a prosecutor. Tell me what you think happened.'

I thought about it. He waited. I thought about it some more.

'I don't know yet,' I said. 'Maybe it's too early to theorize. Maybe we need to gather more facts.'

'And while you do that,' he said, 'a guy like Wayne Steubens kills a few more campers.'

He had another point. I thought about the rape evidence against Jenrette and Marantz. If you looked at it objectively, there was just as much – probably more – against Wayne Steubens.

Or at least there had been.

'He didn't kill Gil Perez,' I said.

'I hear you. So take that out of the equation, for the sake of this discussion. Say he didn't kill the Perez kid.'

He held up both palms to the ceiling. 'What does that leave you with?'

I mulled that over. It leaves me, I thought, wondering what the hell really happened to my sister.

Chapter 29

An hour later I was sitting on a plane. The door had not yet closed when Muse called me.

'How did it go with Steubens?' she asked.

'I'll tell you about it later. How was court?'

'Motions and nothingness from what I hear. They used the phrase "under advisement" a lot. Being a lawyer must be so friggin' boring. How do you not blow your brains out on days like that?'

'It takes work. So nothing happened?'

'Nothing, but you have tomorrow off. The judge wants to see all counsel in chambers first thing Thursday morning.'

'Why?'

'That under-advisement stuff was tossed around, but your assistant whatshisname said it probably wasn't a big deal. Listen, I have something else for you.'

'What?'

'I had our best computer weenie comb through those journals sent to your friend Lucy.'

'And?'

'And they matched what you already knew. At first anyway.'

'What do you mean, at first?'

'I took the information he gleaned and then I made some calls, did some digging. And I found something interesting.'

'What?'

'I think I know who sent her those journals.'

'Who?'

'Do you have your BlackBerry with you?'

'Yes.'

'There's a ton here. Might be easier if I e-mail you all the details.'

'Okay.'

'I don't want to say any more. I'd rather see if you come up with the same answer I do.'

I thought about that and heard the echo of my conversation with Geoff Bedford. 'Don't want me twisting facts to suit theories, eh?'

'Huh?'

'Never mind, Muse. Just send me the e-mail.'

Four hours after I left Geoff Bedford, I sat in the office adjacent to Lucy's, one normally used by an English professor, who was on sabbatical. Lucy had the key.

She was looking out the window when her TA, a guy named Lonnie Berger, came in without knocking. Funny. Lonnie reminded me a bit of Lucy's father, Ira. He had that Peter Pan quality, an outcast wannabe. I am not knocking hippies or far-leftists or whatever you want to call them. We need them. I am a firm believer that you need those on both political ends, even (or maybe more so) the ones you disagree with and want to hate. It would be boring without them. Your arguments wouldn't be as well honed. Think about it at its core: You can't have a left without a right. And you can't have a center without both.

'What's up, Luce? I got a big date with my hot waitress. . . .' Lonnie spotted me and his voice sort of faded away. 'Who's this?'

Lucy was still looking out the window.

'And why are we in Professor Mitnick's office?'

'I'm Paul Copeland,' I said.

I stuck out my hand. He shook it.

'Whoa,' Lonnie said. 'You're the guy in the story, right? Mr. P or whatever. I mean, I read about the case online and . . .'

'Yes, Lucy filled me in on your amateur sleuthing. As you probably know, I have some pretty good sleuths – professional investigators, actually – who work for me.'

He let go of my hand.

'Anything you want to share with us?' I said.

'What are you talking about?'

'You were right, by the way. The e-mail did come from the Frost Library bank of computers at six forty-two p.m. But Sylvia Potter wasn't there between six and seven p.m.'

He started backing away.

'You were, Lonnie.'

He put on the crooked smile and shook his head. Buying time. 'That's a bunch of crap. Hey, wait a second here. . . .' The smile fled as he faked shock and offense. 'C'mon, Luce, you can't believe that I . . .'

Lucy finally turned toward him. She didn't say anything.

Lonnie pointed at me. 'You don't believe this guy, do you? He's . . .'

'I'm what?'

No reply. Lucy just stared at him. She didn't say a word. She just stared until he started to wither. Lonnie eventually collapsed into the chair.

'Damn,' he said.

We waited. He hung his head.

'You don't understand.'

'Tell us,' I said.

He looked up at Lucy. 'You really trust this guy?'

'A lot more than I trust you,' she said.

'I wouldn't. He's bad news, Luce.'

'Thanks for the glowing recommendation,' I said. 'Now why did you send Lucy those journals?'

He started fiddling with an earring. 'I don't have to tell you a thing.'

'Sure you do,' I said. 'I'm the county prosecutor.'

'So?'

'So, Lonnie, I can have you arrested for harassment.'

'No, you can't. First off, you can't prove I sent anything.'

'Sure I can. You think you're knowledgeable with computers and you probably are in some two-bit, impress-the-coeds kind of way. But the experts in my office – now, they're what you call trained professionals. We already know you sent it. We already have the proof.'

He considered that, debating if he should continue to deny it or ride a fresh stream. He chose the fresh. 'So what? Even if I did send it, how is that harassment? Since when is it illegal to send a fictional story to a college professor?'

He had a point.

Lucy said, 'I can have you fired.'

'Maybe, maybe not. But for the record, Luce, you'd have a lot more to explain than I do. You're the one lying about your background. You're the one who changed your name to hide your past.'

Lonnie liked that argument. He sat up now and crossed his arms and looked very smug. I wanted very badly to punch him in the face. Lucy kept staring at him. He couldn't face her straight on. I moved back a little, gave her room.

'I thought we were friends,' she said.

'We are.'

'So?'

He shook his head. 'You don't understand.'

'Then tell me.'

Lonnie started fiddling with the earring again. 'Not in front of him.'

'Yeah, in front of me, Lonnie.'

So much for backing off.

I slapped him on the shoulder. 'I'm your new best pal. You know why?'

'No.'

'Because I'm a powerful and angry law-enforcement official. And my guess is, if my investigators shake your tree, something will fall out.'

'No way.'

'Way,' I said. 'Do you want examples?'

He kept quiet.

I held up my BlackBerry. 'I have your arrest records here. You want me to start listing them for you?'

That made the smug go bye-bye.

'I have them all, my friend. Even the sealed stuff. That's what I mean when I say I'm a powerful and angry cop. I can screw with you five ways to Sunday. So cut the crap and tell me why you sent those journals.'

I met Lucy's eye. She gave me the smallest of nods. Maybe she understood. We had talked strategy before

Lonnie got here. If she was alone with him, Lonnie would fall back on being Lonnie – he would lie and tell stories and tap-dance and skate and try to use their close relationship against her. I knew the type. He would put on the cool, yah-dude exterior, try to use that crooked-smile charm, but if you put enough pressure on him, a guy like Lonnie caves every time. More than that, fear produces a quicker and more honest response with a Lonnie than playing on his supposed sympathies does.

He looked at Lucy now. 'I didn't have a choice,' he said.

Starting to spout excuses. Good.

'Truth is, I did it for you, Luce. To protect you. And, okay, myself. See, I didn't list those arrests on my Reston application. If the school found out, I'd be out. Just like that. That's what he told me.'

'Who told you?' I said.

'I don't know the names.'

'Lonnie . . .'

'I'm serious. They didn't say.'

'So what did they say?'

'They promised me that this wouldn't hurt Lucy. They had no interest in her. They said what I was doing would be for her good, too, that' – Lonnie made a production of turning around toward me – 'that they were trying to catch a killer.'

He looked at me as hard as he could, which wasn't very hard. I waited for him to yell, '*J'accuse!*' When he didn't, I said, 'Just so you know: On the inside I'm quaking.'

'They think maybe you had something to do with those murders.'

'Wonderful, thank you. So what happened next, Lonnie? They tell you to plant these journals, right?'

'Yes.'

'Who wrote them?'

'I don't know. I guess they did.'

'You keep saying they. How many of them were there?'

'Two.'

'And what were their names, Lonnie?'

'I don't know. Look, they were private eyes, okay? Like that. They said they'd been hired by one of the victim's families.'

One of the victim's families. A lie. A bald-faced lie. It was MVD, the private investigation firm in Newark. It was suddenly starting to make a lot of sense. All of this was.

'They mentioned the name of this client?'

'No. They said it was confidential.'

'I bet. What else did they say?'

'They told me that their firm was looking into these old murders. That they didn't believe the official version, blaming them on the Summer Slasher.'

I looked at Lucy. I had filled her in on my visits with Wayne Steubens and Geoff Bedford. We talked about that night, our own role, the mistakes we made, the past certainty that all four were dead and that Wayne Steubens had killed them.

We had no idea what to think anymore.

'Anything else?'

'That's it.'

'Oh, come on now, Lonnie.'

'That's all I know, I swear.'

'No, I don't think so. I mean, these guys sent Lucy those journals to get her to react, right?'

He said nothing.

'You were supposed to watch her. You were supposed

to tell them what she said and did. That's why you came in here the other day and told her how you found out all that stuff online about her past. You hoped that she'd confide in you. That was part of your assignment, wasn't it? You were supposed to exploit her trust and worm your way even deeper into her good graces.'

'It wasn't like that.'

'Sure it was. Did they offer you a bonus if you got that dirt?'

'A bonus?'

'Yes, Lonnie, a bonus. As in more money.'

'I didn't do this for money.'

I shook my head. 'That would be a lie.'

'What?'

'Let's not pretend it was all about fear of being exposed or altruism in finding a killer. They paid you, didn't they?'

He opened his mouth to deny it. I closed it before he bothered.

'The same investigators who dig up old arrests,' I said. 'They have access to bank accounts. They can find, for example, five-thousand-dollar cash deposits. Like the one you made five days ago at the Chase in West Orange.'

The mouth closed. I had to hand it to Muse's investigating skills. She really was incredible.

'I didn't do anything illegal,' he said.

'That's debatable, but I'm not in the mood right now. Who wrote the journal?'

'I don't know. They gave me the pages, told me to feed it to her slowly.'

'And did they tell you how they got that information?'

'No.'

'No idea?'

'They said they had sources. Look, they knew everything about me. They knew everything about Lucy. But they wanted you, pal. That's all they cared about. Anything I could get her to say about Paul Copeland – that was their main concern. They think maybe you're a killer.'

'No, they don't, Lonnie. They think maybe you're an idiot who can muddy up my name.'

Perplexed. Lonnie worked very hard on looking perplexed. He looked at Lucy. 'I'm really sorry. I would never do anything to hurt you. You know that.'

'Do me a favor, Lonnie,' she said. 'Just get the hell out of my face.'

Chapter 30

Alexander 'Sosh' Siekierky stood alone in his penthouse.

Man gets used to his environment. That was how it was. He was getting comfortable. Too comfortable for a man with his beginnings. This lifestyle was now the expected. He wondered if he was still as tough as he once was, if he could still walk into those dens, those lairs, and lay waste without fear. The answer, he was certain, was no. It wasn't age that had weakened him. It was comfort.

As a young child, Sosh's family had gotten ensnared in the horrible siege of Leningrad. The Nazis surrounded the city and caused unspeakable suffering. Sosh had turned five on October 21, 1941, a month after the blockade began. He would turn six and seven with the siege still on. In January of 1942, with rations set at a quarter pound of bread a day, Sosh's brother, Gavrel, age twelve, and his sister, Aline, age eight, died of starvation. Sosh survived eating stray animals. Cats mostly.

People hear the stories, but they can't fathom the terror, the agony. You are powerless. You just take it.

But even that, even that horror – you get used to it. Like comfort, suffering can become the norm.

Sosh remembered when he first came to the USA. You could buy food anywhere. There were no long lines. There were no shortages. He remembered buying a chicken. He kept it in his freezer. He couldn't believe it. A chicken. He would wake up late at night in a cold sweat. He would run to the freezer and open it up and just stare at the chicken and feel safe.

He still did that.

Most of his old Soviet colleagues missed the old days. They missed the power. A few had returned to the old country, but most had stayed. They were bitter men. Sosh hired some of his old colleagues because he trusted them and wanted to help. They had history. And when times were hard and his old KGB friends were feeling particularly sorry for themselves, Sosh knew that they too opened their refrigerators and marveled at how far they'd come.

You don't worry about happiness and fulfillment when you're starving.

It is good to remember that.

You live among this ridiculous wealth and you get lost. You worry about nonsense like spirituality and inner health and satisfaction and relationships. You have no idea how lucky you are. You have no idea what it is like to starve, to watch yourself turn to bones, to sit by hopelessly while someone you love, someone otherwise young and healthy slowly dies, and a part of you, some horrible instinctive part of you, is almost happy because now you will get a bite-and-a-half-size sliver of bread today instead of just a bite size.

Those who believe that we are anything other than animals are blind. All humans are savages. The ones who are well fed are just lazier. They don't need to kill to get their food. So they dress up and find so-called loftier pursuits that make them believe that they are somehow above it all. Such nonsense. Savages are just hungrier. That was all.

You do horrible things to survive. Anyone who believes that they are above that is delusional.

The message had come in on his computer.

That was how it worked nowadays. Not by phone, not in person. Computers. E-mails. It was so easy to communicate that way and not be traced. He wondered how the old Soviet regime would have handled the Internet. Controlling information had been such a large part of what they did. But how do you control it with something like the Internet? Or maybe it wasn't that big of a difference. In the end, the way you rounded up your enemies was through leaks. People talked. People sold one another out. People betrayed their neighbors and loved ones. Sometimes for a hunk of bread. Sometimes for a ticket to freedom. It all depended on how hungry you were.

Sosh read the message again. It was short and simple and Sosh wasn't sure what to do about it. They had a phone number. They had an address. But it was the first line of the e-mail that he kept coming back to. So simply stated.

He read it again:

WE FOUND HER.

And now he wondered what he should do about it.

*

I put a call in to Muse. 'Can you find Cingle Shaker for me?'

'I guess. Why, what's up?'

'I want to ask her some questions about how MVD works.'

'I'm on it.'

I hung up and turned back to Lucy. She was still looking out the window.

'You okay?'

'I trusted him.'

I was going to say I'm sorry or something equally hackneyed, but I decided to keep it to myself.

'You were right,' she said.

'About?'

'Lonnie Berger was probably my closest friend. I trusted him more than anyone. Well, except for Ira, who's got one arm locked in the straitjacket as it is.'

I tried to smile.

'By the way, how's my self-pity act? Pretty attractive, right?'

'Actually,' I said, 'it is.'

She turned away from the window and looked at me.

'Are we going to try again, Cope? I mean, after this is all done and we figure out what happened to your sister. Are we going back to our lives – or are we going to try to see what could happen here?'

'I love when you beat around the bush.'

Lucy wasn't smiling.

'Yeah,' I said. 'I want to try.'

'Good answer. Very good.'

'Thanks.'

'I don't always want to be the one risking my heart.'

'You're not,' I said. 'I'm there too.'

'So who killed Margot and Doug?' she asked.

'Wow, that was a quick segue.'

'Yeah, well, the faster we figure out what happened . . .' She shrugged.

'You know something?' I said.

'What?'

'It's just so damn easy to remember why I fell for you.'

Lucy turned away. 'I am not going to cry, I am not going to cry, I am not going to cry. . . .'

'I don't know who killed them anymore,' I said.

'Okay. How about Wayne Steubens? Do you still think he did it?'

'I don't know. We do know that he didn't kill Gil Perez.'

'Do you think he told you the truth?'

'He said he hooked up with you.'

'Yuck.'

'But that he only got to second base.'

'If he counts the time he intentionally bumped into me during a softball game and copped a feel, well, then technically he's telling the truth. Did he really say that?'

'He did. He also said he slept with Margot.'

'That's probably true. Lots of guys had Margot.'

'Not me.'

'That's because I snagged you as soon as you arrived.'

'That you did. He also said that Gil and Margot had broken up.'

'So?'

'Do you think it's true?' I asked.

'I don't know. But you know how camp was. It was like a life cycle in seven weeks. People were always

going out and then breaking up and then finding someone new.'

'True.'

'But?'

'But the common theory was that both couples went
into the woods to, uh, mess around.'

'Like we were doing,' she said.

'Right. And my sister and Doug were still an item.
Not in love or anything, but you know what I mean.
My point is, if Gil and Margot were no longer together, why would they have been sneaking into the
woods?'

'I see. So if she and Gil were broken up – and we
know Gil didn't die in those woods . . .'

I thought about what Raya Singh had suggested – a
woman who had clearly known and even been close to
Gil Perez, aka Manolo Santiago. 'Maybe Gil killed
Margot. Maybe Camille and Doug just stumbled across
that.'

'So Gil silenced them.'

'Right. Now he's in trouble. Think about it. He's a
poor kid. He has a brother with a criminal record. He'd
be under suspicion as it was.'

'So he faked like he died too,' she said.

We both sat there.

'We're missing something,' she said.

'I know.'

'We might be getting close.'

'Or we might be way off.'

'One of the two,' Lucy agreed.

Man, it felt good to be with her.

'Something else,' I said.

'What?'

'Those journals. What were they talking about – you

finding me covered with blood and me saying we can't tell anyone?'

'I don't know.'

'Let's start with the first part – the part they got right. About how we sneaked away.'

'Okay.'

'How would they know that?'

'I don't know,' she said.

'How would they know you led me away?'

'Or' – she stopped, swallowed – 'how I felt about you?'

Silence.

Lucy shrugged. 'Maybe it was just obvious to anyone who saw the way I looked at you.'

'I'm trying hard to focus here and not smile.'

'Don't try too hard,' she said. 'Anyway, we got part one of the journal. Let's move on to part two.'

'The stuff about me covered in blood. Where the hell did they come up with that?'

'No idea. But you know what really creeps me out?'

'What?'

'That they knew we got separated. That we did lose sight of each other.'

I had wondered about that too.

'Who would know about that?' I asked.

'I never told a soul,' she said.

'Neither did I.'

'Someone could have guessed,' Lucy said. She stopped, looked up at the ceiling. 'Or . . . '

'Or what?'

'You never told anyone about us getting separated, right?'

'Right.'

'And I never told anyone about us getting separated.'

'So?'

'So then there's only one explanation,' Lucy said.

'That being?'

She looked straight at me. 'Someone saw us that night.'

Silence.

'Gil maybe,' I said. 'Or Wayne.'

'They're our two murder suspects, right?'

'Right.'

'Then who murdered Gil?'

I stopped.

'Gil didn't kill himself and move his body,' she went on. 'And Wayne Steubens is in a maximum security facility in Virginia.'

I thought about that.

'So if the killer wasn't Wayne and it wasn't Gil,' she said, 'who else is there?'

'Found her,' Muse said, as she walked into my office.

Cingle Shaker followed. Cingle knew how to make an entrance, but I wasn't sure that was a conscious effort on her part. There was something fierce in her movements, as if the air itself better make way. Muse was no potted plant, but she looked like one next to Cingle Shaker.

They both sat. Cingle crossed the long legs.

'So,' Cingle said, 'MVD is after you big-time.'

'Looks that way.'

'It is that way. I've checked. It's a scorched-earth operation. No expense spared. No lives spared either. They destroyed your brother-in-law already. They sent a guy to Russia. They've put people on the street, I don't know how many. They had someone try to bribe your old buddy Wayne Steubens. In short, they're going to carve out any piece of your ass they can get their blade into.'

'Any word on what they got?'

'Not yet, no. Just what you already know.'

I told her about Lucy's journals. Cingle nodded as I spoke.

'They've done that before. How accurate are the journals?'

'A lot is wrong. I never stumbled across blood or said we have to keep this secret or anything like that. But they know how we felt about each other. They know we sneaked away and how and all that.'

'Interesting.'

'How would they have gotten their information?'

'Hard to say.'

'Any thoughts?'

She mulled it over for a few moments. 'Like I said before, this is how they operate. They want to stir something up. It doesn't matter if it's the truth or not. Sometimes you need to shift reality. Do you know what I mean?'

'No, not really.'

'How to explain . . . ?' Cingle thought about it a moment. 'When I first got to MVD, do you know what I was hired to do?'

I shook my head.

'Catch cheating spouses. It's big business – adultery. My own firm too. It used to be forty percent, maybe more. And MVD is the best at it, though their methods are a tad unorthodox.'

'How?'

'Depends on the case, but the first step was always the same: Read the client. In other words, see what the client really wants. Do they want the truth? Do they want to be lied to? Do they want reassurance, a way to get a divorce, what?'

'I'm not following. Don't they all want the truth?'

'Yes and no. Look, I hated that end of the business. I didn't mind surveillance or background checks – you know, following a husband or wife, checking out credit card charges, phone records, that kind of thing. That's all a tad seedy, but I get that. It makes sense. But then there's this other side of the business.'

'What other side?'

'The side that *wants* there to be a problem. Some wives, for example, want their husbands to be cheating.'

I looked at Muse. 'I'm lost.'

'No, you're not. A man is supposed to be faithful for-ever, right? I know this one guy. I'm talking to him on the phone – this is before we ever met face-to-face – and he's telling me how he would never, ever cheat, how he loves his wife, blah, blah, blah. But the guy is some ugly slob who works as an assistant manager at a CVS or something – so I'm thinking to myself, 'Who is going to come on to him?' Right?'

'I'm still not following.'

'It is easier to be a good, honorable guy when there is no temptation. But in cases like that, MVD would shift reality. By using me as bait.'

'For what?'

'For what do you think? If a wife wanted to nail her husband for cheating, my job would be to seduce him. That's how MVD worked. The husband would be at a bar or something. They would send me out as a' – she made quote marks with her fingers – 'fidelity test.'

'So?'

'So I hate to sound immodest, but take a look.' Cingle spread her arms. Even dressed down in a loose sweater, the sight was indeed impressive. 'If that's not unfair en-trapment, I don't know what is.'

313

'Because you're attractive?'

'Yep.'

I shrugged. 'If the guy's committed, it shouldn't make a difference how attractive the woman is.'

Cingle Shaker made a face. 'Please.'

'Please what?'

'Are you being intentionally dense? How hard do you think it would be for me to get Mr. CVS, for example, to look in my direction?'

'To look is one thing. To do more than that is another.'

Cingle looked at Muse. 'Is he for real?'

Muse shrugged.

'Let me put it this way,' Cingle said. 'I probably ran, oh, thirty or forty of these so-called fidelity tests. Guess how many married guys turned me down?'

'I have no idea.'

'Two.'

'Not great stats, I admit—'

'Wait, I didn't finish. The two that turned me down? Do you know why?'

'No.'

'They caught on. They realized something had to be up. They were both like, 'Wait, why would a woman who looks like this be coming on to me?' They saw the trap – that's why they didn't go through with it. Does that make them better than the other guys?'

'Yes.'

'How so?'

'They didn't go through with it.'

'But shouldn't the why matter? One guy might say no because he's scared he'll get caught. Does that make him any more moral than the guy who isn't scared? Maybe the guy who isn't scared loves his wife more. Maybe he's

314

a better husband and more committed. Maybe the other guy wants to screw around like crazy but he's so meek and timid that he can't go through with it.'

'So?'

'So fear – not love, not wedding vows, not commitment – is the only thing keeping him honest. So which guy is better? Is it the act or the heart?'

'Heavy questions, Cingle.'

'What's your take, Mr. Prosecutor?'

'Exactly. I'm a prosecutor. It's all about the actions.'

'The actions define us?'

'In legal terms, yes.'

'So the guy who is too scared to go through with it – he's clean?'

'Yep. He didn't go through with it. The why is besides the point. No one says he has to maintain his vow out of love. Fear might be as good a reason as any.'

'Wow,' she said. 'I disagree.'

'Fair enough. But is there a point to this?'

'The point is this: MVD wants dirt. Any way they can get it. If the current reality isn't providing any – read: if the husband isn't already cheating – they'll shift the reality – read: get someone like me to hit on the husband. Do you get it now?'

'I think so. I not only have to be careful about what I might have done, but what I look like I'm doing or appear to be doing or might get entrapped into doing.'

'Bingo.'

'And you have no idea who provided them with the information in that journal?'

'Not yet. But hey, you've now hired me to do counterespionage. Who knows what I'll come up with?' She stood. 'Anything else I can help you with?'

'No, Cingle, I think that covers it.'

'Cool. By the way, I have my bill here for the Jenrette-Marantz case. Who should I give it to?'

Muse said, 'I'll take it.'

Cingle handed it to her and smiled at me. 'I liked watching you in court, Cope. You nailed those sons of bitches but good.'

'Couldn't have done it without you,' I said.

'Nah. I've seen a lot of prosecutors. You're the real deal.'

'Thanks. I wonder, though. Based on your definition, did we, uh, engage in reality shifting?'

'No. You had me dig up honest information. No entrapment. Yes, I used my looks to extract the truth. But there's nothing wrong with that.'

'I agree,' I said.

'Wow. We should leave on that note then.'

I laced my hands at the fingers and put them behind my head. 'MVD must miss you.'

'I hear they got a new hottie. Supposedly she's very good.'

'I'm sure she's not you.'

'Don't count on it. Anyway, I might try to steal her from them. I could use a second hottie, and she appeals to a slightly different demographic.'

'How's that?'

'I'm a blonde. MVD's new girl is dark skinned.'

'African-American?'

'No.'

And then I felt the floor underneath me give way as Cingle Shaker added, 'I think she's from India.'

Chapter 31

I called Raya Singh's cell phone. Cingle Shaker was gone, but Muse had stayed behind.

Raya picked up on the third ring. 'Hello?'

'Maybe you're right,' I said to her.

'Mr. Copeland?'

That accent was so phony. How did I buy into it – or had part of me known all along?

'Call me Cope,' I said.

'Okay, uh, Cope.' The voice was warm. I heard that knowing tease. 'What am I maybe right about?'

'How do I know you're not the one? How do I know you wouldn't make me deliriously happy?'

Muse rolled her eyes. Then she mimed sticking her index finger down her throat and vomiting violently.

I tried to make a date for tonight, but Raya would have none of it. I didn't push it. If I pushed, she might get suspicious. We set up a time to meet in the morning.

I hung up and looked at Muse. Muse shook her head at me.

'Don't start.'

'Did she really use that phrase? "Deliriously happy"?'

'I said, don't start.'

She shook her head again.

I checked the clock. Eight-thirty p.m.

'I better get home,' I said.

'Okay.'

'How about you, Muse?'

'I got some stuff to do.'

'It's late. Go home.'

She ignored that. 'Jenrette and Marantz,' Muse said. 'They are really going after you hard.'

'I can handle it.'

'I know you can. But it's amazing what parents will do to protect their children.'

I was going to comment that I understood, that I had a daughter, that I would do anything to keep her safe from harm. But it sounded too patronizing.

'Nothing amazes me, Muse. You work here every day. You see what people are capable of doing.'

'That's my point.'

'What is?'

'Jenrette and Marantz hear that you're looking to seek higher office. They figure it's a weak spot. So they go after you, do all they can to intimidate you. It was smart. Lots of guys would have caved. Your case was only half-assed anyway. They figured you'd see the information and settle.'

'They thought wrong. So?'

'So do you think they're just going to give up? Do you think they'd just go after you? Or do you think there is a reason Judge Pierce wants to see you in chambers tomorrow afternoon?'

When I got home there was an e-mail from Lucy.

Remember how we used to make each other listen to certain songs? I don't know if you've heard this one, but

here. I won't be forward enough to say think of me when
you listen to it.

But I hope you do.

Love,

Lucy.

I downloaded the attached song. It was a fairly rare classic from Bruce Springsteen called 'Back In Your Arms.' I sat there at my computer and listened to it. Bruce sang about indifference and regrets, about all he's thrown away and lost and longs for again and then he achingly begs to be back in her arms again.

I started to cry.

Sitting there, alone, listening to this song, thinking about Lucy, about that night, I actually cried for the first time since my wife died.

I loaded the song on my iPod and brought it into the bedroom. I played it again. And then once more. And after a while, sleep finally found me.

The next morning Raya was waiting for me in front of Bistro Janice in Ho-Ho-Kus, a small town in northeast New Jersey. No one is sure if the name is Hohokus or Ho Ho Kus or HoHoKus. Some people say that the name comes from a Native American word used by the Lenni Lenape, who controlled this parcel until the Dutch started settling in 1698. But there is no definitive proof one way or the other, though that never stops the old-timers from arguing about it.

Raya wore dark jeans and a white blouse open at the throat. A killer. A total killer. Beauty has such an effect, even though I now knew what she was about. I was angry and had been conned and yet I couldn't help feeling an attraction and hating myself for it.

On the other hand, as beautiful and young as she was, I couldn't help thinking that she wasn't in Lucy's league. I liked feeling that. I held on to it. I thought about Lucy and a funny smile crept onto my face. My breathing grew a little shallow. It always had around Lucy. It was again.

Try to figure love.

'I'm so glad you called,' Raya said.

'Me too.'

Raya bussed my cheek. A subtle whiff of lavender came off her. We moved toward a booth in the back of the bistro. A striking mural of life-size diners, painted by the owners' daughter, took up one entire wall. All the painted eyes seemed to follow us. Our booth was the last one, under a giant clock. I had been eating at Bistro Janice for the past four years. I have never seen that clock set on the correct time. The owners' little joke, I guess.

We sat down. Raya gave me her best melt-'em smile. I thought about Lucy. It knocked away the effect.

'So,' I said, 'you're a private eye.'

Subtlety wasn't going to work here. I didn't have the time or the patience for it. I kept going before she could start with the denials.

'You work for Most Valuable Detection of Newark, New Jersey. You don't really work for that Indian restaurant. I should have picked up on that when the woman at the desk didn't know who you were.'

Her smile flickered but it stayed full wattage. She shrugged. 'How did you figure me out?'

'I'll tell you later. How much of what you said to me was a lie?'

'Not much, actually.'

'Are you still going to stick with that story about not knowing who Manolo Santiago really was?'

'That part was true. I didn't know he was Gil Perez until you told me.'

That confused me.

'How did you two really meet?' I asked.

She sat back and crossed her arms. 'I don't have to talk to you, you know. This is work product by the attorney who hired me.'

'If Jenrette hired you through either Mort or Flair, you could make that argument. But here's your problem. You're investigating me. There is no way you can claim that Gil Perez could be work product on Jenrette or Marantz.'

She said nothing.

'And since you feel no qualms about going after me, I will go after you. My guess is, you were not supposed to be found out. There is no reason why MVD needs to know. You help me, I help you, win-win, please add your own cliché.'

She smiled at that.

'I met him on the street,' she said. 'Just like I told you.'

'But not by accident.'

'No, not by accident. My job was to get closer to him.'

'Why him?'

John, the owner of Bistro Janice – Janice being his wife and chef – appeared at our table. He shook my hand, asked me who the lovely lady was. I introduced him. He kissed her hand. I frowned at him. He went away.

'He claimed to have information on you.'

'I don't understand. Gil Perez comes to MVD – '

'He was Manolo Santiago to us.'

'Right, okay, Manolo Santiago comes up to you and says he can help you find dirt on me.'

'Dirt is a bit strong, Paul.'

'Call me Prosecutor Copeland,' I said. 'That was your task, right? Find something incriminating on me? Try to get me to back off?'

She did not reply. She didn't have to.

'And you don't have attorney-client privilege to hide behind, do you? That's why you're answering my questions. Because Flair would never let his client do this. And even Mort, as big a pain in the ass as he is, isn't this unethical. EJ Jenrette hired you guys on his own.'

'I'm not at liberty to say. And frankly, I wouldn't be in a position to know. I work out in the field. I don't deal with the client.'

I didn't care about the inner workings of her office, but it felt like she was confirming what I said.

'So Manolo Santiago comes to you,' I went on. 'He says he has information on me. Then what?'

'He won't say exactly what it is. He gets coy. He wants money, lots of it.'

'And you bring this message to Jenrette.'

She shrugged.

'And Jenrette is willing to pay it. So go on from there.'

'We insist on proof. Manolo starts talking about how he still needs to nail down details. But here's the thing. We've checked up on him now. We know his name isn't really Manolo Santiago. But we also know that he's on to something big. Huge even.'

'Like what?'

The busboy put down our waters. Raya took a sip.

'He told us that he knew what really happened the night those four kids died in the woods. He told us that he could prove you lied about it.'

I said nothing.

322

'How did he find you?' I asked.

'What do you mean?'

But I thought about it.

'You went to Russia to dig up stuff on my parents.'

'Not me.'

'No, I mean, an investigator from MVD. And you guys also knew about those old murders, that the sheriff even questioned me. So . . .'

I saw it now.

'So you questioned everyone involved in that case. I know you guys sent someone down to visit Wayne Steubens. And that means you went to the Perez family too, right?'

'I don't know, but that makes sense.'

'And that's how Gil heard about it. You visited the Perezes. His mother or father or someone called you. He saw a way to score some money. He goes to you. He doesn't tell you who he really is. But he has enough information that you're curious. So they send you to, what, seduce him?'

'Get close to him. Not seduce.'

'You say "tomato," I say "tomahto." So did he take the bait?'

'Men usually do.'

I thought about what Cingle said. This was not a road I wanted to travel down again.

'And what did he tell you?'

'Almost nothing. You see, he told us you were with a girl that night. Someone named Lucy. That's all I knew – what I told you. The day after we met, I called Manolo on his cell phone. Detective York answered. You know the rest.'

'So Gil was trying to get you proof? In order to score this big payday?'

'Yes.'

I thought about that. He had visited Ira Silverstein. Why? What could Ira have told him?

'Did Gil say anything about my sister?'

'No.'

'Did he say anything about, well, about Gil Perez? Or any of the victims?'

'Nothing. He was coy, like I said. But it was clear he had something big.'

'And then he ends up dead.'

She smiled. 'Imagine what we thought.'

The waiter came over. He took our order. I got the salad special. Raya ordered a cheeseburger, rare.

'I'm listening,' I said.

'A man says he has dirt on you. He is willing to give us proof for a price. And then, before he can tell us all he knows, he ends up dead.' Raya ripped a tiny piece of bread and dipped it in olive oil. 'What would you have thought?'

I skipped the obvious answer. 'So when Gil was found dead, your assignment changed.'

'Yes.'

'You were supposed to get close to me.'

'Yes. I thought my helpless Calcutta story would get to you. You seemed like the type.'

'What type?'

She shrugged. 'Just a type, I don't know. But then you didn't call. So I called you.'

'That efficiency suite in Ramsey. The one you said Gil lived in – '

'We rented that room. I was trying to get you to admit to something.'

'And I did tell you some stuff.'

'Yes. But we weren't sure you were being accurate

or truthful. Nobody really believed that Manolo Santiago was Gil Perez. We figured that he was probably a relative.'

'And you?'

'I believed you, actually.'

'I also told you about Lucy being my girlfriend.'

'We already knew about that. In fact, we'd already found her.'

'How?'

'We're a detective agency, that's how. But according to Santiago, she was lying about something that happened back then too. So we figured a direct interrogation wouldn't work.'

'You sent her journals instead.'

'Yes.'

'How did you get that information?'

'That I don't know.'

'And then it was Lonnie Berger's job to spy on her.'

She didn't bother replying.

'Anything else?' I asked.

'No,' she said. 'Actually, this is kind of a relief, you finding out. It felt okay when I thought you might be a killer. Now it just feels sleazy.'

I rose. 'I might want you to testify.'

'I won't.'

'Yeah,' I said. 'I hear that all the time.'

Chapter 32

Loren Muse was doing research on the Perez family. Funny thing she noticed right away. The Perezes owned that bar, the one where Jorge Perez had met up with Cope. Muse found that interesting. They'd been a family of poor immigrants, and now they had a net worth in excess of more than four million dollars. Of course, if you start with close to a million nearly twenty years ago, even if you just invested reasonably well, that number would make sense.

She was wondering what that meant, if anything, when the phone call came in. She reached for the receiver and jammed it up between her shoulder and ear.

'Muse here.'

'Yo, sweetums, it's Andrew.'

Andrew Barrett was her connection at John Jay College, the lab guy. He was supposed to go out this morning to the old campsite and start searching for the body with his new radar machine.

'Sweetums?'

'I only work with machines,' he said. 'I'm not good with people.'

'I see. So is there a problem?'

'Uh, not really.'

There was a funny hum in his voice.

'Have you gotten out to the site yet?' she asked.

'You kidding? Of course we did. Soon as you gave me the okay, I was, like, so there. We drove out last night, stayed at some Motel 6, started working at first light.'

'So?'

'So we're in the woods, right? And we start searching. The XRJ – that's the name of the machine, the XRJ – was acting a little funny, but we got it revved up pretty good. Oh, I brought a couple of the students with me. That's okay, right?'

'I don't care.'

'I didn't think you would. You don't know them. I mean, why would you? They're good kids, you know, excited about getting some field-work. You remember how it is. A real case. They were Googling the case all night, reading up on the camp and stuff.'

'Andrew?'

'Right, sorry. Like I said, good with machines, not so good with people. Of course, I don't teach machines, do I? I mean the students are people, flesh and blood, but still.' He cleared his throat. 'So anyway, you know how I said this new radar machine – the XRJ – is a miracle worker?'

'Yes.'

'Well, I was right.'

Muse switched hands. 'Are you saying . . . ?'

'I'm saying you should get out here pronto. The ME is on her way, but you'll want to see this for yourself.'

Detective York's phone rang. He picked it up. 'York.'

'Hey, it's Max down at the lab.'

Max Reynolds was their lab liaison on this case. This was a new thing down at the lab. Lab liaison. Every time you had a murder case, you got a new one. York liked this kid. He was smart and knew to just give him the information. Some of the new lab guys watched too many TV shows and thought an explanation monologue was mandatory.

'What's up, Max?'

'I got the results back on the carpet-fiber test. You know, the one on your Manolo Santiago corpse.'

'Okay.'

Usually the liaison just sent a report.

'Something unusual?'

'Yes.'

'What?'

'The fibers are old.'

'I'm not sure I follow.'

'This test is usually a given. Car manufacturers all use the same carpet sources. So you might find GM and maybe a five-year window of when it might have been. Sometimes you get luckier. The color was only used in one kind of model and only for one year. That sorta thing. So the report, well, you know this, the report will read Ford-manufactured car, gray interior, 1999 through 2004. Something like that.'

'Right.'

'This carpet fiber is old.'

'Maybe it isn't from a car. Maybe someone wrapped him up in an old carpet.'

'That's what we thought at first. But we did a little more checking. It is from a car. But the car has to be more than thirty years old.'

'Wow.'

'This particular carpeting was used between 1968 and 1974.'

'Anything else?'

'The manufacturer,' Reynolds said, 'was German.'

'Mercedes-Benz?'

'Not that upscale,' he said. 'My guess? The manufacturer was probably Volkswagen.'

Lucy decided to give it one more try with her father.

Ira was painting when she arrived. Nurse Rebecca was with him. The nurse gave Lucy a look when she entered the room. Her father had his back to her.

'Ira?'

When he turned, she almost took a step back. He looked horrible. The color was gone from his face. His shaving was spotty so that there were spiky tufts on his cheeks and neck. His hair had always maintained an unruly air that somehow worked for him. Not today. Today his hair looked like too many years of living among the homeless.

'How are you feeling?' Lucy asked.

Nurse Rebecca gave her an I-warned-you glare.

'Not so good,' he said.

'What are you working on?'

Lucy walked over to the canvas. She pulled up when she saw what it was.

Woods.

It took her back. It was their woods, of course. The old campsite. She knew exactly where this was. He had gotten every detail right. Amazing. She knew that he no longer had any pictures, and really, you'd never take a picture from this angle. Ira had remembered. It had stayed locked in his brain.

329

The painting was a night view. The moon lit up the treetops.

Lucy looked at her father. Her father looked at her.

'We'd like to be alone,' Lucy said to the nurse.

'I don't think that's a good idea.'

Nurse Rebecca thought that talking would make him worse. The truth was just the opposite. Something was locked up there, in Ira's head. They had to confront it now, finally, after all these years.

Ira said, 'Rebecca?'

'Yes, Ira?'

'Get out.'

Just like that. The voice wasn't cold, but it hadn't been inviting either. Rebecca took her time smoothing her skirt and sighing and standing.

'If you need me,' she said, 'just call. Okay, Ira?'

Ira said nothing. Rebecca left. She did not close the door.

There was no music playing today. That surprised her.

'You want me to put some music on? Maybe a little Hendrix?'

Ira shook his head. 'Not now, no.'

He closed his eyes. Lucy sat next to him and took his hands in hers.

'I love you,' she said.

'I love you too. More than anything. Always. Forever.'

Lucy waited. He just kept his eyes closed.

'You're thinking back to that summer,' she said.

His eyes stayed closed.

'When Manolo Santiago came to see you—'

He squeezed his eyes tighter.

'Ira?'

'How did you know?'

'Know what?'

'That he visited me.'

'It was in the logbook.'

'But . . .' He finally opened his eyes. 'There's more to it, isn't there?'

'What do you mean?'

'Did he visit you too?'

'No.'

He seemed puzzled by this. Lucy decided to try another avenue.

'Do you remember Paul Copeland?' she asked.

He closed his eyes again, as though that hurt. 'Of course.'

'I saw him,' she said.

The eyes popped open. 'What?'

'He visited me.'

His jaw dropped.

'Something is happening, Ira. Something is bringing this all back after all these years. I need to find out what.'

'No, you don't.'

'I do. Help me, okay?'

'Why . . . ?' His voice faltered. 'Why did Paul Copeland visit you?'

'Because he wants to know what really happened that night.' She tilted her head. 'What did you tell Manolo Santiago?'

'Nothing!' he shouted. 'Absolutely nothing!'

'It's okay, Ira. But listen, I need to know—'

'No, you don't.'

'Don't what? What did you say to him, Ira?'

'Paul Copeland.'

'What?'

'Paul Copeland.'

'I heard you, Ira. What about him?'

His eyes almost looked clear. 'I want to see him.'

'Okay.'

'Now. I want to see him now.'

He was growing more agitated by the second. She made her voice soft.

'I'll call him, okay? I can bring him—'

'No!'

He turned and stared at his painting. Tears came to his eyes. He reached his hand toward the woods, as if he could disappear into them.

'Ira, what's wrong?'

'Alone,' he said. 'I want to see Paul Copeland alone.'

'You don't want me to come too?'

He shook his head, still staring at the woods.

'I can't tell you these things, Luce. I want to. But I can't. Paul Copeland. Tell him to come here. Alone. I'll tell him what he needs to hear. And then, maybe, the ghosts will go back to sleep.'

When I got back to my office, I got yet another shock.

'Glenda Perez is here,' Jocelyn Durels said.

'Who?'

'She's an attorney. But she says you'll know her better as Gil Perez's sister.'

The name had slipped my mind. I beelined into my waiting area and spotted her right away. Glenda Perez looked the same as she had in those pictures on the fireplace mantel.

'Ms. Perez?'

She rose and gave me a perfunctory handshake. 'I assume you have time to see me.'

'I do.'

Glenda Perez did not wait for me to lead the way. She walked head high into my office. I followed her and closed the door. I would have hit my intercom and said, 'No interruptions,' but I got the feeling Jocelyn understood from our body language.

I waved for her to take a seat. She didn't. I moved around my desk and sat down. Glenda Perez put her hands on her hips and glared down at me.

'Tell me, Mr. Copeland, do you enjoy threatening old people?'

'Not at first, no. But then, once you get the hang of it, okay, yeah, it's kinda fun.'

The hands dropped from her hips.

'You think this is funny?'

'Why don't you sit down, Ms. Perez?'

'Did you threaten my parents?'

'No. Wait, yes. Your father. I did say that if he didn't tell me the truth I would rip his world apart and go after him and his children. If you call that a threat, then yes, I made it.'

I smiled at her. She had expected denials and apologies and explanations. I hadn't given her any, hadn't fueled her fire. She opened her mouth, closed it, sat.

'So,' I said, 'let's skip the posturing. Your brother walked out of those woods twenty years ago. I need to know what happened.'

Glenda Perez wore a gray business suit. Her stockings were that sheer white. She crossed her legs and tried to look relaxed. She wasn't pulling it off. I waited.

'That's not true. My brother was murdered with your sister.'

'I thought we were going to skip the posturing.'

She sat and tapped her lip.

'Are you really going to go after my family?'

'This is my sister's murder we're talking about. You, Ms. Perez, should understand that.'

'I will take that as a yes.'

'A very big, very nasty yes.'

She tapped her lip some more. I waited some more.

'How about if I lay a hypothetical on you?'

I spread my hands. 'I'm all for hypotheticals.'

'Suppose,' Glenda Perez began, 'this dead man, this Manolo Santiago, was indeed my brother. Again just in terms of this hypothetical.'

'Okay, I'm supposing. Now what?'

'What do you think it would mean to my family?'

'That you lied to me.'

'Not just to you, though.'

I sat back. 'Who else?'

'Everyone.'

She started with the lip tap.

'As you know, all of our families engaged in a lawsuit. We won millions. That would now be a case of fraud, wouldn't it? Hypothetically speaking.'

I said nothing.

'We used that money to buy businesses, to invest, for my education, for my brother's health. Tomás would be dead or in a home if we hadn't won that money. Do you understand?'

'I do.'

'And, hypothetically speaking, if Gil was alive and we knew it, then the entire case was based on a lie. We would be open to fines and perhaps prosecution. More to the point, law enforcement investigated a quadruple homicide. They based their case on the belief that all four teenagers died. But if Gil survived, we could also be accused of obstructing an ongoing investigation. Do you see?'

We looked at each other. Now she was doing the waiting.

'There is another problem with your hypothetical,' I said.

'What's that?'

'Four people go into the woods. One comes out alive. He keeps the fact that he's alive a secret. One would have to conclude, based on your hypothetical, that he killed the other three.'

Tapping the lip. 'I can see where your mind might go in that direction.'

'But?'

'He didn't.'

'I just take your word for that?'

'Does it matter?'

'Of course it does.'

'If my brother killed them, then this is over, isn't it? He's dead. You can't bring him back and try him.'

'You have a point.'

'Thank you.'

'Did your brother kill my sister?'

'No, he didn't.'

'Who did?'

Glenda Perez stood. 'For a long time, I didn't know. In our hypothetical. I didn't know that my brother was alive.'

'Did your parents?'

'I'm not here to talk about them.'

'I need to know—'

'Who killed your sister. I get that.'

'So?'

'So I'm going to tell you one more thing. And that's it. I will tell you this under one condition.'

'What?'

'That this always stays hypothetical. That you will stop telling the authorities that Manolo Santiago is my brother. That you promise to leave my parents alone.'

'I can't promise that.'

'Then I can't tell you what I know about your sister.'

Silence. There it was. The impasse. Glenda Perez rose to leave.

'You're a lawyer,' I said. 'If I go after you, you'll be disbarred—'

'Enough threats, Mr. Copeland.'

I stopped.

'I know something about what happened to your sister that night. If you want to know what it is, you'll make the deal.'

'You'll just accept my word?'

'No. I drew up a legal document.'

'You're kidding.'

Glenda Perez reached into her jacket pocket and pulled out the papers. She unfolded them. It was basically a nondisclosure agreement. It also made clear that I would say nothing and do nothing about Manolo Santiago's being Gil Perez and that her parents would be immune from any prosecution.

'You know this isn't enforceable,' I said.

She shrugged. 'It was the best I could come up with.'

'I won't tell,' I said, 'unless I absolutely have to. I have no interest in harming you or your family. I'll also stop telling York or anyone else that I think Manolo Santiago is your brother. I will promise to do my best. But we both know that's all I can do.'

Glenda Perez hesitated. Then she folded the papers, jammed them back into her pocket and headed to my door. She put her hand on the knob and turned toward me.

'Still hypothetically speaking?' she said.

'Yes.'

'If my brother walked out of those woods, he didn't walk out alone.'

My whole body went cold. I couldn't move. I couldn't speak. I tried to say something but nothing came out. I met Glenda Perez's eye. She met mine. She nodded and I could see her eyes were wet. She turned away and turned the knob.

'Don't play games with me, Glenda.'

'I'm not, Paul. That's all I know. My brother survived that night. And so did your sister.'

Chapter 33

Day was surrendering to the shadows when Loren Muse reached the old campsite.

The sign said Lake Charmaine Condominium Center. The land-mass was huge, she knew, stretching across the Delaware River, which separates New Jersey and Pennsylvania. The lake and condos were on the Pennsylvania side. Most of the woods were in New Jersey.

Muse hated the woods. She loved sports but hated the supposedly great outdoors. She hated bugs and fishing and wading and taking hikes and rare antique finds and dirt and general posts and lures and prize pigs and 4-H fairs and everything else she considered 'rural.'

She stopped at the little building that housed the rent-a-cop, flashed her ID, expected the gate to rise. It didn't. The rent-a-cop, one of those bloated weightlifter types, brought her ID inside and got on the phone.

'Hey, I'm in a hurry here.'

'Don't get your panties in a bunch.'

'My panties in a . . . ?'

She fumed.

There were flashing lights up ahead. A bunch of parked police cars, she figured. Probably every cop within a fifty-mile radius wanted in on this one.

The rent-a-cop hung up the phone. He sat in his booth. He didn't come back to her car.

'Yo,' Muse called out.

He didn't respond.

'Yo, buddy, I'm talking to you here.'

He turned slowly toward her. Damn, she thought. The guy was young and male. That was a problem. If you have a rent-a-cop who is on the elderly side, well, it is usually some well-intentioned guy who's retired and bored. A woman rental? Often a mother looking to pick up some extra money. But a man in his prime? Seven out of ten it was that most dangerous of muscle-heads, the cop wannabe. For some reason he didn't make it onto a real force. Not to knock her own profession, but if a guy sets his sights on being a cop and doesn't make it, there is often a reason, and it wasn't something you wanted to get anywhere near.

And what better way to atone for your own worthless life than to keep a chief investigator – a *female* chief investigator – waiting?

'Excuse me?' she tried, her voice an octave gentler.

'You can't enter yet,' he said.

'Why not?'

'You have to wait.'

'For?'

'Sheriff Lowell.'

'Sheriff Lobo?'

'Lowell. And he said no one gets in without his okay.'

The rent-a-cop actually hitched up his pants.

339

'I'm the chief investigator for Essex County,' Muse said.

He sneered. 'This look like Essex County to you?'

'Those are my people in there. I need to go in.'

'Hey, don't get your panties in a bunch.'

'Good one.'

'What?'

'The panties-in-a-bunch line. You've used it twice now. It is very, very funny. Can I use it sometime, you know, when I really want to put someone down? I'll give you credit.'

He picked up a newspaper, ignored her. She considered driving straight through and snapping the gate.

'Do you carry a gun?' Muse asked him.

He put down the paper. 'What?'

'A gun. Do you carry one? You know, to make up for other shortcomings.'

'Shut the hell up.'

'I carry one, you know. Tell you what. You open the gate, I'll let you touch it.'

He said nothing. The heck with touching it. Maybe she'd just shoot him.

Rent-A-Cop glared at her. She scratched her cheek with her free hand, pointedly raising her pinkie in his direction. From the way he looked at her she could tell it was a gesture that hit painfully close to home.

'You being a wiseass with me?'

'Hey,' Muse said, putting her hands back on the wheel, 'don't get your panties in a bunch.'

This was stupid, Muse knew, but damn if it wasn't also fun. The adrenaline was kicking in now. She was anxious to know what Andrew Barrett had found. Judging by the amount of flashing lights, it had to be something big.

Like a body.

Two minutes passed. Muse was just about to take out her gun and force him to open the gate when a man in uniform sauntered toward her vehicle. He wore a big-brimmed hat and had a sheriff's badge. His name tag read lowell.

'Can I help you, miss?'

'Miss? Did he tell you who I am?'

'Uh, no, sorry, he just said—'

'I'm Loren Muse, the chief investigator for Essex County.' Muse pointed toward the guardhouse. 'Small Balls in there has my ID.'

'Hey, what did you call me?'

Sheriff Lowell sighed and wiped his nose with a handkerchief. His nose was bulbous and rather huge. So were all his features – long and droopy, as if someone had drawn a caricature of him and then let it melt in the sun. He waved the hand holding the tissue at Rent-A-Cop.

'Relax, Sandy.'

'Sandy,' Muse repeated. She looked toward the guardhouse. 'Isn't that a girl's name?'

Sheriff Lowell looked down the huge nose at her. Probably disapprovingly. She couldn't blame him.

'Sandy, give me the lady's ID.'

Panties, then miss, now lady. Muse was trying very hard not to get angry. Here she was, less than two hours from Newark and New York City, and she might as well have been in friggin' Mayberry.

Sandy handed Lowell the ID. Lowell wiped his nose hard – his skin was so saggy that Muse half-feared some would come off. He examined the ID, sighed and said, 'You should have told me who she was, Sandy.'

'But you said no one gets in without your approval.'

'And if you told me on the phone who she was, I would have given it.'

'But—'

'Look, fellas,' Muse interrupted, 'do me a favor. Discuss your backwoods ways at the next lodge meeting, okay? I need to get in there.'

'Park to the right,' Lowell said, unruffled. 'We have to hike up to the site. I'll take you.'

Lowell nodded toward Sandy. Sandy hit a button and the gate rose. Muse pinkie-scratched her cheek again as she drove through. Sandy fumed impotently, which Muse found apropos.

She parked. Lowell met her. He carried two flashlights and handed her one. Muse's patience was running on the thin side. She snatched it and said, 'Okay, already, which way?'

'You got a real nice way with people,' he said.

'Thanks, Sheriff.'

'To the right. Come on.'

Muse lived in a crapola garden apartment of too-standard-to-be-standard brick so she wasn't one to talk, but to her amateur eye, this gated community looked exactly the same as every other, except that the architect had aimed for something quasi-rustic and missed entirely. The aluminum exterior was faux log cabin, a look beyond ridiculous in a sprawling, three-level condo development. Lowell veered off the pavement and onto a dirt path.

'Sandy tell you not to get your panties in a bunch?' Lowell asked.

'Yes.'

'Don't take offense. He says that to everyone. Even guys.'

'He must be the life of your hunting group.'

Muse counted seven cop cars and three other emergency vehicles of one kind or another. All had lights flashing. Why they needed their lights on she had no idea. The residents, a mix of old folks and young families, gathered, drawn by the unnecessary flashing lights, and watched nothing.

'How far is the walk?' Muse asked.

'Mile and a half maybe. You want a tour as we go along?'

'A tour of what?'

'The old murder site. We'll be passing where they found one of the bodies twenty years ago.'

'Were you on that case?'

'Peripherally,' he said.

'Meaning?'

'Peripherally. Concerned with relatively minor or irrelevant aspects. Dealing with the edges or outskirts. Peripherally.'

Muse looked at him.

Lowell might have smiled, but it was hard to tell through the sags. 'Not bad for a hunting lodge backwoods hick, eh?'

'I'm dazzled,' Muse said.

'You might want to be a tad nicer to me.'

'Why's that?'

'First, you sent men to search for a corpse in my county without informing me. Second, this is my crime scene. You're here as a guest and as a courtesy.'

'You're not going to play that jurisdiction game with me, are you?'

'Nah,' he said. 'But I like sounding tough. How did I do?'

'Eh. So can we continue to the tour?'

'Sure.'

The path grew thinner until it practically disappeared. They were climbing on rocks and around trees. Muse had always been something of a tomboy. She enjoyed the activity. And – Flair Hickory be damned – her shoes could handle it.

'Hold up,' Lowell said.

The sun continued to dip. Lowell's profile was in silhouette. He took off his hat and again sniffled into his handkerchief. 'This is where the Billingham kid was found.'

Doug Billingham.

The woods seemed to settle at the words, and then the wind whispered an old song. Muse looked down. A kid. Billingham had been seventeen. He had been found with eight stab wounds, mostly defensive. He had fought his assailant. She looked at Lowell. His head was lowered, his eyes closed.

Muse remembered something else – something from the file. Lowell. That name. 'Peripherally, my ass,' she said. 'You were the lead.'

Lowell did not reply.

'I don't get it. Why didn't you tell me?'

He shrugged. 'Why didn't you tell me you were reopening my case?'

'We weren't really. I mean, I didn't think we had anything yet.'

'So your guys hitting paydirt,' he said. 'That was just dumb luck?'

Muse didn't like where this was going.

'How far are we from where Margot Green was found?' Muse asked.

'A half mile due south.'

'Margot Green was found first, right?'

'Yep. See, where you came in? The condos? That used to be where the girls' side of the camp was. You know. Their cabins. The boys were to the south. The Green girl was found near there.'

'How long after you found Green did you locate the Billingham boy?'

'Thirty-six hours.'

'Long time.'

'A lot of land to cover.'

'Still. He was just left out here?'

'No, there was a shallow grave. That's probably why it was missed the first time through. You know how it is. Everybody hears about missing kids and they want to be the good citizen so they come out and help us cover ground. They walked right over him. Never knew he was there.'

Muse stared down at the ground. Totally unremarkable. There was a cross like those makeshift memorials for car-accident deaths. But the cross was old and nearly fallen over. There was no picture of Billingham. No keepsakes or flowers or stuffed bears. Just the beat-up cross. Alone out here in the woods. Muse almost shivered.

'The killer – you probably know this – his name was Wayne Steubens. A counselor, as it turned out. There are a lot of theories on what happened that night, but the consensus seems to be that Steubens worked on the vanished kids – Perez and Copeland – first. He buried them. He started to dig a grave for Douglas Billingham when Margot Green was found. So he took off. According to the hotshot down at Quantico, burying the bodies was part of what gave him his thrill. You know Steubens buried all his other victims, right? The ones in the other states?'

'Yeah, I know.'

'You know two of them were still alive when he buried them?'

She knew that too. 'Did you ever question Wayne Steubens?' Muse asked.

345

'We talked to everyone at that camp.'

He said that slowly, carefully. A bell rang in Muse's head. Lowell continued.

'And yes, the Steubens kid gave me the creeps – at least, that's what I think now. But maybe that's hindsight, I don't know anymore. There was no evidence linking Steubens to the murders. There was nothing linking anybody, really. Plus Steubens was rich. His family hired a lawyer. As you can imagine, the camp broke up right away. All the kids went home. Steubens was sent overseas for the next semester. A school in Switzerland, I think.'

Muse still had her eyes on the cross.

'You ready to keep moving?'

She nodded. They started hiking again.

Lowell asked, 'So how long have you been chief investigator?'

'A few months.'

'And before that?'

'Homicide for three years.'

He wiped the huge nose again. 'It never gets easier, does it?'

The question seemed rhetorical, so she just kept trekking.

'It's not the outrage,' he said. 'It's not the dead even. They're gone. Nothing you can do about that. It's what's left behind – the echo. These woods you're walking through. There are some old-timers who think a sound echoes forever in here. Makes sense when you think about it. This Billingham kid. I'm sure he screamed. He screams, it echoes, just bounces back and forth, the sound getting smaller and smaller, but never entirely disappearing. Like a part of him is still calling out, even now. Murder echoes like that.'

Muse kept her head down, watched her feet on the knotty ground.

'Have you met any of the victims' families?'

She thought about that. 'One is my boss, actually.'

'Paul Copeland,' Lowell said.

'You remember him?'

'Like I said, I questioned everybody at that camp.'

The bell in Muse's head sounded again.

'Is he the one who got you to look into the case?' Lowell asked.

She didn't reply.

'Murder is unjust,' he went on. 'It's like God had this plan and there is this natural order He set up and someone took it upon themselves to mess with that. If you solve the case, sure, it helps. But it's like you crumbled up a piece of aluminum foil. Finding the killer helps you spread it out again, but for the family, it never really regains its form.'

'Aluminum foil?'

Lowell shrugged.

'You're quite the philosopher, Sheriff.'

'Look into your boss's eyes sometimes. Whatever happened in these woods that night? It's still there. It still echoes, doesn't it?'

'I don't know,' Muse said.

'And I don't know if you should be here.'

'Why's that?'

'Because I did question your boss that night.'

Muse stopped walking. 'Are you saying there's some kind of conflict of interest?'

'I think that might be exactly what I'm saying.'

'Paul Copeland was a suspect?'

'It is still an open case. It is still, despite your interference, my case. So I won't answer that. But I will tell you

347

this. He lied about what happened.'

'He was a kid on guard duty. He didn't know how serious it was.'

'That's no excuse.'

'He came clean later, right?'

Lowell did not respond.

'I read the file,' Muse said. 'He goofed off and didn't do what he was supposed to on guard duty. You talk about devastation. How about the guilt he must feel over that? He misses his sister, sure. But I think the guilt eats at him more.'

'Interesting.'

'What?'

'You said the guilt eats at him,' Lowell said. 'What kind of guilt?'

She kept walking.

'And it's curious, don't you think?'

'What is?' Muse asked.

'That he left his post that night. I mean, think about it. Here he is, a responsible kid. Everyone said so. And suddenly, on the night that these campers sneak out, on the night that Wayne Steubens plans on committing murder, Paul Copeland chooses to slack off.'

Muse said nothing.

'That, my young colleague, has always struck me as a hell of a coincidence.'

Lowell smiled and turned away.

'Come on,' he said. 'It's getting dark and you're going to want to see what your friend Barrett found.'

After Glenda Perez left, I didn't cry, but I came awfully close.

I sat in my office, alone, stunned, not sure what to do or think or feel. My body was shuddering. I looked down at my hands. There was a noticeable quake. I actually did that thing when you wonder if you're dreaming. I did all the checks. I wasn't. This was real.

Camille was alive.

My sister had walked out of those woods. Just like Gil Perez had.

I called Lucy on her cell phone.

'Hey,' she said.

'You're not going to believe what Gil Perez's sister just told me.'

'What?'

I filled her in. When I got to the part about Camille walking out of those woods, Lucy gasped out loud.

'Do you believe her?' Lucy asked.

'About Camille, you mean?'

'Yes.'

'Why would she say that if it wasn't true?'

Lucy said nothing.

'What? You think she's lying? What would be her motive?'

'I don't know, Paul. But we're missing so much here.'

'I understand that. But think about it. Glenda Perez has no reason to lie to me about that.'

Silence.

'What is it, Lucy?'

'It's just odd, that's all. If your sister is alive, where the hell has she been?'

'I don't know.'

'So what are you going to do now?'

I thought about that, tried to settle my mind. It was a good question. What next? Where do I go from here?

Lucy said, 'I talked to my father again.'

'And?'

'He remembers something about that night.'

'What?'

'He won't tell me. He said he'd only tell you.'

'Me?'

'Yep. Ira said he wanted to see you.'

'Now?'

'If you want.'

'I want. Should I pick you up?'

She hesitated.

'What?'

'Ira said he wanted to see you alone. That he won't talk in front of me.'

'Okay.'

More hesitation.

'Paul?'

'What?'

'Pick me up anyway. I'll wait in the car while you go in.'

Homicide detectives York and Dillon sat in the 'tech room,' eating pizza. The tech room was actually a meeting space where they wheeled in televisions and VCRs and the like.

Max Reynolds entered. 'How are you guys?'

Dillon said, 'This pizza is awful.'

'Sorry.'

'We're in New York, for crying out loud. The Big Apple. The home of pizza. And this tastes like something that disobeyed a pooper-scooper law.'

Reynolds turned on the television. 'I'm sorry the cuisine does not measure up to your standards.'

'Am I exaggerating?' Dillon turned to York. 'I mean, seriously, does this taste like hobo vomit, or is it me?'

York said, 'That's your third slice.'

'And probably my last. Just to show I mean it.'

York turned to Max Reynolds. 'What have you got for us?'

'I think I found our guy. Or at least, his car.'

Dillon took another riplike bite. 'Less talk, more show.'

'There is a convenience store on the corner two blocks from where you found the body,' Reynolds began. 'The owner has been having problems with shoplifters grabbing items he keeps outside. So he aims his camera out that way.'

Dillon said, 'Korean?'

'Excuse me?'

'The convenience store owner. He's Korean, right?'

'I'm not sure. What's that got to do with anything?'

'Dollars to doughnuts, he's Korean. So he points his camera outside because some asswipe is stealing an orange. Then he starts screaming about how he pays taxes when he probably has like ten illegals working in the place and someone should do something. Like the cops should comb through his cheap-ass, blurry-crap tapes to find Mr. Fruit Stealer.'

He stopped. York looked at Max Reynolds. 'Go on.'

'Anyway, yes, exactly, the camera gives us a partial of the street. So we started checking for cars around that age – more than thirty years ago – and look what we found here.'

Reynolds already had the tape keyed up. An old Volkswagen bug drove by. He hit the freeze button.

'That's our car?' York asked.

'A 1971 Volkswagen Beetle. One of our experts says he can tell by the MacPherson strut front suspension and front luggage compartment. More important, this type of car matches the carpet fibers we found on Mr. Santiago's clothing.'

'Hot damn,' Dillon said.

'Can you make out the license plate?' York asked.

'No. We only get a side view. Not a partial, not even the state.'

'But how many original Volkswagen bugs in yellow can there be on the road?' York said. 'We start with the New York motor vehicle records, move to New Jersey and Connecticut.'

Dillon nodded and talked while chewing like a cow. 'We should get some kind of hit.'

York turned back to Reynolds. 'Anything else?'

'Dillon was right, the quality isn't great. But if I blow this up' – he hit a button and the picture zoomed – 'we can get a partial look at the guy.'

Dillon squinted. 'He looks like Jerry Garcia or something.'

'Long gray hair, long gray beard,' Reynolds agreed.

'That it?'

'That's it.'

York said to Dillon, 'Let's start checking the motor vehicles record. This car can't be that hard to find.'

Chapter 34

Sheriff Lowell's accusations echoed in the still of the woods.

Lowell, nobody's fool, thought Paul Copeland had lied about the murders.

Had he? Did it matter?

Muse thought about that. She liked Cope, no question. He was a great boss and a damned good prosecutor. But now Lowell's words had brought her back. They reminded her of what she already knew: This was a homicide case. Like any other. It leads where it leads, even if that means back to her boss.

No favorites.

A few minutes later a noise came from the brush. Muse spotted Andrew Barrett. Barrett made lanky an art form, all long limbs and elbows and awkward, jerky movements. He was dragging what looked like a baby carriage behind him. It had to be the XJR. Muse called out to him. Barrett looked up, clearly displeased with the interruption. When he saw who it was, his face lit up.

'Hey, Muse!'

'Andrew.'

'Wow, great to see you.'

'Uh-huh,' she said. 'What are you doing?'

'What do you mean, what am I doing?' He put the machine down. There were three young people in John Jay sweatshirts trudging along beside him – students, she assumed. 'I'm looking for graves.'

'I thought you found something.'

'I did. It's up ahead another hundred yards. But I thought there were two bodies missing, so I figured, hey, why rest on my laurels, you know what I'm saying?'

Muse swallowed. 'You found a body?'

Barrett's face had a fervor usually reserved for tent revivals.

'Muse, this machine. Oh my, it's just amazing. We got lucky, of course. There hasn't been any rain in this area in, I don't know, how long, Sheriff?'

'Two, three weeks,' Lowell said.

'See, that helps. A lot. Dry ground. You know anything about how ground-penetrating radar works? I stuck an 800 MHz on this baby. That lets me go down only four feet – but what a four feet! Most of the time, they look too deep. But very few killers dig beyond three, four feet. The other problem is, the current machines have trouble differentiating between like-size items. Like, say, a pipe or deep roots versus what we want – bones. The XJR not only gets you clearer cross-sectional underground images of the soil, but with the new 3-D enhancer—'

'Barrett?' Muse said.

He pushed up his glasses. 'What?'

'Do I look like I give the smallest rat's buttock how your toy works?'

He pushed the glasses up again. 'Uh . . .'

354

'I just care that your toy works. So please tell me what you found before I shoot someone?'

'Bones, Muse,' he said with a smile. 'We found bones.'

'Human, right?'

'Definitely. In fact, the first thing we found was a skull. That's when we stopped digging. The pros are excavating now.'

'How old are they?'

'What, the bones?'

'No, Barrett, that oak tree. Yes, the bones.'

'How the hell would I know? The coroner might have an idea. She's at the site now.'

Muse hurried past him. Lowell followed. Up ahead she could make out big spotlights, almost like a movie set. She knew that lots of excavation teams used powerful voltage even when they were digging in the direct sunlight. As one crime-scene-unit guy had told her, bright lights help differentiate the flotsam from the gold: 'Without the bright lights, it's like judging how hot a chick is by being drunk in a dark bar. You may think you have something, but in the morning, you want to bite your arm off.'

Lowell pointed toward an attractive woman wearing rubber gloves. Muse figured it was another student – she couldn't have been thirty years old. She had long, cave black hair perfectly pulled back, like a flamenco dancer.

'That's Doc O'Neill,' Lowell said.

'She's your coroner?'

'Yep. You know it's an elected position out here?'

'You mean they have campaigns and stuff? Like, hi, I'm Doctor O'Neill, I'm really good with the dead'?'

'I'd make a witty comeback,' Lowell said, 'but you city slickers are too clever for us yokels.'

As Muse got closer, she could see that 'attractive' may have been understating it. Tara O'Neill was a knockout. Muse could see that her looks were something of a distraction to the crew too. The coroner is not in charge of a crime scene. The police are. But everyone kept sneaking glances at O'Neill. Muse stepped quickly toward her.

'I'm Loren Muse, chief investigator for Essex County.'

The woman offered the glove hand. 'Tara O'Neill, coroner.'

'What can you tell me about the body?'

She looked wary for a second, but Lowell nodded that it was okay. 'Are you the one who sent Mr. Barrett out here?' O'Neill asked.

'I am.'

'Interesting fellow.'

'As I'm well aware.'

'That machine works, though. I don't know how on earth he found these bones. But he's good. I think it helped that they ran over the skull first.'

O'Neill blinked and looked away.

'There a problem?' Muse asked.

She shook her head. 'I grew up in this area. I used to play right here, right over this spot. You'd think, I don't know, you'd think I would have felt a chill or something. But nope, nothing.'

Muse tapped her foot, waited.

'I was ten when those teens vanished. My friends and I used to hike out here, you know? We'd light fires. We'd make up stories about how the two kids who were never found were still out here, watching us, that they were the undead or whatever, and that they were going to hunt us down and kill us. It was stupid. Just a way of getting your boyfriend to give you his jacket and put his arm around you.'

Tara O'Neill smiled and shook her head.

'Doctor O'Neill?'

'Yes.'

'Please tell me what you found here.'

'We're still working on it, but from what I can see we have a fairly complete skeleton. It was found three feet down. I'll need to get the bones to the lab to make a positive ID.'

'What can you tell me now?'

'Come this way.'

She walked Muse over to the other side of the dig. The bones were tagged and laid out on a blue tarmac.

'No clothing?' Muse said.

'None.'

'Did they disintegrate or was the body buried naked?'

'I can't say for sure. But since there are no coins or jewelry or buttons or zippers or even footwear – that usually lasts a very long time – my guess would be naked.'

Muse just stared at the brown skull. 'Cause of death?'

'Too early to tell. But there are some things we know.'

'Such as?'

'The bones are in pretty bad shape. They weren't buried all that deep and they've been here awhile.'

'How long?'

'It's hard to say. I took a seminar last year on crime-scene soil sampling. You can tell by the way the ground has been disturbed how long ago the hole was dug. But that's very preliminary.'

'Anything? A guesstimate?'

'The bones have been here awhile. My best estimate would be at least fifteen years. In short – and to answer the question on your mind – it is consistent, *very* consistent, with the time frame of the murders that took place in these woods twenty years ago.'

Muse swallowed and asked the real question that she'd wanted to ask from the beginning.

'Can you tell gender? Can you tell me if the bones belong to someone male or female?'

A deep voice interrupted, 'Uh, Doc?'

It was one of the crime-scene guys, complete with the prerequisite windbreaker announcing such. He was husky with a thick beard and a thicker midsection. He had a small hand shovel and was breathing the labored breath of the out-of-shape.

'What's up, Terry?' O'Neill asked.

'I think we got it all.'

'You want to pack it in?'

'For tonight, yeah, I think. We might want to come out tomorrow, check for more. But we'd like to transport the body now, if that's okay with you.'

'Give me two minutes,' O'Neill said.

Terry nodded and left them alone. Tara O'Neill kept her eyes on the bones.

'Do you know anything about the human skeleton, Investigator Muse?'

'Some.'

'Without a thorough examination, it can be pretty difficult to tell the difference between the male and female skeleton. One of the things we go by is the size and density of the bones. Males have a tendency to be thicker and larger, of course. Sometimes the actual height of the victim can help – males are usually taller. But those things often aren't definitive.'

'Are you saying you don't know?'

O'Neill smiled. 'I'm not saying that at all. Let me show you.'

Tara O'Neill got down on her haunches. So did Muse. O'Neill had a thin flashlight in her hand, the kind that casts a narrow but potent beam.

'I said, pretty difficult. Not impossible. Take a look.' She pointed her light toward the skull.

'Do you know what you're looking at?'

'No,' Muse said.

'First off, the bones appear to be on the lighter side. Second, check out the spot below where the eyebrows would have been.'

'Okay.'

'That's technically known as the supraorbital ridge. It's more pronounced in males. Females have very vertical foreheads. Now, this skull has been worn down, but you can see the ridge is not pronounced. But the real key – what I want to show you down here – is in the pelvis area, more specifically, the pelvic cavity.'

She shifted the flashlight. 'Do you see it there?'

'Yeah, I see it, I guess. So?'

'It's pretty wide.'

'Which means?'

Tara O'Neill snapped off the flashlight.

'Which means,' O'Neill said, getting back to her feet, 'that your victim is Caucasian, about five-foot-seven – the same height as Camille Copeland, by the way – and yes, female.'

Dillon said, 'You're not going to believe this.'

York looked up. 'What?'

'I got a computer hit on that Volkswagen. There are only fourteen in the tristate area that fit the bill. But here's the kicker. One is registered to a guy named Ira Silverstein. That name ring a bell?'

'Isn't he the guy who owned that camp?'

'That's it.'

'Are you telling me that Copeland might have been right all along?'

'I got the address where this Ira Silverstein is staying,' Dillon said. 'Some kind of rehab place.'

'So what are we waiting for?' York said. 'Let's haul ass.'

Chapter 35

When Lucy got into the car, I pressed the button for the CD player. Bruce's 'Back In Your Arms' came on. She smiled. 'You burned it already?'

'I did.'

'You like it?'

'Very much. I added a few others. A bootleg from one of Springsteen's solo shows. 'Drive All Night."

'That song always makes me cry.'

'All songs make you cry,' I said.

'Not "Super Freak" by Rick James.'

'I stand corrected.'

'And "Promiscuous." That one doesn't make me cry.'

'Even when Nelly sings, 'Is your game MVP like Steve Nash?"

'God, you know me so well.'

I smiled.

'You seem calm for a man who just learned that his dead sister might be alive.'

'Partitioning.'

'Is that a word?'

'It's what I do. I put things in different boxes. It's how I get through the craziness. I just put it somewhere else for a while.'

'Partitioning,' Lucy said.

'Exactly.'

'We psychological types have another term for partitioning,' Lucy said. 'We call it "Big-Time Denial."'

'Call it what you will. There's a flow here now, Luce. We're going to find Camille. She's going to be okay.'

'We psychological types have another term for that too. We call it "Wishful or even Delusional Thinking."'

We drove some more.

'What could your father possibly remember now?' I asked.

'I don't know. But we know that Gil Perez visited him. My guess is, that visit stirred something in Ira's head. I don't know what. It might be nothing. He's not well. It might be something he imagined or even made up.'

We parked in a spot near Ira's Volkswagen Beetle. Funny seeing that old car. It should have brought me back. He used to drive it around the camp all the time. He would stick his head out and smile and make little deliveries. He would let cabins decorate it and pretend it was leading a parade. But right now the old Volkswagen did nothing for me.

My partitioning was breaking down.

Because I had hope.

I had hope that I would find my sister. I had hope that I was truly connecting with a woman for the first time since Jane died, that I could feel my heart beating next to someone else's.

I tried to warn myself. I tried to remember that hope was the cruelest of all mistresses, that it could crush your soul like a Styrofoam cup. But right now I didn't want to go there. I wanted the hope. I wanted to hold on to it and just let it make me feel light for a little while.

I looked at Lucy. She smiled and I felt it rip open my chest. It had been so long since I felt like this, felt that heady rush. Then I surprised myself. I reached out with both my hands and took her face in my hands. Her smile disappeared. Her eyes searched for mine. I tilted her head up and kissed her so softly that it almost hurt. I felt a jolt. I heard her gasp. She kissed me back.

I felt happily shattered by her.

Lucy lowered her head onto my chest. I heard her sob softly. I let her. I stroked her hair and fought back the swirl. I don't know how long we sat like that. Could have been five minutes, could have been fifteen. I just don't know.

'You better go in,' she said.

'You're going to stay here?'

'Ira made it clear. You, alone. I'll probably start up his car, make sure the battery is still charged.'

I didn't kiss her again. I got out and floated up the path. The setting for the house was peaceful and green. The mansion was Georgian brick, I guessed, almost perfectly rectangular with white columns in the front. It reminded me of an upscale fraternity house.

There was a woman at the desk. I gave her my name. She asked me to sign in. I did. She placed a call and spoke in a whisper. I waited, listening to the Muzak version of something by Neil Sedaka, which was a little bit like listening to a Muzak version of Muzak.

A redheaded woman dressed in civilian clothes came down to see me. She wore a skirt and had glasses dangling on her chest. She looked like a nurse trying not to look like a nurse.

'I'm Rebecca,' she said.

'Paul Copeland.'

'I'll bring you to Mr. Silverstein.'

'Thank you.'

I expected her to lead me down the corridor, but we walked through the back and straight outside. The gardens were well tended. It was a little early for landscape lights, but they were on. A thick row of hedges surrounded the premises like guard dogs.

I spotted Ira Silverstein right away.

He had changed and yet he hadn't changed at all. You know people like that. They get older, they gray, they widen, they slump, and yet they are exactly the same. That was how it was with Ira.

'Ira?'

No one ever used last names at camp. The adults were Aunt and Uncle, but I just couldn't see calling him Uncle Ira anymore.

He wore a poncho I'd last seen in a Woodstock documentary. He had sandals on his feet. Ira stood slowly and put his arms out toward me. Camp had been that way too. Everyone hugged. Everyone loved each other. It was all very 'Kumbaya.' I stepped into his embrace. He held me tight, with all his strength. I could feel his beard against my cheek.

He let go of me and said to Rebecca, 'Leave us alone.'

Rebecca turned away. He led me to a park bench of cement and green wood. We sat.

'You look the same, Cope,' he said.

He'd remembered my nickname. 'So do you.'

'You'd think the hard years would show on our faces more, wouldn't you?'

'I guess so, Ira.'

'So what do you do now?'

'I'm the county prosecutor.'

'Really?'

'Yes.'

He frowned. 'That's kind of establishment.'

Still Ira.

'I'm not prosecuting antiwar protestors,' I assured him. 'I go after murderers and rapists. People like that.'

He squinted. 'Is that why you're here?'

'What?'

'Are you trying to find murderers and rapists?'

I didn't know what to make of that so I went with the flow. 'In a way, I guess. I'm trying to learn what happened that night in the woods.'

Ira's eyes closed.

'Lucy said you wanted to see me,' I said.

'Yes.'

'Why?'

'I want to know why you've come back.'

'I never went anywhere.'

'You broke Lucy's heart, you know.'

'I wrote her. I tried to call. She wouldn't call me back.'

'Still. She was in pain.'

'I never meant for that to happen.'

'So why are you back now?'

'I want to find out what happened to my sister.'

'She was murdered. Like the others.'

'No, she wasn't.'

He said nothing. I decided to press a little.

'You know that, Ira. Gil Perez came here, didn't he?'

Ira smacked his lips. 'Dry.'

'What?'

'I'm dry. I used to have this friend from Cairns. That's

in Australia. Coolest dude I ever knew. He used to say, 'A man is not a camel, mate.' That was his way of asking for a drink.'

Ira grinned.

'I don't think you can get a drink out here, Ira.'

'Oh, I know. I was never much of a booze man anyway. What they now call 'recreational drugs' was more my bag. But I meant water. They got some Poland Spring in that cooler. Did you know that Poland Spring comes to you straight from Maine?'

He laughed and I didn't correct him on that old radio commercial. He stood and stumbled toward the right. I followed. There was a trunk-shaped cooler with a New York Rangers logo on it. He opened the lid, grabbed a bottle, handed it to me, grabbed another. He twisted off the cap and chugged. The water spilled down his face, turning the white of his beard into something darker gray.

'Ahhhh,' he said when he finished.

I tried to get him back on track.

'You told Lucy that you wanted to see me.'

'Yes.'

'Why?'

'Because you're here.'

I waited for more.

'I'm here,' I said slowly, 'because you asked to see me.'

'Not here here. Here, as in back in our lives.'

'I told you. I'm trying to find out – '

'Why now?'

That question again.

'Because,' I said, 'Gil Perez didn't die that night. He came back. He visited you, didn't he?'

Ira's eyes took on that thousand-yard stare. He started to walk. I caught up with him.

'Was he here, Ira?'

'He didn't use that name,' he said.

He kept walking. I noticed that he limped. His face pinched up in pain.

'Are you okay?' I asked him.

'I need to walk.'

'Where?'

'There are paths. In the woods. Come.'

'Ira, I'm not here – '

'He said his name was Manolo something. But I knew who he was. Little Gilly Perez. Do you remember him? From those days, I mean?'

'Yes.'

Ira shook his head. 'Nice boy. But so easily manipulated.'

'What did he want?'

'He didn't tell me who he was. Not at first. He didn't really look the same but there was something in his mannerisms, you know? You can hide stuff. You can gain weight. But Gil still had that soft lisp. He still moved the same. Like he was wary all the time. You know what I mean?'

'I do.'

I had thought the yard was fenced in, but it wasn't. Ira slipped past a break in the hedges. I followed. There was a wooded hill in front of us. Ira started trudging up the path.

'Are you allowed to leave?'

'Of course. I'm here on a voluntary basis. I can come and go as I please.'

He kept walking.

'What did Gil say to you?' I asked.

'He wanted to know what happened that night.'

'He didn't know?'

'He knew some. He wanted to know more.'

'I don't understand.'

'You don't have to.'

'Yes, Ira, I do.'

'It's over. Wayne is in prison.'

'Wayne didn't kill Gil Perez.'

'I thought he did.'

I didn't quite get that one. He was moving faster now, limping along in obvious pain. I wanted to call him to stop, but his mouth was also moving.

'Did Gil mention my sister?'

He stopped for a second. His smile was sad. 'Camille.'

'Yes.'

'Poor thing.'

'Did he mention her?'

'I loved your dad, you know. Such a sweet man, so hurt by life.'

'Did Gil mention what happened to my sister?'

'Poor Camille.'

'Yes. Camille. Did he say anything about her?'

Ira started to climb again. 'So much blood that night.'

'Please, Ira, I need you to focus. Did Gil say anything at all about Camille?'

'No.'

'Then what did he want?'

'Same as you.'

'What's that?'

He turned. 'Answers.'

'To what questions?'

'The same as yours. What happened that night. He didn't understand, Cope. It's over. They're dead. The killer is in jail. You should let the dead rest.'

'Gil wasn't dead.'

'Until that day, the day he visited me, he was. Do you understand?'

'No.'

'It's over. The dead are gone. The living are safe.'

I reached out and grabbed his arm. 'Ira, what did Gil Perez say to you?'

'You don't understand.'

We stopped. Ira looked down the hill. I followed his gaze. I could only make out the roof of the house now. We were in the thick of the woods. Both of us were breathing harder than we should. Ira's face was pale.

'It has to stay buried.'

'What does?'

'That's what I told Gil. It was over. Move on. It was so long ago. He was dead. Now he wasn't. But he should have been.'

'Ira, listen to me. What did Gil say to you?'

'You won't leave it alone, will you?'

'No,' I said, 'I won't leave it alone.'

Ira nodded. He looked very sad. Then he reached underneath his poncho and pulled out a gun, aimed it in my direction, and without saying another word, he fired at me.

Chapter 36

'What we have here is a problem.'

Sheriff Lowell wiped his nose with a handkerchief that looked large enough to be a clown's prop. His station was more modern than what Muse had expected, but then again her expectations weren't high. The building was new, the design sleek and clean with computer monitors and cubicles. Lots of whites and grays.

'What you have here,' Muse replied, 'is a dead body.'

'That's not what I mean.' He gestured toward the cup in her hand. 'How's the coffee?'

'Outstanding, actually.'

'Used to be crap. Some guys made it too strong, some too weak. It got left on the burner forever. And then last year, one of the fine citizens of this municipality donated one of those coffee pod machines to the station. You ever use one of those things, the pods?'

'Sheriff?'

'Yes.'

'Is this your attempt at wooing me with your aw-shucks, homespun charm?'

He grinned. 'A little.'

'Consider me wooed. What's our problem?'

'We just found a body that's been in the woods, by early estimates, a pretty long time. We know three things: Caucasian, female, height of five-seven. That's all we know for now. I have already combed through the records. There were no missing or unaccounted girls within a fifty-mile radius who match that description.'

'We both know who it is,' Muse said.

'Not yet we don't.'

'You think, what, another five-foot seven-inch girl was murdered in that camp around the same time and buried near the other two bodies?'

'I didn't say that.'

'Then what did you say?'

'That we don't have a definite ID. Doc O'Neill is working on it. We've ordered Camille Copeland's dental records. We should know for sure in a day or two. No rush. We have other cases.'

'No rush?'

'That's what I said.'

'Then I'm not following.'

'See, this is where I have to wonder, Investigator Muse – what are you first and foremost? Are you a law enforcement office or a political crony?'

'What the hell does that mean?'

'You're the county chief investigator,' Lowell said. 'Now, I'd like to believe a person, especially a lady your age, reached that level based on her talent and skill. But I also live in the real world. I understand graft and favoritism and ass kissing. So I'm asking—'

'I earned it.'

'I'm sure you did.'

Muse shook her head. 'I can't believe I have to justify myself to you.'

'But, alas, my dear, you do. Because right now, if this was your case and I came waltzing in and you knew that I was going to run right home and tell my boss – someone who was, at the very least, involved – what would you do?'

'You think I'd sweep his involvement under the rug?'

Lowell shrugged. 'Again: If I was, say, the deputy here and I was given my job by the sheriff who was involved in your murder, what would you think?'

Muse sat back. 'Fair enough,' she said. 'So what can I do to comfort you?'

'You can let me take my time identifying the body.'

'You don't want Copeland to know what we found?'

'He's waited twenty years. What's another day or two?'

Muse understood where he was going with this.

'I want to do right by the investigation,' she said, 'but I don't much relish lying to a man I trust and like.'

'Life's tough, Investigator Muse.'

She frowned.

'Something else I want too,' Lowell went on. 'I need you to tell me why that Barrett guy was out there with that little toy of his looking for long-dead bodies.'

'I told you. They wanted to test this machine in the field.'

'You work in Newark, New Jersey. Are you telling me there are no possible burial sites in that area you could have sent them to?'

He was right, of course. Time to come clean.

'A man was found murdered in New York City,' Muse said. 'My boss thinks it was Gil Perez.'

Lowell dropped the poker face. 'Come again?'

She was about to explain when Tara O'Neill rushed in. Lowell looked annoyed by the interruption but he kept his voice neutral. 'What's up, Tara?'

'I found something on the body,' she said. 'Something important, I think.'

After Cope left the car, Lucy sat alone for a good five minutes with the trace of a smile on her lips. She was still swimming from his kiss. She had never experienced anything like that, the way his big hands held her face, the way he looked at her . . . it was as though her heart had not only started beating again but had taken flight.

It was wonderful. It was scary.

She checked through his CD collection, found one by Ben Folds, put on the song 'Brick.' She had never been sure what the song was about – a drug overdose, an abortion, a mental collapse – but in the end, the woman is a brick and she's drowning him.

Sad music was better than drinking, she guessed. But not much.

As she turned off the engine, she saw a green car, a Ford with New York license plates, pull up right to the front of the building. The car parked in the spot that read no parking. Two men got out – one tall, one built like a square – and strolled inside. Lucy didn't know what to make of it. It was probably nothing.

The keys to Ira's Beetle were in her bag. She rummaged through the purse and found them. She jammed a piece of gum in her mouth. If Cope kissed her again, she'd be damned if bad breath was going to be a factor.

She wondered what Ira was going to say to Cope. She wondered what Ira even remembered. They had never talked about that night, father and daughter. Not once. They should have. It might have changed everything. Then again it might have changed nothing. The dead would still be dead, the living still living. Not a particularly deep thought, but there you go.

She got out of the car and started toward the old Volkswagen. She held the key in her hand and pointed it toward the car. Odd what you get used to. No cars today open with a key. They all have the remote. The Beetle didn't, of course. She put the key into the lock on the driver side and turned it. It was rusted and she had to twist hard but the lock popped up.

She thought about how she had lived her life, about the mistakes she'd made. She'd talked to Cope about that feeling of being pushed that night, of tumbling down a hill and not knowing how to stop. It was true. He had tried to find her over the years, but she had stayed hidden. Maybe she should have contacted him earlier. Maybe she should have tried to work through what happened that night right away. Instead you bury it. You refuse to face it. You're scared of confrontation so you find other ways to hide – Lucy's being the most common, in the bottom of the bottle. People don't go to the bottle to escape.

They go to hide.

She slid into the driver's seat and immediately realized that something was wrong.

The first visual clue was on the floor of the passenger seat. She looked down and frowned.

A soda can.

Diet Coke to be more exact.

She picked it up. There was still some liquid in it. She thought about that. How long had it been since she'd been in the Beetle? Three, four weeks at least. There hadn't been a can then. Or if there had, she had missed it. That was a possibility.

That was when the smell hit her.

She remembered something that happened in the woods near camp when she was about twelve. Ira had taken her for a walk. They heard gunshots and Ira had totally freaked. Hunters had invaded their land. He found them and started yelling that this was private property. One of the hunters had started yelling back. He got close to them, bumping Ira's chest, and Lucy remembered that he smelled horrible.

She smelled that now.

Lucy turned and looked in the backseat.

There was blood on the floor.

And then, in the distance, she heard a crack of gunfire.

The skeletal remains were laid out on a silver table with tiny holes in it. The holes made it easier to clean by simply spraying it with a hose. The floor was tile and tilted toward a drain in the center, like the shower room at a health club, which also made it easier to get rid of debris. Muse didn't want to think what got caught up in such drains, what they used to clean it out, if Drāno did any good at all or if they had to use something stronger.

Lowell stood on one side of the table, Muse on the other with Tara O'Neill.

'So what's up?' Lowell asked.

'First off, we're missing some bones. I'll go out later and take another look. Small stuff, nothing major. That's normal in a case like this. I was about to run some X-rays, check the ossification centers, especially up at the clavicle.'

'What will that tell us?'

'It gives us an idea of age. Bones stop growing as we get older. The last place of ossification is up there, pretty much where the clavicle meets the sternum. The process stops around the age of twenty-one. But that's not important right now.'

Lowell looked at Muse. Muse shrugged.

'So what's the big thing you found?'

'This.'

O'Neill pointed to the pelvis.

Muse said, 'You showed me that before. That's the proof that the skeleton belonged to a female.'

'Well, yes. The pelvis is wider, like I said before. Plus we have the less prominent ridge and smaller bone density – all the signs that she's female. There is no doubt in my mind. We are looking at the skeletal remains of a female.'

'So what are you showing us?'

'The pubic bone.'

'What about it?'

'You see here? We call this notching – or better, the pitting of the pubic bones.'

'Okay.'

'Cartilage holds bones together. That's basic anatomy. You probably know this. We mostly think of cartilage in terms of the knee or elbow. It's elastic. It stretches. But you see this? The marks on the face of the pubic bone? That's formed on the cartilaginous surface where the bones once met and then separated.'

O'Neill looked up at them. Her face was glowing.

'Are you following me?'

Muse said, 'No.'

'The notches are formed when the cartilage is strained. When the pubic bones separate.'

Muse looked at Lowell. Lowell shrugged.

'And that means?' Muse tried.

'That means that at some point in her life, the bones separated. And that means, Investigator Muse, that your victim gave birth.'

Chapter 37

Things do not slow down when you have a gun pointed at you.

To the contrary, they speed up. When Ira pointed the gun at me, I expected to have time to react. I started to raise my hands, the primitive demonstration of being harmless. My mouth began to open to try to talk my way through this, to tell him I would cooperate and do what he wanted. My heart raced, my breathing stopped, and my eyes could only see the gun, nothing but the opening of that barrel, the giant black hole now facing me.

But I didn't have time for any of that. I didn't have time to ask Ira why. I didn't have time to ask him what had happened to my sister, if she was alive or dead, how Gil had gotten out of the woods that night, if Wayne Steubens was involved or not. I didn't have time to tell Ira that he was right, I should have let it lie, I would let it lie now and we could all go back to our lives.

I had no time to do any of that.

Because Ira was already pulling the trigger.

A year ago I read a book called *Blink* by Malcolm Gladwell. I don't dare simplify his arguments but part of what he says is that we need to rely on our instincts more – the animal part of our brain that will automatically jump out of the way if a truck is bearing down on us. He also notes that we make snap judgments, sometimes seemingly based on little evidence, what we used to call hunches, and that they are often right. Maybe that was at work here. Maybe something in Ira's stance or the way he pulled out the gun or whatever made me realize that there would indeed be no talking to him, that he was going to fire and that I was going to die.

Something made me jump right away.

But the bullet still hit me.

He had aimed for the center of my chest. The bullet hit my side, ripping across my waist like a hot lance. I fell hard on my side and tried to roll behind a tree. Ira fired again. He missed this time. I kept rolling.

My hand found a rock. I didn't really think. I just picked it up and, still rolling, threw it in his direction. It was a pitiful move, born out of desperation, something a child lying on his stomach might try.

The throw had no power behind it. The rock hit him but I don't think it mattered. I realized now that this had been Ira's plan all along. This was why he wanted to see me alone. This was why he had taken me into the woods. He wanted to shoot me.

Ira, that seemingly gentle soul, was a killer.

I looked behind me. He was too close. I flashed to that scene in the original *In-Laws* movie, a comedy where Alan Arkin is told to avoid bullets by running 'serpentine.' That wouldn't work here. The man was only six, eight feet away. He had a gun. I was already hit, could feel the blood leaking out of me.

I was going to die.

We were stumbling down the hill, me still rolling, Ira trying not to fall, trying to gain enough balance to take another shot. I knew he would. I knew I only had a few seconds.

My only chance was to reverse direction.

I grabbed the ground and made myself break. Ira was caught off balance. He tried to slow. I grabbed a tree with both hands and whipped my legs toward him. It, too, was a pathetic move, I thought, a bad gymnast on a pommel horse. But Ira was just within striking range and just enough off balance. My feet hit against the side of his right ankle. Not all that hard. But hard enough.

Ira let out a shout and tumbled to the ground.

The gun, I thought. Get the gun.

I scrambled toward him. I was bigger. I was younger. I was in much better condition. He was an old man, his brain half-fried. He could fire a gun, sure. There was still power in his arms and his legs. But the years and the drug abuse had slowed the reflexes down.

I climbed on top of him, searching for the gun. It had been in his right hand. I went for that arm. *Think arm. Only arm.* I grabbed it with both my hands, rolled my body on it, pinned it down and then bent it back.

The hand was empty.

I had been so preoccupied with the right hand that I never saw the left coming. He swung in a long arc. The gun must have dropped when he fell. He had it now in his left hand, gripping it like a rock. He crashed the butt against my forehead.

It was like a lightning bolt had seared through my skull. I could feel my brain jerk to the right, as though ripped from its moor, and start to rattle. My body convulsed.

I let go of him.

I looked up. He had the gun pointed at me.

'Freeze, police!'

I recognized the voice. It was York.

The air stopped, crackled. I moved my gaze from the gun to Ira's eyes. We were that close, the gun pointed straight at my face. And I saw it. He was going to shoot and kill me. They wouldn't get to him in time. The police were here now. It was over for him. He had to know that. But he was going to shoot me anyway.

'Dad! No!'

It was Lucy. He heard her voice and something in those eyes changed.

'Drop the gun now! Do it! Now!'

York again. My eyes were still locked on Ira's.

Ira kept his eyes on me. 'Your sister is dead,' he said.

Then he turned the gun away from me, put it in his own mouth and pulled the trigger.

Chapter 38

passed out.

That was what I was told. I do have dim memories, though. I remember Ira falling on me, the back of his head gone. I remember hearing Lucy scream. I remember looking up, seeing the blue sky, watching the clouds fly by me. I assume I was on my back, on a stretcher, being taken to the ambulance. That was where the memories stopped. With the blue sky. With the white clouds.

And then, when I started to feel almost peaceful and calm, I remembered Ira's words.

Your sister is dead . . .

I shook my head. No. Glenda Perez had told me that Camille had walked out of those woods. Ira wouldn't know. He couldn't.

'Mr. Copeland?'

I blinked my eyes open. I was in a bed. A hospital room.

'My name is Dr. McFadden.'

I let my gaze travel the room. I saw York behind him.

'You were shot in the side. We stitched you up. You're going to be fine, but there will be soreness – '

'Doc?'

McFadden had been using his best doctor singsong, not expecting such an early interruption. He frowned. 'Yes?'

'I'm okay, right?'

'Yes.'

'Then can we talk about this later? I really need to speak to that officer.'

York hid a smile. I expected an argument. Doctors are even more arrogant than attorneys. But he didn't give me one. He shrugged and said, 'Sure. Have the nurse page me when you're done.'

'Thanks, Doc.'

He left without another word. York moved closer to the bed.

'How did you know about Ira?' I asked.

'The lab guys matched carpet fibers found on the body of, uh . . .' York's voice drifted off. 'Well, we still don't have an ID but if you want we can call him Gil Perez.'

'That would be good.'

'Right, anyway, they found these carpet fibers on him. We knew that they came from an old car. We also found a security camera that was near where the body was dumped. We saw it was a yellow Volkswagen, matched it to Silverstein. So we hurried over.'

'Where's Lucy?'

'Dillon's asking her some questions.'

'I don't get it. Ira killed Gil Perez?'

'Yep.'

'No question?'

'None. First off, we found blood in the backseat of the Volkswagen. My guess is, it'll match Perez. Two, the staff at that halfway house confirmed that Perez – signing in as Manolo Santiago – visited Silverstein the day before the murder. The staff also confirmed that they saw Silverstein leave in the Volkswagen the next morning. First time he'd been out in six months.'

I made a face. 'They didn't think to tell his daughter?'

'Staff who saw him weren't on duty the next time Lucy Gold came in. Plus, hey, as the staff told me repeatedly, Silverstein has never been declared incompetent or anything like that. He was free to come and go as he pleased.'

'I don't get it. Why would Ira kill him?'

'The same reason he wanted to kill you, I guess. You were both looking into what happened at that camp twenty years ago. Mr. Silverstein didn't want that.'

I tried to put it together. 'So he killed Margot Green and Doug Billingham?'

York waited a second, as though expecting me to add my sister to the list. I didn't.

'Could be.'

'And what about Wayne Steubens?'

'They probably worked together somehow, I don't know. What I do know is, Ira Silverstein killed my guy. Oh, another thing: the gun Ira shot you with? It's the same caliber as the one used to shoot Gil Perez. We're running a ballistic test now, but you know it'll be a match. So you add that to the blood in the backseat of the Beetle, the surveillance tapes of him and the vehicle near where the body was dumped off . . . I mean, come on, it's overkill. But hey, Ira Silverstein is dead, and as you know, it is very difficult to try a dead man. As for what Ira Silverstein did or didn't do twenty years ago' – York shrugged – 'hey, I'm curious too. But that's someone else's mystery to solve.'

'You'll help, if we need it?'

'Sure. Love to. And when you do figure it all out, why don't you come into the city and I'll take you for a steak dinner?'

'Deal.'

We shook hands.

'I should thank you for saving my life,' I said.

'Yeah, you should. Except I don't think I did.'

I remembered the look on Ira's face, his determination to kill me. York had seen it too – Ira was going to shoot me, consequences be damned. Lucy's voice had been what saved me more than York's gun.

York left then. I was alone in a hospital room. There are probably more depressing places to be alone, but I couldn't think of one. I thought about my Jane, how brave she was, how the only thing that really scared her, terrified her, was being alone in a hospital room. So I stayed all night. I slept in one of those chairs that can be made into the most uncomfortable bed on God's green earth. I don't say that to get applause. It was Jane's one moment of weakness, the first overnight at the hospital, when she grabbed my hand and tried to keep the desperation out of her voice when she said, 'Please don't leave me alone here.'

So I didn't. Not then. Not until much later, when she was back home, where she wanted to die because the thought of being back in a room like the one I'm in now . . .

Now it was my turn. I was alone here. It didn't scare me too much. I thought about that, about where my life had taken me. Who would be here for me in a crisis? Who could I expect to be at my bedside when I woke up in a hospital? The first names that popped into my head: Greta and Bob. When I cut my hand last year slicing open a bagel, Bob had driven me, Greta had taken care of Cara. They were family – the only family I had left. And now they were gone.

I remembered the last time I was hospitalized. When I was twelve years old I came down with rheumatic fever. It was pretty rare then, even rarer now. I spent ten days in the hospital. I remember Camille visiting. Sometimes she brought her annoying friends because she knew that would distract me. We played Boggle a lot. Boys loved Camille. She used to bring the cassette tapes they made for her – groups like Steely Dan and Supertramp and the Doobie Brothers. Camille told me what groups were great, what groups were lame, and I followed her taste as though it were biblical.

Did she suffer out in those woods?

That was what I'd always wondered. What did Wayne Steubens do to her? Did he tie her up and terrify her, like he did with Margot Green? Did she struggle and suffer defensive wounds like Doug Billingham? Did he bury her alive, like those victims in Indiana or Virginia? How much pain had Camille been in? How terrifying were her last moments?

And now . . . the new question: Had Camille somehow gotten out of those woods alive?

I turned my thoughts to Lucy. I thought about what she must be going through, watching her beloved father blow his head off, wondering about the whys and hows of it all. I wanted to reach her, say something, try somehow to comfort her a little.

There was a knock on my door.

'Come in.'

I expected it to be a nurse. It wasn't. It was Muse. I smiled at her. I expected her to smile back. She didn't. Her face couldn't have been more closed.

'Don't look so glum,' I said. 'I'm fine.'

Muse moved closer to the bed. Her expression didn't change.

'I said—'

'I already talked to the doctor. He said you might not even have to stay overnight.'

'So what's with the face?'

Muse grabbed a chair, pulled it next to the bed. 'We need to talk.'

I had seen Loren Muse make this face before.

It was her game face. It was her I'm-gonna-nail-da-bastard face. It was her try-to-lie-and-I'll-spot-it face. I had seen her direct this look at murderers and rapists and carjackers and gangbangers. Now she was aiming at me.

'What's the matter?'

Her expression didn't soften. 'How did it go with Raya Singh?'

'It was pretty much what we thought.' I filled her in briefly because, really, talking about Raya felt almost beside the point at this stage. 'But the big news is, Gil Perez's sister came to see me. She told me Camille was still alive.'

I saw something change in her face. She was good, no doubt, but so was I. They say that a true 'tell' lasts less than a tenth of a second. But I spotted it. She wasn't necessarily surprised by what I said. But it had jolted her nonetheless.

'What's going on, Muse?'

'I talked to Sheriff Lowell today.'

I frowned. 'He hasn't retired yet?'

'No.'

I was going to ask her why she'd reached out to him,

but I knew Muse was thorough. It would be natural for her to have contacted the lead from those murders. It also explained, in part, her behavior toward me.

'Let me guess,' I said. 'He thinks I lied about that night.'

Muse did not say yes or no. 'It is odd, don't you think? You not staying on guard duty the night of the murder.'

'You know why. You read those journals.'

'Yes, I did. You sneaked off with your girlfriend. And then you didn't want to get her in trouble.'

'Right.'

'But those journals also said that you were covered with blood. Is that true too?'

I looked at her. 'What the hell is going on?'

'I'm pretending that you aren't my boss.'

I tried to sit up. The stitch in my side hurt like hell.

'Did Lowell say I was a suspect?'

'He doesn't have to. And you don't have to be a suspect for me to ask these questions. You lied about that night – '

'I was protecting Lucy. You know this already.'

'I know what you've already told me, yes. But put yourself in my position. I need to handle this case with no agenda or bias. If you were me, wouldn't you ask these questions?'

I thought about it. 'I get it, okay, fine, fire away. Ask me whatever you want.'

'Was your sister ever pregnant?'

I just sat there, stunned. The question had hit me like a surprise left hook. Probably her intent.

'Are you serious?'

'I am.'

'Why the hell would you ask that?'

'Just answer the question.'

'No, my sister was never pregnant.'

'Are you sure?'

'I think I'd know.'

'Would you?' she asked.

'I don't understand. Why are you asking me that?'

'We've had cases where girls have hidden it from their families. You know that. Heck, we had a case where the girl herself didn't know until she delivered the baby. Remember?'

I did.

'Look, Muse, I'm pulling rank here. Why are you asking if my sister was pregnant?'

She searched my face, her eyes crawling on me like slimy worms.

'Cut that out,' I said.

'You have to recuse yourself, Cope. You know that.'

'I don't have to do anything.'

'Yeah, you do. Lowell is still running the show. It's his baby.'

'Lowell? That hick hasn't worked on this case since they arrested Wayne Steubens eighteen years ago.'

'Still. It's his case. He's the lead.'

I wasn't sure what to make of this. 'Does Lowell know about Gil Perez being alive this whole time?'

'I told him your theory.'

'So why are you suddenly ambushing me with questions about Camille being pregnant?'

She said nothing.

'Fine, play it that way. Look, I promised Glenda Perez that I would try to keep her family out of it. But tell Lowell about it. Maybe he'll let you stay involved – I trust you a lot more than the backwoods sheriff. The key thing is, Glenda Perez said my sister walked out of those woods alive.'

'And,' Muse said, 'Ira Silverstein said she was dead.'

The room stopped. The tell was more obvious on her face this time. I looked at her hard. She tried to hold my gaze, but eventually she broke.

'What the hell is going on, Muse?'

She stood. The door opened behind her. A nurse entered. With nary a hello, she strapped a blood pressure collar around my arm and started pumping. She stuck a thermometer in my mouth.

Muse said, 'I'll be right back.'

The thermometer was still in my mouth. The nurse took my pulse. The rate had to be off the charts. I tried to call out around the thermometer.

'Muse!'

She left. I stayed in bed and stewed.

Pregnant? Could Camille have been pregnant?

I couldn't see it. I tried to remember. Did she start wearing loose clothes? How long was she pregnant for – how many months? My father would have noticed if she was showing at all – the man was an ob-gyn. She couldn't have hid it from him.

But then again maybe she didn't.

I would say this was nonsense, that it was absolutely impossible that my sister had been pregnant, except for one thing. I didn't know what the hell was going on here, but Muse knew more than she was saying. Her question wasn't haphazard. Sometimes a good prosecutor needs to do that with a case. You need to give the crazy notion the benefit of the doubt. Just to see. Just to see how it could possibly fit.

The nurse finished up. I reached for the phone and dialed home to check up on Cara. I was surprised when Greta answered with a friendly 'Hello.'

'Hi,' I said.

The friendly fled. 'I hear you're going to be fine.'

'That's what they tell me.'

'I'm here with Cara now,' Greta said, all business. 'I can have her stay at my place tonight, if you'd like.'

'That would be great, thanks.'

There was a brief lull.

'Paul?'

She usually called me Cope. I didn't like that. 'Yes?'

'Cara's welfare is very important to me. She is still my niece. She is still the daughter of my sister.'

'I understand that.'

'You, on the other hand, mean nothing to me.'

She hung up the phone.

I sat back and waited for Muse to return, trying to turn it over in my aching head. I went through it step-by-step.

Glenda Perez said my sister walked out of those woods alive.

Ira Silverstein said she was dead.

So who do I believe?

Glenda Perez appeared to be somewhat normal. Ira Silverstein had been a lunatic.

Point: Glenda Perez.

I also realized that Ira had kept talking about wanting things to stay buried. He killed Gil Perez – and was about to kill me – because he wanted us to stop digging. He would have figured that as long as I thought my sister was alive, I would search. I would dig and raze and do whatever was necessary, consequences be damned, if I thought there was a chance I could bring Camille home. Ira clearly didn't want that.

That gave him a motive to lie – to say she was dead.

Glenda Perez, on the other hand, also wanted me to stop digging. As long as I kept my investigation active, her family was in real danger. Their fraud and all the other quasi-crimes she'd listed could be exposed. Ergo, she too would have realized that the best way to get me to back off was to convince me that nothing had changed from twenty years ago, that Wayne Steubens had indeed killed my sister. It would have been in her interest to tell me my sister was dead.

But she didn't do that.

Point: Glenda Perez.

I felt the hope – there was that word again – rise in my chest.

Loren Muse came back into the room. She closed the door behind her. 'I just talked to Sheriff Lowell,' she said.

'Oh?'

'Like I said, it's his case. I couldn't talk about certain things until I got his okay.'

'This is about your pregnancy question?'

Muse sat down as if she were afraid the chair might break. She put her hands in her lap. That was weird for her. Muse usually gestured like an amphetamine-fueled Sicilian who's nearly gotten clipped by a speeding car. I had never seen her so subdued. She had her eyes down. My heart went out to her a little bit. She was trying so hard to do the right thing. She always was.

'Muse?'

She raised her eyes. I didn't like what I saw.

'What's going on here?'

'Do you remember my sending Andrew Barrett up to the campsite?'

'Of course,' I said. 'Barrett wanted to try out some new ground-penetrating radar gizmo. So?'

Muse looked at me. That was all she did. She looked at me and I saw her eyes go wet. Then she nodded at me.

It was the saddest nod I have ever seen.

I felt my world drop with a splat.

Hope. Hope had been gently cradling my heart. Now it spread its talons and crushed it. I couldn't breathe. I shook my head but Muse just kept nodding.

'They found old remains not far from where the other two bodies were found,' she said.

I shook my head harder. Not now. Not after all this.

'Female, five-foot-seven, probably been in the ground between fifteen and thirty years.'

I shook my head some more. Muse stopped, waiting for me to get my bearings. I tried to clear my thoughts, tried not to hear what she was saying. I tried to block, tried to rewind. And then I remembered something.

'Wait, you asked me if Camille was pregnant. Are you saying this body . . . that they can tell that she was pregnant?'

'Not just pregnant,' Muse said. 'She gave birth.'

I just sat there. I tried to take it in. I couldn't. It was one thing to hear that she'd been pregnant. That could have happened. She could have had an abortion or something, I don't know. But that she carried to term, that she delivered a baby, and that now she was dead, after all this . . .

'Find out what happened, Muse.'

'I will.'

'And if there is a baby out there . . .'

'We'll find that too.'

Chapter 39

'I have news.'

Alexei Kokorov was still an impressive, though hideous, specimen. In the late eighties, right before the Wall came down and their lives changed forever, Kokorov had been Sosh's underling at InTourist. It was humorous when you thought about it. They had been elite KGB men back home. In 1974, they'd been in 'Spetsgruppa A' – the Alfa Group. The group was supposedly counterterrorism and crime, but on a cold Christmas morning in 1979, their unit had stormed the Darulaman Palace in Kabul. Not long after that, Sosh had gotten the InTourist job and moved to New York. Kokorov, a man Sosh had never particularly gotten along with, had gone too. They had both left their families behind. This was how it was. New York was seductive. Only the most hardened Soviet would be allowed to go. But even the most hardened needed to be watched by a colleague he didn't necessarily love or trust. Even the most hardened needed to be reminded that there were loved ones back home who could be made to suffer.

'Go on,' Sosh said.

Kokorov was a drunk. He had always been one, but in his youth, it almost worked to his advantage. He was strong and smart and drink made him particularly vicious. He obeyed, like a dog. Now the years had crept up on him. His children were grown and had no use for him. His wife had left him years ago. He was pathetic, but again, he was the past. They had not liked each other, true, but there was still a bond. Kokorov had grown loyal to Sosh. So Sosh kept him on the payroll.

'They found a body in those woods,' Kokorov said.

Sosh closed his eyes. He had not expected this and yet he was not totally surprised. Pavel Copeland wanted to unearth the past. Sosh had hoped to stop him. There are things a man is better off not knowing. Gavrel and Aline, his brother and sister, had been buried in a mass grave. No headstone, no dignity. It had never bothered Sosh. Ashes to ashes and all that. But sometimes he wondered. Sometimes he wondered if Gavrel would rise up one day, point an accusing finger at his little brother, the one who'd stolen an extra bite of bread more than sixty years ago. It was just a bite, Sosh knew. It hadn't changed anything. And yet Sosh still thought about what he'd done, the stolen bite of bread, every morning of his life.

Was that how this was too? The dead crying out for vengeance?

'How did you learn of this?' Sosh asked.

'Since Pavel's visit, I've been watching the local news,' Kokorov said. 'On the Internet. They reported it.'

Sosh smiled. Two old KGB toughies using the American Internet to gather information – ironic.

'What should we do?' Kokorov asked.

'Do?'

'Yes. What should we do?'

'Nothing, Alexei. It was a long time ago.'

'Murder has no statute of limitations in this country. They will investigate.'

'And find what?'

Kokorov said nothing.

'It's over. We have no agency or country to protect anymore.'

Silence. Alexei stroked his chin and looked off.

'What is it?'

Alexei said, 'Do you miss those days, Sosh?'

'I miss my youth,' he said. 'Nothing more.'

'People feared us,' Kokorov said. 'They trembled when we passed.'

'And what, that was a good thing, Alexei?'

His smile was a horrible thing, his teeth too small for his mouth, like a rodent's. 'Don't pretend. We had power. We were gods.'

'No, we were bullies. We were not gods – we were the dirty henchmen of the gods. They had the power. We were scared, so we made everyone a little more scared. That made us feel like big men – terrorizing the weak.'

Alexei waved a dismissive hand in Sosh's direction. 'You're getting old.'

'We both are.'

'I don't like this whole thing coming back.'

'You didn't like Pavel coming back either. It's because he reminds you of his grandfather, doesn't he?'

'No.'

'The man you arrested. The old man and his old wife.'

'You think you were better, Sosh?'

'No. I know I wasn't.'

'It wasn't my decision. You know that. They were reported, we took action.'

'Exactly,' Sosh said. 'The gods commanded you to do it. So you did. Do you still feel like such a big man?'

'It wasn't like that.'

'It was exactly like that.'

'You'd have done the same.'

'Yes, I would have.'

'We were helping a higher cause.'

'Did you ever really buy that, Alexei?'

'Yes. I still do. I still wonder if we were so wrong. When I see the dangers freedom has wrought. I still wonder.'

'I don't,' Sosh said. 'We were thugs.'

Silence.

Kokorov said, 'So what happens now – now that they found the body?'

'Maybe nothing. Maybe more will die. Or maybe Pavel will finally get the chance to face his past.'

'Didn't you tell him that he shouldn't do that – that he should let the past stay buried?'

'I did,' Sosh said. 'But he didn't listen. Who knows which one of us will be proven right?'

Doctor McFadden came in and told me that I was lucky, that the bullet went through my side without hitting any internal organs. It always made me roll my eyes when the hero gets shot and then goes on with his life as though nothing ever happened. But the truth is, there are plenty of gunshot wounds that do heal like that. Sitting in this bed wasn't going to make it any better than resting at home.

'I'm more worried about the blow to your head,' he said.

'But I can go home?'

'Let's let you sleep awhile, okay? See how you feel when you wake up. I think you should stay overnight.'

I was going to argue but there was nothing to be gained by going home. I felt sore and sick and achy. I probably looked like hell and would scare Cara with my appearance.

They had found a body in the woods. I still couldn't wrap my brain around that one.

Muse had faxed the preliminary autopsy to the hospital. They didn't know much yet, but it was hard to believe that it wasn't my sister. Lowell and Muse had done a more thorough examination of missing women from that area, seeing if there were any other women unaccounted for who could possibly fit this bill. The search had been fruitless – the only preliminary match for the computer records of the missing was my sister.

So far the coroner had come up with no cause of death. That wasn't unusual in a skeleton of this shape. If he had sliced her throat or buried her alive, they probably would never know. There would be no nicks on the bone. The cartilage and internal organs were long gone, the victims of some parasitic entity that had feasted on them long ago.

I skipped down to the key item. The pitting of the pubic bone.

The victim had given birth.

I again wondered about that. I wondered if that was possible. Under normal circumstances, that might give me some hope that it wasn't my sister they'd dug up. But if it wasn't, what could I conclude exactly? That around the same time some other girl – a girl no one can account for – had been murdered and buried in the same area as the ones at that camp?

398

That didn't make sense.

I was missing something. I was missing a lot.

I took out my cell phone. There was no service in the hospital but I looked up York's number on it. I used my room phone to make the call.

'Anything new?' I asked him.

'Do you know what time it is?'

I didn't. I checked the clock. 'It's a few minutes after ten,' I said. 'Anything new?'

He sighed. 'Ballistics confirmed what we already knew. The gun Silverstein shot you with is the same one he used to kill Gil Perez. And while DNA will take a few weeks, the blood type in the back of the Volkswagen Beetle matches Perez's. In sports terms, I'd call that game, set, match.'

'What did Lucy say?'

'Dillon said she wasn't much of a help. She was in shock. Said her father was not well, that he probably imagined some kind of threat.'

'Dillon buy that?'

'Sure, why not? Either way our case is closed. How are you feeling?'

'Peachy.'

'Dillon got shot once.'

'Only once?'

'Good one. Anyway, he still shows every woman he meets the scar. Turns them on, he says. You remember that.'

'Seduction tips from Dillon. Thanks.'

'Guess what line he uses after he shows them the scar?'

' "Hey, babe, want to see my gun?" '

'Damn, how did you know?'

'Where did Lucy go after you finished talking to her?'

'We drove her back to her place on campus.'

'Okay, thanks.'

I hung up and dialed Lucy's number. It went into her voice mail. I left a message. Then I called Muse's mobile.

'Where are you?' I asked.

'Heading home, why?'

'I thought maybe you'd be going to Reston U to question Lucy.'

'I already went.'

'And?'

'She didn't open the door. But I could see lights on. She's in there.'

'Is she okay?'

'How would I know?'

I didn't like it. Her father died and she was alone in her apartment. 'How far are you from the hospital?'

'Fifteen minutes.'

'How about picking me up?'

'Are you allowed out?'

'Who's going to stop me? And it's just for a little while.'

'Are you, my boss, asking me to drive you to your girlfriend's house?'

'No. I, the county prosecutor, am asking you to drive me to the home of a major person of interest in a recent homicide.'

'Either way,' Muse said, 'I'm so very there.'

No one stopped me from leaving the hospital.

I didn't feel well, but I had felt worse. I was worried about Lucy and I realized with growing certainty that it was more than normal worry.

I missed her.

I missed her the way you miss someone you're falling

in love with. I could run around that statement, soften it somehow, say that my emotions were on hyperdrive with all that was going on, claim that this was nostalgia for a better time, a more innocent time, a time when my parents were together and my sister was alive, and heck, even Jane was still healthy and beautiful and somewhere happy. But that wasn't it.

I liked being with Lucy. I liked the way it felt. I liked being with her the way you like being with someone you're falling in love with. There was no need to explain further.

Muse drove. Her car was small and cramped. I was not much of a car guy and I had no idea what kind of car it was, but it reeked of cigarette smoke. She must have caught the look on my face because she said, 'My mother is a chain smoker.'

'Uh-huh.'

'She lives with me. It's just temporary. Until she finds Husband Five. In the meantime I tell her not to smoke in my car.'

'And she ignores you.'

'No, no, I think my telling her that makes her smoke more. Same with my apartment. I come home from work, I open my door, I feel like I'm swallowing ashes.'

I wished that she'd drive faster.

'Will you be okay for court tomorrow?' she asked.

'I think so, yeah.'

'Judge Pierce wanted to meet with counsel in his chambers.'

'Any idea why?'

'Nope.'

'What time?'

'Nine a.m. sharp.'

'I'll be there.'

'You want me to pick you up?'

'I do.'

'Can I get a company car then?'

'We don't work for a company. We work for the county.'

'How about a county car?'

'Maybe.'

'Cool.' She drove some more. 'I'm sorry about your sister.'

I said nothing. I was still having a hard time reacting to that. Maybe I needed to hear that the ID was confirmed. Or maybe I had already done twenty years of mourning and didn't have that much left. Or maybe, most likely, I was putting my emotions on the back burner.

Two more people were dead now.

Whatever happened twenty years ago in those woods . . . maybe the local kids were right, the ones who said that a monster ate them or that the boogeyman took them away. Whatever had killed Margot Green and Doug Billingham, and in all likelihood Camille Copeland, was still alive, still breathing, still taking lives. Maybe it had slept for twenty years. Maybe it had gone somewhere new or moved to other woods in other states. But that monster was back now – and I'd be damned if I was going to let it get away again.

The faculty housing at Reston University was depressing. The buildings were dated brick and shoved together. The lighting was bad, but I think that might have been a good thing.

'You mind staying in the car?' I said.

'I have to run a quick errand,' Muse said. 'I'll be right back.'

I headed up the walk. The lights were out, but I could hear music. I recognized the song. 'Somebody' by Bonnie McKee. Depressing as hell – the 'somebody' being this perfect love she knows is out there but will never find – but that was Lucy. She adored the heart-breakers. I knocked on the door. There was no answer. I rang the bell, knocked some more. Still nothing.

'Luce!'

Nothing.

'Luce!'

I knocked some more. Whatever the doctor had given me was wearing off. I could feel the stitches in my side. It felt exactly like it was – as though my very movements were ripping my skin apart.

'Luce!'

I tried the doorknob. Locked. There were two windows. I tried to peer in. Too dark. I tried to open them. Both locked.

'Come on, I know you're in there.'

I heard a car behind me. It was Muse. She pulled to a stop and got out.

'Here,' she said.

'What is it?'

'Master key. I got it from campus security.'

Muse.

She tossed it to me and headed back to the car. I put the key in the lock, knocked one more time, turned it. The door opened. I stepped in and closed the door behind me.

'Don't turn on the light.'

It was Lucy.

'Leave me alone, Cope, okay?'

The iPod moved on to the next song. Alejandro Escovedo musically asked about what kind of love destroys a mother and sends her crashing through the tangled trees.

403

'You should do one of those K-tel collections,' I said.

'What?'

'You know, like they used to advertise on TV. Time Life presents *The Most Depressing Songs of All Time*.'

I heard her snort a laugh. My eyes were adjusting. I could see her sitting on the couch now. I moved closer.

'Don't,' she said.

But I kept walking. I sat next to her. There was a bottle of vodka in her hand. It was half empty. I looked around her apartment. There was nothing personal, nothing new, nothing bright or happy.

'Ira,' she said.

'I'm so sorry.'

'The cops said he killed Gil.'

'What do you think?'

'I saw blood in his car. He shot you. So yeah, of course, I think he killed Gil.'

'Why?'

She didn't answer. She took another long swig.

'Why don't you give me that?' I said.

'This is what I am, Cope.'

'No, it's not.'

'I'm not for you. You can't rescue me.'

I had a few replies to that but every one reeked of cliché. I let it go.

'I love you,' she said. 'I mean, I never stopped. I've been with other men. I've had relationships. But you've always been there. In the room with us. In the bed even. It's stupid and dumb and we were just kids, but that's the way it is.'

'I get it,' I said.

'They think maybe Ira was the one who killed Margot and Doug.'

'You don't?'

'He just wanted it to go away. You know? It hurt so much, caused so much destruction. And then, when he saw Gil, it must have been like a ghost was coming back to haunt him.'

'I'm sorry,' I said again.

'Go home, Cope.'

'I'd rather stay.'

'That's not your decision. This is my house. My life. Go home.'

She took another long draw.

'I don't like leaving you like this.'

Her laugh had an edge. 'What, you think this is the first time?'

She looked at me, daring me to argue. I didn't.

'This is what I do. I drink in the dark and play these damn songs. Soon I'll drift off or pass out or whatever you want to call it. Then tomorrow I'll barely have a hangover.'

'I want to stay.'

'I don't want you to.'

'It's not for you. It's for me. I want to be with you. Tonight especially.'

'I don't want you here. It will just make it worse.'

'But—'

'Please,' she said, and her voice was a plea. 'Please leave me alone. Tomorrow. We can start again tomorrow.'

Chapter 40

D r. Tara O'Neill rarely slept more than four, five hours a night. She just didn't need sleep. She was back in the woods by six a.m., at first daylight. She loved these woods – any woods, really. She'd gone to undergrad and medical school in the city, at the University of Pennsylvania in Philadelphia. People thought that she'd love it. You're such a lovely girl, they said. The city is so alive, so many people, so much happening.

But during her years in Philadelphia, O'Neill had returned home every weekend. She eventually ran for coroner and made extra money working as a pathologist in Wilkes-Barre. She tried to figure out her own life philosophy and came up with something she once heard a rock star – Eric Clapton, she thought – say in an interview about not being a big fan of, uh, people. She wasn't either. She preferred – as ridiculous as it sounded – being with herself. She liked reading and watching movies without commentary. She couldn't handle men and their egos and their constant boasting and their raging insecurities. She didn't want a life partner.

This – out in the woods like this – was where she was happiest.

O'Neill carried her tool case, but of all the fancy new gizmos that the public had helped pay for, the one she found most useful was the simplest: a strainer. It was nearly the exact same as the kind she had in her kitchen. She took it out and started in the dirt.

The strainer's job was to find teeth and small bones.

It was painstaking work, not unlike an archeological dig she had done after her senior year in high school. She had apprenticed in the Badlands of South Dakota, an area known as the Big Pig Dig because, originally, they had found an Archaeotherium, which was pretty much a huge ancient pig. She worked with pig and ancient rhinoceros fossils. It had been a wonderful experience.

She worked through this burial site with the same patience – work most people would find mind-deadeningly tedious. But again Tara O'Neill thrived.

An hour later, she found the small piece of bone.

O'Neill felt her pulse quicken. She had expected something like this, realized that it was a possibility after the ossification X-rays. But still. To find the missing piece . . .

'Oh my . . .'

She said it out loud, her words echoing in the stillness of the woods. She couldn't believe it, but the proof was right there, right in the palm of her rubber-gloved hand.

It was the hyoid bone.

Half of it anyway. Heavily calcified, brittle even. She went back to her search, sifting as fast as she could. It didn't take long now. Five minutes later, O'Neill found the other half. She held up both pieces.

Even after all these years, the bone fragments still fit together like a jigsaw.

Tara O'Neill's face broke into a beatific smile. For a moment, she stared at her own handiwork and shook her head in awe.

She took out her cell phone. No signal. She hurried back half a mile until two bars appeared. Then she pressed Sheriff Lowell's number. He picked up on the second ring.

'That you, Doc?'

'It is.'

'Where are you?'

'At the burial site,' she said.

'You sound excited.'

'I am.'

'Why?'

'I found something in the dirt,' Tara O'Neill said.

'And?'

'And it changes everything we thought about this case.'

One of those random hospital beeping noises woke me. I stirred slowly, blinked open my eyes and saw Mrs. Perez sitting with me.

She had pulled the chair right next to my bed. The purse was in her lap. Her knees touched. Her back was straight. I looked into her eyes. She'd been crying.

'I heard about Mr. Silverstein,' she said.

I waited.

'And I also heard that they found bones in the woods.'

I felt parched. I looked to my right. That yellow-brown plastic water pitcher, that one unique to hospitals and specifically designed to make the water taste awful, sat on the stand next to me. I was about to reach for it, but Mrs. Perez was up before I could do so much as lift my hand. She poured the water into a cup and handed it to me.

'Do you want to sit up?' Mrs. Perez asked.

'That's probably a good idea.'

She pressed the remote control and my back began to curl into a sit.

'Is that okay?'

'That's fine,' I said.

She sat back down.

'You won't leave this alone,' she said.

I didn't bother responding.

'They say that Mr. Silverstein murdered my Gil. Do you think that's true?'

My Gil. So the pretense was down. No more hiding behind a lie or a daughter. No more hypothetical.

'Yes.'

She nodded. 'Sometimes I think Gil really did die in those woods. That was how it was supposed to be. The time after that, it was just borrowed. When that policeman called me the other day, I already knew. I'd been expecting it, you see? Part of Gil never escaped from those woods.'

'Tell me what happened,' I said.

'I thought I knew. All these years. But maybe I never learned the truth. Maybe Gil lied to me.'

'Tell me what you do know.'

'You were at the camp that summer. You knew my Gil.'

'Yes.'

'And you knew this girl. This Margot Green.'

I said that I did.

'Gil fell for her hard. He was this poor boy. We lived

409

in a burnt-out section of Irvington. Mr. Silverstein had a program where children of workers got to attend. I worked in the laundry room. You know this.'

I did.

'I liked your mother very much. She was so smart. We talked a lot. About everything. About books, about life, about our disappointments. Natasha was what we call an old soul. She was so beautiful but it was fragile. Do you understand?'

'I think so, yes.'

'Anyway, Gil fell very hard for Margot Green. It was understandable. He was eighteen. She was practically a magazine model in his eyes. That's how it is with men. They are so driven by lust. My Gil was no different. But she broke his heart. That too is common. He should have just suffered for a few weeks and then moved on. He probably would have.'

She stopped.

'So what happened?' I asked.

'Wayne Steubens.'

'What about him?'

'He whispered in Gil's ear. He told him that he shouldn't let Margot get away with it. He appealed to Gil's machismo. Margot, he said, was laughing at Gil. You need to pay that tease back, Wayne Steubens whispered in his ear. And after a while – I don't know how long – Gil agreed.'

I made a face. 'So they slit her throat?'

'No. But Margot had been strutting all over camp. You remember this, yes?'

Wayne had said it. She was a tease.

'There were many kids who wanted to knock her down a peg. My son, of course. Doug Billingham too. Maybe your sister. She was there, but that might have been because Doug talked her into it. It's not important.'

A nurse opened the door.

'Not now,' I said.

I expected an argument but something in my voice must have worked. She backed up and let the door close behind her. Mrs. Perez had her eyes down. She stared at her purse as though afraid someone would snatch it.

'Wayne planned it all very carefully. That's what Gil said. They were going to draw Margot out to the woods. It was going to be a prank. Your sister helped with the lure. She said that they were going to meet some cute boys. Gil put a mask on his head. He grabbed Margot. He tied her up. That was supposed to be the end of it. They'd leave her there for a few minutes. She'd either escape from the rope or they'd untie her. It was dumb, very immature, but these things happen.'

I knew that they did. Camp was full of 'pranks' back then. I remembered one time we'd taken a kid and moved his bed into the woods. He woke up the next morning alone, outside, terrified. We used to shine a flashlight in a sleeping camper's eyes and make a train noise and shake them and yell, 'Get off the tracks!' and watch the kid dive off his bed. I remembered that there were two bully campers who used to call the other kids 'faggots.' Late one night, when both were deep in sleep, we picked one up, took off his clothes, put him in bed with the other. In the morning, the other campers saw them naked in the same bed. The bullying stopped.

Tying up a total tease and leaving her in the woods for a little while . . . that wouldn't have surprised me.

'Then something went very wrong,' Mrs. Perez said.

I waited. A tear escaped Mrs. Perez's eye. She reached into her purse and pulled out a wad of tissues. She dabbed her eyes, fought them back.

'Wayne Steubens took out a razor blade.'

I think my eyes widened a little when she said that. I could almost see the scene. I could see the five of them out in the woods, picture their faces, their surprise.

'You see, Margot knew what was going on right away. She played along. She let Gil tie her up. Then she started mocking my son. Made fun of him, said he didn't know how to handle a real woman. The same insults women have thrown at men throughout history. But Gil didn't do anything. What could he do? But suddenly Wayne had the razor blade out. At first, Gil thought it was part of the act. To scare her. But Wayne didn't hesitate. He walked over to Margot and slashed her neck from ear to ear.'

I closed my eyes. I saw it again. I saw the blade going across that young skin, the blood spurting, the life force leaving her. I thought about it. While Margot Green was being slaughtered, I was only a few hundred yards away making love to my girlfriend. There was probably poignancy in that, in that most horrible of man's actions running adjacent to his most wondrous, but it was hard to see it now.

'For a moment no one moved. They all just stood there. Then Wayne smiled at them and said, 'Thanks for the help.''

I frowned, but maybe I was starting to understand. Camille had drawn Margot out, Gil had tied her up . . .

'Then Wayne lifted the blade. Gil said they could see how much Wayne liked what he had done. How he stared at Margot's dead body. He had a thirst now. He started toward them. And they ran. They ran in different directions. Wayne chased them. Gil ran for miles and miles. I don't know what happened exactly. But we can guess. Wayne caught up to Doug Billingham. He killed him. But Gil got away. And so did your sister.'

The nurse returned.

'I'm sorry, Mr. Copeland. I need to take your pulse and blood pressure.'

I nodded for her to come in. I needed to catch my breath. I could feel my heart hammering in my chest. Again. If I didn't calm down, they'd keep me in here forever.

The nurse worked quickly and silently. Mrs. Perez looked around the room as if she'd just entered it, as if she'd just noticed where she was. I was afraid I was going to lose her.

'It's okay,' I said to her.

She nodded.

The nurse finished up. 'You're being released this morning.'

'Great.'

She gave me a tight smile and left us alone. I waited for Mrs. Perez to continue.

'Gil was terrified, of course. You can imagine. So was your sister. You have to see it from their viewpoint. They were young. They were nearly killed. They had watched Margot Green get slaughtered. But maybe most of all, Wayne's words haunted them. 'Thanks for the help.' You understand?'

'He had made them a part of it.'

'Yes.'

'So what did they do?'

'They just hid. For more than twenty-four hours. Your mother and I were worried sick. My husband was home in Irvington. Your father was at camp too. But he was out with the search parties. Your mother and I were together when the call came in. Gil knew the number of

413

the pay phone in the back of the kitchen. He dialed it three different times but he hung up when someone else answered. Then, more than a day after they went missing, I picked it up.'

'Gil told you what happened?'

'Yes.'

'You told my mother?'

She nodded. I was starting to see it.

'Did you approach Wayne Steubens?' I asked.

'We didn't have to. He'd already approached your mother.'

'What did he say?'

'Nothing incriminating. But he made it clear. He had set up an alibi for that night. And you see, we knew already. Mothers are like that.'

'You knew what?'

'Gil's brother, my Eduardo, was serving time. Gil had a small arrest record – he and some friends stole a car. Your family was poor, my family was poor. There would be fingerprints on the rope. The police would wonder why your sister had led Margot Green into the woods. Wayne had gotten rid of the evidence against him. He was rich and well liked and could hire the best attorneys. You're a prosecutor, Mr. Copeland. You tell me. If Gil and Camille came forward, who would have believed them?'

I closed my eyes. 'So you told them to stay hidden.'

'Yes.'

'Who planted their clothes with the blood?'

'I did that. I met Gil. He was still in the woods.'

'Did you see my sister?'

'No. He gave me the clothes. He cut himself, pressed his shirt against the wound. I told him to stay hidden until we came up with a plan. Your mother and I tried to

414

figure a way to turn it around, to get the police to learn the truth. But nothing came to us. Days passed. I knew how the police could be. Even if they did believe us, Gil was still an accomplice. So was Camille.'

I saw something else.

'You had a handicapped son.'

'Yes.'

'And you needed money. To take care of him. And maybe to pay for Glenda to go to a decent school.' My eyes found hers. 'When did you realize that you could cash in with that lawsuit?'

'That wasn't part of our original thinking. That came later – when Billingham's father started screaming about how Mr. Silverstein didn't protect his son.'

'You saw an opportunity.'

She shifted in her seat. 'Mr. Silverstein should have watched them. They would have never gone in those woods. He wasn't blameless in this. So yes, I saw an opportunity. So did your mother.'

My head was spinning. I tried to make it stop just long enough to accept this new reality. 'Are you telling me . . .' I stopped. 'Are you telling me that my parents knew that my sister was alive?'

'Not your parents,' she said.

And I felt the cold gust hit my heart.

'Oh no . . .'

She said nothing.

'She didn't tell my father, did she?'

'No.'

'Why not?'

'Because she hated him.'

I just sat there. I thought about the fights, the bitterness, the unhappiness. 'That much?'

'What?'

'It's one thing to hate a man,' I said. 'But did she hate my father so much that she'd let him think his own daughter was dead?'

She didn't respond.

'I asked you a question, Mrs. Perez.'

'I don't know the answer. I'm sorry.'

'You told Mr. Perez, right?'

'Yes.'

'But she never told my father.'

No answer.

'He used to go out in those woods and search for her,' I said. 'Three months ago, as he lay on his deathbed, his last words were that he wanted me to keep looking. Did she hate him that much, Mrs. Perez?'

'I don't know,' she said again.

It started to hit me, like heavy raindrops. Big thuds. 'She bided her time, didn't she?'

Mrs. Perez didn't respond.

'She hid my sister. She never told anyone – not even . . . not even me. She was waiting until the settlement money came through. That was her plan. And as soon as it did . . . she ran. She took enough money and ran and met up with my sister.'

'That was . . . that was her plan, yes.'

I blurted out the next question. 'Why didn't she take me?'

Mrs. Perez just looked at me. I thought about it. Why? And then I realized something. 'If she took me, my father would never stop looking. He'd get Uncle Sosh and all his old KGB cronies on it. He might let my mother go – he had probably fallen out of love with her too. He thought my sister was dead so that wouldn't be a draw. But my mother knew that he'd never let me go.'

I remembered what Uncle Sosh said, about her

returning to Russia. Were they both there? Were they both there right now? Did that make sense?

'Gil changed his name,' she went on. 'He traveled around. His life was less than spectacular. And when those private detectives came around to our house and asked questions, he got wind of it. He saw it as a way of cashing in again. You see, it was odd. He blamed you too.'

'Me?'

'You didn't stay on guard duty that night.'

I said nothing.

'So part of him blamed you. He thought that maybe this was a good time for payback.'

It added up. It fit in perfectly with what Raya Singh had told me.

She stood. 'That's all I know.'

'Mrs. Perez?'

She looked at me.

'Was my sister pregnant?'

'I don't know.'

'Did you ever see her?'

'Excuse me?'

'Camille. Gil told you she was alive. My mother told you she was alive. But did you ever see her yourself?'

'No,' she said. 'I never saw your sister.'

Chapter 41

didn't know what to think.

There was almost no time either. Five minutes after Mrs. Perez left my room, Muse entered.

'You got court.'

We checked out of the hospital without fuss. I had an extra suit in my office. I changed into it. And then I headed to Judge Pierce's chamber. Flair Hickory and Mort Pubin were already there. They had heard about my episode the night before, but if they cared, they weren't about to show it today.

'Gentlemen,' the judge said. 'I'm hoping we can find a way of settling this case.'

I was in no mood. 'That's what this is about?'

'It is.'

I looked at the judge. He looked at me. I shook my head. It made sense. If they had tried to pressure me by digging up dirt, what would have stopped them from doing the same with the judge?

'The People aren't interested in a deal,' I said.

I stood.

'Sit down, Mr. Copeland,' Judge Pierce said. 'There may be problems with your DVD evidence. I may have to exclude it.'

I started for the door.

'Mr. Copeland!'

'I'm not staying,' I said. 'It's on me, Judge. You did your part. Blame me.'

Flair Hickory frowned. 'What are you talking about?'

I didn't reply. I reached for the doorknob.

'Sit down, Mr. Copeland, or be in contempt.'

'Because I don't want to settle?'

I turned and looked at Arnold Pierce. There was a quiver in his lower lip.

Mort Pubin said, 'Will somebody explain to me what the hell is going on?'

The judge and I ignored him. I nodded to Pierce that I understood. But I wasn't about to give in. I turned the knob and left. I started down the hallway. My wounded side ached. My head throbbed. I wanted to sit down and cry. I wanted to sit down and ponder what I had just learned about my mother and my sister.

'I didn't think it would work.'

I turned. It was EJ Jenrette.

'I'm just trying to save my son,' he said.

'Your son raped a girl.'

'I know.'

I stopped. He had a manila folder in his hand.

'Sit a second,' Jenrette said.

'No.'

'Imagine your daughter. Your Cara. Imagine that one day she grows up. Maybe she has too much to drink at a party. Maybe she drives and hits someone with the car. Maybe they die. Something like that. She makes a mistake.'

'Rape is not a mistake.'

'Yeah, it is. You know he'd never do it again. He screwed up. He thought he was invincible. He knows better now.'

'We're not getting into this again,' I said.

'I know. But everyone has secrets. Everyone makes mistakes, commits crimes, does whatever. Some people are just better about burying them.'

I said nothing.

'I never went after your child,' Jenrette said. 'I went after you. I went after your past. I even went after your brother-in-law. But I never went near your child. That was my own personal line.'

'You're a prince,' I said. 'So what do you have on Judge Pierce?'

'It's not important.'

He was right. I didn't need to know.

'What can I do to help my son, Mr. Copeland?'

'That horse is out of the barn,' I said.

'You really believe that? You think his life is over?'

'Your son will probably serve five, six years tops,' I said. 'What he does while he's in there and what he does when he gets out – that'll decide what his life is.'

EJ Jenrette held up the manila envelope. 'I'm not sure what to do with this.'

I said nothing.

'A man does what he can to protect his children. Maybe that was my excuse. Maybe that was your father's.'

'My father's?'

'Your father was KGB. Did you know that?'

'I don't have time for this.'

'This is a summary of his file. My people translated it into English.'

'I don't need to see that.'

'I think you should, Mr. Copeland.' He held it out. I didn't take it. 'If you want to see how far a father might go to make a better life for his children, you should read this. Maybe you'll understand me a little better.'

'I don't want to understand you.'

EJ Jenrette just held the file out. Eventually I took it. He walked away without another word.

I headed back to my office and closed the door. I sat at my desk and opened the file. I read the first page. Nothing surprising. Then I read the second page and yet again, just when I thought I couldn't hurt any more, the words tore open my chest and shredded me apart.

Muse came in without knocking.

'The skeleton they found at that camp,' she said. 'It's not your sister.'

I couldn't speak.

'See, this Dr. O'Neill found something called a hyoid bone. That's in the throat, I guess. Shaped like a horseshoe. Anyway, it was snapped in half. That means the victim was probably manually strangled. But see, the hyoid bone isn't this brittle in young people – it's more like a cartilage, I guess. So O'Neill ran some more ossification tests with X-rays. In short, it is much more likely that the skeleton belonged to a woman in her forties, maybe even her fifties, than someone Camille's age.'

I said nothing. I just stared at the page in front of me.

'Don't you get it? It's not your sister.'

I closed my eyes. My heart felt so damn heavy.

'Cope?'

'I know,' I said.

'What?'

'It's not my sister in the woods,' I said. 'It's my mother.'

Chapter 42

Sosh wasn't surprised to see me.

'You knew, didn't you?'

He was on the phone. He put his hand over the mouthpiece.

'Sit down, Pavel.'

'I asked you a question.'

He finished his call and put the phone back in the cradle. Then he saw the manila envelope in my hand. 'What's that?'

'It's a summary of my father's KGB file.'

His shoulders slumped. 'You can't believe everything in those,' Sosh said, but there was nothing behind his words. It was as though he'd read them off a teleprompter.

'On page two,' I said, trying to quiet the tremor in my voice, 'it says what my father did.'

Sosh just looked at me.

'He turned in my Noni and Popi, didn't he? He was the source that betrayed them. My own father.'

Sosh still wouldn't speak.

'Answer me, dammit.'

'You still don't understand.'

'Did my own father turn my grandparents in, yes or no?'

'Yes.'

I stopped.

'Your father had been accused of botching a delivery. I don't know if he did or not. It makes no difference. The government wanted him. I told you all the pressure that they can apply. They would have destroyed your entire family.'

'So he sold out my grandparents to save his own skin?'

'The government would have gotten them anyway. But yes, okay, Vladimir chose to save his own children over his elderly in-laws. He didn't know it would go so wrong. He thought that the regime would just crack down a little, flex a little muscle, that's all. He figured they'd hold your grandparents for a few weeks at the most. And in exchange, your family would get a second chance. Your father would make life better for his children and his children's children. Don't you see?'

'No, I'm sorry, I don't.'

'Because you are rich and comfortable.'

'Don't hand me that crap, Sosh. People don't sell out their own family members. You should know better. You survived that blockade. The people of Leningrad wouldn't surrender. No matter what the Nazis did, you took it and held your head high.'

'And you think that was smart?' he snapped. His hands formed two fists. 'My God, you are so naive. My brother and sister starved to death. Do you understand that? If we had surrendered, if we'd given those bastards that damn city, Gavrel and Aline would still be alive. The tide still would have turned against the Nazis eventually. But my brother and sister would have had lives – children, grandchildren, grown old. Instead . . .'

He turned away.

'When did my mother find out about what he'd done?' I asked.

'It haunted him. Your father, I mean. I think part of your mother always wondered. I think that was why she had such contempt for him. But the night your sister vanished, he thought that Camille was dead. He crumbled. And so he confessed the truth.'

It made sense. Horrible sense. My mother had learned what my father had done. She would never forgive him for betraying her beloved parents. She would think nothing of making him suffer, of letting him think that his own daughter was dead.

'So,' I said, 'my mother hid my sister. She waited until she had enough money from the settlement. Then she planned on disappearing with Camille.'

'Yes.'

'But that begs the central question, doesn't it?'

'What question?'

I spread my hands. 'What about me, her only son? How could my mother just leave me behind?'

Sosh said nothing.

'My whole life,' I said. 'I spent my whole life thinking my mother didn't care enough about me. That she just ran off and never looked back. How could you let me believe that, Sosh?'

'You think the truth is better?'

I thought of how I spied on my father in those woods. He dug and dug for his daughter. And then one day he stopped. I thought that he stopped because my mother ran off. I remembered the last day he had gone out to those woods, how he told me not to follow him:

'*Not today, Paul. Today I go alone. . . .*'

He dug his last hole that day. Not to find my sister. But to bury my mother.

Was it poetic justice, placing her in the ground where my sister supposedly died, or was there also an element of practicality – who would think to look in a place where they had already searched so thoroughly?

'Dad found out she planned to run.'

'Yes.'

'How?'

'I told him.'

Sosh met my eye. I said nothing.

'I learned that your mother had transferred a hundred thousand dollars out of their joint account. It was common KGB protocol to keep an eye on one another. I asked your father about it.'

'And he confronted her.'

'Yes.'

'And my mother . . .' There was a choke in my voice. I cleared my throat, blinked, tried again. 'My mother never planned on abandoning me,' I said. 'She was going to take me too.'

Sosh held my gaze and nodded.

That truth should have offered me some small measure of comfort. It didn't.

'Did you know he killed her, Sosh?'

'Yes.'

'Just like that?'

Again he went quiet.

'And you didn't do anything about it, did you?'

'We were still working for the government,' Sosh said.

'If it came out that he was a murderer, we could all be in danger.'

'Your cover would have been blown.'

'Not just mine. Your father knew a lot of us.'

'So you let him get away with it.'

'It was what we did back then. Sacrifice for the higher cause. Your father said she threatened to expose us all.'

'You believed that?'

'Does it matter what I believed? Your father never meant to kill her. He snapped. Imagine it. Natasha was going to run away and hide. She was going to take his children and disappear forever.'

I remembered now my father's last words, on that deathbed . . .

'*Paul, we still need to find her . . .*'

Did he mean Camille's body? Or Camille herself?

'My father found out my sister was still alive,' I said.

'It's not that simple.'

'What do you mean, it's not that simple? Did he find out or not? Did my mother tell him?'

'Natasha?' Sosh made a noise. 'Never. You talk about brave, about being able to withstand hardships. Your mother wouldn't speak. No matter what your father did to her.'

'Including strangling her to death?'

Sosh said nothing.

'Then how did he find out?'

'After he killed your mother, your father searched through her papers, through phone records. He put it together – or at least he had his suspicions.'

'So he did know?'

'Like I said, it's not that simple.'

'You're not making sense, Sosh. Did he search for Camille?'

Sosh closed his eyes. He moved back around his desk. 'You asked me before about the siege of Leningrad,' he said. 'Do you know what it taught me? The dead are nothing. They are gone. You bury them and you move on.'

'I'll keep that in mind, Sosh.'

'You went on this quest. You wouldn't leave the dead alone. And now where are you? Two more have been killed. You learned that your beloved father murdered your mother. Was it worth it, Pavel? Was it worth stirring up the old ghosts?'

'It depends,' I said.

'On what?'

'On what happened to my sister.'

I waited.

My father's last words came to me:

'Did you know?'

I'd thought he was accusing me, that he saw guilt on my face. But that wasn't it. Did I know about the real fate of my sister? Did I know what he'd done? Did I know that he murdered my own mother and buried her in the woods?

'What happened to my sister, Sosh?'

'This is what I meant when I said it's not so simple.'

I waited.

'You have to understand. Your father was never sure. He found some evidence, yes, but all he knew for certain was that your mother was going to run with the money and take you with her.'

'So?'

'So he asked me for help. He asked me to look into his evidence. He asked me to find your sister.'

I looked at him.

'Did you?'

'I looked into it, yes.' He took a step toward me. 'And

428

when I was finished, I told your father that he got it wrong.'

'What?'

'I told your father that your sister died that night in the woods.'

I was confused. 'Did she?'

'No, Pavel. She didn't die that night.'

I felt my heart start to expand in my chest. 'You lied to him. You didn't want him to find her.'

He said nothing.

'And now? Where is she now?'

'Your sister knew what your father had done. She couldn't come forward, of course. There was no proof of his guilt. There was still the matter of why she had disappeared in the first place. And of course, she feared your father. How could she just return to the man who murdered her mother?'

I thought about the Perez family, the charges of fraud and all that. It would have been the same with my sister. Even before you add my father into the equation, it would have been difficult for Camille to come home.

Hope again filled my chest.

'So you did find her?'

'Yes.'

'And?'

'And I gave her money.'

'You helped her hide from him.'

He didn't answer. He didn't have to.

'Where is she now?' I asked.

'We lost touch years ago. You have to understand, Camille didn't want to hurt you. She thought about taking you away. But that was impractical. She knew how much you loved your father. And then later, when you became a public figure, she knew what her return, what

429

this scandal, would do to you. You see, if she came back, it would all have to come out. And once that happened, your career would be over.'

'It already is.'

'Yes. We know that now.'

We, he said. We.

'So where is Camille?' I asked.

'She's here, Pavel.'

The air left the room. I couldn't breathe. I shook my head.

'It took a while to find her after all these years,' he said. 'But I did. We talked. She didn't know your father had died. I told her. And that, of course, changed everything.'

'Wait a second. You . . .' I stopped. 'You and Camille talked?'

It was my voice, I think.

'Yes, Pavel.'

'I don't understand.'

'When you came in, that was her on the phone.'

My body went cold.

'She's staying at a hotel two blocks away. I told her to come over.' He looked at the elevator. 'That's her now. On her way up.'

I slowly turned and watched the numbers climb above the elevator. I heard it ding. I took one step toward it. I didn't believe it. This was another cruel trick. Hope was having its way with me again.

The elevator stopped. I heard the doors begin to open. They didn't slide. They moved grudgingly as though afraid to surrender their passenger. I froze. My heart hammered hard against my chest. I kept my eyes on those doors, on the opening.

And then, twenty years after vanishing into those woods, my sister, Camille, stepped back into my life.

Epilogue

One Month Later

Lucy does not want me to take this trip.

'It's finally over,' she says to me, right before I head to the airport.

'Heard that before,' I counter.

'You don't need to face him again, Cope.'

'I do. I need some final answers.'

Lucy closes her eyes.

'What?'

'It's all so fragile, you know?'

I do.

'I'm afraid you'll shift the ground again.'

I understand. But this needs to be done.

An hour later, I am looking out the window of a plane. Over the past month, life has returned to quasi-normal. The Jenrette and Marantz case took some wild and weird twists toward its rather glorious ending. The families did not give up. They applied whatever pressure they could on Judge Arnold Pierce and he broke. He threw out the porno DVD, claiming we didn't produce it in a timely enough fashion. We appeared to be in trouble. But the jury saw through it – they often do – and came back with guilty verdicts. Flair and Mort are appealing, of course.

I want to prosecute Judge Pierce, but I'll never get him. I want to prosecute EJ Jenrette and MVD for blackmail. I doubt I'll get that either. But Chamique's lawsuit is going well. Rumor has it that they want her out of the way quickly. A seven-figure settlement is being bandied about. I hope she gets it. But when I peer into my crystal ball, I still don't see a great deal of happiness for Chamique down the road. I don't know. Her life has been so troubled. Somehow I sense that money will not change that.

My brother-in-law, Bob, is out on bail. I caved in on that one. I told the federal authorities that while my recollections were 'fuzzy,' I do believe Bob told me that he needed a loan and that I approved it. I don't know if it will fly. I don't know if I'm doing the right thing or the wrong thing (probably the wrong) but I don't want Greta and her family destroyed. Feel free to call me a hypocrite – I am – but that line between right and wrong grows so blurry sometimes. It grows blurry here in the bright sunshine of the real world.

And, of course, it grows blurry in the dark of those woods.

Here is the quick yet thorough update on Loren Muse: Muse remains Muse. And I'm thankful for that. Governor Dave Markie hasn't called for my resignation yet and I haven't offered it. I probably will and I probably should, but as of right now, I'm hanging in.

Raya Singh ended up leaving Most Valuable Detection to partner up with none other than Cingle Shaker. Cingle says that they're looking for a third 'hottie' so they can call their new agency 'Charlie's Angels.'

The plane lands. I get off. I check my BlackBerry. There is a short message from my sister, Camille:

Hey, bro – Cara and I are going to have lunch in the city and shop. Miss and love you, Camille

My sister, Camille. It is fantastic to have her back. I can't believe how quickly she had become a full-fledged and integral part of our lives. But the truth is, there is still a lingering tension between us. It is getting better. It will get better still. But the tension is there and unmistakable, and sometimes we go over the top in our efforts to combat it by calling each other 'bro' and 'sis' and saying that we 'miss' and 'love' each other all the time.

I still don't have Camille's entire backstory. There are details she is leaving out. I know that she started with a new identity in Moscow, but didn't stay long. There were two years in Prague and another in Begur on the Costa Brava of Spain. She came back to the United States, moved around some more, got married and settled outside Atlanta, ended up divorced three years later.

She never had kids, but she is already the world's greatest aunt. She loves Cara, and the feeling is more than reciprocated. Camille is living with us. It is wonderful – better than I could have hoped – and that truly eases the tension.

Part of me, of course, wonders why it took so long for Camille to come home – that's where the majority of the tension comes from, I think. I understand what Sosh said about her wanting to protect me, my reputation, my memories of my father. And I know that she understandably was afraid of Dad while he still breathed.

But I think that there is more to it.

Camille chose to keep silent about what happened in those woods. She never told anyone what Wayne Steubens had done. Her choice, right or wrong, had left Wayne free to murder more people. I don't know what would have been the right thing to do – if coming forward would have made it better or worse. You could argue that Wayne still would have gotten away with it, that he might have run off or stayed in Europe, that he would have been more careful about his killings, gotten away with more. Who knows? But lies have a way of festering. Camille thought that she could bury those lies. Maybe we all did.

But none of us got out of those woods unscathed.

As for my romantic life, well, I am in love. Simple as that. I love Lucy with all my heart. We are not taking it slow – we plunged right in, as if trying to make up for lost time. There is a maybe unhealthy desperation there, an obsession, a clinging-as-though-to-a-life-raft quality in what we are. We see a lot of each other, and when we're not together I feel lost and adrift and I want to be with her again. We talk on the phone. We e-mail and text-message incessantly.

But that's love, right?

Lucy is funny and goofy and warm and smart and beautiful and she overwhelms me in the best way. We seem to agree on everything.

Except, of course, my taking this trip.

I understand her fear. I know all too well how fragile this all is. But you can't live on thin ice either. So here I am again, in Red Onion State Prison in Pound, Virginia, waiting to learn a few last truths.

Wayne Steubens enters. We are in the same room as our last meeting. He sits in the same place.

'My, my,' he says to me. 'You've been a busy boy, Cope.'

'You killed them,' I say. 'After all is said and done, you, the serial killer, did it.'

Wayne smiles.

'You planned it all along, didn't you?'

'Is anyone listening in to this?'

'No.'

He puts up his right hand. 'Your word on that?'

'My word,' I say.

'Then, sure, why not. I did, yes. I planned the killings.'

So there it is. He too has decided that the past needs to be faced.

'And you carried it out, just like Mrs. Perez said. You slaughtered Margot. Then Gil, Camille and Doug ran. You chased them. You caught up to Doug. You murdered him too.'

He raises his index finger. 'I made a miscalculation there. See, I jumped the gun with Margot. I meant her to be last because she was already tied up. But her neck was so open, so vulnerable . . . I couldn't resist.'

'There are a few things I couldn't figure out at first,' I say. 'But now I think I know.'

'I'm listening.'

'Those journals the private detectives sent to Lucy,' I say.

'Ahh.'

'I wondered who saw us in the woods, but Lucy got that one right. Only one person could have known: the killer. You, Wayne.'

He spreads his hands. 'Modesty prevents me from saying more.'

'You were the one who gave MVD the information

they used in those journals. You were the source.'

'Modesty, Cope. Again I plead modesty.'

He is enjoying this.

'How did you get Ira to help?' I ask.

'Dear Uncle Ira. That addle-brained hippie.'

'Yes, Wayne.'

'He didn't help much. I just needed him out of the way. You see – and this might shock you, Cope – but Ira did drugs. I had pictures and proof. If it came out, his precious camp would have been ruined. So would he.'

He smiles some more.

'So when Gil and I threatened to bring it all back,' I say, 'Ira got scared. Like you said, he was somewhat addle-brained then – he was a lot worse now. Paranoia clouded his thinking. You were already serving time – Gil and I could only make things worse by bringing it all back. So Ira panicked. He silenced Gil and tried to silence me.'

Another smile from Wayne.

But there is something different in the smile now.

'Wayne?'

He doesn't speak. He just grins. I don't like it. I replay what I'd just said. And I still don't like it.

Wayne keeps smiling.

'What?' I ask.

'You're missing something, Cope.'

I wait.

'Ira wasn't the only one who helped me.'

'I know,' I say. 'Gil contributed. He tied Margot up. And my sister was there too. She helped get Margot into those woods.'

Wayne squints and puts his forefinger and thumb half-an-inch part. 'You're still missing one teensy-weensy thing,' he says. 'One itsy-bitsy secret I've kept all these years.'

I am holding my breath. He just smiles. I break the silence.

'What?' I ask again.

He leans forward and whispers, 'You, Cope.'

I can't speak.

'You're forgetting your part in this.'

'I know my part,' I say. 'I left my post.'

'Yes, true. And if you hadn't?'

'I would have stopped you.'

'Yes,' Wayne says, drawing out the word. 'Precisely.'

I wait for more. It doesn't come.

'Is that what you wanted to hear, Wayne? That I feel partially responsible?'

'No. Nothing that simple.'

'What then?'

He shakes his head. 'You're missing the point.'

'What point?'

'Think, Cope. True, you left your post. But you said it yourself. I planned it all out.'

He cups his hands around his mouth and his voice drops to a whisper again.

'So answer me this: How did I *know* you wouldn't be at your post that night?'

Lucy and I drive out to the woods.

I already got permission from Sheriff Lowell, so the security guard, the one Muse had warned me about, just waves us through. We park in the condo lot. It is strange – neither Lucy nor I had been here in two decades. This housing development hadn't existed back then, of course. But still, after all this time, we know just where we are.

Lucy's father, her dear Ira, had owned all this land. He had come up here all those years ago, feeling like Magellan discovering a new world. Ira probably looked out at these woods and realized his lifelong dream: a camp, a commune, a natural habitat free from the sins of man, a place of peace and harmony, whatever, something that would hold his values.

Poor Ira.

Most crimes I see start with something small. A wife angers her husband over something inconsequential – where the remote control is, a cold dinner – and then it escalates. But in this case, it was just the opposite. Something big got the ball rolling. In the end, a crazy serial killer had started it all. Wayne Steubens's lust for blood set everything in motion.

Maybe we all facilitated him in one way or another. Fear ended up being Wayne's best accomplice. EJ Jenrette had taught me the power of that too – if you make people fearful enough, they will acquiesce. Only it hadn't worked in his son's rape case. He hadn't been able to scare Chamique Johnson. He hadn't been able to scare me either.

Maybe that was because I had already been scared enough.

Lucy carries flowers, but she should know better. We don't place flowers on tombstones in our tradition. We place stones. I also don't know who the flowers are for – my mother or her father. Probably both.

We take the old trail – yes, it is still there, though it's pretty overgrown – to where Barrett found my mother's bones. The hole where she lay all these years is empty. The remnants of yellow crime-scene tape blow in the breeze.

Lucy kneels down. I listen to the wind, wonder if I

hear the cries. I don't. I don't hear anything but the hollow of my heart.

'Why did we go into the woods that night, Lucy?'

She doesn't look up at me.

'I never really thought about that. Everyone else did. Everyone wondered how I could have been so irresponsible. But to me, it was obvious. I was in love. I was sneaking away with my girlfriend. What could be more natural than that?'

She puts the flowers down carefully. She still won't look at me.

'Ira didn't help Wayne Steubens that night,' I say to the woman I love. 'You did.'

I hear the prosecutor in my voice. I want him to shut up and go away. But he won't.

'Wayne said it. The murders were carefully planned – so how did he know I wouldn't be at my post? Because it was your job to make sure that I wasn't.'

I can see her start to grow smaller, wither.

'That's why you could never face me,' I say. 'That's why you feel like you're still tumbling down a hill and can't stop. It's not that your family lost the camp or their reputation or all the money. It's that you helped Wayne Steubens.'

I wait. Lucy lowers her head. I stand behind her. Her face drops in her hands. She sobs. Her shoulders shake. I hear her cries, and my heart breaks in two. I take a step toward her. The hell with this, I think. This time, Uncle Sosh is right. I don't need to know everything. I don't need to bring it all back.

I just need her. So I take that step.

Lucy holds up a hand to stop me. She gathers herself a piece at a time.

'I didn't know what he was going to do,' she says. 'He

439

said he'd have Ira arrested if I didn't help. I thought . . . I thought he was just going to scare Margot. You know. A stupid prank.'

Something catches in my throat. 'Wayne knew we got separated.'

She nods.

'How did he know?'

'He saw me.'

'You,' I say. 'Not us.'

She nods again.

'You found the body, didn't you? Margot's, I mean. That was the blood in the journal. Wayne wasn't talking about me. He was talking about you.'

'Yes.'

I think about it, about how scared she must have been, how she probably ran to her father, how Ira would have panicked too.

'Ira saw you in blood. He thought . . .'

She doesn't speak. But now it makes sense.

'Ira wouldn't kill Gil and me to protect himself,' I say. 'But he was a father. In the end, with all his peace, love and understanding, Ira was first and foremost a father like any other. And so he'd kill to protect his little girl.'

She sobs again.

Everyone had kept quiet. Everyone had been afraid – my sister, my mother, Gil, his family, and now Lucy. They all bear some of the blame, and they all paid a stiff price. And what about me? I like to excuse myself by claiming youth and the need to, what, sow some wild oats. But is that really any excuse? I had a responsibility to watch the campers that night. I shirked it.

The trees seem to close in on us. I look up at them and then I look at Lucy's face. I see the beauty. I see the damage. I want to go to her. But I can't. I don't know why. I want to – I know it is the right thing to do. But I can't.

I turn instead and walk away from the woman I love. I expect her to call out for me to stop. But she doesn't. She lets me go. I hear her sobs. I walk some more. I walk until I am out of the woods and back by the car. I sit on the curb and close my eyes. Eventually she will have to come back here. So I sit and wait for her. I wonder where we will go after she comes out. I wonder if we will drive off together or if these woods, after all these years, will have claimed one last victim.

Acknowledgments

I'm not an expert in much, so it's a good thing I know generous geniuses who are. This might sound like namedropping, but I was helped by my friends and/or colleagues Dr. Michael Baden, Linda Fairstein, Dr. David Gold, Dr. Anne Armstrong-Coben, Christopher J. Christie, and the real Jeff Bedford.

Thanks to Mitch Hoffman, Lisa Johnson, Brian Tart, Erika Imranyi, and everyone at Dutton. Thanks to Jon Wood at Orion and Françoise Triffaux at Belfond. Thanks to Aaron Priest and everyone at the creatively dubbed Aaron Priest Literary Agency.

Lastly, I would like to give a special thanks to the brilliant Lisa Erbach Vance, who has learned over the past decade to deal splendidly with my moods and insecurities. You rock, Lisa.

If you have enjoyed

The Woods

Don't miss

TELL NO ONE

Now a critically acclaimed film

Also available in Orion paperback
price £6.99
ISBN: 978-0-7528-4471-8

There should have been a dark whisper in the wind. Or maybe a deep chill in the bone. Something. An ethereal song only Elizabeth or I could hear. A tightness in the air. Some textbook premonition. There are misfortunes we almost expect in life—what happened to my parents, for example—and then there are other dark moments, moments of sudden violence, that alter everything. There was my life before the tragedy. There is my life now. The two have painfully little in common.

Elizabeth was quiet for our anniversary drive, but that was hardly unusual. Even as a young girl, she'd possessed this unpredictable melancholy streak. She'd go quiet and drift into either deep contemplation or a deep funk, I never knew which. Part of the mystery, I guess, but for the first time, I could feel the chasm between us. Our relationship had survived so much. I wondered if it could survive the truth. Or for that matter, the unspoken lies.

The car's air-conditioning whirred at the blue MAX setting. The day was hot and sticky. Classically August. We crossed the Delaware Water Gap at the Milford Bridge and were welcomed to Pennsylvania by a friendly toll collector. Ten miles later, I spotted the stone sign that read Lake Charmaine—private. I turned onto the dirt road.

The tires bore down, kicking up dust like an Arabian stampede. Elizabeth flipped off the car stereo. Out of the corner of my eye, I could tell that she was studying my profile. I wondered what she saw, and my heart started fluttering. Two deer nibbled on some leaves on our right. They stopped, looked at us, saw we meant no harm, went back to nibbling. I kept driving and then the lake rose before us. The sun was now in its death throes, bruising the sky a coiling purple and orange. The tops of the trees seemed to be on fire.

"I can't believe we still do this," I said.

"You're the one who started it."

"Yeah, when I was twelve years old."

Elizabeth let the smile through. She didn't smile often, but when she did, *pow*, right to my heart.

"It's romantic," she insisted.

"It's goofy."

"I love romance."

"You love goofy."

"You get laid whenever we do this."

"Call me Mr. Romance," I said.

She laughed and took my hand. "Come on, Mr. Romance, it's getting dark."

Lake Charmaine. My grandfather had come up with that name, which pissed off my grandmother to no end. She wanted it named for her. Her name was Bertha. Lake Bertha. Grandpa wouldn't hear it. Two points for Grandpa.

Some fifty-odd years ago, Lake Charmaine had been the sight of a rich-kids summer camp. The owner had gone belly-up and Grandpa bought the entire lake and surrounding acreage on the cheap. He'd fixed up the camp director's house and tore down most of the lake-front buildings. But farther in the woods, where no one went anymore, he left the kids' bunks alone to rot. My sister, Linda, and I used to explore them, sifting through their ruins for old treasures, playing hide-and-seek, daring ourselves to seek the Boogeyman we were sure watched and waited. Elizabeth rarely joined us. She liked to know where everything was. Hiding scared her.

When we stepped out of the car, I heard the ghosts. Lots of them here, too many, swirling and battling for my attention. My father's won out. The lake was hold-your-breath still, but I swore I could still hear Dad's howl of delight as he cannonballed off the dock, his knees pressed tightly against his chest, his smile just south of sane, the upcoming splash a virtual tidal wave in the eyes of his only son. Dad liked to land near my sunbathing mother's raft. She'd scold him, but she couldn't hide the laugh.

I blinked and the images were gone. But I remembered how the laugh and the howl and the splash would ripple and echo in the stillness of our lake, and I wondered if ripples and echoes like those ever fully die away, if somewhere in the woods my father's joyful yelps still bounced quietly off the trees. Silly thought, but there you go.

Memories, you see, hurt. The good ones most of all.

"You okay, Beck?" Elizabeth asked me.

I turned to her. "I'm going to get laid, right?"

"Perv."

She started walking up the path, her head high, her back straight. I watched her for a second, remembering the first time I'd seen that walk. I was seven years old, taking my bike—the one with the banana seat and Batman decal—for a plunge down Goodhart Road. Goodhart Road was steep and windy, the perfect thoroughfare for the discriminating Stingray driver. I rode downhill with no hands, feeling pretty much as cool and hip as a seven-year-old possibly could. The wind whipped back my hair and made my eyes water. I spotted the moving van in front of the Ruskins' old house, turned and—first pow—there she was, my Elizabeth, walking with that titanium spine, so poised, even then, even as a seven-year-old girl with Mary Janes and a friendship bracelet and too many freckles.

We met two weeks later in Miss Sobel's second-grade class, and from that moment on—please don't gag when I say this—we were soul mates. Adults found our relationship both cute and unhealthy—our inseparable tomboy-kickball friendship morphing into puppy love and adolescent preoccupation and hormonal high school dating. Everyone kept waiting for us to outgrow each other. Even us. We were both bright kids, especially Elizabeth, top students, rational even in the face of irrational love. We understood the odds.

But here we were, twenty-five-year-olds, married seven months now, back at the spot when at the age of twelve we'd shared our first real kiss.

Nauseating, I know.

We pushed past branches and through humidity thick enough to bind. The gummy smell of pine clawed the air. We trudged through high grass. Mosquitoes and the like buzzed upward in our wake. Trees cast long shadows that you could interpret any way you wanted, like trying to figure out what a cloud looked like or one of Rorschach's inkblots.

We ducked off the path and fought our way through thicker brush. Elizabeth led the way. I followed two paces back, an almost symbolic gesture when I think about it now. I always believed that nothing could drive us apart—certainly our history had proven that, hadn't it?—but now more than ever I could feel the guilt pushing her away.

4

My guilt.

Up ahead, Elizabeth made a right at the big semi-phallic rock and there, on the right, was our tree. Our initials were, yup, carved into the bark:

E.P.

+

D.B.

And yes, a heart surrounded it. Under the heart were twelve lines, one marking each anniversary of that first kiss. I was about to make a wisecrack about how nauseating we were, but when I saw Elizabeth's face, the freckles now either gone or darkened, the tilt of the chin, the long, graceful neck, the steady green eyes, the dark hair braided like thick rope down her back, I stopped. I almost told her right then and there, but something pulled me back.

"I love you," I said.

"You're already getting laid."

"Oh."

"I love you too."

"Okay, okay," I said, feigning being put out, "you'll get laid too."

She smiled, but I thought I saw hesitancy in it. I took her in my arms. When she was twelve and we finally worked up the courage to make out, she'd smelled wonderfully of clean hair and strawberry Pixie Stix. I'd been overwhelmed by the newness of it, of course, the excitement, the exploration. Today she smelled of lilacs and cinnamon. The kiss moved like a warm light from the center of my heart. When our tongues met, I still felt a jolt. Elizabeth pulled away, breathless.

"Do you want to do the honors?" she asked.

She handed me the knife, and I carved the thirteenth

line in the tree. Thirteen. In hindsight, maybe there had been a premonition.

It was dark when we got back to the lake. The pale moon broke through the black, a solo beacon. There were no sounds tonight, not even crickets. Elizabeth and I quickly stripped down. I looked at her in the moonlight and felt something catch in my throat. She dove in first, barely making a ripple. I clumsily followed. The lake was surprisingly warm. Elizabeth swam with clean, even strokes, slicing through the water as though it were making a path for her. I splashed after her. Our sounds skittered across the lake's surface like skipping stones. She turned into my arms. Her skin was warm and wet. I loved her skin. We held each other close. She pressed her breasts against my chest. I could feel her heart and I could hear her breathing. Life sounds. We kissed. My hand wandered down the delicious curve of her back.

When we finished—when everything felt so right again—I grabbed a raft and collapsed onto it. I panted, my legs splayed, my feet dangling in the water.

Elizabeth frowned. "What, you going to fall asleep now?"

"Snore."

"Such a man."

I put my hands behind my head and lay back. A cloud passed in front of the moon, turning the blue night into something pallid and gray. The air was still. I could hear Elizabeth getting out of the water and stepping onto the dock. My eyes tried to adjust. I could barely make out her naked silhouette. She was, quite simply, breathtaking. I watched her bend at the waist and wring the water out of her hair. Then she arched her spine and threw her head back.

6

My raft drifted farther away from shore. I tried to sift through what had happened to me, but even I didn't understand it all. The raft kept moving. I started losing sight of Elizabeth. As she faded into the dark, I made a decision: I would tell her. I would tell her everything.

I nodded to myself and closed my eyes. There was a lightness in my chest now. I listened to the water gently lap against my raft.

Then I heard a car door open.

I sat up.

"Elizabeth?"

Pure silence, except for my own breathing.

I looked for her silhouette again. It was hard to make out, but for a moment I saw it. Or I thought I saw it. I'm not sure anymore or even if it matters. Either way, Elizabeth was standing perfectly still, and maybe she was facing me.

I might have blinked—I'm really not sure about that either—and when I looked again, Elizabeth was gone.

My heart slammed into my throat. "Elizabeth!"

No answer.

The panic rose. I fell off the raft and started swimming toward the dock. But my strokes were loud, maddeningly loud, in my ears. I couldn't hear what, if anything, was happening. I stopped.

"Elizabeth!"

For a long while there was no sound. The cloud still blocked the moon. Maybe she had gone inside the cabin. Maybe she'd gotten something out of the car. I opened my mouth to call her name again.

That was when I heard her scream.

I lowered my head and swam, swam hard, my arms pumping, my legs kicking wildly. But I was still far from the dock. I tried to look as I swam, but it was too dark now, the moon offering just faint shafts of light, illuminating nothing.

I heard a scraping noise, like something being dragged.

Up ahead, I could see the dock. Twenty feet, no more. I swam harder. My lungs burned. I swallowed some water, my arms stretching forward, my hand fumbling blindly in the dark. Then I found it. The ladder. I grabbed hold, hoisted myself up, climbed out of the water. The dock was wet from Elizabeth. I looked toward the cabin. Too dark. I saw nothing.

"Elizabeth!"

Something like a baseball bat hit me square in the solar plexus. My eyes bulged. I folded at the waist, suffocating from within. No air. Another blow. This time it landed on the top of my skull. I heard a crack in my head, and it felt as though someone had hammered a nail through my temple. My legs buckled and I dropped to my knees. Totally disoriented now, I put my hands against the sides of my head and tried to cover up. The next blow—the final blow—hit me square in the face.

I toppled backward, back into the lake. My eyes closed. I heard Elizabeth scream again—she screamed my name this time—but the sound, all sound, gurgled away as I sank under the water.